Introducing . . .

MAURICE QUAIN . . . Once idealistic, he had been betrayed too often. The loss of his estates, his wife, and his ideals leaves him alone with only his ambition to sustain him.

PATRICK NORTH . . . Quain's handsome and gallant young secretary. Patrick has all the humanity and warmth that Maurice has so long denied himself. It is through Patrick that Blount begins his attack.

SIR EDWARD BLOUNT . . . As Maurice becomes a powerful Northern merchant, Blount, the cause of his former ruin, sets out to undo him again. He sees a chance to acquire Quain's vast commercial holdings.

LADY KATHERINE PERROT . . . Maid of honor to the Queen. When Maurice and Patrick go to London after Patrick's release, they meet Katherine. Her perilous position at Court has made her seek security in Blount's arms, but Patrick loves her hopelessly.

SIR JOHN PERROT . . . Natural son of Henry VIII, he is the Deputy Warden of the Tower of London. He has no illusions about his future. Lusty, though embittered, he hopes only to protect himself and his daughter.

SIR FRANCIS WALSINGHAM . . . The Queen's rugged, faithful Foreign Secretary. His only desire is to safeguard the Tudor Queen and serve the cause of Protestant England.

The times are troubled with change and peril. Elizabeth is insecure on her throne, threatened always by plots to replace her with Mary of Scotland. Men of vision and daring are exploring the great trade routes. Quain, aloof and bitter, is a man of his time; he serves the House of Quain first, and England after. Join us in this grand novel of gripping intrigue, and violent passion.

Pinnacle Books by Anne Powers:

RACHEL
THE GALLANT YEARS
THE IRONMASTER
THE ONLY SIN
THE PROMISE AND THE PASSION
ROYAL BONDAGE

Royal Bondage

by Anne Powers

PINNACLE BOOKS   LOS ANGELES

ROYAL BONDAGE

A Pinnacle Books edition, published by special arrange-
ment with the author.
Originally published under the title NO WALL SO HIGH
Originally published by Bobbs-Merrill Co., Inc.

ISBN: 0-52340-188-4

First printing, April 1973
Second printing, December 1977

Cover illustration by Charles Copeland

Printed in the United States of America

PINNACLE BOOKS, INC.
One Century Plaza
2029 Century Park East
Los Angeles, California 90067

The first of gold, who this inscription bears;—
Who chooseth me shall gain what many men desire.
The second, silver, which this promise carries;—
Who chooseth me shall get as much as he deserves.
This third, dull lead, with warning all as blunt;—
Who chooseth me must give and hazard all he hath.
How shall I know if I do choose the right?

—*Merchant of Venice*

ROYAL
BONDAGE

Part I

WHAT MANY MEN DESIRE

1

Katherine Perrot gave the ruff at the neck of her wine-red dress a vicious pull, tossed the delicately fluted cambric onto the table as it came unfastened. A wanton wind stirred through the open casement window, touching her bare slim throat coolly and loosening dark tendrils of hair from the stiffly jeweled net on her head.

Edward Blount closed the door and followed the young woman into the room. He said plaintively, "You don't seem glad to see me, Kit." The light gleamed on the gold chain across his stiffly padded doublet, on his fair hair and short jaunty beard.

Katherine laughed. "You've been away only a fortnight!" She spoke lightly, but she felt as though every nerve in her body were drawn too tightly today like the strings of an overtuned viol. Ned was always difficult after an absence.

Blount slid his hand up her throat to lift her chin, kissed her on the mouth. "Only a fortnight? It seemed forever to me, sweetheart." She yielded to him one moment, then turned away. She moved with a quick grace in spite of the monstrous farthingale with its whalebone hoops that held the wide skirt out from her waist, let it fall in heavy folds to the floor.

Blount looked at her sullenly, the delicate coloring of her small face, her rounded chin and dark eyes under winglike brows. "But of course you were not lonely. There are always other gallants about you. Too many. One wonders what favors they're promised or given that they do not get discouraged dancing attendance on you."

Katherine said nothing, feeling his anger as though it were rough hands upon her. His sporadic jealousy tore like cat's claws through the fabric of his devotion. She shook her head. "Don't hurt yourself, Ned. You know whom I——" She stopped the breadth of a moment. She was fond of him, yes, in many ways, though mostly selfish ones, she thought with a catch of remorse. But love him? "You know to whom I am faithful. Did your affairs go well?"

He shrugged. "The only things you can do these days without permission are to be born and to die. I'd hoped to enclose the common land next to my estates and buy more sleep, but I must have a license. Perhaps you'd mention my need to the Queen."

"I'll try to speak to Her Majesty tomorrow. We've been at Hampton Court only a week, but already she is planning to go down to Richmond, so the chance may not arise at once." Katherine looked at him with amused affection. "Last month you wanted to transport troops to the Netherlands. What will it be next month?"

Blount scowled. "You don't understand me, Kit. Why do you think I struggle so hard to win the royal favor, to make a fortune, except that we may marry?"

"I might say, Ned, for almost any reason else!" She glanced at him piquantly. "So don't fear I'll hold you to your rash words." He could not afford now to wed a woman without a dowry. And if any of his schemes prospered, would he be content with a wife who could not match him with money or land? She looked down, idly touched a lute that lay on the dark table. The note of music swelled sweetly against the paneled walls of the high-ceilinged room and died away, leaving a little pool of silence. It was broken by the sound of a brisk knock.

Katherine could hear her waiting woman outside open the door, then cross to the inner room. She turned her head. "Who is it, Mattie?"

Mattie, a middle-aged woman with a thin humorless face which tightened disapprovingly when she looked at Blount, whispered, "Sir Francis Walsingham, mistress, to see Sir Edward."

Blount, not waiting for Katherine's nod, said sharply, "Bid Sir Francis in, woman" He crossed the room to meet the Queen's Secretary at the door.

Walsingham was a dark grave man with a firm-set mouth and tired eyes. The light fell on the flat plane of his indrawn face from cheekbone to graying beard, on his black unadorned doublet with its narrow ruff which was his only concession to fashion. He bowed vaguely to Katherine and held out his hand to the clerk who had followed him into the room, his arms full of documents.

"The papers, Poley." Walsingham put them on the table, ruffled through the sheets. "I am sorry to bother you, Lady Katherine, Sir Edward, but it seemed less trouble to stop in on my way to the Queen's Chamber than to send for you later as I do not know how long the royal audience will be. I had a request here for a renewal of a trading permit in the Netherlands that I wanted your opinion on. A small matter, but as I am returning to London tonight I want to clear up these details."

He had a brisk precise voice that seldom changed its intonation. Katherine felt nothing was a small matter to him. He would take care of the pettiest affairs of state or the question of the succession to the Crown with neither idleness nor haste but with firm attention to details, losing sight of nothing, giving favor to no one. "The letter is from a merchant in North England. What is his name? You knew him."

Blount looked up in surprise. "A tradesman, Sir Francis, that I would know? Perhaps you speak of one of my creditors. I'll be glad to put in a word for any of them of course." He fingered a diamond in his ear.

Walsingham said dryly, "He's not exactly a creditor of yours, Sir Edward. Where is the letter?" The rustle of the papers was the only sound in the quiet room. "Ah, here it is." He glanced down at the crabbed writing on a sheet of fine vellum. "The name is Maurice Quain."

Blount, waiting indifferently for Walsingham to speak, froze for one moment, hand as though glued to the jewel in his ear. He turned his head slowly. "Mau-

3

rice Quain? Why, I did once know a man called that. But a tradesman——"

"A merchant, Sir Edward, and a very prosperous one."

"The man I was acquainted with would be even less likely to be a merchant than a tradesman from what I knew of him. Maurice Quain? Impossible."

Katherine glanced up quickly at some note in Ned's voice, a faint uneasiness under his bluff denial.

"I don't know," Walsingham said, "how many Maurice Quains there are in the world. The one I speak of was a friend—or should I say a neighbor?—of yours once. He was involved in one of those plots to free the royal whore Mary of Scotland and was sentenced to death until some whim of Her Majesty's prompted her to pardon him. He moved north to Blyth in Northumberland and started shipping ventures that now reach from the Baltic to Greece. I have no further actual knowledge of him, but I've heard stories lately that make me hesitate to renew this permit he asks for. We are speaking of the same man, are we not?"

Blount weighed the Secretary for a moment with his eyes, then he laughed. "It must be, Sir Francis. I lost sight of Quain after his trial. Still it is difficult to believe he is a sober merchant now. Of all the hotheaded rash young fools I've ever known, he's the one I'd think would be least likely to make a success out of anything. But in what way can I help you?"

"I wanted an opinion on this trading permit from a man who knew him. He is too close to the Scotch border and too far from London. One wonders why he should live there out of the way of the trade routes if all his dealings could bear investigation. What cargo does he carry besides wool and fish and lace and hemp?"

"If you have any reason at all to believe his commerce is other than it seems, Sir Francis, it would be best of course to deny him the permit. His mother was a Scotswoman I know, and a distant kin to that Mary Stuart."

Katherine said carelessly, though there was a note of

4

faint distaste in her voice, "Surely it is unfair to condemn a man for his parentage?"

"You are overhasty, Lady Katherine," Walsingham retorted. "Condemn? No one knows better than I the solid bulwark of England that our merchants are—if they are loyal. But it is not a simple matter of a yes or a no. Quain has served Her Majesty, but I have heard he also sells war supplies to Philip of Spain. I had the tale from an agent of mine, but he had no other news and may have given me the story to make himself worth his pay. Do you think it's true, Sir Edward?"

Blount moved to the window, stood gazing down a moment at the exquisite and sharply formal garden Henry the Eight had made for Queen Elizabeth's mother, Anne Boleyn. He turned back into the room. "I do not know what to answer, Sir Francis. To say the truth, no one was more astounded than I to find him involved in the plot to free Mary Stuart. And that was years ago."

"Still you were the one who discovered it and were well rewarded with his lands for your trouble."

Blount brushed that aside with a gesture of his hand. "He was a headlong young man who talked too much. Finding he was a rebel was no credit to my discernment."

Katherine's eyes were on him, judging him. She thought, No credit to your discernment? Informing on a friend is no credit to you at all, Ned.

He said angrily, answering her look, "Would you have had me play the traitor too, Katherine, by concealing another's treason?"

"I? Not at all! I was just unaware you had come into your estate so." Maurice Quain—a man she might like, set against the caution, the self-interested intriguing, the prudent pushing of so many gentlemen at Court.

Walsingham said, "Should Quain be loyal now, of course, he could be most valuable to us."

"Yes. If he would."

"You don't like him, Sir Edward?"

Blount hesitated, then smiled charmingly. "I would not go that far, Sir Francis. I really do not know him—I have not seen him for well onto fifteen years. It

5

is only . . . naturally I do not quite trust him. Or perhaps someone like me cannot understand an esquire turned merchant. I want to harm no innocent man, Sir Francis, but it would bear looking into."

Walsingham agreed. "We have too many enemies within and without to chance putting our friends with them. I had thought of giving the permit and in return we would demand a heavy pledge of Quain for his good behavior."

Blount repeated. "The matter would bear looking into—by someone you trust. He's very wealthy now you say?"

"Yes."

Blount looked down at the toe of his gilt leather shoe. "I always have business at home. I wouldn't be far from Blyth, and this affair sounds serious. A man who didn't know Quain might bungle so that, instead of unraveling the question of his loyalty, he would succeed only in putting Quain on guard."

Katherine stirred, feeling a subtle emanation of savagery. Walsingham eyed her shrewdly. "Don't spin to yourself some romantic story about this merchant because he was once in a wild plot to free Mary Stuart. Treason, mistress, is a disease that invades the body insidiously. At any cost it must be checked."

Katherine laughed. "I cry for mercy, Sir Francis. I have sympathized with a queen imprisoned. But say no more or you will have me convinced I too harbor traitorous thoughts."

"It is no matter for jest, Kit," Blount turned to Walsingham. "I should be happy if you would trust me, sir." He added slowly, "If I should bring back an ill report of this merchant, his possessions—"

Walsingham took him up before he could finish. "His possessions, Sir Edward, are scattered over half of Europe. It is this very point that strengthens my suspicions. Why substantial holdings in foreign countries if one is a true and loyal Englishman?"

"Still if his properties are confiscated, surely there are means to recover them?"

Walsingham said quietly, "So that we draw his fangs if he is a traitor, I am content. There may be means,

6

there usually are ways, to recover wealth from prisoners." He bowed slightly, crossed the room to the outer door. "Come into my house in London tomorrow. I will have Master Poley give you final details then as I may not be free." He drew his hand across his tired eyes, stumbled slightly as he went through the door which Blount, following him, held open.

Blount waited till the latch clicked, pale-blue eyes alight in a bronzed face that seemed to grow more purposeful as he stood there. Katherine felt a faint pulse of excitement, knowing without further words the temptation that was twisting his thoughts. Blount said, "Ships to the Mediterranean, black cargo to the Indies, privateers striking against Spanish galleons, the English flag planted on the far coasts of China. Dull merchant ships, sweetheart, transformed to war and fame and power."

And now it had been said. A little shiver ran through her, the excitement in her warming to pity for this merchant Ned would ruin. When Blount put his heart on one particular star, one undeviating course, he was a man to be feared. Yet he had no understanding of others, no knowledge even of her beyond her body and his need for her. Men didn't have to be careful, understanding. Life didn't load the dice against them. If one man failed them, they were always assured of another, while women had to stand or fall by their first and only cast. Not little Deborah, though. At the thought of her small daughter fear stabbed Katherine so that the pain of it sickened her. She could do well enough for herself, but this life was not good enough for Deborah. She felt a vast sympathy for all the weak and defenseless in the world.

"This merchant, Ned—do him no injustice even though your cause may be greater than his."

There was so long a pause she thought he hadn't heard her. Then he turned with a laugh. "You seem to dwell long on him, Kit. Do you never think of me fighting always for both of us, trying to make my way when a single slip, the wrong word at the wrong time, and I'm over the precipice into ruin and disfavor? Am

I an unjust man? Would I harm anyone without reason? Kit, Kit, I hoped you would understand me."

Katherine said gently, "I love you. Is that not enough?" If she didn't love him, well, she had a quiet affection for him. "Does he have a wife?"

"Who? Maurice?" Blount moved back sharply. Pale eyes narrowed. He said harshly, "You talk too much."

They were on the edge of one of their senseless quarrels with some darker depth in it because she had shown a casual interest in this stranger. "Don't, Ned. You'll be leaving soon again. I'll miss you."

He forgot his annoyance for a moment. "You do talk too much, Kit—especially before Walsingham."

Katherine looked skeptical. "Why? What did I say that was wrong?"

"Almost everything you could have said! I think he was trying to warn you in his own way."

"Of what?"

"That injudicious sympathy can ruin a man or a woman. You'd pity a Turk you thought unfortunate. That can be dangerous."

Katherine lifted her shoulders indifferently. "I think you see for me, Ned, dangers that are not there. But you did not answer me. Does Maurice Quain have a wife?" She wondered, even as she spoke, why she insisted on knowing, trying to feel out this darkness in him that was so disturbing. Still, was it worth chancing his explosion into anger?

He didn't show anger at her question. He looked at her and through her, but with his first word she knew that in her careless curiosity she had harmed this unknown merchant, had somehow steeled Ned's hostility toward him. What chance would this man have against Walsingham's coldly appraising eyes, against Blount's enmity and his need for money?

Blount said, "I will find out everything about him, sweetheart, everything, and report to you and to Sir Francis. But let us not waste golden moments in unpleasant talk." His fingers fumbled with the silver brooch at the breast of her gown.

A wave of repugnance broke over her. It spent its force quickly. No, she thought, this was only Ned, whom she cared for, and she must find herself again in the sweetness of his love, herself and him. She turned up her face to him, felt the warmth of his arms about her, while she let the world and the Court and the thoughts of a merchant far to the north slip from her with a little sigh.

2

The clerk's spine hugged the back of his chair as his gaze shifted from the short swarthy man before him to the closed door at his right. "You tell him, Captain Fox. I wouldn't bring his lordship bad news. Not today I wouldn't."

The title set the spark to the captain's narrowly held temper. "His lordship!" he snarled. "Maurice Quain gets grander every time I see him. Why, he's no closer to a lordship than my dog." His face reddened above his silky black beard and his figure, splendid in black and crimson satin and lace of tarnished gold, swelled alarmingly.

A young man leaning over a high desk across the room broke off a melody he had been humming to grin at the speaker. "You have to call him something," he said reasonably. "And with the kind of tale, you're bringing him today, the best you can say is hardly good enough."

Through the open window in the east wall could be heard the thundering of waves against the rocky shore below, the scream of a gull, the blustering spring wind shrilling around the corners of the stone house.

The captain swung about on his heel. "So our songster's with us. I didn't see you before, Patrick." There was a thin note of contempt in his voice.

"You mean you didn't hear me," Patrick retorted, "and you bellowing like a bull at matingtime." He was a dark supple young man with a contagious grin.

The captain ignored Patrick. "Ye're all in fear of your master. We go out to make money for him, get shot at, have our ships blown up by Turk and Spaniard and Englishman, and now, by the wounds of Christ, his

9

own cutthroat kinsmen steal the cargo out of the hold and you're afraid to annoy my fine merchant with the news! Well, *Madre de Dios,* I'm not!"

The captain moved across the room with a rolling gait. His fist crashed on the panels of the closed door. At an "Enter!" from within he put his hand to the latch and strode truculently into the room. The long oak-paneled office was lighted coolly from wide windows facing to the north, neutralizing the warmth of the wainscoting and of the Turkish carpet on the floor.

Maurice Quain looked up from the papers outspread on the table before him. He was big-boned and lean with a square impassive face, thinly set mouth and chill blue eyes. He flicked an imaginary speck from the sleeve of his dark Florentine serge doublet while his eyes rested on the trail of mud the captain's boots were leaving across the Eastern carpet. "Well, Captain Fox?"

"Name of a Name!" The captain, who had involuntarily followed Maurice's gaze, dragged his eyes from the muddied floor and began to bluster. "Italy—Turkey—Tripoli—Spain—we beard the pirates, we drive off the Infidels, we outsail the Christians——"

"I didn't know you were back in the Mediterranean trade route," Maurice interrupted coldly. "In fact, I was under the impression you were returning from Antwerp."

"We was," Fox admitted.

"I'm glad to see you landed safely then. May I have the list of cargo? Your prowess in your earlier days I will hear another time."

Captain Fox spread his hands flat on the polished surface of the table while his mouth opened and closed like a fish's. Though he prided himself on being able to swear in every civilized and several uncivilized languages, it was a full minute before a word came out of his mouth. "My earlier days! *Ventre-saint-gris!* We was rounding the Head yesterday—we was blown out of our course—and a fleet belonging to your own Scottish kinsmen came out from under the cover of the point there and opened fire. A galleon and two pinnaces against us."

"Three ships? But you of course," Maurice said sardonically, "fought to the death."

"Not when it's useless, I don't, Quain. We surrendered and they rifled everything in the hold and took half our men."

The silence in the room was thick and unpalatable as cold porridge. A window rattled in its frame under a sudden gust of wind. "What flag were you flying?"

"What flag do you think? The Tudor, as you told us, or we'd never have got the cargo past Drake's men—if he's in the North Sea and not back in the West Indies. If he's not here, some other pirates is always hanging on and off watching the trade ships."

Maurice leaned back in his chair, a big gilded one with high carved back and wide arms. His face was imperturbable. The drumming of his fingers on the ornately carved table was the only sign of his annoyance. "Any fool born of imbecile parents and bred among savages could have told you what flag to fly when you're off the Scottish coast. How soon can you be ready to sail again?"

"Two weeks. There was a shot below the water line and part of the mainmast was blown away."

"Speak to Patrick on your way out. He'll see the shipbuilder for you."

"But a crew?"

"Need I teach you your own trade, Captain? Any night in any tavern you can persuade half again as many men as you need. Or perhaps, having been so near death as you say you were yesterday, your conscience has grown overtender?"

The captain smiled, not pleasantly, showing a gap where three upper teeth were missing. "I thought in your own town, Master Quain—but perhaps none of your friends drink in taverns?"

Maurice brushed that aside. "I'll expect you to be ready to sail within the week. The warehouse is full of linen yarn to be brought to Antwerp and wool for Duckett of London."

Captain Fox shifted from one booted foot to the other. "Look here, Master Quain," he burst out. "What about my pay for this trip?"

"I'll put the amount you should have made to your account, Captain. Let us hope on your next voyage you will earn it." Maurice smiled, but with no flicker of warmth. "Now if we're both done venting our spleen, sit down. As I said, your return will be to the Netherlands and London. After that Hart in London has plans for you to sail again to Spain."

Captain Fox pulled up a chair, threw himself into it and stretched out his legs. His movements were quick and catlike, though his black doublet slashed with crimson silk and padded across the chest made his short figure look square and unwieldly. "Spain . . . I don't know, Master Quain. It's not only the trouble you have in getting paid—"

"For the cordage we shipped Philip two months ago I had half the price before our ships left port, and a manor house in Sussex that the Spanish ambassador owns as security for the rest. You need not look for a new employer yet."

Captain Fox grinned reluctantly. "I might have known, Master Quain. But there's more. You're here in Blyth out of the sound of what's going on in the world. I know your reasons—so that you may have a free hand to ship where you will without danger of seeing half your cargoes confiscated. But you don't know the violence of feeling in London. The English hate the very name of Spain. And when a Scotsman, or half a Scotsman, does business with Philip—well, it's dangerous. I've heard talk about this dabbling of yours with Spain."

Maurice said coldly, "You have? And what kind of talk do you hear when I'm doing business with Elizabeth Tudor?"

"The kind I like to hear. But cordage for the Armada—that's no good."

"The stakes are something bigger, Captain, than cordage for a fleet that may never weigh anchor. I have men now in London, Antwerp, Paris, Madrid, Rome. Would you have me withdraw them every time some fool speaks his mind in a city street?"

Fox regarded the young merchant complacently.

12

"You're probably right, Master Quain. You usually are or I'd not be sailing for you."

Maurice looked at the swarthy face, the shrewd restless eyes of the seaman with a momentary passion of distaste. "I am detaining you, Captain. You must want to see to the repair of your ship."

Fox pushed back his chair as he rose without any sign of annoyance at the blunt dismissal. "Aye."

Maurice's eyes followed the return track of mud across the carpet as Fox left. Patrick came in before the door could close. "You have two more visitors, Master Quain—a messenger from some London gentleman whose name he refuses to give to anyone but you, and your cousin Donald Stuart. Do you wish to see them?"

"Let them wait. I want a letter sent Hart at the Royal Exchange." Maurice pushed quill and inkhorn across the table toward the young man. "I would like to know why this business of buying a membership in the Turkey Company has not been completed. This Hart isn't the man his father was in handling my investments. I wonder—— But to change to another house I would have to go to London myself and I'm not ready for that yet. Well, tell him he can put into it any sum up to two hundred pounds to buy a share for me. If my money's invested elsewhere, he can borrow any part of that. The terms . . ."

There was a flame alight in Maurice's eyes. A house of business in every country in Europe and Western Asia so that no matter where merchants went, his company would be there. No matter what governments rose or fell, he would grow richer, selling either side what it needed—at a price. But Turkey and the overland trade routes to the Far East which the Sultan controlled were closed to all English merchants outside the Turkey Company which held the Crown monopoly.

Patrick's quill paused above the paper he was writing on as Maurice's gaze went past him. His lips began to form soundlessly the words of the song he had been singing, stopped as he caught an irritable glance from Maurice whose attention had swung back to him. "What was I saying there? The terms? Put down that if

13

he must raise the cost of the membership he's not to pay over eleven or twelve percent interest. My name alone should be security enough for a reasonable rate. . . . By the way, the shipment of linen is ready for Sir John Perrot. He's at Hartley now. You might ride over when the linen's delivered Thursday. Perrot is hard to please and harder to get payment out of—like all government officials. Get his signature down for every yard of cloth. If we don't get paid, we'll at least have the thin pleasure of knowing what our losses are."

Patrick smiled. "From what I hear of Perrot, Master Quinn, that's hardly safe. They say he's throwing anyone he claps eyes on into prison trying to get every last rebel into his net."

Maurice said coldly, "Should so regrettable an incident occur, Patrick, we will endeavor to free you. Send in the messenger." He glanced up with indifferent interest at the jaunty young man who came in a moment later and whose eyes roved about the office as though in bored approval of the expensive furnishings. "You had business with me?"

The thin young man looked at Maurice for the first time. "Ah yes, Master Quain."

His lips kept on moving, but Maurice heard no further word. He was staring at the short cape the man wore. On the left shoulder was embroidered an otter, the badge of the Quains. Maurice leaned back in his chair, feeling a little sick, and there was a noise in his ears like the sound of a high wind. He wet his lips with the tip of his tongue. "Would you repeat yourself? I didn't hear what you said. I'm afraid my mind was on another matter."

The messenger stared haughtily. "I merely brought a request from my master. He would like to see you later today."

As Maurice did not answer, the other tapped his foot impatiently. Maurice said quietly, "And his name?"

"Sir Edward Blount. No doubt even in this lost corner of the world you have heard of him."

"Blount? The name has a familiar ring. I believe I had the pleasure of meeting the gentleman once."

14

Maurice's brittle voice was emotionless. "I shall be honored to have him dine with me tomorrow night. At six. We keep merchants' hours here."

The messenger shrugged eloquently. "I will give him your petition, Master Quain. If he does not accept, I——"

Maurice said freezingly, "I think Sir Edward will accept. Was there any futher message? No?" He nodded in dismissal.

The man crossed the room, annoyance in the rigid set of his shoulders. Maurice looked after him with unseeing eyes. Edward Blount. What did he want after all these years? And on top of that the thought: Blount was always something of a fool. Maurice could probably buy every possession of Ned Blount's twice over and not notice it.

He shrugged and rang for Patrick to show in his last visitor. Before Patrick could answer, Donald swung the door open and was halfway into the office. Maurice said, "Good morning!" in a voice that stopped him short. "Well, since you are so far, come in and sit down."

Donald hooked one of the backless chairs about with his foot and dropped down on the velvet-covered seat. He was almost as tall as Maurice, but heavier, with eyes as blue as the sea and pale reddish hair. "I'm happy to see you looking so well, cousin."

Maurice's brows rose at the stiff phrasing. "Is there any reason I shouldn't be?"

Donald made a wide geture to include the high pile of papers on the desk, the closed windows, the severe office. "Enough to kill the healthiest man!" He leaned forward in sudden eagerness. "Maurice, I've bad news. Last night Perrot—he was appointed Deputy Warden lately you know—captured Gerald and Lane. You remember them?"

"No."

"Good men they are. Maybe they did a little trading over the border, lifted the purses of a merchant or two, but they've been taken and it'll mean hanging. They were with us in our younger days, Maurice. We owe them something."

15

Maurice murmured politely, "Do you?"

Donald said doggedly, "They were friends of mine and I intend to free them."

"For your sake I hope you change your mind before you plan further. I can guess what sort of treasonous plots led to your friends' being in prison waiting for the rope, but I'm not interested."

"I could almost forget, Maurice," Donald put in slowly, "the days you were willing enough to dare the gallows yourself for less than the freedom of two friends."

"Was I? I have forgotten." Maurice glanced at the papers before him. "Well, it's always pleasant to talk over old times, Donald, but there's a ship sailing for France in the morning and I want to look these over before she leaves. Will you excuse me if I return to my work?"

Donald jumped to his feet. His chair went over with a soft thud on the thick carpet. "That's all you care for now. Money! Money and women!"

Maurice said indifferently, "You may be right. And now if you've done—— I'm a plain merchant and busy."

"As you will. I'll ask only this of you. I heard that you've been supplying cloth to Perrot. I thought if you'd send one of your clerks to see him I could get into Hartley with him."

Maurice might have been contemplating the Great Wall of China for all the response in his manner.

Donald said eagerly, "You know what shrift these prisoners will get when they're dispatched to London if they live long enough to be sent, Maurice. I could free them. I could go in as one of your retainers—Patrick North perhaps."

Maurice came alive. "Keep away from Patrick or anyone else in my office, Donald."

"There was a time when already you'd be halfway to Harley, a better plan than mine in your mind. You aren't the man you were. Sometimes I think you aren't a man at all."

Maurice laughed. "You may again be right."

Donald said, "Maurice!" Their eyes met. Donald's

eyes wavered and withdrew from Maurice's hard unreadable gaze. "Don't you remember when you—"

Maurice spoke stonily. "I was young then."

"Yes. You were young and a human being. You risked even Lucy——"

At the mention of his wife Maurice stood up slowly, walked across to the door and held it open for his cousin to leave. The scratching of quills in the outer room, a rustle of paper, were the only sounds for a moment. "I'll be glad to see you again, Donald, if ever you want to work for me——" He broke the sentence off, leaving unspoken but clear that otherwise there was no hurry at all for his cousin to return.

Donald looked at the outer office, then back into the dark quiet of the inner room. He shook his head. "When I'm that dead, Maurice, I'll be buried at sea!" He went out into the sunlight, a big man who left a breath of the outdoors behind him. Maurice returned to his cargo listings.

"Eating," Maurice said indolently, "is one of the few pleasures in life we can always depend on." He stood waiting for Edward Blount to take his place at the table. Silver and crystal and gold glittered in the candlelight against the diapered damask cloth. The hard and shining newness of service and linen jarred on Maurice's fastidious taste even while it satisfied some bitter arrogance in him.

Blount slid into the high-backed chair at the foot of the table. "As I was saying, Maurice, it seems to me that this North Country is a hotbed of treason." His stiffened lace ruff, open in the front in the latest fashion, flared back to frame his heavy-jowled face and blond curling hair.

Maurice turned his head toward his guest with chill disapproval. "I am sure, Sir Edward, you do not wish to ruin your dinner with talk of business. Would you try those capons?" He indicated an enormous silver dish on which the roasted birds were swimming in a golden sauce. The first page held the platter for Blount, the next followed with quail, pheasant and golden jellies with exotic Eastern flavors.

17

Blount looked at the dishes, the preserved fruits, pastes, marchpanes and comfits, with an envious expression that did not escape Maurice's coldly observant eyes. "I am used to plainer living myself, Maurice, especially when traveling for the government. And one hears tales around here of rebellion and treason—well, really they would take the hunger from the least royal of men."

Maurice's voice had a touch of boredom. "I never believe what I hear until I see the proof of it and even then I doubt. Perhaps the lamb would appeal to you. No? My new cook is from Spain and rather a credit to his country."

Blount, with a meat pasty halfway to his mouth, looked at it a moment indecisively. "I don't trust these foreign devils myself. Italian, Spaniard, Frenchman, they're all the same and all hostile to us. I wonder you would have an enemy cook for you."

"You mistake the matter, Sir Edward. I have no enemies." Maurice's eyes caught and held his guest's blandly.

Blount felt the pasty rise within him at that look. He pushed the remainder on his plate to one side and cut a leg from a capon with his dagger. "No enemies? You're likely to have no friends then either, Maurice."

A neat retort, Blount thought, and one that gave him back some confidence in himself. He had expected from Maurice a savage refusal to see him or, when his messenger returned instead with an invitation to dine, an eager if not servile desire to be friendly, forget the past. He had come swaggering slightly, arrogant, prepared to accept the bribes or promises of a man broken once and afraid now. Instead, from the first moment he had entered the house he had been made to feel like a blunderer and an imbecile by this stranger who was sauve and courteous and ice-cold.

"Friends?" Maurice asked smoothly. "What would a man who would not be betrayed do with freinds?"

Blount, lifting his goblet, started slightly. The wine slopped over the edge, making a scarlet pool on the white cloth. Maurice glanced at the page to refill the glass. "You must taste that wine, Sir Edward. One of

18

my factors in Greece shipped it to me. But perhaps you have some amusing court talk? We are so far behind the times up here that the story of that French courtier—what was his name? Monsieur de Simier?—and the Queen is still fresh."

Blount looked blankly at Maurice, trying to see in him again the young man he had once known, gay and impetuous, speaking carelessly of whatever concerned himself, not using words as now to fill up the void about them with an impenetrable wall of sound. "The story escapes me at the moment, Maurice."

"Oh, it was not any one story—just general gossip, for instance, of the rather remarkable way the Queen has of dressing, forgetting a button here, a brooch there, letting her skirts slip aside to the thigh, not in private. And Elizabeth did not, we hear, seem too outraged when Simier kissed the white skin since his master was not there to trade a year of his life for the privilege. I suppose such tales as these might be one reason Henry of France was but indifferently interested in becoming King of England."

Blount scowled. "Really, Maurice—"

"Ah yes, she's a great queen no doubt as you would say. But something too much Anne Boleyn's daughter to be a lady."

"What I would say, Maurice, is that those are ungrateful words about the woman who pardoned you, gave you a second life."

"It reminds one, does it not, Sir Edward, of those Eastern religions where one lives through a whole cycle of lives. Reincarnation, isn't it? Rather wasteful I think when one life is more than enough for any sane man."

This dinner was beginning to take on something of the quality of a nightmare, Blount thought. He had said nothing he had intended to say, had not threatened, nor bribed, nor extracted promises or confessions. His head ached. That Grecian wine was overstrong, and he felt he had been battered with some smooth blunt weapon. He reached for a marchpane of powdered almonds and sugar. "This sweetmeat is delightful, Maurice." There was a hint of patronage in his voice, though he was crumbling the sweet savagely between his fingers. He would at least show his rank by calling this merchant by his first name! "You believe in the new way, I see, of dining alone?"

Maurice shrugged his wide shoulders. "Why have your meals disturbed by the prating of fools and the talk of braggarts? I pay my servants. I don't have to listen to them as well and spoil one of the finer pleasures of life."

Blount reached for his glass, took a hasty gulp of wine before a "Pleasures, Jesus Christ!" could be wrung out of him. He said abruptly, "I came here, Maurice, to discuss an important matter with you. If you can stomach only trivialities while you dine, let us forgo the rest of this meal. Can we talk in your office?"

Maurice bowed courteously. "Where you will, Sir Edward, and when you will." He nodded to a page to bring basin and rose water. Then he stood up, his face expressionless, betraying no trace of how he flinched from this meeting. He looked down at his hands. There was a time when he would have killed Edward Blount with no weapon but these.

Blount half-turned as they went out. "I hope my haste has not offended you?"

Maurice's brows lifted sardonically. Blount wondered if Maurice were a man you *could* offend. Or one you could please.

Maurice said, "In here, Sir Edward," and threw open the door of his library. "This should be pleasanter than the office."

A fire crackled on the hearth throwing out a glow of warmth and light in the chilly drafts of the room. On the paneled walls above a row of low bookshelves were great square maps showing all Europe, the Mediterranean, the north coast of Africa. The trade routes were inked in, from the monopoly of the Muscovy Company in Russia to the Portuguese routes pointing south around Africa. Westward the lines were only arrows toward the Spanish possessions in the Americas, and eastward they linked England with Turkey, and beyond Turkey were shown the caravan roads to Samarkand and China and southeastward to Persia. Maurice stood back, a tall big-boned man against the

20

black and white spread of the parchment world behind him.

Blount was drawn to the maps irresistibly. "The world on your wall, Master Quain—Maurice—and you with ships and cargo to send where you will and see return with gold and merchandise. In so short a time to have risen so high—" He turned away decisively. "But I did not come to discuss your past, successful as it undoubtedly has been—at least your later years."

He smiled charmingly at Maurice, feeling himself Edward Blount again, a knight from Whitehall visiting a wealthy but dangerously situated merchant whose future depended on him, whom he could spare or destroy. He sat down in a big chair, elbow on the wide arm, chin resting on the palm of his hand. The evidences of Maurice's wealth would make a saint ache to lay his hands on it, to send ships on those trade routes for himself and for England. . . . But he must go more warily, not blunder as he had been doing.

"Before we can take up the present, Maurice, perhaps we should clear away any small misunderstandings there may have been between us in the past." He let his smile fade, his expression become anxious.

Maurice stiffened. He said coldly, "Do not trouble yourself. I am sure there is nothing of moment to concern ourselves with."

"I was afraid you might have heard some foolish and malicious story about Lucy and me and given credence to it. But of course you knew when she came to me there at the last, it was for you."

Maurice said, "My wife has been dead almost fifteen years. There is no need to speak of her." He looked down to adjust a loose lace on his doublet so that Blount might not see the anguish in his eyes. He should never have left her that day. Every time he had gone out with the undisciplined, desperate rebels, disaster had fallen, bringing on the ones he loved best a red flame of destruction. Lucy had been afraid. What young girl would not have been? She had gone to Blount thinking the cause lost. Maurice tried to believe that was the only time she had gone to Blount's arms, though he knew better. She had been too young and

21

tender to be the wife of a man who had wanted to right the injustices of the world.

That was the night he and his friends, Gerard and Lane and Donald with him, had marched against the government force led by Blount, and young Lucy had been killed by a stray musket shot. It had been his last mistake. He had been taken, and then by the mad chance that governs men's fate he was pardoned. Or rather because the gentry were usually pardoned and their estates forfeited, while better men had hanged. He had turned to trade and prospered, and gold had never injured him. What else could you lose and get again and it not be tarnished in the exchange? Not a woman, nor a friend, nor a faith.

"Fifteen years," Maurice repeated harshly. "And whatever blame there might have been was all mine."

"Not at all, not at all," Blount said generously. "I only brought up the subject lest you have felt your honor unsatisfied."

"You have another matter to discuss?"

"Yes. Sir Francis Walsingham sent me here." Blount let his words hang in the air a minute.

Maurice said, "Francis Walsingham?"

Blount shifted himself in his chair to look up at Maurice. He said impatiently, "God's wounds, Maurice, let us be open with each other and have done with this business!"

"By all means."

"Sir Francis sent me about that permit you begged to have renewed for your trade in the Netherlands."

"Yes?"

Blount chewed at his underlip viciously, slid his hands back and forth along the carved arms of the chair. Then he smoothed out his frown and smiled. "Yes, indeed, Maurice. And he wants to renew it for you. He thinks merchants are the bulwark of England's power, and as always he is right." He paused.

Maurice waited politely for him to go on. Blount hung onto his smile doggedly. "Of course Sir Francis can deny you the license and ruin your trade."

Maurice smiled faintly. "He can withhold the license," he conceded.

"Sir Francis is in fact considering doing so," Blount snapped, "unless I can bring a better report of your trading than we have had up till now." Maurice looked bored. "The reports have not been what I'm sure you would wish them to be. Sir Francis feels that if he should give you a license——"

"Give?" Maurice murmured.

"—sell you one then, he should have some pledge in return that would assure us of your good faith."

"And the pledge?"

Blount said impressively, "A ship of one hundred and fifty tons. Unless of course, as I said, I can assure him your commerce is above question."

"And you feel you can do so?" Maurice's brows lifted.

Blount shrugged. "Perhaps." He twisted the gold chain about his neck with long sinewy fingers. "The particular point in question is a story I've had confirmed here about your selling supplies to Philip of Spain."

"You do not approve, Sir Edward?"

"Approve?" Blount exploded into anger. "Selling war material to the man who will turn it against us by next——" He stopped.

"Surely," Maurice said mockingly, "you do not believe that Philip Hapsburg's famous Armada, which has worn out the hopes of her friends and the fears of her enemies, will carry an invading army to England next summer?"

Blount sat up straight. "How did you know the time was next summer?"

"If the Armada creaks into action within two years or ten, I'll give you leave to bring a dozen ships to Walsingham."

"You can jest. You will not be facing the guns. Or will you be with the landing parties?"

Maurice spoke thoughtfully. "Philip of Spain has promised, I believe, twenty regiments to be landed in the North—which would turn out to be a hundred lone soldiers. That would be five thousand men less than you need or a hundred more than you want. No. I not be one to light the beacon fires for Philip Hapsburg."

"Though he's of your own faith?"

"My faith? I'm like Elizabeth, Sir Edward. I am what it profits me to be."

"But you sent Philip cordage?"

"Of course I sent Spain cordage. The Spaniards can use it to hang themselves or rig their ships. I'll send cordage to Elizabeth tomorrow for the same price Philip paid."

"I could have you thrown into prison tonight for that statement." Blount felt bland, sure of himself.

Maurice smiled. "There might be questions asked. I've made myself valuable to a few people, and can make myself so to you if I understand you right."

Blount looked up sharply. He said with slow emphasis, "Perhaps. You are suggesting——"

"I?" Maurice retorted. "Nothing. I'll be happy to send Sir Francis a ship. I've two in the harbor. They seem to be of Dutch design."

"You mean you attacked and captured the ships of a small nation who is England's ally, the outpost of England's fortress aginst Spain?"

"Sir Edward, I'm a merchant. I buy what others have to offer. Yesterday it was two ships. They need repairs and new sails and they were too hastily constructed. Still, they're something between a sailor and the floor of the ocean."

Blount said, "I don't know that we can be of the value to each other that I'd hoped, Maurice. You seem to be a man who knows nothing of honor, of love of country, not even of gratitude to a kindly Queen who saved you from death."

"It's a safe sort of life."

Blount snapped, "A coward too?"

"I see your price rising every minute, Sir Edward." Maurice suppressed a yawn. "You're right of course. But—you will forgive me?—I must confess this prating of honor and country and patriotism palls on me. I was a brave-enough soldier, and once I played with wooden horses. I have outgrown both forms of entertainment. The horse amuses the child, and the heroics must cause laughter among the gods."

Blount felt an angry bewilderment, though Maurice

24

had said one word he could understand. He instantly disclaimed his awareness of it. "I do not quite know what you mean, Maurice. My price——"

"Let us not puruse this useless discussion. You know I invited you here with the unfounded hope that you'd changed since last I knew you. We might then have been of the use to each other you evidently desired when you came so far. You at Court, I here in the North. But you haven't fulfilled any of your . . . ah, brilliant promise."

Blount felt as though a naked rapier had been plucked out of the air and flashed before his eyes. He looked at Maurice stupidly.

Maurice added smoothly, "I don't like being threatened, Sir Edward. A business suggestion I might have listened to, but awkwardly phrased insinuations salted down with hypocrisy are not to my taste—which might be a little too fastidious."

Blount came to his feet, a bright outraged figure. He thought irrelevantly of Katherine. Why, he had flattered this man by being jealous of him. How Katherine would despise him! "I think you overreach yourself, Maurice. You cannot expect your license if I am against you."

Maurice smiled contemptuously and did not trouble to answer.

Blount's color rose. "Would you ruin yourself again, Maurice? You may not be so lucky as you were once."

"On the other hand you may be more fortunate. Confiscation this time would be of far more value than the poor stretch of land you received fifteen years ago. Not enough greater however to make it worth your while doing the work any common informer could do."

"I don't think, Maurice, you are quite in a position to hurl names about. I would have been your friend. You choose to place us among your foes."

"No. I wish merely to remain neutral. Enemies I find are a burden, though of course not so dangerous as one's friends."

At that last word Blount smiled, regaining his composure. "That reminds me of a small matter, Maurice. Perhaps I should have brought it up before. I met your cousin in town yesterday. He needed some slight assistance for a venture, something to do with Perrot, so I gave him a few pounds."

Maurice started to lift his head, then held himself rigid. "I cannot quite believe there is not some misunderstanding. I bear you no grudge, but Donald wouldn't talk to you down in hell."

"I didn't tell him my name, Maurice. But I heard a word or two in the common room at the inn and gave the landlord a small sum for your cousin. It doesn't take much to buy enough rope for a man set on self-destruction. You know, Maurice, when I came here today I would have been satisfied with some small profit such as a share of your business. But you were right earlier. My price has gone up. To conceal any indiscretions of your cousin as well as your own questionable trading I think I would ask——" He paused thoughtfully. "Or would you care to make a suggestion?"

Maurice smiled. "Not yet, Sir Edward." Blount had found the one vulnerable point in his armor, and he had not even troubled to ask Donald yesterday exactly what wild plan he had in mind. Whatever it was, it was too late now to reach and stop him. Maurice felt a nausea thick in his throat, and a sickness too dull for pain surged through him. "If I should change my mind, I'll let you know."

Blount bowed in his most gallant manner. "Not yet" and "if I should change my mind" were phrases not so stonily assured as Maurice's first contemptuous refusals. He should have brought up Donald Stuart's name earlier. That had been a blunder. Maurice might have been more amenable. Ah, well, you could not expect success at the very first venture! And he would yet hold Maurice and his vast possessions in the hollow of his hand. He lifted his eyes to Maurice's and felt shock at the hard gaze they met. Still, the merrier the day, he thought, when Maurice would come begging.

Maurice rang for a servant to show Blount to the door, snuffed out the candles in the library and stood there staring into the darkness beyond the light from the hearth. His hands were twisted together as though

he could hold tightly in their clasp the hard emotionless core of his being that he had fashioned out of the
odds and ends of his life.

3

Maurice could hear from the common room of the
Red Lion the sound of laughter, a scuffle, a snatch of
song. Then the opened door clicked to and Meg came
in. Her eyes were drowsy, and her round face soft with
sleep. "You weren't here Monday, Maurice. I missed
you." She spoke with a shade of petulance.

"But you'd not have noticed my absence tonight,
Meg?"

She smoothed back her disheveled hair, smothered a
yawn. "I'm not sleepy for the reason you believe."
There was a hopeful lift to her voice.

Maurice was not, however, drawn to ask questions
of her. He never asked questions. Even if he had cared
for the girl he would not have, and he found Meg no
trouble to forget. But he felt a sharp relief in her
presence. The small chamber was oppressive, with a
brazier of coals burning in one corner and the single
window shuttered against the dangerous night air. It
closed in about him, deepening the sense of uneasiness
engendered by Blount's threat against Donald last
night.

He shrugged his disquiet aside impatiently and
turned to bar the door. Meg watched him with hard
eyes. He never could be the same as other men. What
if another couple or two did come in? She liked people
about her, and noise and lights. If he were so fine, why
didn't he have his women in his own house?

He put his finger lightly on a loose curl. "Don't
leave me, Meg." He smiled, but his voice was young
and urgent, though he was aware that the very taw-
driness of this girl was to him a thin veneer of safety.
Where there was no faith there could be no betrayal.

She laughed and kissed him. "How you talk, Maurice! And me always here when you want me. It's you
who don't love me enough."

His hand slid up to her bare shoulder. The flesh was warm and moist. Outside there was a sudden pounding of feet, then a fist crashed on the door. Meg's hands flew to her mouth as she let out a little scream of terror. Maurice shot back the bolt with annoyance. A young groom stood in the dark hall trying to catch his breath after his haste. "You're wanted at your house, Master Quain."

"What is it?"

"That I don't know at all, sir. I was told to get you quick. I brought your gelding."

Maurice glanced back at Meg, then followed the boy down corridor and stairs. The vague foreboding rose within him. Outside, the night wind, salty and tasting of the sea, stung his face. The sound of it, tearing through the branches of the trees lining the road and rattling the shutters of houses, and the rhythmic pounding of hoofs on the stones were the only noises to disturb the dark. They galloped down the short stretch of road to his house, tall and gabled, the stained lath and white plaster and gray stone gleaming in the moonlight.

A small group of men were huddled near the door in the courtyard. Maurice went past the whispering servants within and up the wide staircase, ignoring the patter of voices that rose behind him. Donald was waiting in the hall above. His face was haggard.

Maurice said, "Well?"

The chill question made Donald shrink farther within himself. "Say what you will, Maurice. I deserve anything. If a worthless thing like my life would help, you'd be welcome to it."

"I don't doubt, Donald, that your sentiments are excellent. But none too clear. You would say——" Maurice didn't want to hear, not even if it broke the intolerable suspense of this moment.

Donald said, "It's worse than you think."

"Well?"

"This time I've ruined you."

"It's not that easily accomplished."

"And Patrick too."

28

"You went into Hartley with Patrick?" Maurice's voice was like a blow.

"Yes. He didn't know I had any plans—that there wasn't any reason I shouldn't join him." He didn't look at Maurice as he spoke. The torches along the stairway and on the upper landing flung wavering lights on the timbered floor and up the high walls to the carved rafters. "I got my friends free—well, what does it matter to you? Patrick was taken as an accomplice since I went in with him and Perrot sweats he'll make him suffer enough for the three of us. And as Patrick went on your business, your name is in it."

Maurice said bitterly, "For just one night's work you did well, Donald." Blount, he thought, had done far better than even he could have hoped.

"I wish I were in hell before I had to tell you this. But, Maurice, there is one chance to save Patrick at least. I can raise men from near the border. I sent a boy into the town and found out Perrot is sending him south to London. If they do not have Patrick North in their hands, what can they do against you?"

"Nothing—except put out a proclamation against me." Maurice stared at Donald scornfully. Then the contempt died out of his face. He frowned. "Donald! Perhaps . . ." His voice warmed. "You get what men you can. I have the crew of Fox's ship at my command. He hasn't sailed yet." His black mood was washed away by a swift and shining spirit of resolve. "Wait! I'll get sword and helmet. We'll ride to Hartley this night."

Donald moved swiftly after Maurice to the bedroom, a big square chamber with walls paneled in dark oak to a ceiling of molded plaster that shone in the light of branched candelabra. Shadows slid out across the floor, wavered, fell back before slithering silent out again.

Maurice tossed his cloak onto the table. The shadows leaped at the wild spurt of flame from the draft of the thrown garment, moved forward again as though waiting. The iron bound lid of a chest at the side of the room clanged when Maurice threw it open. He flung a visorless helmet to Donald, pulled out scabbard and sword. The leather was dark from the sifted

29

dust of years and stiff under his fingers as he buckled the belt about his narrow hips. There was one bright moment more heady than wine when the scabbard struck against his leg as he turned to face Donald Then he stopped. The candles were pale tongues of light licking against the vastness of the shadows closing about them.

Maurice's fingers fumbled with the battered silver buckle at his waist. The belt loosened. He walked across the carpeted floor, laid the sheathed sword quietly on the silk and velvet coverlet of the bed. Had he thought to take up a weapon again? He would destroy the man he wanted to save, he would ruin himself. He felt for one moment the deadness that had been within him when he had made his last mistake and his young wife had died. No!

Maurice said, "I'm afraid, Donald, I have been precipitate. I forgot I am only a merchant and of little use to you. If you need any of my servingmen, take them."

It was a moment before Donald realized what Maurice had said. "But you—I almost thought, Maurice, you were a man again, Maurice!" He put his hand out blindly toward the door and went out of the room. Maurice heard the clank of his spurred boots down the stairs, doors opening, the shouting of men, a deep-voiced command, and the thudding of hoofs—too few hoofs charging into the blackness of the night.

The silence closed about him again. He turned. He was very tired. The weapon on the bed caught his eye. With cold deliberation he walked over, took up the scabbard, unsheathed the blade, watched the fire of light run down the steel. He would make no more mistakes. He put his booted foot on the blade and broke it neatly in half before he flung it back into the still open chest. What need had he of a sword? He was a rich man. He could buy what he wanted.

The porter closed the door behind Maurice and shuffled off quickly. Maurice looked about the square hall of the house Perrot had taken for his headquarters at Hartley. A young womanservant went hastily past him. A page had been loitering on the steps of the wide staircase that swept up into dimness. He came running down, unconscious of Maurice's presence. A roar sounded from the regions overhead. Maurice had never seen John Perrot, but from the stories he had heard of his choleric temper, he gathered that the man he was looking for was not far away.

Maurice crossed to the boy. "I want to see Sir John."

The page jumped at the unexpected sound of Maurice's voice, grinned impudently as he turned his head to look at the merchant. "You, sir, are the only one in this house who does. Up the steps, turn down the corridor, and through the second floor door to your right."

Maurice eyed him coldly. "Announce me to Sir John. Quain of Blyth."

The page shrugged resignedly and went gingerly up the stairs again with Maurice at his heels. The boy stopped with his hand on the latch as a volume of curses came from the room within. He looked at the coin in his hand that Maurice had given him. "You want to see Sir John, but does he want to see you, Master Quain? As no ill-wisher of yours, it's a point I'd be sure about before you go farther."

"He will."

The page hunched his shoulders up about his ears, opened the door. A deep voice snarled, "What do you want?" At the same moment a pewter mug came flying across the room. The boy stepped neatly aside as he announced Maurice. There was a silence. Then: "Show him in!"

Sir John Perrot, seated behind a long oak table, lifted a haggard face to the visitor. His eyes were bloodshot, and the skin under his jaw was loose and flabby. He was a heavy middle-aged man, and in his leather jerkin and soiled ruff he looked more like a common soldier than the Deputy Warden of the North. But the green eyes in the mottled face were direct and piercing in spite of his seemingly far-from-sober condition. "What in the name of the Seven Wounds of Christ do you want?" He threw back his head, draining a mug that was a companion to the one he had hurled at the page. "I told 'em I didn't want to be disturbed."

31

Maurice crossed the room, tossed his cloak onto a bench and sat down unbidden in a carved walnut chair. Perrot suddenly pulled himself upright. "Quain! I heard your name yesterday. I didn't like it. I like it less today. Well, plenty of room in the cell with that man of yours."

Maurice pulled off his gauntlets indolently, finger by finger. Before he could answer, the door opened again. Maurice did not turn. He knew who it was before he heard the quick clipped voice—"Did you send for me, Sir John?"—before he saw the blue satin doublet slashed with crimson, bright against the oaken door, the fair hair and beard, the charming smile. Maurice's eyes flicked from Edward Blount to the casement windows closed against the sunlight that sifted through the thick greenish glass of the small leaded panes.

Perrot's voice rolled across the room. "Send for you? Get out! Body of Christ, I told you, Blount, to get out of here today and stay out!"

Blount said, "If you should need me, Sir John, you have but to ring. I will wait." He glanced towards Maurice. "Shall I assume you want the guards?"

Perrot's hand closed purposefully about his tankard. "All you have to assume, Blount, is that I want you to get out. Now!" Blount bowed gracefully and withdrew. "That bastard knew I hadn't sent for him. He's just one of Walsingham's men spying on me. I'm sending him home tomorrow. I'll wager he's at the keyhole now hoping to find out why you're here." His bloodshot eyes turned to Maurice. "Why are you?"

Maurice said smoothly. "I thought, since you were so close, Sir John, I would see you about the shipments of cloth sent you three months ago."

Perrot's mouth dropped open. "Well, I'll be damned! The very words your man used yesterday. At least Blount says he was your man."

"North? We'll speak of him later. Now as to the cloth——"

The color in Sir John's face mounted ominously. "If you purposed to come here to force payment out of me, it was an ill day for you. If this house had gold

32

stuffed to its rafters, I wouldn't pay you for a bale. So you know this Master North?"

Maurice ignored the question. "You mistake me, Sir John. The payment for the cloth is of no consequence. I wished only to learn if the material suited you or if the next shipment should be of heavier linen."

"Ship what you will. It doesn't matter to me if the soldiers all go naked. I'm set upon by every fool and knave in England and Scotland." He glared at Maurice, including him in either category or perhaps both. "Just what makes you think you'll be shipping anything to anybody? If you're done with this nonsense, Quain, may I put in a word?" He stopped to refill his tankard from a leather sack on the table. "I was about to send for you to answer a few questions."

Maurice's brows rose in polite inquiry while he looked at the knight speculatively. The gossip of Sir John's birth seemed to have more truth than most tales—Henry the Eighth's bastard by Mary Berkeley. The Tudor temper, the green eyes, the same tall frame as Queen Elizabeth, though where Elizabeth was angular Sir John had their father's heaviness.

"Two men escaped yesterday while I was talking here to some scurvy young clerk from your shop about cloth and uniforms."

Maurice said, "An odd coincidence."

Sir John started to choke, loosened the enormous ruff at his throat and tore off the supporting standard with a jerk of his powerful hand. "But I have your clerk, Quain, and he's being sent to London today to hang. I'm hemmed in on every side by enemies, and he'll probably be my ruin. But he aided in the escape of prisoners and, body of God, he'll hang!"

"Your ruin?"

"But not mine alone. You won't come out of this well either."

Maurice looked bored. "Really, Sir John! My downfall perhaps, though I doubt it, or yours. But not the ruin of both of us. What possible connection is there between you and me?"

"None, except that we're both in the way of bigger men. You don't believe it? If you think Edward Blount

33

intends you should walk through that door again a free man, you are not so shrewd as I'd think you. As for me, have I not fought for this England and bled for her? Yet I'm always thrown to some outpost—North England this year; I've heard rumors it'll be Ireland next year. I make enemies because I do not fear to tell the truth no matter who gets hurt. Walsingham doesn't like that. Burghley doesn't like it. A lot of people don't like it."

Maurice felt that whatever the reasons for Perrot's making enemies, there was no question of his ability to do so. But he only said, "Blount?" dismissing him contemptuously.

Perrot tilted back in his chair, gulped down his liquor as he looked at Maurice across the rim of his tankard. "Don't underestimate your enemies, Quain. A snake isn't large, but it's dangerous."

Maurice, starting to lean forward, was motionless as his eyes caught the speaker's. A cold breath of wind blew over him. Perrot and he, two doomed men— strangers and yet caught together in some deadly web? He said briefly, "But now, Sir John, you and this clerk of mine. I fail to see how he will either aid or injure you."

"If I do my duty and have him hanged, Quain— which rest assured I shall—someone will use the story when it's too late to help you or any man else, and turn it against me, saying how I oppressed the poor and weak; how I couldn't hold two criminals under lock and key and—oh, you know how it goes."

"Well then, an unlocked door, a drunken guard— the matter's simple enough."

"Simple! And the next step for me will be toward the Tower. Let three prisoners escape! Master Quain! Either way I'm trapped. Hang the man and there will still be my probable destruction. But his escape would make it certain, though the Queen of England's my own——" He stopped.

"Yes. You are right. I had not thought so far. Another escape from a town overflowing with your soldiers would not sound well. Better I can see to go back to the original suggestion; an odd coincidence North

34

was here at the moment the rebels broke prison. Does that have a better ring? All at a price of course, Sir John."

Perrot's hand crashed against the top of the table as he pulled himself to his feet. "I believe now all I have heard of you, Quain. You bribe John Perrot, attempt to buy my honor! My name has not yet been bandied about by idle tongues. I have never been branded timeserver or seller of favors. But that it would please Blount so much I'd have had you long before this in chains yourself." He was breathing hard, leaning slightly forward from his hips as he glared at Maurice, who had not moved.

"An excellent-sounding defense, Sir John. The Queen herself would believe it. Now the terms——"

Perrot snarled, "You persist in a pretense—" he stopped a moment, the words he'd chosen following one another ill after drinking—"a pretense that we are agreed on a mad scheme of treason. If you do not give me some satisfaction on your part in this before I drain this cup, you'll be put under guard."

Maurice smiled at the way the threat shaped itself. He moved across deliberately to the table, picked up the mug of wine and walked over to empty it onto the hearth. The liquid hissed in the flames and a cloud of smoke spiraled blackly upward. "I think we understand each other. No official can live on the wages the Queen doles out, the Deputy Warden least of all. Debts mount. Creditors are grossly importuning."

Perrot lowered himself slowly onto his great chair while almost unconsciously he refilled the returned mug from the leather sack.

Maurice went on: "Perhaps I'm wrong, Sir John, but I've heard that your officers, in order to get their penny a day from the Exchequer for each of their men, fill up their ranks with Scotch rebels so that they can report one hundred, a hundred and fifty, two hundred men, under them. When the money's in the captains' hands, the rebels disappear with their new liveries and muskets, and the captains pocket the silver."

Perrot growled, "What else could they do if they'd live?"

35

"Precisely, Sir John. And for, well, say two hundred pounds, a Deputy could send his moneylenders packing, could live a little closer to his position."

The tip of Perrot's tongue ran about his lips. "Two hundred pounds you said?"

"And as for the shipments of cloth, consider them a small gift in evidence of my gratitude." Maurice drew up his chair to the table.

"Two hundred pounds and two shipments of cloth. Why? For less than that you could probably get your name left completely off the record."

Maurice said coldly, "I'm paying for the favor. My reasons are my own."

"It doesn't make sense. You serve Elizabeth, I'm told, and Philip of Spain, Henry of France, the Flemish burghers—but always for a profit. Is a clerk worth two hundred pounds in the North?" He looked up with a leer. "Or does he have a wife who will be grateful?"

"As I said, Sir John, my reasons are my own. If I may use this parchment and quill, I'll make out a bill of exchange to my agent in London for the money." He wrote rapidly, signed his name, and under it the twentieth of May, 1584.

Perrot pushed the wine toward Maurice. "Seal it with a drink?"

"No, thank you."

Perrot drew back with distaste. Bribery did not look so bad when done with a laugh, a wink, a lusty drink. But carrying it out as though it were a cold business deal did nothing to soften its hard lines.

Maurice handed the piece of parchment he had made out across the table to the knight. "If there should be questions on this, you can say you forced a loan out of me."

Sir John looked the writing over carefully, then rolled it up and put it under his doublet. He snorted, "Who'll believe anyone got money out of you for nothing? You with a foot in every camp in Europe. Oh, I keep myself advised."

"I had not thought," Maurice retorted, "to keep my affairs private. People want to be paid, then, to hold

36

their tongues. Now as to Master North—he will be released at once?"

"Yes. I'll give the captain instructions." Perrot laughed suddenly, an unexpected bellow in the quiet room. "It's worth it just to spite Blout, who thought to get a reward for the lad's capture. Burghley won't like this; he won't like it at all. I wish I could see his face when he's told the rebels escaped. He thinks he's King of England. And so," he added flatly, "he is, or I'd not be kicked about, enemies on every side——" His voice broke off into an almost indistinguishable grumble. "If he's not put down, my deputyship will end as too many others have ended their office here—a march from the border to the Tower." Apropos of nothing that had gone before, he added, "You should be married, Quain."

Maurice stood up. "I was married. Once is enough for any man of sense."

Perrot looked into the golden depths of his mug. "I have a daughter."

Maurice almost laughed. "Do you think I'd take a woman without any fortune and inherit her father's debts?"

Perrot said simply. "You can afford to. I couldn't. I had to take my pleasure away from the marriage bed. Katherine's not a bad-looking lass either." Maurice did not even trouble to scorn the offer. "She's of the blood royal through me, though that is not always an easy heritage. Before I die I'd like to see her safely married to a commoner."

"The Tudors, upstarts, kings since yesterday, a hundred years!" Maurice did not try to keep the offense out of his voice by softening the words with a conciliatory tone.

"She has a Scottish mother."

"French I heard it."

"All right," Perrot snapped. "Her mother was a French maid of honor. I just thought Scottish might appeal to you more, and you part Scottish yourself."

"I am not interested."

Perrot had brought up his daughter's betrothal merely on the spur of the moment, and as he had been

37

known to do before with any single man not staring a debtors' prison in the face. He gave over the attempt without demur. "I thought you might just possibly be looking for a wife. Katherine's a nice armful. I hear her name linked with Blout's and I don't like it. What do women see in men like that?"

Maurice looked up at the words, then down at the knuckles of his hands, white as he clenched them. "I don't know," he said softly. . . . Lucy.

"I suppose you never thought of running a sword through him?"

There was so long a pause that Sir John opened his mouth to repeat his question. Maurice stooped to adjust his boot, then pulled on his gauntlets before answering. The silver and golden eagles embroidered on the leather caught the light slanting through the leaded panes. "No," he said easily. "Why bother with a task any mercenary who can hold a weapon would perform for you?" He started to turn away. "I trust I'll have no trouble getting leave out of Hartley?"

Perrot waved his big hand carelessly. "Not at all, not at all. Just ask whoever has his ear against the keyhole to see you past the guards." He shook with sudden laughter. "Learned a lot myself at a keyhole once."

Maurice smiled faintly. "You have my gratitude, Sir John, for your help today. I may be able to return the favor sometime."

Perrot looked up from under heavy brows at the impassive clean-shaved face above him. "I hope, Master Quain, I'll never be so desperate as to need to ask for it!"

Patrick handed the listings of cargo to the customs official at the warehouse and walked down to the shore to wait for Captain Fox. The *Falcon* had anchored a cable's length off the quay and the gig with a half dozen men at the oars was working its way in against the ebbing tide. A high wind drove puffs of clouds across the blue arch of sky, sang through the branches of the scrubby pines edging the path to the wharf, plucked at the wide sleeves of his doublet. Patrick narrowed his eyes against the sun which glinted on the green waters of the bay and splintered on the white broken crests of the long waves rolling in almost to his feet. He watched the small boat come smartly about and glide up the long incline.

Captain Fox walked gingerly up the slippery stones of the ramp. His finery was wet through so that the tarnished lace looked like tangled seaweed about his throat. He scowled at Patrick. *"Ventre-saint-gris!* Of all the godforsaken harbors I ever put into, this is the scurviest! I hope your cargo's ready to load damn fast. I'm sailing in the morning."

Patrick said gravely, "Why, Captain, we don't want to be cheated of your charming company so soon when you haven't been here for over two months. Besides, the cannon for La Rochelle isn't here yet. There's a delay for a special license."

"A plague on the license! If this wind gets stronger and drives the *Falcon* onto the shoals the cannon will never get to France."

"When we start to do business for the convenience of ship captains, we'll send you word. Where's the dispatch from London?"

The captain put his horny hand into his doublet, pulled out a packet of letters. "That agent of yours—I never can remember his name—belly . . . liver . . . Hart!—he said to give them to Quain the moment I saw him. He also said things isn't so good at the Exchange."

Patrick laughed. "What things? And not good for whom?" He took the dispatches, broke the seal and started to ruffle through, but rolled the papers up again quickly ast he wind tore along the edges. "I see what you mean, Captain. I suppose the breeze is a little strong for a boat like the *Falcon* held together with hope, faith and a smearing of pitch."

Fox forgot his mention of London news. "Why, you trullibub, you barley pudding full of maggots, that's the best ship that ever rode out a storm in the North Sea, the Atlantic or the Mediterranean! But I don't like this harbor."

"Well, come up later today and tell Master Quain all your troubles, Captain. He'll be much interested." Patrick went up the slope to untie his horse from the post near the warehouse.

As Patrick entered the office half an hour later, Maurice turned from the window that faced the sun-splattered land reaching toward the northern hills. Patrick tossed a sheaf of parchment on the table. "The usual routine except for this triple sealed letter which is marked for your attention."

Maurice took the document, read through it swiftly, then again slowly, incredulously. "You'll have to change the orders I gave you this morning, Patrick. We won't be in Blyth in August. We'll be on our way to London."

Patrick looked up in astonishment. "London? Why?"

Maurice said grimly, "Because Hart is the most stupid man east of the Indies. The muddleheaded idiot lost what little wits he had and transferred all my money to Antwerp for safekeeping. I'll have to go south to straighten out my affairs."

"Hart must have had some reason for such a move," Patrick spoke reflectively, but he smiled. Go down to London? There was magic in the very name of the city.

"Don't try to excuse him. He heard rumors in the Burse about me—cordage to Philip for instance, and that Perrot and I were together two months ago and two traitors escaped hanging and after that Perrot paid his debts. A few odd words started by Blount no doubt and Hart jumps like a frightened rabbit. I dislike stupidity."

Patrick frowned. "Cordage? That's not new. Of course Perrot—your cousin didn't do you too good a turn with him, but it was not from malice."

Maurice said shortly, "You can always depend on your friends to deal with you faithlessly. And aside from business I didn't care for the way Donald risked the neck of an employee of mine in his schemes."

"I didn't enjoy being used as a pawn myself," Patrick admitted. "But I suppose Donald Stuart had other things than me on his mind. Do you want an order sent your agent in Antwerp countermanding the transfer?"

"Yes, though it may be too late. I hope Hart is

stricken with the pox." Maurice eyed his secretary with annoyance as Patrick showed no false sorrow at the necessity of a journey to London.

The cries of the vendors, the screeching of wagons and the clanging of iron from blacksmith's shops crashed about his ears as Maurice walked up the quay at Billingsgate. The crowd surged around him—ragged urchins, harlots, sailors with red kerchiefs about their heads and hoops of gold in their ears, and bustling customs officials. Maurice stepped behind the high wheels of a water cart, disliking the pressure of people. And the stench—were all the fish in London at Billingsgate?

Patrick, coming toward him past two fish peddlers, narrowly escaped having a tray of herring on his head. Maurice said coldly, "If you think you can get safely by the London vendors, hire one of these boys idling around to take you to the Royal Exchange. Tell Hart I want to see him at once." The wind, warm and damp, stirred through his hair.

Patrick smiled. "Yes, sir!" He added with zest, "I'll like London, Master Quain."

"Will you?" Maurice looked indifferently at the spectacle that had impressed Patrick. To the east the Tower of London with its great curtain walls and towers was massive against the gray sky. Houses, with their upper stories jutting out so that scarcely a finger of light could seep through to the streets below, were crowded together leading toward St. Paul's on the hill. Beside them the Thames flowed out to sea. The ships at anchor rocked gently in the waves, their masts and rigging creaking from the movement. He turned back. "Captain Fox mentioned the Saracen's Head is a good place to stay. I'll be there."

Patrick nodded and moved quickly out of the press while Maurice waited impatiently for one of the crew to be sent him to act as guide through the city. Captain Fox himself was holding his own against customs officials and inspectors from the London Livery Companies and, Maurice suspected, enjoying it thoroughly.

After almost an hour's delay a household servant came up with a particularly villainous-looking sailor, scarred and bearded. Maurice eyed him with a dry humor. "I'm going to the Saracen's Head, Hans. Do you think you can find me the way without frightening the natives to death?"

Hans, who caught only the words "Saracen's Head," made a guttural sound of assent and nodded vigorously.

The stones of the narrow twisting streets were slippery with drying slops and rubbish flung from the windows overhead. Maurice found the stench hanging acrid and heavy in the airless way. The houses huddled wall to wall so that no inch of space was wasted. Prentices outside the shops shouted their masters' wares of leather goods, shoes, silverwork, foreign laces, cloth of linen and serge and velvet—boys with breaking voices that met and clashed and outshrilled one another.

The Saracen's Head was distinguished by a seven-foot pole from which swung a huge square board. On the board was painted in blatant reds and blues and greens the head of a vicious-looking Oriental in a monstrous turban. Maurice looked at the picture and then at his guide with a fleeting smile for an underlying resemblance of savagery in the products of East and West. He dismissed the sailor and opened the door. It was early in the afternoon and few groups were at the tables. Maurice glanced about, went across the timbered floor to a corner table near an open casement window.

The landlord bustled up, a thin man who looked as though he never had time to enjoy his own cookery. "Nice roast capon we have today, sir, with honey sauce. Or a young goose, pheasant, young suckling pig, mutton, lamb, beef ribs, whatever your desires are. And wines, ah——" He rubbed his hands. "We have a fresh shipment from France, Gascony, Burgundy, golden wines from the South."

Maurice deliberated. "Goose if it's really young and tender, and a light wine."

The landlord looked offended at the lack of appreciation in Maurice's tone. "Yes, sir, right away, sir." He backed away.

A man's voice behind him made an angry exclamation, and the landlord just avoided colliding with the young woman the newcomer was escorting. The girl laughed lightly. "Do not mind, sir. No harm done."

Maurice did not turn his head at her laughter or the low amused voice. He glanced up at the inn door opened again and Patrick and Hart entered. As they came up, Maurice said, "Good day, Master Hart! You are most prompt. I hope this does not inconvenience you."

"No. Why, no, not at all, sir." Hart was a round, portly little man with lanky brown hair. "But, God in heaven, you're the last person this side of hell I thought to see in London! Do you think it's wise? Surely you leave again when Captain Fox sails out?"

The servitor brought up the meal Maurice had ordered and waited for the requests of the other two. Maurice said, "From the looks of this goose, I'd advise you to try the beef. There isn't much the worst cook can do do that except to forget to bake it entirely." When the servingman moved away, he turned back to his agent. "Tomorrow is a little early when Fox leaves. I thought you would prefer to meet here rather than at your offices in the Exchange since you seemed so—" he suppressed a harsher word and said—"unduly worried over my business affairs." He picked up his wine. The light breaking through the glass made patterns of gold on the nicked table.

Hart's fingers laced together. "Most kind of you, Master Quain. I suppose you got my letter? About Antwerp I mean. I . . . well, I just used my best judgment."

"I don't doubt it was your best."

"While beyond my duty, Master Quain, I felt I should handle your money as I would want you to handle mine if our positions were reversed."

Maurice's voice did not become warmer. "It's a pity to spoil even so mediocre a dinner with talk of business, but it seems to me we are somewhat at cross purposes. I've sent a man to Antwerp countermanding your order. I'm presuming you had a bill of exchange conveyed out of the country. You did not chance moving gold?"

"Yes. Of course a bill of exchange. You meant confirmed? You said countermanded." Hart laughed.

" 'Countermanded' was the word I used and meant, Master Hart. I hope my clerk was in time. Any man is entitled to be a fool once. But no agent of mine is entitled to be a fool twice. I trust we have now reached an understanding?"

The servingman put their platters before Hart and Patrick and moved to the table where the man and girl were sitting. Maurice did not even glance at them. Patrick's eyes, following the servingman, found the girl. He stared at her, catching his breath at her unexpected beauty. A slim young woman with shining dark hair and a vivid mobile face. Her glance crossed his. She seemed no more aware of him than if he were part of the chair he was sitting on.

Hart turned incredulously toward Maurice. "You mean you don't want your holdings secured? If you will pardon me, sir, I think you are mad."

Maurice shrugged and picked up a piece of tired-looking watercress. Patrick withdrew his gaze reluctantly from the girl to grin at Hart. "You must admit, Master Hart, it is worth some small risk not to lose all our connections in London."

Hart hung grimly onto the knowledge of being in the right. "Better to lose half your fortune—or all of it, Master Quain—than your life. The trouble is you don't know what dangers are. You sit on your rock in North England, trade with Spain or the devil and think you've no troubles but from pirates and storms. You forget how when cargo comes into port the Court of the Livery Companies decides whether the quality is good or if the cargo should just be burned out of hand. You know how you've escaped that once or twice and only by—"

Maurice said, "Bribery is a harsh word. Let us say we saved our cargo by persuading the Court of the Livery Companies to inspect the goods again and see

44

they were of an excellent quality. Which they always are. Inferior products are seldom worth the trouble involved with them. Inferior products or inferior employees."

Hart looked at Maurice resentfully. "If you will not leave London, Master Quain, let us settle our accounts tomorrow."

Maurice glanced from Hart to his wine in a bored fashion. "Good! I'll not detain you if you find my company dangerous."

Though his dinner was scarcely touched, Hart got to his feet with alacrity at the unexpected opportunity to leave. Patrick, suppressing a smile at the little man's haste, lifted his wine to his mouth in a gesture that was never completed. A chair scraped gratingly across the floor and the man at the nearby table rose and came toward them. Edward Blount here! Patrick put his glass down with exaggerated care so that its foot fitted exactly in the wet ring where it had stood earlier.

Blount's heavy voice said, "A moment, Hart!" The knight's neat mustache and short jaunty beard were golden against the starched ruff at his throat. Patrick noticed fleetingly how the girl turned her head, how her brows lifted in surprise at her companion's sudden movement. "We have been watching you for some time, Hart. Not without reason, it seems."

Hart made a strangled sound in his throat. His skin was a sickly grayish-white. Maurice turned to eye the intruder with much the same expression of distaste as he had looked at his food earlier. "I wondered if the voice were yours, Sir Edward. But I had not thought to see you. Who is looking after North England, and you in London?"

"I'll wager you hadn't expected me, Maurice," Blount retorted, "or you would never have dared come here."

"My dear sir, do you cut so large a figure against the English sky?"

Edward Blount flushed angrily. Maurice, now that Hart had moved, could see Blount's companion. Her glance caught his unexpectedly. Her lashes swept against her cheeks as she looked down at her hands

45

folded loosely together on the table in front of her. Slim, delightful looking hands. But a girl unmasked in a public place. Careless of her reputation? Or had she more likely none to be careless of? But there was something in and beyond her beauty that stirred a faint response.

Blount made a graceful movement to one side so that his silken body blocked the girl's view. He said, "It is not I who cut so large a figure, Maurice; but you. It is only fair to tell you I have reported to Sir Francis Walsingham—" Blount stopped, showing his annoyance at Maurice's remaining seated.

"You were saying?"

"It is only fair to tell you, Maurice," Blount started again stiffly, "that I reported seeing you with Sir John Perrot in Hartley where two rebels escaped. It doesn't sound well."

"It doesn't?"

"I do my duty to my country as I see it, Master Quain . . . Maurice. But I do it honestly and openly. I have no personal quarrel with you." Maurice looked at him so bleakly that Blount caught his breath, stumbled over his words. "I thought it but honorable to tell you what your position is here."

"Thank you!" Maurice dismissed him with a turn of his head toward his agent. "We will settle our affairs tomorrow then, Master Hart." Blount did not move. Hart ran the tip of his tongue about dry lips unable to speak.

Patrick was on his feet. He had read more into Blount's words than Maurice troubled to do. The muscles of his throat were rigid. For one moment the tension was fine as a hair and brittle as thin glass. There was a rustle from behind and the young woman came across the floor toward them. She was taller than Maurice had expected. Her black hair, piled high on her proudly held head, was set off by a small velvet cap looped with pearls, the plume at the side curving down to her shoulder. She touched Blount's arm. Maurice came slowly to his feet, approval in his eyes for the fine lines of her young body, her lovely piquant face, the dark eyes and painted red mouth.

Blount shook off her hand, frowning. "My dear Katherine! I am sorry to have had to interrupt our dinner but I have my duties, however they may interfere with our pleasure. You do not understand me, Maurice."

Katherine glanced from Blount to the men he was facing: Hart whom fear had reduced to a jelly; Patrick—the color was returning to his cheeks at her quick warm glance and there was an attempt at a grin on his thin mouth. She smiled at him, and then looked at Maurice. From the moment Blount had gone to their table she had been sure it was Maurice Quain. She felt she knew this man as though they had met before. She was sorry for him and knew a tinge of disloyalty in her pity. For if Ned had been against this merchant when first he'd planned to go to North England, that had been but a faint shadow of his hostility when he returned.

Maurice met her eyes. His own recognized the sympathy in her mobile face, recognized and rejected it with a chill scorn before he turned back to Blount. The unspoken rebuff made her tingle with anger for a moment, then her shoulders lifted in an indifference that matched his.

Blount said, "You do not understand me, Maurice. There is no need for me to tell you why you are being placed under arrest. Some men have been in the Tower for years without being brought to trial or hearing the reason for their imprisonment."

The small noises in the common room, a laugh, a quick retort, the cry, "Score at the bar!" the breathless "Anon, sir, anon!" the sound of dish striking against dish, all seemed to swell, filling in the space about them that had been sucked empty at Blount's words.

Maurice's voice was contemptuous. "Arrest? Me? Don't be a fool, Blount. One would think to hear you that you were on the stage or in Northumberland."

"My men are at the door. You do not suppose this is a chance meeting. I came prepared. I have ways, Maurice, of knowing where the enemies of the State are, their plans——"

Maurice made a gesture of impatience. "I don't

47

doubt you will be so ill-advised as to carry out your threat, Sir Edward. But I trust you will allow me to finish my dinner. Thank you. It is poorly cooked and worse served, but a hungry man cannot be too fastidious. You will not, of course, insult your intelligence by also arresting my companions."

Patrick turned his head sharply at Maurice's words.

Conscious of Katherine at his elbow and himself not cutting so fine a figure as he had hoped, Blount spat out, "No! We let the small fish through the meshes in the net."

Patrick said quietly, "Except for me."

Maurice waited for Katherine to leave so he might be seated. "Let me return your kindness, Sir Edward, by informing you that while I do not pretend to know the thoughts of her ministers, the Queen will not be pleased with your work this day."

Edward Blount's hope of seeing Walsingham dwindled with the fading light of day. He stood at the window opening on St. James's Park, which stretched toward the palace of St. James. A frown of impatience creased his brows as he stared at grass and trees, a pale green under the mist coming up from the Thames on which Whitehall fronted. Light clouds in the western sky obscured the sun. He wiped his forehead with a fine cambric handkerchief. It had been a warm oppressive day. His padded doublet sat heavily on his shoulders. He wondered in exasperation what vagary of the Queen's made her decide to have the court in London at this time of year.

He should have been happy, pleased with himself, and he was not. He couldn't understand it. Maurice Quain had come to London, walked into his arms openly and carelessly. The credit for his arrest need be divided with no one, nor the reward. But something vital was missing. Was it just uneasiness because Maurice had been so sure of himself? By heaven, he'd be glad to see the end of that man! He would like to see the arrogance wiped off his face, the icy self-assurance torn away, and only a broken shell left, yellowish with fear. What good would his money be then? Or Katherine's sympathy do him? That was the sore spot which had the exquisite torture of an aching tooth.

Katherine had been odd over this whole affair. She had not said much. But then, unlike a woman, she seldom did. There had been about her, however, a curious withdrawal. Women! He checked his thoughts. Katherine had set eyes on Maurice only once, had not even spoken to him. He had no reason in the world to be jealous. And yet somehow he felt bruised from the whole encounter. He hooked his thumb in his belt. The reward. The sweetness of the thought of Maurice's money made him smile involuntarily.

He turned his head as the door swung open. There was a clank of arms of the body guard and the Queen's Principal Secretary came into the anteroom. His face was gray with fatigue, but his eyes had a sharpened intensity in their very weariness. Blount stood stiffly outlined against the window waiting for Sir Francis to see him, or rather to admit seeing him. Walsingham missed nothing.

A young secretary lifted the mantle from Walsingham's shoulders as he answered the unspoken question, "Nothing at all, Sir Francis, except two routine dispatches, one from Antwerp begging for an answer to their appeal for aid to the Northern Provinces, and the other from Madrid complaining about the piratical raids of Drake and Hawkins." His anxious eyes dwelt on Walsingham, who always looked ten years older after a difficult audience with the Queen.

Walsingham glanced around. "You wished to see me, Sir Edward?"

"At your convenience, sir."

Walsingham nodded and motioned him to follow as the secretary held the door to the inner office open for them. "Yes?" Walsingham sat down behind a wide paper-strewed desk.

Blount searched for the term that would rivet attention. "It's about one of those rebels from the North, sir."

At the word "rebels" the Principal Secretary winced. The word had been hurled back and forth all afternoon between him and that red-haired green-eyed daughter

49

of Henry or of the devil. The Dutch were only rebels, she had snapped at him, rebels against their rightful monarch Philip of Spain. She would not countenance them. Give them aid, and they'd be an example to any of her own subjects who might be dissatisfied. No! No! No! To his bald statement that Drake and Hawkins and their privateers were at war with Spain whether England was or not, she had only laughed—cackled would be closer. That was the kind of war she liked. Drake's ventures sometimes paid a thousand percent return. When did outright warfare pay even the expenses poured into the armies and supplies? What if the Dutch rebels had the only true religion, as Walsingham said? She was tired of extremists who found so little in this life they had to quarrel and die over the next. She was tired of the Dutch demands. She was tired of Walsingham.

Walsingham moved a document a hairbreadth to get it into line with the quill beside it, lifted his dark eyes to Blount. "A Northern rebel?" he asked sourly. "Who is it?"

"Maurice Quain of Blyth, sir."

Walsingham repeated the name slowly, appeared to go through his mind as a man might ruffle through his papers for data, then nodded. "Yes. I remember your report."

"The story of his bribing Sir John Perrot."

"The report coupled his name with Perrot," Walsingham corrected.

"However it is put, Sir Francis, it is certain he is carrying on his treason under the name of commerce."

Walsingham lifted his hand. "Sir Edward, I like it no better than you. But Perrot is not a man we can touch easily, at least not yet. As for the Spanish supplies, unless we declare war with Spain, traffic with the country is not a crime though it would seem to be injudicious."

"Worse than that, Sir Francis. You remember the pledge you demanded? That ship the *Wilhelm* and its companion were Dutch vessels and not honestly come by, I'll swear. Do you consider such a merchant a friend of the State? No."

Walsingham looked up at Blount. He did not like others answering for him. "With enemies on every side, English subjects like this Quain are our worst enemies because they are not always recognized as such. But you say you have a man watching him in Blyth?"

"I have done better than that, Sir Edward. Maurice Quain is in London. I will say I'd hoped for some time—but I did not really expect his arrival here. A blunder for so clever a man, don't you think?"

"That is good, Sir Edward. It is much easier to control his shipping from here than far in the North. But is he staying in London?"

Blount smiled. "Quain has been committed to a sheriff's home in Cheapside waiting for your signature to send him to the Tower. His secretary, who is a young fool, also is there—on his insistence, not mine."

Walsingham did not speak for a moment. Then: "No! On what grounds did you have Quain taken into custody?"

Blount sat up straight in surprise. "But I have just told you, sir!"

Walsingham shook his head. "We might hold him on that. But a man with his wealth does not disappear so easily. If you recall, Sir Edward, I mentioned when we first spoke of him that he'd been of service to Her Majesty. Never move openly against a man unless you have enough proof to hang him twice over."

"But, Sir Francis! The escape of those rebels . . . the Dutch ships . . ."

"I said *proof*. Or of course the Queen's ill will. She does not yet see eye to eye with us on foreign affairs. And Maurice Quain is within the law."

"Am I to understand I am to have Quain released?"

"For the time."

Blount said dully, "If a man's wealthy, I see he can do anything he wills."

The strained look of fatigue about Walsingham's eyes lifted. "Make no such mistake as that, Sir Edward. But it takes time and foresight. No least detail is unimportant. No subject in the realm is overlooked. I may be called a spinner of webs, but without constant care and thought and planning, without counterplots to fight the eternal intrigues of our enemies, England would be a chaos open to the first invader of our shores." He paused, gazing past Blount, eyes on some distant object invisible to lesser men. "I have in mind a plan that will put an end forever to constant plottings. It will attract traitors as honey draws flies, and we will be finished with the archplotter of them all."

"Mary of Scotland!"

"Yes. While she lives, every discontented man has a standard to rally under against our Sovereign Queen, every firebrand or fanatic has reason to jeopardize Elizabeth's life. Elizabeth knows that while Mary lives her throne is not safe, yet she cannot be brought to sign the death warrant. That day must come or she might as well sign her own."

Blount started to speak, then stopped. Walsingham glanced at him. "This is not so far off the subject of Quain as you might think. Instead of working against our enemies, we will work with them. You once sent me a report on Anthony Babington, a hothead who talks too much of Mary Stuart. I have enough to put hands on him even now, but we will let him get further entangled, him and others, from the least to the highest in the land and be done with this Hydra-headed monster of dissension. If Quain is innocent, he's safe. If he's not, we'll make sure of him."

Blount's eyes narrowed in thought. "But if he is taken so——"

"You'll get your share of the reward. I do not forget loyal servants of the State." He put his head on his hand, his fingers shading the evening light from his eyes. "Speaking of Mary Stuart, do not let your personal feelings sway you a hairbreadth. As you know, treason is ever paid for with hanging, drawing and quartering. Past service does not mitigate the sentence."

Blount was on his feet. "My personal feelings! Sir Francis! I . . . Mary, she's less to me than the dust underfoot."

"To you now, yes. But this light o' love of yours—what's her name? Katherine—Perrot's daughter. I don't like her parentage, and she has been heard to

52

make remarks about the Scotch Queen that border on treason."

Blount, at the breath of danger to Katherine, retorted with a show of spirit. "It's only misplaced pity. Katherine's a softhearted lass. Is that a crime?"

"It could be," Walsingham said meaningly.

Blount said heavily, "I will speak to her."

"I would do so. Unless you've tired of her. If so, let her approach this Quain. We must not forget how he was tried once. Old loyalties die hard. In the warmth of Katherine's eyes he might find the Scotch Queen's plight peculiarly distressing." Walsingham looked at Blount, whose face was contorted with an effort at self-control. He said regretfully, "But I see you haven't tired of her. A pity. We'll send someone else. There's a woman Alicia I've used before. But speak to Katherine. I don't like Stuart sympathizers about the Queen."

"I will answer for Katherine's loyalty, Sir Francis, as for my own."

"Never speak for a woman, Blount. One would not think to look at you that you were so young." Walsingham struck a gong on his desk for his secretary. "I have work to do. Tell the sheriff to release Quain in the morning."

Blount bowed, went briskly out of the room. The smile on his face was forced and his fingernails made half circles in his palms. He had thought Maurice's fortune in his grasp. He must discipline himself to wait for the right moment to pluck the fruit of his loyal work. Only last year he had been given a share in a Paris establishment, the House of Gascony, for his help with the Court of the Livery Companies when their London agent had been caught smuggling goods into the country. Perhaps some similar agreement might be reached with Maurice. The returns on the Gascony house had been excellent, but they were not enough; they were nothing compared with his hopes yesterday when Maurice had been arrested. He felt defeated. He must see Katherine. He hoped she would be in her own chamber and not in attendance on the Queen.

She was in her own room in the palace. She lifted her head with smile as he knocked and entered the

53

room. Against the tall window that reached from ceiling almost to the floor, she was a slight figure in the half-light, almost ghostlike in a pale dressing gown of taffeta that rustled with her slightest movement. Her unbraided hair was a black cloud about her small face and slim straight shoulders.

His hand lost itself in the silk of that hair as he kissed her lightly. The sleeve of her gown slipped back, revealing a rounded forearm whiter than the taffeta. Its slenderness stirred him with a troubling awareness of beauty and the transience of beauty.

"Kit, Kit, you're too lovely a lass for me! Sometimes I wonder you have stayed with me so long." It was not a question and Katherine did not take it so. Her eyelashes swept up as she returned his gaze, not provocatively but with a quiet thoughtfullness. "If you should leave me, Katherine!" Perhaps he should make sure of her. Marriage? No. Not such madness as that when with Quain's fortune he might wed an heiress. Even Katherine's title was but a matter of courtesy extended to her by the Queen. He turned, walked half across the room and back again. He said abruptly, "I was with Sir Francis this evening."

"I'll wager you it was no pleasant interview then. I saw him earlier when he was talking to Her Majesty. I hope he didn't meet some poor Spaniard on his way home or he'd have hanged him out of hand." The tips of her fingers touched her soft neck, moved tentatively along the clean line of her jaw. She shook her head.

Blount said, disgruntled, not looking at her, "No. I had as good as a Spaniard for him—well, you know—and he's to be released in the morning! For the time."

Katherine's smile and lift of brows were frozen for a half minute at Blount's last words. "You mean, I take it, the man you had arrested at the Saracen's Head? I'm glad he's to be free. I cannot say I liked your part in that. But what do you mean—for the time?"

He was about to mention Babington, hesitated and said instead. "A man who is a traitor to Her Majesty like this merchant, if he does not get discovered one day, will another. You're glad, my dear, that he's to be freed?"

54

"Of course. I'm not one to cage even a blackbird. Besides," she added teasingly, "isn't he much too handsome to put behind stone walls?"

Blount turned on her, caught her roughly by the shoulders. "'Fore God, Kit, if you should even smile——"

"Oh, Ned, Ned, you're such a child! I've seen this merchant once. I'm not likely to see him again. You're troubled tonight over other matters. You were perhaps too hasty making that arrest. What are the odds? There's no harm done." She laughed up at him, a kind laughter that salved his hurts.

He dropped his hands to his sides. "I'm not worthy of you, Kit. I know that. I cannot bear to think of any other having your love. But I am disturbed." He stopped short. He would not tell her his plans about Maurice Quain. God only knew how she would act. Women were capricious creatures, delightful but undependable. He remembered Walsingham's warning. "Katherine!"

She did not hear him. Maurice Quain. She felt an involuntary attraction to him. A troubling man, big, with a tense, controlled power, a coldly handsome face. She would not want to see him often. Was her reason because he had evaluated and despised her? She turned slowly toward Ned. He loved her as she was, asked nothing of her but to be herself. At the expression on his face, fear twisted momentarily within her, but she said gaily, "Smile, Ned! You can't feel so depressed over losing one poor prisoner!" She leaned toward him, brows high, eyes laughing.

"Not that, Kit. It's you. Sir Francis said, hinted rather, you were too sympathetic toward the Scotch Queen for your own safety."

"Is that all? Of course I pity her. I thought at the least you had a warrant for my arrest."

"All! A suspicion of treason." Blount stared at her, then put an arm about her waist. "From suspicion to the Tower—— Oh God, Kit, be careful! I could not bear it if anything should happen to you."

The feel of her warm flesh through the thin silk surged through him. He swept her off her feet, head

55

bent to kiss her on her soft mouth. She turned from him a moment, then she looked up into his face. He seemed defenseless somehow, and it was a kind face really under the hardness the years had brought to him. She touched his cheek caressingly with her fingers. "Oh, Ned, love me always!"

Elizabeth Tudor tapped one foot restlessly as she glanced at the bronze and jeweled clock on the wall of the royal bedchamber. "My lords of the Council will meet in an hour. Is there no entertainment for us while we wait?" She moved over to sit down in her great chair. Its gilt wood and red velvet were unkind to the new wig she was wearing.

The ladies who had picked up their embroidery bent their heads over their work. Their needles made splinters of light as their well-cared-for hands created intricate patterns of thread on the shining lengths of cloth. One young woman started to tune a lute while the others waited for a cue to what would please Elizabeth this morning—court gossip, foreign intrigues, London talk, Burbage's theater in Holywell where he was producing the most delightful play about the Grand Turk Suleyman and his favorite slave the red-haired Roxane. One said, "Like our good Queen Bess the lady must have been." Unfortunately the young woman laughed nervously.

Elizabeth looked at the speaker coldly. "Do not compare me to some harlot in an Eastern harem, mistress."

"I meant, Your Highness, how you inspire lifelong devotion, consummate love."

"Love!" Elizabeth said. Her green eyes sparkled in her heavily painted face. "Ah yes, love." She swept the circle about her mockingly, stopped as she met Katherine's gaze. "A new brooch you have there, Kit. Let me see it!"

Katherine unfastened the jewel at her throat and brought it to the Queen, hoping desperately Elizabeth would not go into one of her jealous rages. She should never have been so indiscreet as to let Ned stay the night with her. Because the Queen scandalized all Europe did not mean she would forgive her ladies having even an attentive suitor, much less so personable a lover as Ned. "A pretty ornament. Where got you that?"

Katherine said smoothly, "Aztec, is it not, Your Highness? I thought it must be from the sale of some of Sir Francis Drake's Spanish treasures."

The mention of Drake brought on a spatter of excited talk. Such a man! Black and harsh . . . never two words where one would do . . . stern-looking . . . he killed men like flies . . . and as for women! Well, he was really primitive, my love. But so brave and fearless!

Katherine fingered her brooch and said nothing. She felt a deep dissatisfaction with herself this morning. She lacked courage. It seemed easy enough to be brave if you were a man like Drake with swords flashing in front, yes, but with your followers behind you and you knew who was foe and who was friend. It was no battle with insubstantial shadows, no struggle without weapons to protect a child, to rest some kind of security out of her life. Little Deborah. She could not bear to think there should ever be for her small daughter this quiet despair that lay cold on her heart. The brooch cut into her flesh.

She heard her name, glanced up. Elizabeth said, "A friend of yours, Kit, Edward Blount, begs audience with me. Would he be thinking now of . . . ah, permission to marry?"

"I would not hazard a guess, Madam, what Sir Edward's thoughts——" And then she knew. He must have asked for the audience after Maurice Quain had been arrested. With his release, Ned would have to change whatever petition he'd had in mind. But however he worded it, it would not be to the merchant's advantage. Maurice Quain in spite of his cold assurance would not have any chance at all if Elizabeth were set against him. Ned had a ridiculous dislike of the man, his need for money sharpening his hostility on the grindstone of jealousy. She said aloud, "Unless, Madam, it is about a merchant we met yesterday. He's from North England. He might amuse you—the mer-

57

chant I mean, not Ned!" She wondered momentarily how Maurice Quain would like to be described as an amusement for the Queen.

There was a flicker of interest on Elizabeth's face. "A merchant? Why should he be entertaining? Is he young?"

"Young for a merchant. In his thirties I would guess. He's a Northerner," she added as though that explained something. "His name is Maurice Quain."

"Quain? So he's in London. I do know the name. He's done me good service in getting shipments from the Continent. I suppose he's a barbarian since he's from the North, but, yes, I would like to see this merchant, Kit." Elizabeth smiled. "He's young, you say?"

There was a stir among the ladies. One bit her lip not to laugh. Another yawned. Katherine thought the courtiers might flatter Elizabeth to her face and jeer behind her back, yet there was a force about her, something unbreakable and vigorous, that would be more alive and younger than youth no matter how old she grew. Perhaps because no matter how she threw away her reputation, let her few finenesses wither among her vulgarities, allowed her moods to swing from jest to savagery, she lived for something greater than herself—England.

From that devotion, if Elizabeth did not change her mind and refuse him audience, Maurice Quain would have a measure of safety, at least more than he could hope for from Walsingham's unsleeping suspicions or Ned's enmity. But Kit wondered if she would regret her precipitate sympathy.

5

"I have an option on the *Plymouth Rose*. She's sailing from Southhampton in thirty days. Cargo out of Africa to the West Indies, returning with rum." Maurice paused on his way across the inner courtyard of the Royal Exchange in the heart of London to listen to the speaker haranguing the crowd about him.

Someone called out, "What are the shares?"

"Fifty pounds each. Twenty shares are up for sale. Twenty shares, gentlemen, and one hundred, two hundred, three hundred precent returns the least you can expect. You there, Webster, how many shares will you have? Five and your fortune's made!"

The man spoken to, a thin man of middle age with a shrewd humorous face, retorted. *"The Plymouth Rose?* Rotten timbers, drunken captain—she's as good as at the bottom of the Atlantic now!" He laughed and turning away collided with Maurice. He swept off his flat cloth cap. "Your pardon, sir!"

Maurice nodded absently, his eyes still on the trader calling out his venture. "You think it a poor risk?"

Webster said, "This slave running to the Indies, unless you have a Drake or a Hawkins on the captain's deck, is dangerous business. If they get across the Atlantic, the Spanish authorities will probably impound the vessel at the least and the crew will row their lives away in Mediterranean galleys. Of course if they're lucky—" he shrugged—"your money will come back to you three times over. But my real objection to buying a share—" he glanced at Maurice with a dry smile—"is that I haven't the fifty pounds."

Maurice looked at the speaker reflectively a moment. "I'm new at the Exchange here, sir. I wonder if you would do me the kindness to point me the way to Hart's offices? I understand the shops and offices are above. Is that right?"

"Yes, sir! When Sir Thomas Gresham finished the Exchange sixteen years ago he tried to rent all the space for shops but it was too dark and damp below. You can't even use those rooms for storage for any length of time. But Gresham was one of the wealthiest men in England before he died, so his disappointment must have been moderate." He eyed Maurice shrewdly, the expensive sober doublet, the only light touch the white satin panes in the sleeves and the narrow conservative ruff at the throat, the dark hose and gauntlet boots of tooled leather. "I will do better, sir, than point the way to Hart. I'll take you to his office." He shouldered a way through the throng that was gathering

59

about them, alert at the word of African cargo and West Indies rum.

Maurice glanced about for Patrick, motioned with his head for the young man to follow. Webster led the way across the paved inner yard, up the stone steps to the gallery above. He stopped a few feet from a closed door. "If, sir, it is to do business with Hart that you are here, perhaps I should advise you that another day you will be apt to get more satisfaction out of an interview with him."

Maurice looked at him, coldly inquiring.

Webster said, "Hart may not be facing bankruptcy, but one of his richest investors has been ruined. He won't swagger it about the Exchange for a while again."

There was the least trace of malice in the man's voice. It amused Maurice. "What house are you with?"

"The Africa Company when it's in operation. But they just sell shares for each voyage, disband when the enterprise is over and sell shares again for the next shipping sometimes months and sometimes years later. Through my work with them I know what kind of a ship the *Plymouth Rose* is. We've used her."

"Where are your offices?"

Webster grimaced. "In my own home on the bridge, third house from the left if you ride in from the Southwark side. I come over here every day to pick up a little business and sell my knowledge of ships and ventures."

Maurice said briefly, "Wait out here if you have the leisure," and opened the wide planked door into the office.

Webster, choosing to hear only Maurice's suggestion to wait, followed him into the room. Patrick shrugged and went after them though unwilling to leave his precarious perch on the gallery. He had been leaning over the balustrade to watch the raucous crowd below with its shifting patterns of light and dark, English merchants mingling with the traders and captains of Europe, Africa and Asia in their gaudy dress. Guttural German speech rose and clashed with the Italian, French and Moorish.

60

A clerk who had been jotting down figures on huge sheets came forward at their entrance. "Sir? Master Hart? Right this way if it pleases you, sir."

Hart turned from the window at their entrance into the small cramped inner room that gave a confused impression of scriveners and counters. The clerk said, "This gentleman, Master Hart, says he wants to see you about—what was it about, sir?" He turned toward Maurice not noticing the expression on his employer's face.

"Quain! You! I thought you were in the Tower."

Maurice said curtly. "You choose the most impractical times to think, Master Hart. Since you sent no messenger to the Saracen's Head, I thought I would settle my accounts with you here."

Hart turned toward a door at his left. "If you'll come in here, Master Quain, we can speak in private. Your man can wait out in front." He noticed Webster standing with Patrick as Maurice moved forward from where his big body had hidden the thin figure. "What are *you* doing here?"

Webster, who had realized at once what the situation was, made a depricatory gesture to indicate he was with Maurice, while his eyes sparkled with a malicious humor. "I'll wait with this young man."

Hart gave him a suspicious look as he pushed open the door and held it for Maurice to enter. "Sit down, Master Quain, sit down. You!" He turned toward a clerk. "Bring in the Quain papers."

Maurice lowered himself into a straight-backed chair near the one small window as the clerk jumped to do Hart's bidding.

"Here are your accounts as close as we can reckon them so quickly, Master Quain." Hart loosened several sheets of parchment from a brassbound book and brought them to Maurice. "I bought the additional shares in the Muscovy Company that you ordered. But you know, Master Quain, I don't like this new way of doing business—selling shares. Why, the London merchants are beginning to carry on half their export trade on other people's capital. The old way like the Merchant Adventurers is better where only the most eminent merchants may trade and the fee for membership is so high the riffraff can't enter their ranks. In those joint-stock affairs like the Muscovy Company everybody's money buys the ships and half of the stock in trade. Ridiculous! Any man with twenty-five pounds to spare will soon think himself a financial agent."

Maurice raised his brows. "Does that explain why I have had scarcely a word from you on the preliminary work for the founding of my Eastern Company, and no reports at all on the Turkey Company?"

Hart said flatly, "I have discussed the matter of buying a membership in the Turkey Company with Osborne himself who is the director but there are only sixteen members and two appointed by the Crown. So far there has been no vacancy."

"No matter for the moment." Maurice spoke with surprising equanimity. "Just what steps have you taken for this company I want to start?"

Hart interlaced his pudgy fingers. "It is this way, Master Quain. I have not found many houses interested in coming in on the venture. They're all willing to use your investments and agents, but they want to get more control in their hands."

Maurice smiled contemptuously at the suggestion. "How much money do I have at the moment from recent cargo returns?"

Hart smirked. "It's my belief that money, like prentices, should never be idle. It is all reinvested, but I can raise any amount you might need against your French shipment at probably not more than eighteen percent interest or even——" He looked at Maurice craftily. How long would the luck hold which had delivered Quain from prison in twelve hours? "Or I might even give you the loan of it myself."

"I thank you, Master Hart. But as you suggested, it is no doubt better that we close our accounts. Make out a list of your expenses and fees. I expected indeed to see it completed by now. I'd like also a copy of these sheets so that I will know exactly how my London affairs stand. When may I expect both?"

Hart said resentfully, "Tomorrow, sir. But do not . . . I mean . . . perhaps we should think of this awhile longer. We have done business together for many years."

"I've done business with your father," Maurice corrected him. "I had no cause for complaint while he lived. Your father would never have told me he could find no house interested in a sound venture nor suggested that instead I finance it by borrowing money at a ruinous rate of interest. If you had not given me your decision before to sever connections—— But enough." He rose. "I will expect those papers this afternoon."

Hart stood up also. "You cannot come into London a stranger, Master Quain, and go out in the Exchange and find a new agent. You'll not discover my like easily."

"That is exactly what I'm depending on." As Hart started to protest further, Maurice added, "I cannot have an agent who would cut off my affairs every time there is, or he thinks there is, the smell of danger in the wind. I bid you good day, Master Hart."

He walked to the outer room where Patrick and Webster waited. The clerk opened the door for them to leave. Webster bowed to Hart and went out after Maurice.

"Master Quain, you have this morning made an enemy." Webster gestured toward the closed door behind them. "But you have more than offset your loss, sir. You have also made a friend. Me."

Maurice raised his brows slightly as he glanced at Webster. "Good! Could you prove your value by pointing out to me the most important directors in the Turkey Company?"

"I can do better for you than that. I can get an invitation for you to an exclusive dinner some of the merchants hold weekly. There's one tomorrow night at the Sign of the Swan and Cygnet. Should you care for my valuable company, I can go with you."

Patrick looked at Webster with some amusement. "I'd have you know, Master Webster, if that's your name, this is not a post I give up to every talkative beggar we meet in London."

Webster threw a malicious smile at the young man, but said only, "It will be difficult enough to get Master

Quain in without another foreigner to account for. But while we're about the business of London, I can point out to you where you will find some of its pleasures."

"Can you now?"

"That's right. You've plenty of years left before you for commerce." He leaned toward Patrick confidentially. "At the Blue Cat just north of Bishopsgate you'll find the prettiest girls—and a tavern hostess who is most careful whom she employs. Not one of the lasses will return your favors with the French disease. Downstairs is a little quiet gaming. Another word and I'll probably be off with you."

Patrick grinned. "Why not take that post instead? With that long face of yours, you look in need of any pleasures you can find."

Maurice interrupted him. "Since you offer your services, Master Webster, I'll use them and thank you. Come to the Saracen's Head tomorrow." There was a note of finality in Maurice's voice that Webster took correctly as dismissal. He bowed with a certain saturnine humor and walked off down the gallery.

Patrick whistled a snatch of a gay tune that was lost in the cacophony as they went down the steps. Maurice stopped a moment to watch the scene before him, listen to the cries. Ships sailing to the legendary East, the lands of the Great Khan, of dark-skinned natives, of exotic secrets, dark continents and ships sailing to the golden West, across an ocean alive with monsters of the deep, peopled with a thousand unknown terrors, to the fabulous wealth of the Indies. This was his world, intoxicating, challenging, so that one wanted to let no offer pass—black cargo out of Africa, grains to ice-locked Russia, copper and tin to Turkey.

Merchandise moving across seas and continents, pushing back barriers among the peoples of the earth so that Christian or Moslem or pagan in the East should go clothed in wool, eat English wheat, wear Irish linen, sail their ships with timbers from Norway; so that men of the West should have strange spices in their foods, dress in silks so fine a shining length could be crumpled in the hand and no bright thread show through the fingers, walk on thick-piled carpets that

64

gave beauty to the colorless homes of the Occident. Maurice smiled.

Maurice looked approvingly about the apartment when they returned to the Saracen's Head. He had had the host's furniture replaced with his own, and gilt and velvet and polished wood gleamed in the golden flames of wax candles on tables and desk and in sconces against the walls.

The landlord, who had come up immediately to inquire about dinner, came farther into the room. "A pity to eat alone," he said, letting one eyelid droop. "The best appetizer for a meal is laughter, a gay companion with a saucy tongue and ways to give you pleasure."

Jacques, the valet, entered at the same moment with a wild flurry of gestures and speech, apologizing for his lateness in a language that had some faint resemblance to French. He had been born James and a good Yorkshireman, but he had not prospered in his trade until it was borne in on him that all valets were from the Continent. After that his name had become Jacques and the broad Yorkshire tongue was forced into foreign phrases that had the smoothness and ease of a fat man thrust into too tight hose.

Maurice frowned him silent. "Do you have someone who fits your description?"

"I have a—" the landlord, catching Maurice's skeptical glance, decided not to mention his daughter—"I have knowledge of such a one. I'm sure this person will more than please you." He lifted his head suddenly, eyes sly. Neither of them had mentioned the sex desired. "I presume . . . you do want a young lady?"

Maurice stared, not taking the meaning at once. Then he said shortly, "Yes."

"It doesn't matter. Either sex I can have for you. A young spirited boy? No? I thought you being a merchant . . . sometimes after they have been long in the East . . . why, I could tell you tales of a merchant adventurer who took this very room . . ."

Maurice shrugged his shoulders as Jacques lifted off the heavy doublet revealing the fine white linen shirt

65

underneath. "Why not instead," he asked pleasantly, "have this paragon you mentioned relate any stories in her own pretty fashion?"

A knock sounded at the door half an hour later. Maurice had not expected the girl yet. He wanted companionship tonight to put the crown on the anticipation of his future. A little warmth of excitement stirred in his blood as the landlord came in, a red-haired woman half a step behind him.

Maurice glanced at her. Let us hope, he thought sardonically, that her wit makes up for her years, and her skill by long practice matches both. Ten years ago she had probably been a beauty, but that had been a long ten years and a hard ten years ago. She had a defiant way of carrying herself as though half expecting a rebuff. There was a certain animal high spirit about her, however, and she had a look of readiness to savor any good things that might come her way.

Maurice's instant annoyance with both her and the landlord began to fade. He nodded to the latter, who had been waiting in the doorway, to leave. "Your dinner will be up at once, sir, at once. The finest cooking, the headiest wines in London."

Maurice watched the woman appraisingly as she crossed the room to him. She had a low-necked dress edged with tawdry lace that barely confined her full breasts, a waist made small by painfully tight lacing, and broad hips.

With quick sidelong glances she acquainted herself with every object in the room. Real gold handles those were on the desk, and this carpet underfoot, truly a sin to walk on it. Rich gentlemen didn't come her way often any more, but the landlord was something of a friend and would get his share of whatever Master Quain would pay. There was a sober lavishness here that impressed her. The tip of her tongue ran about her lips with something feline and contented in the gesture as she lifted her eyes to the tall man before her.

Maurice said bluntly, "You're satisfied, madam, I can pay your price?"

So he had not liked the way she'd looked the room

over. "With a fine gentleman like you," she retorted pertly, "half the pay is the privilege of——" She hesitated. Some of these men didn't like plain speaking. They wanted to pretend she was there just for dinner, for chatter to pass the time away. "Of serving you," she finished. "The other half is left to your heart." She waved a plump hand vaguely toward her own generous bosom.

Maurice smiled faintly. "Sit down, my dear." He had his hand on the back of a gilded chair beside the table. She sank down into it with gusto. "The wine from Andalusia, Jacques, and then you may go." He rather liked the wench. It was a pity, though, that this sort of woman never thought of washing herself. The strong female odor dulled the fine edge of his senses.

His distaste was erased by the excitement within him, by the wine Jacques poured into silver goblets for them before he left, by the dinner which the woman— Alicia she said her name was—served that they might be alone. Her eyes grew brighter with the food and the drink. When they finished she moved back in her chair with a gasp of delight. "A feast for a king!" She sighed. Her eyes slid sidelong to meet his.

Maurice, forearms on the table, leaned toward her. Her gesture then stopped him cold, jarringly. She made the sign of the cross over her heart. He said harshly, "Why that, Alicia?"

"What? What did I do?" Her hand flew to her throat. "Virgin Mary! You will not—Master Quain, you'll never tell the authorities?"

He did not answer her, and his eyes were cold as granite. She said flutteringly, "You will not, Master Quain. It's a dangerous custom, but in our family we like to keep some little remnants of the ancient faith. But perhaps. . . . I wonder if you do not understand. There are some of your name I've heard have held to the old ways of worship. Perhaps you . . ." Still he said nothing. "We're Papists." She spoke with her eyes down while her fingers made little pleats in her green skirt. Maurice wondered how many if any Catholics called themselves Papists. "That's why I . . . this life

67

. . . we had money once. It all went in fines for not attending the Anglican services. I was forced to this."

"Now I've always heard that girls in such circumstances fled to the convents on the Continent?"

It had not gone off right, Alicia realized. It would take more than one evening, a few glasses of wine and a pair of bright eyes to get this man to talk easily. She'd done her best. Now she'd enjoy herself. She giggled at his words. "Oh, Master Quain! What would *I* do in a convent!" She went to him.

A gray mist was all about him, pressing down on his eyes and ears, muffling his senses, while distorted figures from his dreams whirled on the edge of consciousness. Maurice opened his eyes slowly. The mist began to dissolve. There was a faintly sour taste in his mouth. He gazed at the embroidered canopy of blue velvet across the top of the bed. Curtains of the same material fell in folds about the sides so that he was in a dim blue world, pierced by a shaft of gray light when the drafts in the room swayed the draperies.

He could still feel Alicia's heavy warm body beside him and smell the faint acrid odor of her flesh. But her skill in the ways of love had been above his expectations. She had given him pleasure, taken delight from him, knowing how to satisfy without satiation, or almost. He had said to come back in two nights, and yet there was this sour aftertaste. She had been so blundering and obvious with her religious prattle it could have been nothing less than deliberate. But why? Well, what did it matter? She did well enough as a bed companion.

Jacques came forward with a heavy dressing robe. Maurice slipped his arms into it, shrugged it over his shoulders. The crimson wool gown, with a darker shade of velvet in the wide sleeves, fell in folds to his feet. He shook his head to get the last of the sleep out of his eyes. Today, if Webster did not disappoint him, he would see the directors of the Turkey Company, and he would not take the refusal Hart had accepted so easily.

There was a peremptory knock at the door. The boy sitting drowsily on the bench jumped up to draw the bolt. Maurice glanced across the room. The landlord came in, bustling and officious. Behind him was a tall man in the livery of the House of Tudor, with the Tudor rose on his sleeve. A small group of people had gathered curiously outside the door before it swung to. Jacques stepped forward gaping.

Patrick, who had been sitting at the window waiting for Maurice to waken, crossed to stand beside him. He felt blood pounding to his finger tips. Edward Blount first, this time a royal guard. Maurice waited while the messenger came forward.

"You are Master Quain. I have a summons for you." He handed a rolled parchment to Maurice. Patrick in response to Maurice's glance fumbled in the pouch at his belt and brought out two rose nobles. The messenger eyed them twice, grinned, bowed again and withdrew.

"Maurice, breaking the seal to unroll the dispatch, said, "Two rose nobles are rather ample payment, aren't they, as a reward to come from Whitehall to the Saracen's Head?"

"He was from the Queen! Besides—" Patrick looked at Maurice with a whimsical lift of his brows—"I thought, Master Quain, he was here to take us all to prison this time and would have the whole purse!"

A trace of exasperation showed on Maurice's face. "If you can but disabuse your thoughts on the wild tales about the dangers of London you must have heard somewhere and put your mind on your duties instead, you won't jump at every shadow."

Patrick forebore to retort that little more than an hour after landing at Billingsgate, Maurice had been under arrest. He had been freed, but who knew for how long?

Maurice looked down the page, taking the meaning at a glance, then reread the message more slowly. "Her Majesty will give me an audience this week Friday." There was a controlled smile on his lips. A summons from Elizabeth. She would want something of him, something no other merchant could bring her. Such an open showing of favor should be more powerful than money with the London merchants.

Patrick grinned. "After seeing the expense sheets of any London venture, I didn't think Her Majesty was in the habit of giving anything away, even an audience!"

Maurice said, "True! We'll earn it."

Patrick took the dispatch to put it on the desk. He said carelessly, "I saw her again from a distance. She's one of the Queen's ladies. Her name is Katherine Perrot."

"Whose name?" But Maurice knew. Since he'd seen her she had stayed in the corner of his mind as though she mattered to him in some way. Not alone the perfect shoulders, the firm breasts and slim waist—the farthingale had concealed further charms or defects of her figure—haunted him, but some elusive quality about her.

"The young woman at the Saracen's Head with Blount."

Maurice laughed. "Sir John's daughter! Which proves her . . . no better than I thought her."

Webster came up to the apartment at noon, but not before the clerk Vincent had returned with his report of the trader—honest enough, a willing worker but eccentric. The kind of man who'd serve you with his life if he liked you and pay a shilling to see you hang if he didn't.

Maurice had not particularly cared for what he heard. If his employees had feelings, it was a pity. But if they let those feelings interfere with their work, they no longer served him. Loyalty, bought and well paid for—Maurice expected not more and not less than that of any man.

Webster said, "Master Quain, the dinner's at seven. For the price of it you are welcome. But don't be forgetting you are a Northerner and a foreigner to these merchants. No one else will forget it."

"Well? The London merchants do business every day with foreigners who cannot even speak their tongue."

"Yes, Master Quain, but I'm guessing you want more than to do business with them. You want to enter the exclusive circle of the city's commerce—the kind that the London merchants carry on together for their own profit and fame."

Maurice eyed him expressionlessly. "You think rather too much, Master Webster, or else you listen at keyholes. Either is unnecessary if you care to be in my employ."

The last sentence was half a question. Webster smiled. "I would be very much interested in working for you sir. Should you wonder at the source of my suggestion that you want to enter into London business, Hart has been talking at the Exchange about a membership in the Turkey Company. Which last, as you know, has still not been acquired."

At that Maurice stood very still. He gazed with seeming intentness out the open casement window at the people moving below. Heads bobbed along the narrow cobbled street, the flat caps of prentices who were bawling their masters' wares, the plumed hats of gallants walking mincingly by in their velvet and ruffs, the white starched caps of housewives who were stepping briskly down the street to buy food for their family dinners or making little eddies in the stream of people while they stopped to exchange news with a neighbor. The stench rose up and smote his nostrils—from rubbish steaming on the cobbles and from the carcass of a dead dog kicked to one side.

The idea of his being outside the magic circle had never occurred to him. He had expected only to offer money and receive the stock as soon as a vacancy could be managed. The Turkey Company had secured the usual monopoly from the Queen and the Privy Council preventing independent merchants from buying or selling in Turkey except through it. Was he to be robbed of his far-flung plans so early in the fight? He turned to Webster. "Edward Osborne is the man to see, isn't he?"

"He has the final word, Master Quain, because of his position and wealth. But if it weren't for Dick Staper there wouldn't be such a company. They'll both be at the dinner. I've been to Constantinople," he said dreamily. "I'd like to go again."

71

Patrick said, "Nobody goes without me, Master Webster!"

Webster shot a look at him. "The East, Master Secretary, is strong drink for boys like you."

Maurice made a gesture for silence. "What are Osborne's weaknesses?"

Webster's underlip jutted out. He rubbed his chin with the back of his hand. "To say the truth, Master Quain, he has none that will profit you. His ambition is to be the biggest name in the Turkey Company. How can you trade on that? Every reason you advance for being admitted though you're an outsider will make a stronger reason for his keeping you out. Nevertheless, I'm your man."

Patrick murmured, "Quain's man? Why? Won't Osborne hire you?"

Webster looked at him from under heavy lids. "I know where I could go and get a fine price for my services, young man, should I care to serve two masters, Master Quain and—another who does not like him."

Patrick said sharply, "What do you mean by that?"

Maurice dismissed the matter contemptuously. "There may be someone who is not my friend. But no one serves me and any man else."

Maurice thought with cold approval that the dinner had been the most civilized one he'd had since leaving Blyth. He twirled a goblet of Canary idly in his fingers as members and guests moved back their chairs, regrouped themselves about the table, but with no slackening of a heated discussion on the trade route northwestward around the Americas.

One merchant said doggedly, "Frobisher would have found the passage to Cathay if all the subscribers in the company that sent him hadn't demanded he bring back a lot of worthless rock to be assayed instead of letting him explore westward to the Pacific."

Osborne spoke up. Maurice glanced across the table at him—a portly man, sleek with good living, a pleasant round face with a pointed beard and shrewd blue eyes. "The whole fault there, Piper, was that the

Court backed the project. All the gallants can see is getting gold and silver to hang from their ears or their noses, like dancing bears. Trade, trade, trade is worth more than the whole Spanish plate fleet from the Americas. But the Court, bah! Rock! Two ships of rock sent back, and the admiral not some inexperienced captain but Martin Frobisher himself. Keep away from the Court and courtiers. That's what Frobisher should have done. We had trouble getting the good will of Queen and Privy Council for our Turkey Company because our goal of commerce was too tame, but our members will grow wealthy while the courtiers pile up debts." Osborne stopped abruptly as he caught Maurice's gaze and remembered several strangers were present.

Everyone's eyes turned to Maurice. Webster, sitting at a lower table, stiffened warily. Maurice said smoothly, "I do not know the ins and outs of Court subscriptions on the venture around the Americas, but this Turkey Company of yours has an honorable and profitable reputation for so young a business."

A frown creased Osborne's smooth brow. "I do not believe I have the pleasure of your acquaintance?"

"Maurice Quain, Master Osborne, late of Blyth in Northumberland."

There was a stir about the table. The name was known to most of them. Too well known. Osborne's eyes hardened. "You may have been slandered, Master Quain, but according to what I have heard, you know too well the ins and outs, as you term them, of Courts in commercial ventures. And not alone the Court of our glorious Queen Elizabeth, serving whom is an honor, but the government of the greatest enemy of our trade and of our country—Spain who convets the world."

Webster looked unhappy. Maurice said carelessly, "Your reports are justified by the facts, Master Osborne. I find such ventures highly profitable, just as you find it profitable to compete sometimes murderously with Christian allies for the trade of the Infidel."

Two or three voices started an angry defense of their rivalry in the East with France and Italy, stopped at

73

the cold scorn on Maurice's face. One man laughed. He was middle-aged with receding hair brushed back so that it stood out above his ears like the wings of Mercury's cap. As the talk swerved sharply back to Frobisher's unsuccessful ventures, he moved over and pulled up a chair briskly beside Maurice. He spoke confidentially. "Richard Staper, Master Quain. You may have heard my name. Good. I also know something of you."

Maurice smiled with the least trace of warmth. "Good or bad?"

"Good. That your word is better than many a man's signed contract. That there is always quality in your merchandise. I understand from the inquiries of your London agent Hart that you're interested in becoming a member of the Turkey Company.

"My affairs seem well known."

Staper made a gesture of dissent. "Merchants with money to invest largely are so few they are always gossiped about. What these men buy or sell in the Exchange, every trader has his eyes on. I noticed, for instance, that you bought only a small subscription in Frobisher's venture for the Northwest Passage to Cathay. None of the big merchants put in money on the venture except Sanderson and he'd married Sir Walter Raleigh's niece, as you may know." Staper laughed. "Don't let Raleigh talk to you. He could persuade St. Peter to buy a share in hell in case matters should go badly in the heavenly regions. Why, he almost convinced me I should put money into this Virginia venture of his. Fortunately any profits have all gone to the Turkey Company or I'd have half my wealth invested in his next expedition. It may reward map makers and discoverers, but the knowledge of a New World would be small pleasure to me if I heard of it in a debtors' prison!"

Maurice said nothing. Staper went on musingly: "The West—it's a dream, Master Quain. It might even come true one day. But hardheaded businessmen like me will never push it forward. Dreams are made into reality by the dreamers and the explorers who are driven on toward the unknown by some inner compelling need that I cannot even understand. By adventurers like Drake and Hawkins and Frobisher who must have action served up to them every day as I have my dinner. And by gamblers and riffraff who feel any change may make their lot better since it cannot be worse. But never by men like me who must have their returns in gold or cargo. My sons, my grandsons, may trade across the Atlantic with a New World. It may be—though I can believe that in my heart only after a good dinner and too much wine.

"I talk too much, I'm told, Master Quain. I've wandered too far from our discussion. As I said, I understand you are interested in buying into the Turkey Company. Is that right?"

Maurice said carelessly, "I've thought of it."

Staper ran his hands through his hair so that the sides looked more winglike than ever. "There are only twelve memberships, you know, besides the original group of four according to the charter the Queen and Privy Council gave us, and two members more to be appointed by them. They have not insisted on their prerogative, and we have had no trouble. You know from what you've heard that we're not too anxious to have the Court mixing in our business affairs. Unfortunately we have no vacancies now, but I wanted to talk to you because there's a chance there'll be a place to be filled soon. In a company so small in numbers as ours and so vast in enterprise we like to select our future brother adventurers carefully. Shall we see Osborne?"

Osborne turned aside from his companions as they came up. Staper said, "Master Quain would like to talk to you."

Osborne's genial face hardened. "Well?" He signaled to one of the servingmen to fill the glasses.

Maurice looked at the golden-brown ale foaming from the jug, shook his head with an expression of distaste. "Canary if you please."

Osborne's eyes grew colder. "You wanted to speak with me?"

Maurice waited until his wine had been poured and

the servingman had moved away. "Yes. About your Turkey Company."

"You seem to take quite an interst in my—our—company, Master Quain."

"I do. I've been trying to buy a share in it for some time now. My agent had not informed me that your membership was so limited. However, Master Staper tells me there may be a vacancy soon. I'd like to buy that share."

Osborne glanced at Staper, a line of annoyance between his brows. "Aren't you being hasty, Dick?"

Staper shrugged. "I like to look ahead. A merchant like Quain would be valuable to us."

"Valuable? Well, it is possible." Osborne's dislike showed plainly in his face.

Maurice said, "This is a business venture, Master Osborne. I presume your personal feelings will not sway you. To become a member I'm willing to pay double for the share. Does that content you?"

"Master Quain, you seem to be under the misapprehension that given enough money you can buy anything."

Maurice's brows rose. "You don't think that true?"

"No! To be more specific: in no circumstances nor for any amount of money would I sell you a share in the Turkey Company. It is better to be plain with you now."

Maurice answered smoothly, "I cannot complain you are not open with me. And if the last as well as the first word is yours, there is little more to be said."

Staper shrugged his shoulders resignedly. "A pity, Osborne. I think Master Quain would be useful to us."

Osborne held up his hand irritably. "I have heard too much of this. Now about the shipment of tar and hemp from Russia, Piper." He turned his back on Maurice.

Maurice's mouth thinned to a line. He said coldly, "I am sorry if you are already weary of the discussion, Master Osborne, because I must warn you it's one you're not yet done with. Good evening, sir."

Staper said, "I should tell you, Master Quain, Osborne never changes his mind. Once your friend, always your friend. But the reverse is also true. I regret this. Could I help you in some other matter?"

"Yes. I'm taking my business out of the hands of my former agent. I do not know where to place it. Perhaps you might have a suggestion?"

"Why don't you stay in London and handle it yourself? Otherwise I would say the House of Bowyer. They have been in the trade for themselves for generations and lately have gone into merchandising for others as well. Their credit is excellent and their business sense seldom at fault."

"Thank you. I will see them, But as for staying in London myself—" Maurice shook his head. "The thought of markets with the Hapsburgs in Madrid and with the Valois in Paris which might be interfered with by our government here prevents me. A pity you do not make use of such opportunities?"

Staper's eyes twinkled. "Master Quain, I'm a man who is easily satisfied. Give me the wealth of the East and I am content."

Maurice said, "But to obtain this wealth we must sell as well as buy. My warehouses are filled with material of value to the Sultan for his constant wars— tin and copper from Cornwall, timber from Norway, cordage. . . . With the present state of affairs, the East offers the best markets where these products can be disposed of at a satisfactory profit. Besides, to develop a truly international business an Eastern outlet is essential. Attempting expansion without one is like driving a cart with three wheels. I have houses through Europe. The next logical step is Asia."

Staper eyed him with concern. "Don't feel too bitter about this business, Master Quain. There are other ways to the East. The Muscovy Company or around the Cape of Good Hope."

"When the ships are built that will carry goods safely around the Cape I'll buy a share in them in ten, twenty years," Maurice said briefly. "I'll pay for them with my profits in the Turkey Company."

"I hope you do, Master Quain."

"Thank you." Maurice looked around for Webster,

77

who came forward at once. "Would you get a serving-man to provide a linkboy?"

"You aren't leaving so early! A little cheer, you know, adds pleasure to life, softens hard feelings, makes one forget any unpleasant discussions."

Maurice smiled coldly at the small man with the hair like Mercury's cap. "It just happens, Master Staper, that I do not want to forget."

6

Maurice looked about the immense room of gold and white with the Tudor arms on every wall and the Tudor rose embroidered on hangings at windows and doors. Courtiers expecting an audience with the Queen and petitioners hoping for it stood about in little groups, talking gaily or earnestly, their voices rising, clashing lightly as rapiers, falling away into laughter. The discordant amusement sounded strained and un-natural.

Maurice was weary to death of the Presence Cham-ber at Whitehall. In the last six weeks he had spent more time waiting for the royal audience than he had on his commercial affairs, and Elizabeth, surrounded by her ladies, a bouquet of exotic flowers, had not even glanced at him. He stood alone and withdrawn a little, his nerves tightening at something in the atmosphere he sensed but could not quite determine. The shifting scarlet and green and blue of doublets and hose, the gold and silver cloth, the glitter of jewels embroidered on farthingales, of jewels inset in brilliant fans, the gleaming white of lace or fine linen ruffs—some memory they evoked that he shrank from, something that had in it a nostalgic evocation at once of pleasure and of pain.

Mary Stuart's Court—another queen of another country and himself another man. He had been very young that first time he had seen her, too young and impressionable. Mary had been lovely. No, she had not been lovely. He remembered now how he had been dis-appointed at his first glimpse of her. That tall young woman with the plain features, the commonplace brown hair, was this the celebrated Mary of Scotland? But he had come away as smitten with her beauty as the next young man. She wasn't fragile but she gave the impression of fragility. She wasn't helpless either, but those long fine hands of hers had a broken gesture of resistless appeal when she spoke to each man as though all the fate of her frail beauty lay in him.

They had all failed her. And she was an old woman, aged with prison life—the wild fragile sweetness enclosed in four walls, the gay spirit and lithe body fettered by the will of another woman. Betrayed by them all just as she—had not Mary betrayed them too? Had she not one by one brought down in ruins the Scottish lords who would have been her friends—Mary who could never tell friend from enemy until too late? So trusting, so easily swayed a nature should never have been royal, nor a girl who was so much more woman than queen. In any walk of life she would have had the fatal spark that enkindles ruin. As a queen it was a nation she destroyed, Scotland torn by wars, the massacre of the rebels when the wave of blood had broken over North England at the rising of the lords to free her.

He heard his name spoken, turned his head sharply to see Katherine Perrot standing beside him. His brows rose. She smiled at him. "Would you come this way, Master Quain?" She put a hand on his sleeve and drew him toward a window niche. It was a slim competent hand that somehow surprised him. With that fine cambric ruff at the wrist he unconsciously expected long tapering fingers, an appearance of graceful helplessness. She was a tall girl. The top of her head reached to his mouth so that he might easily have touched with his lips the shining dark waves of her hair.

She answered his unspoken question. "Her majesty feared she had done you too much honor or perhaps she changed her mind on some other count, but today I think she will speak with you." Katherine colored slightly, afraid he might guess it had been she who had caused the Queen to favor him again. "If you are over here away from the throng, she will be more likely to notice you."

79

Maurice said coldly. "This aping of a courtier's ways hardly befits a man of business."

"True enough, I suppose. I'm so used to them that this weighing and judging of the royal whims becomes as natural as eating. There may be other ways to live——" Her voice trailed off, a hint of wistfulness under the level tone. She glanced out the windows to the garden below. "Does it matter much to you, this audience? You're a wealthy man, Master Quain. You need nothing." She smiled at him piquantly. "You need nothing, Master Quain, except a friend at Court."

"That should be easy enough," Maurice said. "There are few friendships not for sale at Whitehall."

Katherine laughed. "If you speak of me, sometimes my friendship is bought and sometimes it is given."

Maurice drew a ring from his finger. "I appreciate your help, madam." He handed her the ring, a gold band with three exquisitely cut diamonds, with the same air he would have paid off a prentice.

Katherine let it lie in her palm one moment. "Thank you, Master Quain, but I'm afraid I could not take so much for only a friendly word of advice. I would feel myself under obligation to you. And you are not a man whose debt I'd care to be in." She spoke lightly that he should not know how deeply he had hurt her. Not with his offer of a jewel, but the scorn with which he had given it. Of all men this Maurice Quain in whom somehow she sensed a need for pity and whom she wanted to like her.

Maurice shrugged and put the ring back on his finger. No doubt it was something else she wanted of him. He glanced up as she strangled a sound in her throat, turned to follow her gaze and saw Edward Blount watching them. Blount's face was expressionless but there was a black fury in his eyes. He disappeared among the courtiers.

Katherine smiled a little shakily. "Perhaps it was as well I returned the ring! Ned is inclined to be jealous."

"Blount? He's inclined to be a fool."

Katherine had started to move away but she swung back at that. "Unless you enjoy danger for its own sake, do not underrate Edward Blount, Master Quain.

He may not have your—your hard bright edge or swiftness of decision, but once he has his teeth in a man, he never lets go. Not ever." And then she was gone.

A few minutes later the chamberlain Sir Christopher Hatton, magnificent in white velvet, read out Maurice's name and inclined his head graciously for the merchant to come forward. Elizabeth watched him. The heavy paint on her face emphasized rather than concealed the wrinkles and her red wig was slightly awry. At her slightest movement the light splintered along the diamonds sewed into the bodice of her dress, gleamed at the network of pearls in the huge farthingale she wore. The narrow face and gaunt frame seemed lost in the dazzle of velvet and jewels and gold, but there was a force here Maurice had not felt at a distance. "You have not been pressing for an audience, Master Quain." Her wide mouth turned down at the corners.

"We do not ask, Your Majesty, for the favor of the sun," he said. "We can but wait and hope for the warming rays."

Her heavy lids drooped over her green eyes as she looked at him, a big erect man with a wide spread of shoulders, a lean figure, hard eyes in a hard almost expressionless face. Her gaze almost unconsciously went to the Earl of Leicester who was beside her, to his bloated face with purplish veins about his nose and high about his cheekbones, to the loose skin under his jaw. His extravagantly costumed figure was sunk at the moment in lethargy. Leicester smiled and put his hand on her knee. Elizabeth giggled. "Robin!" And then she said, "What will we do with this solemn merchant here. Have him in on our project or shall we look for a merrier fellow?"

Leicester deliberated while he stared insolently at Maurice. "They're all sober, my love, from the getting of so much gold. It weights a man's spirits."

"That is a burden, Robin, I'd gladly bear." She turned to Maurice. "You have been of service to us in the past, Master Quain. We hope you now will at least equal those efforts."

She glanced about at the people straining to hear the

least word that fell from her lips while they judged the exact intonation of her voice: by just what degree was it more or less friendly than to the petitioner who had preceded this tall merchant or the one who'd come next? Her long fingers drummed on the carved arm of the chair.

"I'll see you privately in my cabinet in an hour, Master Quain." She looked at the chamberlain. Hatton was glaring at Leicester who was receiving more of the royal smiles today than he. "Sir Christopher, whom else do we have waiting for audience today?"

As Hatton murmured the names, Maurice moved back through the crowd. A private audience with Her Majesty? He wondered skeptically if it would take less time from business than this futile public reception.

His hopes, which had not been high, vanished after three hours in the anteroom to the royal cabinet. Leicester went in to Elizabeth and did not come out. Hatton went in and came out again. A goldsmith was allowed to enter, and after that two men who looked like tradesmen but were probably aldermen in London, sent for no doubt that the Council might raise another loan from the people of London.

Maurice shifted in the chair that was not designed for comfort, stretched out his long legs. He had turned over his accounts to the House of Bowyer as Staper had suggested. The house had indeed not only been eager to handle his business but had promised to buy shares in his Eastern Company and pledged further purchases from merchants whose credit was good. There might be, Bowyer mentioned, some slight disagreement over Maurice's keeping more than the usual directorship powers in his hands, but his own backing was already assured. It was Bowyer's belief that the man whose brain and enterprise had created a daring venture could best bring it to a profitable conclusion.

Bowyer, a warmhearted elderly merchant, had begun discussing Maurice's enterprises with enthusiasm and ended with a cold respect for Maurice's business acumen. He said warningly that Maurice, not being a Londoner and not given to trying to win the liking of others, would find it hard to convince members that he should hold such absolute powers. Maurice said carelessly that any reasonable sums Bowyer thought should be spent on good will would be acceptable to him. Bowyer had shrugged in despair of making this young merchant understand the human aspects of gaining the confidence of associates, and said he'd undertake the business.

Maurice looked up casually as two newcomers entered, breaking into his reflections. The first, a quiet man, dark and withdrawn, who seemed to be looking both inwardly and outwardly at the one moment, had been pointed out to him as Francis Walsingham. Edward Blount was just behind the Queen's Secretary. Sir Francis was shown into the cabinet. Aldermen and goldsmith came out. Even Leicester came through the oaken door finally. There was a scowl on his face as he stumped out.

Blount and Maurice, except for the halberdiers just outside the open door leading to the staircase, were alone in the high-ceilinged room. The silence was thick about them. Maurice bowed. No greeting seemed to him quite suitable for a man who had tried to threaten him for money and then had placed him under arrest. Blount gave no indication for a moment of having seen Maurice though they were scarcely a score of feet apart. Perhaps he also felt a certain inadequacy of speech.

Maurice rested his elbow on the narrow arm of the chair, chin on the palm of his hand. He could sense Blount's eyes on him, was aware of how Blount moved across the room. He glanced up as a shadow fell between him and the window he was facing.

Blount said, "You're a brave man, Maurice."

"Is that right?" Maurice's voice was bland.

"Yes. Or a fool. But I don't think you're that, though you were so once in Blyth when you did not come to terms with me. And perhaps now again because whatever you are doing here, whatever falseness you are trying to sell to Her Majesty, it will do you no good. But I wish you no ill. I will give you one word of warning. Go back to Blyth, bury yourself there out of

English politics and business and you will perhaps be safe—at a price."

Without changing his position Maurice looked at Blount's blue velvet shoes, slashed and lined with silver, at his dark hose, his crimson doublet, the huge starched ruff, and finally at his face again with an astonished contempt that needed no words to express it.

Blount said, "I have given you warning. Expect no further mercy from me or anyone."

Maurice's brows lifted. "The other day, Sir Edward, I saw a play in the yard at the Tabard. It was a ranting strutting play, good enough, you understand, but full of overblown passions and wild words. You sound just a trifle as though you were copying a few lines from it. In fact, if I may point it out without offense, aren't you making rather a habit of such talk?"

Blount's face showed an effort at self-control. He spoke carefully and slowly. "Perhaps I blurted out my mind too quickly in an effort to get a distasteful task done with, Maurice. We need not go again into your background—rebellion, treason, the questionable ways you have made your fortune. The Queen is now aware of it and will not, I swear, even grant you private audience. The Turkey Company is closed to you. You escaped arrest once. You are not likely to be so lucky twice. If I were you, I'd go back to Blyth."

"You are beginning to weary me, Sir Edward." He gave Blount his title scornfully.

Blount drew in his breath. "I've only one word more to say and that is about Katherine Perrot. We have already proved which of us can win and hold a woman. Let one lesson suffice you."

Maurice could feel the carving of the chair arm cut into his flesh but he said only, "Katherine Perrot? A lovely young woman, Sir Edward. Let us hope her future fortune is closer to her deserts than her present appears to be." He looked away without interest.

Some of Blount's remarks might have been inaccurate, but he was right about the audience. The Queen did not see Maurice that day.

Maurice tossed a sheath of papers toward Patrick.

"Make me a copy of these holdings. Whatever Bowyer's other virtues are, his clerk's can't write." This wearing away of time at Whitehall for an audience that was no closer today than a month ago was bad. He was losing touch with the news at the Exchange, and, with religious wars tearing Europe apart, an investment one day was a ruin the next. He looked up decisively. "Do you remember Katherine Perrot, Patrick?"

"Remember Katherine Perrot? Yes. Who, Master Quain, could forget her?"

Maurice noted the tinge of color in Patrick's face, the attempt at a light tone. "She's just another woman. But I want you to see her. I've a ring that she would not accept. Give it to her in such a way that she will not refuse it again. She will know what I want of her."

Patrick picked up the jewel as though he were touching white-hot metal. There was a savage undernote in his voice. "Before I deliver this, what do you want of her?"

Maurice stared at the tone, then laughed. "Not what you think. An audience with Elizabeth." He turned back to his papers. "But if with the gift you can also have your will of the wench, take her and welcome."

Patrick's chair scraped back. He caught it automatically as it started to fall to the floor. It diverted his angry retort. Maurice did not even trouble to look up. Patrick's mouth thinned, but, he admitted wryly, he was glad of the chance to see Katherine Perrot on any terms.

Patrick went through the great stone entrance gate to Whitehall, threaded his way past a troop of men in half-armor, steel headpieces and breastplates gleaming in the misty light of the early October evening. Groups of servingmen in a variety of liveries lolled about waiting for their masters within the palace. The cognizances on their sleeves proclaimed them Leicester's, Hatton's, Burghley's or Walsingham's men, or the retinue of lesser gentry. In spite of the gambling and drinking corners there was a rather orderly air about the courtyard. The Queen was at Whitehall, and her impatience with brawlers was well known to go so far that an offender might lose his right hand. Quarrels were usually settled outside the palace precincts.

An idle page, seeing Patrick's hesitation at which way to turn, offered to act as guide. The corridors gleamed darkly, and the wide staircase with its broad low treads and heavy newel posts of oak curved upward into dim spaces lighted by torches flaring in bronze sconces along the wall. The page brought him to Katherine's door.

Patrick hesitated a moment, then knocked sharply on the panels. A voice called out to enter and he swung the door wide. Katherine stood across the room near the window, her head bent over a scrap of paper. She looked up and saw him.

The back of her hand went to her mouth to suppress an almost soundless cry. "I thought . . . Mattie . . . who are you?" There was only a single candle, and the gray light through the windows left the corners of the room in shadow.

The words struck Patrick like a blow. Katherine did not know him. Worse, she was afraid of him. She regained command of herself at once. "I . . . was startled, sir. I thought it was my waiting woman at the door." She moved slowly toward the table, twisting the paper in her hand absently, all the time holding him with her eyes. Still casually she put the crumpled sheet into the flame of the candle, pale gold in the half-light, and watched it flake into ash before she spoke again. "You seem a little familiar. Perhaps I do know you."

The tension had gone out of her face and she smiled easily at him. Patrick started to say his business, stopped. He did not want to be thought of as Maurice Quain's secretary, but as himself. He said, "We did not exactly meet before, madam. But I saw you once at the Saracen's Head when Sir Edward Blount——" Well, he couldn't keep Maurice out after all, he saw, as no flicker of memory lighted her face. "Sir Edward tried to—rather did—arrest Master Quain."

"Oh, yes, the big merchant. I do recall you now." She remembered she had liked him. "Do you come for him or for yourself?" She made a pattern with her forefinger in the fine ashes on the table.

He hesitated at her direct question. "Let us say for both, Lady Katherine!" Take your chance, my lad, he thought. So good a one will not come again soon, but the waiting woman will!

There was a faint elusive perfume about her, and her dark eyes and the beauty of her small piquant face at once drew him and yet held him away. She had on a soft robe of blue brocade cut low at the throat. The gown clung to her waist, was molded about the smooth curve of her hips. Without her farthingale and with the robe clinging to her body, she looked small and delicate.

Katherine smiled, moved over to a chair to sit down and gestured to him to do the same. "I do not even know your name."

He felt suddenly at ease, the warmth of her voice drawing him into a magic circle with her. "Patrick North, madam. I came here to bring you a gift from Master Quain for your very kind services." He crossed the room to give her the packet. In the half-light Katherine gleamed like some jewel from the sea, dark hair, fair skin and blue satin robe.

She turned back the linen wrapping, looked at the golden circlet against the fine white cloth and looked again, not seeing the blue-white of the diamonds but Maurice's face, chill and expressionless. She held the ring uncertainly in her hands, shook her head.

Patrick said, "You must accept it, Lady Katherine. I would not dare return with it."

She smiled at that but with a trace of uneasiness. "If I can convince Her Majesty that she should see Master Quain I will earn this jewel! But Edward——" She stopped.

At that name Patrick said, "I have thought that ever since we've come to London, Lady Katherine, there has been some hostile force against us. I think I know who is behind it. Perhaps you do. Master Quain did not ask me to bring it up." He hesitated.

"You would say?" She looked up at him, standing there lithe and dark with a wryly humorous expression twisting his mouth.

"No. I cannot ask your favor toward us at the expense of Edward Blount who is——" He stopped.

"My lover?" She looked at him calmly.

"I was about to say an older friend."

Katherine laughed. "You imply by that you are equally a friend if of newer vintage? I think, Master North, you would be a good friend to have."

Color mounted to his face. "You are too kind, Lady Katherine!" Only the stiff phrase came to his lips but his heart hammered at her careless, good-humored remark. He thought how idiotic it was of him to make so much of a pleasant phrase she would have spoken to anyone.

There was surprise and then a quick pity in her eyes as she saw how he had taken her words. "Forget what I said! We are not likely to meet again, but I will help your suit so far as I can with Her Majesty."

Patrick looked down at her. The color was still in his face but he felt confidence hardening in him. He smiled. "Forget, Lady Katherine? Not anything I ever hear you say, nor your least glance or gesture."

"Now, Master North, it is you who are being kind, too kind." She twisted the linen in her hands about Maurice's ring. Somehow she wanted to cry. She started to rise, hoping he would leave.

At her move Patrick took his courage in his hands. "I may as well say this now. I might not have the chance again, at least not soon. I have held you in my heart, Lady Katherine, since the first moment I saw you."

Katherine shook her head, a bittersweet taste in her mouth. "Don't!"

"Why not?" There was a challenging note in his voice. "Like every gallant in the Court, can I not hope?"

There was only bitterness within her now. She said in a hard voice, "And just what do you hope for, Master North?"

His brows went up in surprise. "To marry you, of course."

Katherine stared at him, her face softening in spite of herself, her eyes winking back unshed tears. "Oh,

88

God, Master North, you're so young! Go! I wish you would go now."

He kissed the tips of her fingers. "I will. But I'll come back, Lady Katherine." He turned as he put his hand on the latch, grinned a little ruefully. "Even though your hope may be that I won't."

Katherine waited, not moving until the door closed after him. Then she bent to pick up the ring that had fallen to the floor when she had risen. She went slowly across the room to place it in her jewel box, moving mechanically, her underlip caught in her teeth. A new conquest. She had no reason to cry. She forced herself to smile. But the smile did not reach her eyes as the ring winked up at her in the light and reminded her of Maurice Quain. The metal of the brassbound jewel case was cold under her hand. She shivered. Then she lifted her lovely shoulders in a shrug.

Elizabeth Tudor leaned back in her chair. One thin shoulder was slightly higher than the other under the heavy satin of her gown. Her eyes watched Maurice with catlike intensity. She raised her right hand in a gesture to silence Walsingham's protests. "Perhaps I misplace my trust, Master Quain, but I look to you for the success of this affair."

Maurice returned her gaze coldly and warily. She had been talking around the subject for a quarter of an hour and was still no nearer the heart of it. At every word the Queen's Principal Secretary, facing him with an open hostility, tried to dissuade her from her course. "Rather than to send this merchant abroad on your business, Your Majesty, you might do better to exile him."

Maurice eyed Walsingham speculatively. The Queen's Secretary did not seem to hold any feeling against him in London, but he evidently did not feel Maurice a safe man to send abroad. That was the reason no doubt he'd had to wait so long for this audience. It was over a month since he'd enlisted Katherine's aid. The Queen had probably been hoping as usual that, if she put off making her decision long enough, the problem, whatever it was, would mend itself. From the fact of his being here it had evidently not been solved.

Elizabeth laughed at Walsingham. "If he does not do this for us, Sir Francis, whom can we send? Enough of this prating, I beg you."

Walsingham said doggedly, "If we send no one, Madam? So? Is that not better than to let this foreigner into Spanish dominions?"

"Foreigner? Oh, you mean Quain?"

"Yes, Your Majesty. Perhaps you forget his Northern birth and Northern loyalties. Half a Scotsman, and in Spain's pay for all we know. Once in Mary Stuart's. Yet you'd give him leave into their dominions to tell your plans, let them know your armies, your fortifications, how many troops you'll send abroad against them. I do not trust this man."

Elizabeth chuckled. "You've made yourself clear enough, Sir Francis! But we must send someone to Antwerp."

Maurice lifted his head at the mention of Antwerp. Walsingham noted the movement. "How, Your Majesty, do you know he'll return?"

Elizabeth looked at Maurice again. "He will. He is a man of business. Already I see in his face that he intends to make a good thing out of this! Do you not, Master Quain?"

Maurice smiled with his mouth only. "Madam, I have not yet heard what my duties are. But you can be assured that what I undertake I will complete as well as I am able. No one has yet questioned my integrity in commerce. As for the pay, one half will be the glory of being able to serve the most beautiful princess in Europe."

"And the other half?" Elizabeth was pleased.

"Will be what a merchant should demand if his services are to your satisfaction." He knew what the price would be, but he would not name it yet.

Elizabeth tapped him on the arm with her jeweled fan. "Ah, that's not so gallant. But I am satisfied to begin with, though nothing you can say will satisfy my Moor." Her nickname for Walsingham seemed peculiarly apt. Maurice thought there was a darkness about him as though he moved in unlighted rooms, suspicious of prying eyes.

Maurice said, "Madam, if the means are not to the liking of Sir Francis, let us hope the end will be. You mentioned Antwerp?" God's bones, they could go on for weeks and be none the closer to the reason for this royal audience!

Elizabeth closed her fan with a decisive click. "Yes, Master Quain, Antwerp. We need a loan raised, to be paid in gold or silver or jewels. As you may know, we have had difficulties of late trading in the Netherlands and our merchants have moved north to Hamburg. Yet with the turmoil through Europe, Antwerp is the only exchange where enough silver can be raised for our needs. We must have thirty thousand pounds."

Maurice said consideringly, "Even at the commercial capital of the world, thirty thousand pounds is—well, I'd say impossible to raise quickly."

"How do you know it must be raised soon?"

"Sir Francis, I have seen reports out of Antwerp. The money must be raised quickly if at all. As you no doubt know, before William the Silent was assassinated by the Spanish this last summer he warned the merchants that the Prince of Parma would move in on the city. With the death of their leader, the Dutch have forgotten his counsel. I haven't. Parma has been building forts along the Schelde to prevent Brussels and Ghent from giving aid to Antwerp. Now with Ghent, Dendermonde and Vilvorde surrendering, Antwerp is shut off from all help of neighboring cities. There can be but one conclusion—Parma will beseige Antwerp soon and with every weapon at his command. Not alone to capture a strategic city but to put down at last the Dutch rebellion against their Spanish King. Antwerp has the best port in the Netherlands. Philip Hapsburg must control it before he can go farther in his well-known enterprise for conquering England. I sent orders to have my own investments transferred to Paris and Hamburg."

Elizabeth said in a dangerous voice, "And why have I not been told of this serious situation, Sir Francis?"

Walsingham threw up his hands. "Not told! Madam,

for months the Dutch have been at your feet pleading with you for help."

"I beg you, Sir Francis—we will not go into that now. After all they are rebels against their lawful lord and king, Philip of Spain. I don't like rebels." Her eyes flicked over Maurice momentarily. "Though why Philip drives them to such lengths over religion——— A strange man, Philip."

Walsingham said sharply. "You will find one day, Madam, there is not room in the world for that devil's spawn Philip Hapsburg and those of us who profess the purer religion. If you did not think so, why did you sign the laws against those of the Catholic faith who follow that perverted sinful man, that man who perjures himself swearing he sits in the chair of St. Peter in Rome?"

"I wonder myself sometimes, Sir Francis. One does what one thinks best at the time, and then one doubts. But I'm only a woman and growing old." The pathos in her voice was denied by the sparkle in her green eyes. "Your Dutch friends would drive too hard a bargain with me. When their promises are backed with four seacoast towns to be put in my possession, I think—I do not say I will—but I think I may understand somewhat better your rather tiresome ranting, Sir Francis."

"You will do as you will, Your Majesty. Before we go farther into this affair with Quain, may I ask him one question? How much do these 'reports' of yours cover business and how much diplomatic affairs?"

Maurice looked uninterested. "Sir Francis, you overrate my poor abilities. I am an ordinary merchant with the usual ways of communication. Government, policy, call it what you will, are above my understanding and outside the interest of a man of business except where they jeopardize my investments."

"Your investments?" Walsingham turned his head toward Elizabeth. "Until this man returns, Your Majesty, may I suggest one precaution? Should we not handle Quain's affairs in London until we see the money he raises under your seal given into your hands?"

"Before God, Sir Francis, I would not stir a step on this mission under such conditions!"

"You are speaking," Walsingham said with a deadly quiet, "to the Principal Secretary of England."

"And you," Maurice retorted coldly, "to the one man who can raise a loan in Antwerp." He looked at Elizabeth. "Your Highness, I cry your pardon for so hasty a remark in your presence. I have no need to fear an outrage before the very font of justice. I was in the wrong."

Elizabeth nodded absently. "What percent do you think will have to be paid, Master Quain? Those niggardly money-changers on the Continent take the full interest before ever they send the coin."

"Their first offer will be twenty percent. I might get them down to sixteen, fifteen, not less than that probably."

"Well, do what you can. But make sure you tell them the loan will be repaid within the year."

Maurice said, "And how soon, Your Majesty, will it be repaid?"

Elizabeth shrugged. "How can we tell?" She laughed infectiously. "If Drake captures the Spanish plate fleet, it will be repaid the next day."

Maurice permitted himself a faint smile. "However, Madam, unless I have some assurance of a reasonable chance that the loan will be returned in the year, I cannot undertake to raise the money."

Elizabeth stared at him. "God's pittikins, Quain, but you grow fine! I have heard stories of your business dealings—how many men you have ruined, how you let your own townsmen be impressed for your ships, and half a dozen more tales with none to your credit. Yet you cavil at a slight glossing over of the truth. I do not like such jests." Her voice rose stridently.

Maurice listened unmoved. "They are all true," he agreed. "But never have I given my word or signed my name on any contract and not fulfilled it. Any other way is poor business. This uncertain repayment is why England's credit is so low on the Continent and the interest so high."

"But sixteen, eighteen percent for two years. Why,

you'd have to raise at least five thousand pounds more to cover the interest."

"If I get a lower rate, it will be on the reputation of my name, Your Majesty. That I cannot hazard. If I get the loan at all it will be so. But of course," he added sardonically, "you have other financial agents."

An angry color crept up Elizabeth's face, showing faintly under the layers of paint on her cheeks. "As you know, there's no man else in England who can get past Parma's army as you can—you who have so well served his master and my royal brother, Philip of Spain. But on the other hand, if we are not pleased with you, sir, we can confiscate every shilling you hold and commit you to the Tower."

Walsingham made a half-arrested movement. "Perhaps an excellent thought, Your Majesty."

Maurice murmured, "Every shilling in England. That would not do my fortune mortal hurt."

Elizabeth ignored both remarks. "I want thirty thousand pounds raised for one year. Your payment will be eight percent of the silver delivered into our hands."

Maurice weighed her words unhurriedly. "I have perhaps a better plan, Your Majesty. My reputation, as I said, is worth money to me. I will forgo any payment beyond undue expense. That will take care of part of the second year's interest. The wages I would have—" he looked at her and then at her gaunt body suggestively—"could be paid only by you."

Elizabeth glanced down and then up at him like a young girl. "Master Quain, you are too forward!"

"Beauty," said Maurice, "blames men for being drunk when she has intoxicated us. It is not just. Though your beauty inflames, chastity guards you. No man would dare ask anything unseemly of the Virgin Queen."

"Well, well," Elizabeth said, "let us hear what your petition is then."

"Perhaps, Your Majesty, when I come back it will sound better in your ears. May I wait until my return to see whether or not I have been successful? The giving or withholding of your favor I leave in your gracious hands."

94

Katherine Perrot looked up from her embroidery frame as Maurice went through the outer room of the Queen's suite. "Good morning, Master Quain!"

Maurice had not noticed her among the four young women seated in a half circle under the mullioned windows, suave young gentlewomen who gazed at him from under drooping lids while one smiled, another pouted prettily and the third sighed. Katherine gave him only a straightforward rather amused glance and stood up to cross to him. She drew him with the lift of a brow to the far corner of the room where the tapestry caught the light slanting through the windows. The figures of scarlet, azure and green glowed softly against a silver-gray background. "Did your affairs go well, Master Quain?"

"Yes. Your help, Lady Katherine, was invaluable. Please accept my thanks."

She shrank from the chilly tone. "A small matter, sir, and vastly overpaid. I might have done as much for the asking." She raised her eyes filled with sudden mischief, a subtly sensuous overtone in the lift of her shoulders. "The ring, Master Quain, is of far more worth than my poor services today."

Maurice smiled down at her without warmth though he could feel his blood quickening within him. She was being deliberately provocative, he thought, not because she was interested in him, but out of sheer idle curiosity. He said indifferently, "If a wench comes easily, good. But there's no woman in the world for whom I'd have the madness to risk the Queen's anger." One day, he thought, he'd have this girl for a night and then be free of her witchery. She made every other woman he took into his arms pallid and tawdry.

Katherine looked at him meditatively from under half-closed lids while beneath her cool composure she felt a savage desire to strike him across the face. She wondered if he would even notice it. Unaccountably she wanted to cry. Her voice was husky with disdain. "I'm afraid you are reading into my words, Master Quain, a meaning that is not there. Not even the Queen wants so much for her money. You of course would not ask anything money could not purchase.

95

You know only of the merchandise on sale in every market stall."

Maurice said, "I once thought there were some things not to be bought—love or loyalty or honor. Do not be betrayed by such illusions. With gold you can buy them all, my dear." He looked at her with hard cynical eyes, then bowed to kiss her hand. The flesh was warm and firm under her lips. What was in these slim fingers—muscle and bone and blood—that the feel of her hand in his should tear at his heart? "If I come back, Lady Katherine, you will have done me more of a service than you know. If I do not——" So great a venture as his Eastern Company, with which he would one day perhaps outdistance the Turkey Company, was worth the risk of being caught between Spanish fire and Flemish resistance. "But I will return."

Katherine rose from the deep curtsy with which she had returned his bow, looked after him with opaque eyes, her head high, as he went through the wide arched door. She crossed the room, took up her embroidery frame again. The three women eyed her, leaning forward in their eagerness for gossip. "Who's the handsome gentleman?"

"Did you see that doublet? The buttons were diamonds and the clasp at the throat was of ruby. My dear Kit, your Edward Blount might glitter more brightly, but for a man of substance—well, if you aren't interested in him, tell me."

"Not interested? Kit? Look at her color! Not interested!" They did look, half maliciously, half pleased for her.

"Who is he?"

Katherine held up the linen she was working on. There was a pucker between her brows as she examined it. "Don't you think a crimson flower here in the design instead of a yellow? You won't care about him when I tell you. Maurice Quain, a merchant from the North."

One of the women laughed. "Then he has the money he seems to have! With that ruby clasp I'd be interested if he were a chimney sweep."

Another said, "It's not like the old days. Now every nobleman is trying to marry a merchant's daughter to pay his debts."

The third girl sighed. "He walks as though he owned Whitehall. And the way he wears his clothes! You can see Master Quain has been used to wealth all his life."

From the silken skein on her lap Katherine drew out a thread of scarlet that looked like a thin line of blood, held it against the white linen square to see how the colors blended and contrasted. She did not think Maurice wore fine clothes with a careless grace, but as a man wore a suit of armor, and for the same reason—whether he shrank or swaggered within, there would be no change in the look of impregnability to the world. Maurice, Maurice—but was that what he wanted? No. Perhaps that was what he was, the real man, steel to his bones, instead of flesh.

She was always aware of sensitive defenseless humanity at the core of each person she met under the hard eyes, the bones and skin, whether scoffer or bully or insolent courtier. She smiled at her three companions. They were women who had always had everything they needed, with ample dowries so that they could marry well. Their lives were built on a dais so that they never felt the cold drafts of life about their pretty expensively shod feet. But under velvet and jewels and brocade in each one of them there was perhaps some bitterness, an unhealed wound, a blind groping for an unattainable desire.

One said, "You can well smile, Kit, with this wealthy merchant at your feet. We envy you."

"What merchant?" The words fell heavy as a stone into the light ripple of the women's voices.

Katherine twisted the end of the thread between her fingers, put it through the eye of her needle before she looked up slowly to Edward Blount. She felt a tremor run through her. His face was completely expressionless. She had been prepared for annoyance, black anger even, but this went beyond anger.

Someone laughed, said in a tone too high and too thin, "Why, Master Quain of course. He was in with the Queen."

Blount turned to look at the speaker. "I wasn't asking you."

The young woman started to retort angrily. Her voice died away.

Katherine said, "My friends are overkind, Ned. They think if I talk to a man, he's at my feet." She held up her embroidery, glanced from it to Blount. "I was working on this for a shirt for you. I wonder . . . perhaps a little more blue to finish the edges? What do you think, dear?"

With a sweep of his hand Blount knocked linen and frame to the floor, caught Katherine's arm and jerked her to her feet. There was a smothered gasp of indignation from the women.

Katherine twisted her arm free. "You're hurting me."

"I want to talk to you."

Katherine looked at him wearily. "If you must, come in here."

She moved across to open the door of a small inner chamber. It was airless and lighted only by a narrow window high in the wall. She followed him in, stood with her back to the door. "I hope you have some good reason for a scene like that, Ned. I didn't like it."

He stayed across the width of the stone room from her, barely in control of his anger. "So he had audience with the Queen? And you talked to him? I need not guess who persuaded Her Majesty to listen to whatever treasonous lies he poured into her ears."

Katherine looked at him, not answering. His rage somehow degraded her.

"I found this——" he opened his hand to show her the diamond ring Patrick had brought her—"in your jewel box yesterday. I had begun to wonder. Quain's, isn't it? He'll get it back, and if ever again——" He paused. The unspoken threat from a man who liked to air his fury gathered edge in the silence. "What was he paying you for?"

Katherine looked at the ring in his open palm and thought of Elly and Deborah. "What you know in your heart he paid me for. An audience with the Queen. Don't quarrel with me about Maurice Quain. He means

98

nothing to me, nor I to him." Especially, she thought, I mean nothing to him.

Blount's eyes narrowed. "It really matters little, I suppose. I will have him soon—" his hand closed over the ring—"where I want him."

Katherine's heart jerked and stilled. That was why he had not finished his threat. Already he was carrying it out. Her eyes questioned him.

"Yes, my dear, where you'll not see him again. He'll be in the Tower on treason, and he'll come out to ride to the gallows."

"No." Katherine smiled confidently. "He is too prudent a man to be involved in treason." She knew from his answering look that this was his own fear. Her voice was clear and cutting. "What harm have you done Maurice Quain, Ned, that you should hate him so?"

At that he took two steps toward her, raised his hand to strike her, let it drop to his side as he met her eyes. "What harm have I done him? He stands in my way at every turn. He is the enemy of England. If he should rise, where will I be? You think it is only on business he sees the Queen? When he has her favor he will use it to get his lands back and ruin me. And what will happen to you then? Or perhaps I see. You have thought of this already. At my downfall you'll have a new lover and lose nothing in the exchange except good blood for base! How could one like you judge, who is not certain of her own father or her child's?"

The sickness that started at the pit of her stomach crawled upward, constricting her heart, filling her throat to nausea. "I can at least be grateful for one thing, Edward Blount: you are not Debbie's father."

She thought he would strike her now, but he only gave a short laugh. "We'll correct that with the next brat. But let us have no more of these gifts from Quain, or even thoughts of him."

Suddenly his mood changed, affected by her beauty, his passion shifting to desire. "I would never have looked in your jewel box, but I was putting a new bracelet there for a surprise for you, Kit. You do not know how you are hurting me. If I could be sure of your love——" There was pathos in his voice.

Her anger against him slipped away as though it were not worth holding. He seemed so pathetic—so big and fair and needing her so much, buffed by storms both within and without that he did not understand. There was a helplessness in him that always went to her heart. She shrugged. "Return the ring if you wish, Ned. It's of no importance."

In spite of her pity for him she looked at him across a gulf. Ned had destroyed today some delicate cord in their relationship. While necessity and remembered hours of pleasure bound them together, even promised them future joys, an essential had been finally spoiled by his jealousy, his lack of trust. It seemed as though he were Ned and yet another man too, or perhaps it was that some part of him that had been just below the surface had come into the light now.

Blount put his hand under her chin, lifted her face to him. "I'm sorry, sweet. I'll bring you some other bauble for this jewel I'm sending back. One kiss to show that you forgive me! Whatever my faults, Kit, you know they are all because I love you so much." He put his hands on her shoulders, slid them down her back to her waist so that she must come closer to him. "Sometimes I think, sweetheart, a quarrel is worth the bitterness for the joy of being friends again."

"Oh, Ned, Ned!" She tucked back a curl, touched her ruff to be sure it was not disarranged, smoothed out her wide skirt, then put a hand on the latch. "Her Majesty may send for me." She went slowly out.

Blount watched her go. He was rather pleased with himself. He had shown Katherine he would stand no nonsense about Maurice Quain. And Quain himself—Sir Francis had told him Elizabeth Tudor's plan to send Maurice to Antwerp. If Walsingham did not close on Maurice and he went abroad—didn't the House of Gascony have an outlet in Antwerp? And there were other ways. 'Fore God he could watch Maurice Quain die slowly, by inches, and warm himself in the sight! He looked at the diamond ring in his hand. He'd send it back to Maurice, but it would be his again one day.

100

Maurice drew the silver inkhorn closer, poised his quill above it while he weighed the instructions he would send Bowyer. If Parma planned to move more closely about Antwerp, the burghers would start to store grain. He must have—— He became aware suddenly of a faint knocking at the door. He looked up for someone to answer, called impatiently to Jacques.

"Yes, monsoor, yes, monsoor." Jacques put down the clothes he was packing, went to the door, came back a moment later. Behind him Maurice could hear the footsteps of the visitor. He turned with annoyance. It was Alicia. "You may go, Jacques. Well, Alicia, what do you want?"

She twisted her hands together, big bony hands but finely shaped. "Master Quain, I don't know how to say it . . . I . . ."

"Who sent you?"

Alicia's eyes lighted up at that. "That is it! How did you know? It's this way . . . I . . ."

"My dear Alicia, I'm a busy man. I expect to leave London tomorrow, and I have my affairs to get in order."

"Yes, I know."

Maurice put his quill down and gave her his full attention. "You know? How?"

"My brother, sir. He . . . he works in the kitchens at Whitehall and hears gossip."

"All right. You have a brother. I am leaving the city. He feels I have tarnished his sister's honor. How much does he want?"

Alicia put one hand on her hip, moved toward him with a pathetic semblance of coquetry. "It's not like that at all, sir. It's honored I am to be of service to you. But I . . . I just mentioned you to a fine gentleman and he begs to meet you. He's a very fine gentleman."

"I'm sure he is. When I return——"

"No, no, no. That wouldn't do. He must see you before you leave, Master Quain. Please."

"Who is he?"

"I'm not supposed to say. But he's a very fine gentleman, and his name is Anthony Babington."

101

Maurice said coldly, "Babington? I've never heard of him."

"But you will see him?"

"Where is he?"

"He's waiting down in the common room. You will——"

Maurice threw out his hands. "It will probably take less time than listening to you plead for him. Tell him to come up. You need not return with him."

"Why, sir, I wouldn't interfere with gentlemen's business! But . . . aren't you going to say good-by to me?" She leaned over him.

Maurice gave her two rose nobles and glanced at the silver clock on the wall. "Tell this Babington my time is short."

Anthony Babington came striding in, a whirl of brave colors, green velvet cloak lined with scarlet, crimson doublet laced with silver, a plume held with a gold aigrette on his broad-brimmed hat which he swept off as he bowed to Maurice. "Sir! You are most kind to see me. But I would not have dared presume so on your good nature if this were not as much to your advantage as to mine, to all ours, to England's!" He smiled, a young, good-humored smile, confident of Maurice's approval.

It was a confidence Maurice did not share. "Well?"

Babington, not waiting for an invitation, pulled up a chair, sat down and leaned forward earnestly. "Master Quain, it is a simple thing I am going to ask of you, but it is only fair to tell you as much as I can of our side. I am assured you will be eager—I know you will feel honored to help." His voice faltered on the last sentence as he met Maurice's coldly indifferent eyes.

"My time is brief, Master Babington."

"Yes, I know. I'm sorry. Now, sir, there are six of us who have formed an association to rescue Mary Stuart, the rightful Queen of England, from her prison and escort her in safety to France." He stood up as he spoke her name, sat down again at once not to interrupt his story. Maurice opened his mouth to stop the young man, closed it again as Babington rushed on.

"Now, Master Quain, Mary's escape is as far as some of my friends care to go. But as for me—I was her page once and I made a vow then to rescue her though I gamble life and property. I——"

Maurice interrupted icily: "The chances seem excellent that you'll lose both. Now if that is all, Master Babington——"

Anthony Babington was scarcely aware of the interruption. "As for me, Master Quain, I have resolved not only that she shall go free but that she shall grace the throne she rightfully owns. To crown her in England we must have Spain's help. You are going to Antwerp. You could deliver a message to the great Prince of Parma."

Maurice stared at the speaker unbelievingly. "Do you run around pouring into every man's ear this tale of treason? I think you're mad."

Babington's laugh rang out, clear and boyish. "You must indeed. Gods me, there are not above half a score men in England, friends of mine of long standing, to whom I would speak so freely. You, you can take a small part in this by delivering my message to Parma about the code we shall use. Any other man I could send might be stopped, but you're beyond suspicion. Later, when the time comes, you will be a captain in our army."

"I am a merchant, Master Babington."

"Yes, yes, I know. I understand that. A most ingenious concealment. But we know you were at Mary Stuart's right hand when she was taken. We know you are in London now to strive to get her freed. I can assure you it can be accomplished only by force of arms. This mission of yours to Antwerp is providential, nothing less than the benevolent hand of Providence."

"The only providence I see in this, sir," Maurice rejoined coldly, "Is that you have done your raving to someone who is not going to turn you over to Walsingham for high treason. If you wish to put your head in the lion's mouth, it is of no moment to me, except as a fellow human being to warn you it is there—which you in your foolishness seem not aware of." His voice warmed slightly. "Master Babington, enough ruin and disgrace and blood have been sacrificed to this queen you would serve. Let those suffice. Go home, marry, live out your own life as a sane man. You are young to die."

Babington stared at Maurice. "Am I to understand, Master Quain, that you will not deliver this message to Parma?"

"Do I look like the kind of fool who would? Before you go—" the young man had made not the slightest move to leave—"I would like one question answered: Why did you come to me?"

"I told you."

"You told me what you know. Not how you know it."

"I was informed of your background and mission by a good friend of mine, Master Quain. As you can understand, I name no names beyond my own. Walsingham thinks this man is in his pay as a clerk, but he is in ours."

"If you mean that this man you speak of is taking your money, that does not mean he's loyal to you. I do not like having my business so much public property that for a shilling anyone may learn of it."

Babington smiled. "It takes more than a shilling, Master Quain! Do not let it concern you."

"On the contrary I feel it should concern me very much."

Babington's voice dropped to a confidential whisper. "I'll tell you this, Master Quain. It is my belief that Walsingham himself, indeed the government, wishes Mary Stuart to escape. She is a constant embarrassment to them. Walsingham was kind enough to give me an audience and hinted as much. They do not, of course, expect we'll rise with Spain and France and put the loveliest lady in Christendom on the throne."

"I doubt if she is the loveliest lady in Christendom now. And if Walsingham wants Mary Stuart out of prison, let him find less dark and devious ways to free her. You are, if you do not mind plain speaking, a fool to do it for him. I would not trouble to give you the advice, but I served her once as you know. I'm wiser now."

Babington came to his feet. "You are pleased to sneer, Master Quain. But all this, all this you have earned——" He indicated the luxurious room with a sweep of his arm. "I see it now. I thought it was a concealment, but I see now it is no doubt the price of treachery. You got more than thirty pieces of silver for betraying Mary Stuart, didn't you?"

"Mary Stuart needs no one to betray her. She always betrays herself. You are a rash and foolhardy young man, Master Babington. I hope you live long enough to attain some wisdom, though I cannot see it as much of a possibility. Do you mind . . . your elbow . . . you are spilling wax on the table." Maurice moved the tall light he had kept burning for any documents he wanted sealed. "But I have spent more time than I have to spare. Good day to you!"

Babington stood stiffly beside his chair. "When Mary Stuart rides into London at the head of a conquering army, do not expect more mercy than you show now."

"If that is your dream and you cannot forget it, do yourself a kindness and buy a rope from a friend to put around your neck. It is better than the rack and quartering knife. Good day!"

Babington bowed without a further word and went out, swaggering just a little, a brave mock-heroic figure to Maurice's eyes, a knight-errant born too late into a practical hardheaded world.

Thirty thousand pounds of silver out of Antwerp. To move that much silver, if he could raise it, would present a problem. He must have a ship waiting. So Walsingham had set spies on him. Alicia no doubt. That was Blount's doing, of course. He was more of an idiot than this young Babington, and that was saying a good deal.

He looked down at the paper under his hand, remembered where his plans had been interrupted. If Parma were to move against Antwerp, grain could be sold the citizens at double the usual price. He would have Bowyer send every bushel of wheat he could lay hands on from the warehouses to the Flemich city. The grain he might not sell to the patriots of Antwerp, he would send to Parma for victualing his army. Beef too the Spanish would need—and pay for. Wisdom was a hard lesson but, once learned, how profitable!

Part II

AS MUCH AS HE DESERVES

7

Sleet beat against the diamond-shaped panes of the windows, and the winter wind howled about the inn making the austere room seem brighter by contrast. The flames on the hearth reflected on the tiles framing the fire, gleamed on the scrubbed floor with its single small mat serving for a rug, warmed the plain, paneled walls and deepened the blue and red of the Delft pottery on the table.

Maurice, sensitive to his surroundings, felt first a pleasure in the apartment and then an ironic amusement. Somehow it depicted Antwerp itself—keep the fires blazing, clean your boots, rise early, do your business at the Burse, driving a good bargain, and drink down your good or ill fortune with vast quantities of ale, though daily the food that went with the ale was growing a little more spare, the beef stringier, the loaves of bread smaller.

On the Scheldt the Prince of Parma was driving his pilings fifty feet deep out from the banks, placing huge timbers across them to form a roadway twelve feet wide fortified by blockhouses. The citizens watched the Spanish form the walls with a shrug, a laugh. Maurice had heard their comments too often. The river was half a mile wide, sixty feet deep in the middle. Parma could never close it. The tide rose eleven feet. The Spanish would grow tired and move on, or ships would come to their aid from England, or an army march north to Antwerp from France. Antwerp was in a strategic position between the southern provinces which had made peace with Philip Hapsburg and the northern provinces still carrying on their fight for independence from Spanish rule. Neither England nor France could afford to let Antwerp fall. Parma's success in the Netherlands would place a Hapsburg strangling cord around France and leave England without her Dutch outpost against Spanish aggression. It was merely a matter of waiting. Besides the river could not be bridged to blockage the city.

Maurice did not know whether the river could be bridged or not and cared something less. But he wanted the thirty thousand pounds before he found out. Foreign merchants from Germany, France and Italy were leaving the city. In the midst of packing their effects they were not interested in negotiating a loan with the representative of a small country that would, if the Spanish reduced Antwerp, soon be facing her most powerful enemy across a few miles of sea.

A personal loan on the strength of the Quain name and backed with the property of the House of Quain in Hamburg, Paris, Rome, any amount up to the value of that property. A loan to the Queen of England with no collateral but the Royal Seal, absurd! If times were normal, they would talk about it—at eighteen percent interest. But payment was always uncertain, and with Antwerp under Parma's hostile eyes their hasty departure was costing them enough now without an added strain on their finances. Should the Scheldt not be bridged and Parma march his soldiers elsewhere, good! Master Quain must return and they would discuss this loan.

Maurice thanked them sardonically and turned his attention to the Flemish burghers. The burghers were willing to lend the silver, five hundred pounds here, another five hundred there, but the interest would be twenty percent. After all, when could they expect to be paid? It was beyond experience that the Royal House of England would make complete repayments in the month promised, or even the year. They had to protect themselves. Twenty percent—really you could call it charity. Maurice said fourteen percent. Fourteen! The only reason for their generosity in not demanding twenty-five percent in the Queen's need was that she might one day accept the sovereignty of the Netherlands. Why, the Emperor of Austria had paid them twenty-one percent! Maurice said fourteen for the Queen of England.

Fourteen? Well now, they might come down to nineteen, even eighteen if he'd back the loan with his personal resources. Where he gave his name, everyone knew the investment was the same as in their hands again. But the word of crowned heads through Europe—they began on their woes, how this commercial house had been ruined, another was tottering, because of childlike faith in the Valois in Paris, the Hapsburgs in Vienna and Madrid, the Tudors in London.

Maurice said fourteen percent backed by the Royal Seal only. They asked in retort how much Maurice was gambling on so slim a collateral. Maurice said, "Fourteen percent, gentlemen, my last word. But—" here he'd leaned forward with a quick gesture—"you seem to have forgotten the most important point of all. At the moment Antwerp's future is not bright. Think of it: thirty thousand pounds of your silver reposing safely in the Tower of London instead of paying Parma's soldiers if he should be successful. If he is, you lose nothing. Every shilling is ready to be returned with interest. If I were sure Antwerp would be forced to surrender, I would ask to be paid, gentlemen, for getting your silver out of the country. If Parma withdraws, your money is still in good keeping and you'll make a handsome profit to boot. Well?"

"Fifteen percent and we'll sign the agreement."

So he had thirteen thousand pounds at fifteen percent interest to be transported somehow to London. He could, like the citizens, scoff at the young general's folly in attempting to put a rein on the ocean's tide. He was more inclined to curse the burghers for not having opened the Blauw-garen dike before it was too late and flooded the meadows to the city, making Antwerp a seaport vulnerable only to a naval attack. He did neither, but weighed coldly his chances for moving the silver.

Ghent had fallen. Vilvorde was taken, cutting off commerce by water between Brussels and Antwerp, and in any case Brussels itself was under siege. The

109

Scheldt was the only possibility, and Parma had it guarded by St. Mary's and Philip's forts.

Maurice looked across at Patrick who was sitting at the table under the window. If the silver were captured, the burghers would say it was the Queen's. Elizabeth would declare the money still the burghers' since she had not laid eyes on it. In short the silver would be his own—if it were lost.

Patrick, feeling Maurice's eyes upon him, glanced up. "It looks, Master Quain, as though we'll see some fighting yet. I was outside the walls last night with a scouting party. The timbers are built several hundred feet out from the riverbanks. Do you think they can close the gap?"

Maurice said mechanically, "A floating bridge might do it if strong enough to resist the tide. Parma does not have to worry over the resistance of the citizens. With half the energy they use in scoffing they could blow his defenses to hell. You'll not see them doing it. God, but I'd like——" He stopped abruptly. "That is neither here nor there. As you know from your listings, Patrick, we have almost half the loan raised. It should be shipped to England while there's assurance of getting the silver out of Antwerp."

"You aren't returning to London!"

"No. You are."

"Leave Antwerp? Why, I've never been in a besieged city and I may not have the chance again."

Maurice said dryly, "Why bother? You can save time and lose nothing by just going without your meals for three days and then quartering a rat and eating it raw. A besieged town runs out of firewood. But do not forget to order pheasant and malmsey for me."

Patrick grinned, shrugged in resignation. "How will you get the silver past Parma?"

"With the town fathers' permission we'll have to acquire some sort of boat to brave the batteries on the riverbanks. It could be done on a moonless night with a trained pilot. The ships from Zeeland are at Lillo below the bridge. At a price you could have one take you across to England or at least to one of the seacoast towns. The rest is easy enough. Get me an appointment with Sainte-Aldegonde as soon as possible. Today or tomorrow morning at the latest."

"Your name, Master Quain, is familiar to me. I am happy for the opportunity to become acquainted with you." A heavy man beginning to wear thin like a much used sword, Philip de Marnix, Baron de Saint-Aldegonde and Burgomaster of Antwerp, rose courteously to receive his guest.

Maurice bowed, murmured a thank you for his lordship's graciousness and flicked a look about the white-washed room. It was Sainte-Aldegonde's own scantily furnished chamber, not one of the state apartments. A broken lance crossed with a rusted sword hung on one wall. A chain fastened to an iron stake lay in the corner, no doubt a reminder of the years the Burgomaster had spent in Spanish prisons.

Maurice felt this room was Sainte-Aldegonde, purposeful, plain, straightforward and open, with a core of steel—no, of inflexible iron. Maurice knew that he was also a scholar, a poet and a diplomat, but was not this the essential man? He sat down, turned back his cloak showing the lining of martens' skins. Flakes of snow drifted against the small-paned windows, ridging the leaded frame.

Sainte-Aldegonde said, "Master Quain, I'm sorry to be blunt, but I can give little time to any one person. You had some pressing affair?"

"I'm fully aware of the honor you do me, my lord Burgomaster. I would not trouble you but my need touches the service of my most gracious sovereign, Queen Elizabeth."

"I will count it a privilege to give you any assistance at my disposal." Sainte-Aldegonde waited, his shrewd eyes on the merchant.

My request is for a flatboat to go down the Scheldt before the unseasonable weather is upon us. As you no doubt know, my lord, I have been raising a loan for Her Majesty, and I'd like to have my secretary convey the silver I have raised to England before we are in the grip of winter. You could send a man with him."

111

"Before there is ice on the river, Master Quain, or before the bridge is closed?"

Maurice said, "I have hoped with your citizens that the Prince of Parma will·soon tire of his useless labors and take his troops elsewhere."

"You do not believe the bridge can be closed across the Scheldt?"

"It can, my lord, of course. One could move mountains if one could keep up the heart for it. A floating bridge of cabled barges for instance would do the trick. But money comes slowly out of Spain, I've heard, supplies are difficult to get, soldiers besieging a city have not the spirit of the besieged fighting for their lives and homes."

Sainte-Aldegonde nodded. "You are a soldier, Master Quain?"

"I? No, my lord."

"Yet that was a soldier's judgment you used. Well, well. What you want is a ship?"

It was on Maurice's tongue to sway Sainte-Aldegonde's favor with a bribe. He closed his teeth on the words. Sainte-Aldegonde would not be an easy man to offer money to. No one with sense would refuse money, but it took time to bribe with a finesse befitting a Burgomaster. "I do, sir."

Sainte-Aldegonde deliberated. "We have boats, of course. But once it was down the river, we'd never get it back again, and God knows what our needs will be before we're through." He looked up suddenly. "You would stay in Antwerp?"

Their eyes met and clashed, and Maurice read hostility in the other's gaze. Perhaps the Burgomaster knew of his profiteering. He had made three hundred percent on the cargoes of grain he had sent in until the leaders of the city had in a flurry of civic dignity made such profits illegal. Then the shipments had stopped promptly. No captain for ten or twelve percent profit would risk sailing by the Spanish guns or chance the fate that overtook those who were captured—having their arms and legs cut off and their mutilated bodies sent on down to Antwerp instead of the hoped-for grain. Maurice said, "I came here to raise a loan for

112

Her Majesty. I am staying until the whole amount is in my hands."

Sainte-Aldegonde leaned forward. "Is that your only reason for coming to Antwerp, Master Quain?"

"What other possible purpose, my lord, could I have?"

"If I must tell you what you know—to keep Parma informed of the city's defenses. You talk like a soldier, your eye discerns exactly what a military man would be looking for, and now you come with some thin excuse about wanting a boat to get your secretary to England. You are sure he wants to go to England? He doesn't want to stop at a Spanish fort to speak to the Prince of Parma?"

Maurice thought it was well he had trusted his instinctive judgment not to offer Sainte-Aldegonde a bribe. "My dear sir, do you seriously consider thirteen thousand pounds of silver a thin excuse? It could buy a hundred men, body and soul. Would it be asking too much of you to point out what I could possibly gain by so clumsy a contrivance?"

Sainte-Aldegonde said, "To a blunt soldier, nothing. But shall I be honest with you?" And now Maurice was aware of that core of iron. There was a sense of danger in the air.

"Why not indeed?"

"I have heard of you as I said, Master Quain. I have been waiting for you to call on one pretext or another. The man who sent me the information I cannot name to you, but I am well aware of how you are up to the hilt in the conspiracies to free Mary of Scotland, and with the help of Parma and the Spanish, plan to place her on the throne of England."

"By God's wounds," Maurice said, "I think I will cast in my lot with the Scottish Queen and save myself the trouble of refuting the charges of my enemies. It takes time I cannot spare from my business."

"It would seem a little strange," Sainte-Aldegonde admitted, "for one in your commercial position to risk everything on such a gamble. But I have known men do it." His eyes scraped over Maurice trying to penetrate the mask of his face. "I would do it myself if I

113

were convinced of the rightness of the lady's cause. I am not convinced of course. The victory of Mary Stuart with the aid of Spanish arms would be the deathblow to all I have worked for my whole life—which is reason enough to keep you in irons until our victory is assured."

"Reason enough for a hothead, yes. Not for a diplomat and leader like you when half your hopes of success are founded on good relations with Elizabeth Tudor. I cannot see you imprisoning her financial agent. If I felt any hostility to you, I would urge you to make so gross an error."

Sainte-Aldegonde said, "How can I be sure whether you are raising this loan for Elizabeth or for Mary? My correspondent——"

"I am sure I can name your correspondent, my lord. Is it not Edward Blount? Or perhaps, not having complete confidence in you, he did not sign his name. He was always a fool and never more so than now. I have the Royal Seal of England. But that to my mind carries less weight than the unquestioned acceptance of my word among the traders at the Burse. A merchant's reputation, my lord, is no less dear to him than honor to a soldier. To be brief, I do not like the reflections cast on my integrity."

Sainte-Aldegonde pounced at that. "It was surmise. But do you deny you have sold supplies to our enemies?"

"Deny? I sell to any man who can pay me. I'm not a politician. I'm not a soldier. I was once, but I gave it up as a poor profession. I am merely, my lord, a merchant who takes sides in no controversy. It's a pity in this modern day common sense is a crime."

Sainte-Aldegonde said slowly, "I am inclined to believe you. I would respect you more if I did not."

"Your respect," Maurice rejoined coldly, "I will gladly forgo for the hire of a ship for Her Majesty's service."

Sainte-Aldegonde, irritated by Maurice's words, hesitated. "I must see this Royal Seal, Master Quain. If I am satisfied, your secretary will be allowed to proceed to England. But we will beg you to remain in Antwerp until our representative, whom we will send to London on the same ship, comes back with his report."

Maurice bowed sardonically, forbearing to point out that this had been his suggestion a quarter of an hour ago before a strain had been put on their relationship.

Maurice smothered a yawn, tossed papers onto the small table and drew over a candle. Under his fatigue was a restlessness that would not let him sleep. He felt dissatisfied with himself, with the slow progress of the royal loan. He glanced down the first sheet with the names of the wealthiest burghers of the city. Grotte, Van Artweldt, Strauss—he had seen them all except Strauss, who had refused even to meet him. Joseph Strauss. Maurice stiffened suddenly. The name had a familiar ring to it. Only it was not associated with Antwerp. He groped for that faint recollection. Some gossip, not savory.

The East—an official bribed, a murder, some great French company had fallen. Afterward Joseph Strauss had been an enormously wealthy man. The details escaped him annoyingly. The East—Persia? Turkey? He heard someone moving about in the next chamber and called out. Patrick opened the door between the two rooms, looked surprised at seeing Maurice there with a paper in his hands and alone. "You called, sir?"

"Yes. Where have you been?"

Patrick was wiping his hands on a towel. His face was damp and his brown hair was dripping. "I was down looking at the river. If we could sail on a night like tonight with a pilot who knows the water, I think we could get by the Spanish batteries."

"Good. What do you know of Joseph Strauss?"

"Strauss?" Patrick tossed the towel back into his room and came in, rolling down his sleeves. "That man we went to last week who would not even see you? Nothing at all, sir, except that the manners of his attendants were surly."

"Doesn't the name recall some old gossip, something about a French company in the East?"

Patrick shook his head. "I'm sorry. I've never heard the name before, Master Quain."

"See if Webster's around. He might know odd scraps of rumors."

Webster entered a few minutes later wearing a night-cap pulled down to his brows and an enormous blue dressing robe that would have looked large on a man twice his size. He rubbed his eyes to get the sleep out of them. "You wanted me, Master Quain?"

Maurice looked at him skeptically. "I do—if you've more of your wits about you than you seem to have. Do you remember this Joseph Strauss at whose home we were refused entrance? Do you know anything about him?"

Webster came wide-awake. "Strauss? I was wondering about him myself. There was a man, only his name wasn't Strauss. It was—wait—Josef Stryss. It's an old story. How did it go? I remember hearing it, oh, ten years ago, when a French company went bankrupt. The Le Roux Company. This Stryss, or Strauss if that's who he is, sold them out. He sent their chief factor in Constantinople into some Turkish trap—Stryss was one of the Le Roux agents in Turkey, you understand. Anyway, the factor was murdered, and Stryss and the Turkish officials divided the Le Roux money and he retired. He hasn't been heard of since though he has large holdings in France, I think. It might be the same man."

"How much do you surmise, how much can you prove, Master Webster?"

Webster said maliciously, "I know enough names and dates so that I could seem to have the truth."

"Provide me with them in the morning, and while you're in London with Patrick anything you can discover about this Strauss may help if you can get back to Antwerp. Holdings in France? I wonder——"

"A nice thought there," Webster said promptly, "if your meaning is that you could persuade this gentleman to advance a slight loan on them. French silver would go to Elizabeth Tudor to be used against France at the royal convenience. You could serve Her Majesty worse."

"I am raising money for Elizabeth Tudor. My service begins and ends with that task. What comes of it, good or ill, is no concern of mine."

Webster looked thoughtful. "Strauss. I don't know, Master Quain. You might do better to forget him. He's dangerous, as more than one man, including the whole Le Roux Company, can tell you."

"If the Queen grants a petition I have in mind, it will more than repay any slight trouble I may have."

Webster shrugged. "If you will then, I shall try to get information of Strauss, though it seems little sense to me to get a new employer and let someone cut his throat so soon."

Sainte-Aldegonde, standing at the northern angle of the city wall, looked down the Scheldt toward the sea. He said bitterly, "Well, Master Quain, you were right. The impossible has succeeded. The bridge has been rebuilt."

Maurice waved a deprecatory hand. "On the contrary it was your belief long before it was mine that the city could be encircled." To break the monotony of life in a besieged city, Maurice had accepted the Burgomaster's invitation to accompany him on his daily tour of the wall and outposts. Patrick and Webster had been gone well over two months. In that time the bridge had been completed, breached by fire ships and rebuilt. "A pity you could not have had a free hand in the defenses of Antwerp."

Sainte-Aldegonde looked fiercely at him. "A pity hardly states the case." He brought his hand down hard on the parapet, not noticing the way the stones cut the flesh. "Antwerp! Antwerp!"

The early spring wind roared across the flat land, scooped up the tops of the waves on the Scheldt, flinging the water against the stone walls rising from the river. Maurice wiped the spray from his face with the cuff of his gauntlet as he gazed critically at Parma's bridge. The piles with their huge timbers fortified by blockhouses reached out into the water from either bank until they were about four hundred yards apart. Barges over sixty feet long, anchored at bow and stern with cables and bound together with enormous chains,

117

bridged the center of the Scheldt. A timbered pathway was made across the parapets at the side for defense, and on each barge a heavy artillery was placed with thirty-two guns pointing up and the same number pointing down the river. It was a masterwork, Maurice thought. The burghers of Antwerp against the genius of Parma—but sometimes brilliance was not enough.

Sainte-Aldegonde said abruptly, "What do you think of it? Impregnable?"

"As a merchant I'd say yes, and that surrender now is the only sane plan, while the city still has its industries and the citizens aren't ravaged by the plague. As a man I'd say to wait and hope. Antwerp is well garrisoned and stocked, though you should have bought more shiploads of grain. As a soldier——" He stooped.

"Do not forget that Ghent, Dendermonde and Vilvorde surrendered, and Brussels has fallen. But as a soldier you say?"

"Fire ships again or open the sluices of the Kowenstyn dike."

Sainte-Aldegone nodded. "Our one hope now." He added puzzled, "If you had counseled only surrender——"

"Your suspicions of me would have been heightened?" Maurice sighed. "A pity common sense is so rare it is looked on as a trait of villainy." He gazed across the flat earth to the great Blauw-garen and the Kowenstyn dikes holding back the gray tossing sea that seemed to hunger for the land. A stretch of stormy water, and then England. And in England a dark-haired wench with a slim vibrant body, a gay and vivid face, provocative, and yet holding some remote passionless suspense behind the invitation in her dark eyes that was more challenging than an unmixed flame of desire.

Sainte-Aldegonde said abruptly, "I shall see Gianibelli again. He's the Italian, you know, who engineered the fire ships which destroyed the bridge." He stared a moment at Maurice.

Maurice's voice was sardonic. "When your plans are completed, my lord, remind me to send the details of your attack to the Prince of Parma that he may get his

118

defenses ready. As a spy no less than that could be expected of me."

The night of Gianibelli's fire ships to which Sainte-Aldegonde referred came before him. Eight fire ships, one every half hour, were to be sent and after them two explosive vessels to blow up the bridge. Once a breach was made, Justinus of Nassau could sail his Zeeland fleet up the Scheldt to prevent the rebuilding of the Spanish bridge. As the time dragged by, the name of the admiral in charge went among the watchers with oath or prayer, Jacob Jacobzoon. However it was said, with anger or pleading, it was not, Maurice noted, said with hope. Why he had been appointed to manage the affair, only the gods who drive men mad would ever know.

Suddenly a spark had been seen, and the first ship sailing down the river burst into flaming beauty. Then the whole fleet, instead of being in an orderly procession, was afire. Some of the vessels burned themselves out on the river. Others touching the bridge were leaped upon by the Spanish soldiers and the fires beaten out. The men on the parapets of the city walls waited, rigid in their tension.

The last two, Gianibelli's "hell ships," the *Hope* and the *Fortune*, had floated down, the creeping flame on their decks marking their progress in the river. One ran aground, its seven thousand pounds of gunpowder wasted. The spark went out. A groan went up.

The other ship had continued to the bridge. Hell indeed broke loose. Noise, noise carried to a degree that went beyond sound into evil action It roared over the crowd, seemed to smash bone and muscle into pulp, to tear the earth from under them. A glare lighted up the sky from horizon to horizon.

The river, sixty feet deep, was scooped out as with a giant ladle and swept over dikes and meadows. An empty house outside the citadel trembled and crashed. Chain shot, iron hooks, paving stones, plowshares, mutilated bodies and torn limbs filled the air. How much was seen, how much the distorted imagination conjured, none could know. A flying missile struck one of

119

the men near Maurice. There was a shuddering, long-drawn scream hardly heard in the horror about them. A chip of stone grazed Maurice across the cheek.

As the roar receded like the tide going out, one and then another had lurched to his feet to watch for the rocket Admiral Jacobzoon was to send up when a gap was made in the bridge. No signal had lighted the air as the watchers waited in an intolerable suspense, and the Zeeland vessels below sailed back and forth ready to dash for the opening and sail through to Antwerp.

Not until three days later was it learned that Jacobzoon had run off without waiting for the report. The boatman he'd sent down rowed about, afraid to go too close, and returned with the word the fire ship had failed. By the time it was discovered that the bridge had been torn apart, Parma, working night and day, had repaired it and mounted more guns. The citizens of Antwerp drew their belts a notch tighter and cursed their leaders.

Sainte-Aldegonde had not taken his eyes from Maurice. "There may be more truth in your words than an honest man would like."

Maurice turned his head to look at Baron de Sainte-Aldegonde. For a moment he groped back past the memory of the night of the attack to their talk about the next offensive move and his acid comment on his sending the Patroit's plans to the Prince of Parma. He lifted his brows inquiringly.

"Because if you are not one of Parma's agents, how does it happen two of your men returned this morning through the Spanish lines?"

"Patrick and Webster? Impossible! I have not seen them."

"The younger one is in the guardroom at the moment."

"By the innocence of Christ, what will you think of next! By what right do you lay a hand on an employee of mine?"

"One moment, Master Quain. Your secretary is not under arrest but speaking with the captains on the disposition of the Spanish troops. He's below here." They

120

went down from the parapet to the ground floor of the gatehouse where a small group of Dutch officers were gathered.

Patrick was giving them little news they had not learned themselves these hard months of the siege. Old Count Mansfeld, through whose lines he had come, held Stabroek for the Spanish. Colonel Capizucca, the brilliant Italian officer, was on his left flank. Parma was extending his lines toward Beveren.

Sainte-Aldegonde and his captains exchanged glances. "A final and desperate measure: the sluices of the Kowenstyn dike must be opened."

"De dijk, ja, kapitein!" No more was said. The garrison on the three-mile dike must be held somehow while a breach was made so that the sea could inundate the land and give the Zeeland vessels a waterway to the city.

One officer shot a look at Maurice. "How does *de heer* happen to be in on a military discussion?"

Maurice said, "So long as you hold a man of mine, I feel obliged to have you suffer my presence. Besides, you can hardly call it a strictly military matter when your decision affects every person in Antwerp, and every citizen in Antwerp will no doubt have a word to say to it himself."

Sainte-Aldegonde raised his old hands, dropped them hopelessly. "There's the fault of our whole defense: as many decisions as there are souls. That is why we go hungry now—because half the citizens would not let the Blauw-garen dike be opened. No, they had oxen grazing in the meadows. Where are their oxen now? In Spanish bellies. But this time, my friends, a military matter will be decided by military men. The people of Antwerp elected me their Burgomaster, though I would not have taken the office if William of Orange had not begged me to accept it. Now with their wills or not, I shall serve them as I see fit. There is but one way out for them and for us, and it is a desperate chance."

Patrick said, "Whatever you do, my lord, you must count me one of your men."

"Fijn, mijnheer! We need every soldier. You shall be among the first with me in the attack."

An officer sitting at Maurice's right turned to look at him. "You, Master Quain, say nothing. Yet I'll wager you can handle a weapon as well as the next man."

Every eye was on the big man, erect, hard and flexible as steel.

Maurice shrugged. "My only ability is that I can stop a musket shot as well as the next one. So if it does not displease you over-much, or even if it does, I think that while you are fighting for your dike, I shall be safely ensconced behind the walls of Antwerp." He rose to his feet, an ironical enjoyment on his face at the fury in the officer's eyes. "Your servant, gentlemen!"

As they went out, Maurice said, "I expected your return to be somewhat earlier."

"I did myself, Master Quain, but there was a delay hiring a ship across the Channel—we got passage in Sluys—and then there was a stormy fortnight, if you recall, when it was impossible to leave port. In London Sir Francis didn't want to give us permission to return, and his reluctance was more than matched on this side of the water by Count Mansfeld's objections to allowing us through the Spanish lines into Antwerp. As soon as we saw Parma, however, there was no more trouble. In fact, now I think of it, I'm rather surprised we're here at all. But you have not asked about the silver. It is safely in the Tower of London and the Queen is grateful."

"I was sure you would not have so easy a bearing if anything had gone wrong, nor would you have come back breathing heroic fire to fight against the enemies of Antwerp."

Patrick shrugged. "I'm an Englishman, and the Dutch Patriots are fighting our battles on their soil." He added abruptly, "Doesn't that mean anything to you?"

"I can't say it does, Patrick! Did Webster find out anything more about Strauss?"

"Yes, sir! He must be at the inn by now and can tell you."

122

Joseph Strauss lived in a high narrow house. Its upper stories jutted across the street, and its small windows, frowned down on passers-by. The heavy door was opened, after a clanking of chains, the scraping back of a bolt. Following the porter, Maurice and Webster went down a long dark corridor past two men who looked more like soldiers than servitors, and up curving steps to a small room furnished only with benches, and with but one window high in the wall and barred. The door was closed on them.

Webster did not like this. Every minute dragged leadenly past. There was something unearthly about this place, as palpable as the clammy feel of fog. He shot a glance at Maurice. That man wasn't human! He'd look imperturbable in hell. Webster finally got up, moved about the room. His footfall was light, restless. As the minutes wore it made Maurice think of the tread of a caged animal.

Antwerp. If it were not a weakness, he would wish he had never come here. Maurice could feel some dim parallel to his spirit in the spirit of the city. The concern of the merchants over commerce, the butchers over their oxen, while catastrophe in the person of Parma drew nearer and nearer; the reluctance to take the offensive as a defense, the incompetence and cowardice and fate that fought against the fire ships—he had a premonition that if Antwerp should go out to fight she would never win, would lose always, as he had lost. Fighting she would not win, and if she did not fight, the devil or Parma or Blount would still be successful. Antwerp was doomed as someday——

He glanced up at his companion. "Strauss is discourteous. There must be someone in the corridor, Master Webster. Would you ask how long we're expected to wait?"

Webster jumped at the sound of Maurice's cold voice in the silence. "Yes, sir! If I don't get a knife in me, I'll be back before you can say a prayer." He opened the door.

The servingman who had brought them up was outside and instantly blocked the way with a surly growl.

Maurice spoke with chill displeasure. "Be good

123

enough, sirrah, to tell Master Strauss that if his time is not valuable, mine is. I will see him at once or tomorrow he will have to come to me. You may add that this reception does not please us."

He glanced at Webster as the door closed. "This play acting of theirs is ridiculous, but it has the advantage of proving Strauss has something on his mind and lives in fear of being discovered. I think he's the man we're looking for."

He had hardly finished speaking when the door was opened again. The servingman said, "This way, *mijnheer.*" He waved Webster back. "Not you. He'll have but one person with him at a time."

Joseph Strauss leaned over his desk to peer at Maurice out of red-rimmed nearsighted eyes. Almost as tall as Maurice, he was thin to emaciation, and his black velvet robe with its wide sleeves gave the impression of being hung on a skeleton whenever he moved. "Quain?" His voice was high and asthmatic. "You're from England? What do you want?"

The room was large and luxurious in the light that cut between the drawn draperies at the long narrow window. The dimness gave it the impression of being moistly dark, like a place dug out underground. Maurice without waiting to be bidden sat down in a big chair piled with Turkish cushions. "As I believe you understood from my message last week, Master Strauss, I am in Antwerp to raise a loan for the Queen of England. A large share has been met, but I still have need of seventeen thousand pounds. I thought you might wish to lend Her Majesty that amount at twelve percent interest."

Strauss's laughter cackled out, and to Maurice's ear it had a note of relief. "Is that all? Well, sir, you had my answer. I am not interested." He picked up a silver bell. "I'll have my attendant show you to the door. *Goeden dag!*"

Maurice did not move. "Perhaps we should discuss the matter——"

"No!" Strauss started to ring the bell.

"Master Stryss."

124

The bell clanged to the carpeted floor. Across the table a pair of old, fear-ridden eyes looked at Maurice. "What do you want of me?"

Maurice said, "I have stated my terms."

"I can't meet them. You know I can't meet them. Twelve percent!"

Maurice said thoughtfully, "You cannot? Come now, Master—do you prefer to be called Strauss? I've lost half a morning here already. It's possible the delay was unavoidable. Whatever the reason, let us at least conclude our business now without further waste. On August 16, 1574, a German in the employ of a French company spoke with a eunuch in the Seraglio in Constantinople. On August 17 all the Le Roux possessions in Turkey were seized, the factor and his assistant murdered. The next spring a wealthy merchant by the name of Stryss took up residence in Hamburg. Later there was talk. He appeared in other cities, but there was still gossip. Finally a merchant named Joseph Strauss settled in Antwerp, six, seven years ago. He felt quite secure, justifiably so. There had been no gossip at all about him recently."

Strauss stretched forward across the desk like something reptilian, inhuman, out of the darkness of the earth. Maurice thought in self-contempt he had more fancies today than a woman, but he watched with hawk's eyes. Strauss said, "You would drive a man too far. You are in my hands. What makes you think that I'll not value my good name and seventeen thousand pounds more than your life?"

Maurice looked at him with scorn. "Do you think Elizabeth Tudor's financial agent could disappear and no questions asked? Nor could you save yourself by leaving Antwerp. A besieged city is not easy to get out of."

Strauss extended a bony hand, changing his tactics abruptly. "You make a great to-do, *mijnheer,* about how much harm a lying rumor will do me. Do you think I hand over seventeen thousand pounds to any man who has the effrontery to throw some old fable in my teeth? You insult your intelligence as well as mine."

125

Maurice said, "Let me correct two false impressions. First, I am not asking you to give but to lend the silver to the royal House of Tudor. And secondly, I wouldn't trouble to spread a rumor, true or untrue. I would merely send your name and residence to some of the survivors of the Le Roux family in Paris. You would not believe how long a memory for wrongs, fancied or real, some men have. I think that after that the best your seventeen thousand pounds could do for you would be to provide a most handsome funeral."

Strauss huddled back in his chair shaking so the velvet robe fluttered over his bony frame as though it moved of itself. "You're a devil out of hell. May the curse of God follow you back! May your friends desert you in your need and your loved ones betray you!" He spoke in an odd whispering voice.

Maurice smiled bleakly. "You are a few years late with your good wishes, Master Strauss. Now this loan—will it be in silver, gold, or a bill of exchange?"

"A bill of exchange on a Parisian house." The air crackled with words not spoken.

Maurice stood up. "Thank you, Master Strauss. You can send the letter to my lodgings at the Dolphin when it is drawn up. The interest will not be deducted now. It will be repaid with the loan."

The old man bent down to pick up his bell which had fallen to the floor earlier, rang for an attendant. "Show *Mijnheer* Quain out." He looked ten years older than when Maurice had entered. He did not glance at his visitor as Maurice bowed, but only stared in front of him as though he saw in the air shapes that others could not see.

In the corridor below Webster was waiting. He drew a long breath as they went out into the cobbled street. "There were moments, Master Quain, when I did not think we would see the outside of that house again."

Maurice said absently, "Why not? A dog too old to bite will often growl the loudest."

Paris . . . he sensed danger there. The person who handled that bill of exchange would be noticed. He shrugged. He had long ago gone past fear for his body. Perhaps that was why he had killed some part of a

126

man today. As he had made Strauss afraid of death and terrified of life, he knew he had done him a mortal hurt.

The drums rolled, were silent, rolled again. The darkening city throbbed to the rhythmic beating. The air was alive and tense as Patrick went through the streets. His booted feet rang loud on the cobblestones. His half-armor gleamed in the twilight. Small companies of soldiers and bands of armed citizens were drawing in like the spokes of a wheel toward the ships warped against the banks of the river. Patrick, swept into the crowd, began to feel out of place in the confusion. He shouldered his way toward a group of officers about Sainte-Aldegonde who was watching the embarking of the militia. The Burgomaster's eyes were keen under his bushy brows; a flame of excitement seemed to lick up his face, giving it a mottled color.

Sainte-Aldegonde called Patrick to join them. *"Een Engelschman, kapitein,* who can report to Queen Elizabeth how we defend our homes in the Provinces. Stay with us, Master North."

Below them the waters spread out from the river across the flat land on the right bank of the Scheldt so that boats could be sailed from the city directly to the Kowenstyn dike near the mouth of the river. Sail followed sail across the inundated land, some down the river toward the bridge to divert the troops there, a larger number to the dike to the right and beyond the bridge.

To see the ships taking the wind and cutting through the water where meadow should be gave Patrick a feeling of fantastic unreality, like Noah with many arks watching the waters rising over the earth. Patrick laughed. An older officer glanced at him inquiringly, blue eyes round in a fair round face. Patrick started to explain, hesitated at the inability to convey his impression, and remarked instead, "It's just funny."

The other, only half understanding the words, frowned at him. The eternal struggle between sea and land funny? He shrugged and turned back to watch the loading of the last ships. The officers went down to the

127

pier. It was completely dark now, and Patrick had to feel his way into the boat, grope to an empty place near the bulwarks. The creak of rigging, the slapping of the sail sounded loud in the darkness. Overhead the stars were diamond-sharp against the blue-black sky and far away, farther than God.

Someone whispered, "Another hour and the fire ships from Lillo will be sent out."

An hour. It seemed too long, and then too short a time. He had a momentary nausea. Fear and excitement and a heady sense of danger blended and fought and blended again within him. The lapping of the water against the sides of the slow-moving boat, the blackness so deep that his companions were a blur of hands and faces in the night, the faint fresh wind stirring his hair made him feel time had stopped.

There was an indrawing of breath as a glare lighted the western sky. It threw into relief the Kowenstyn dike below them. The five forts built on the palisaded earthworks looked like the stubby fingers of a hand pointing upward. Three more flaming ships came quickly after the first. The drums of the Spaniards beat insistently, clamorously, filling the night.

Behind the fire ships came the Zeeland war vessels. The masts above the dike were just visible to the soldiers in the ships coming down from Antwerp. Figures, black against the glare, could be seen scrambling up the barricade between Fort St. George and the Fort of the Palisades. The Spanish streamed out from the forts. The light glinted on their armor. The beating of the drums never stopped. A trumpet sounded above the shouting, the screams of wounded men. The Zeelanders began to give back.

The first boats from Antwerp touched the dike. Patrick groped his way out of the vessel after the others. The Spanish in the flush of victory turned to find the Patriots at their rear as well as before them. Patrick, in a dense mass of humanity, was pushed from behind up the slippery sides of the dike. The piles of planking Parma had used for fortification made a slimy handhold. He reached the top, sword in hand. He felt his blade ringing against steel. He cut and stabbed. There

128

was a choked cry. The light from the burning ships cast a reddish glow on dark faces and bright metal. The Spaniards drew back foot by foot to the forts.

Instantly spades and picks were out. Half the Patroits began to dig with a grim fury. The rest fortified themselves with sacks of sand and lengths of timber they had brought on the boats. Patrick stood at the edge in the line handing up the materials for breastworks.

A warning shout rang out, then a clash of steel. From Fort St. George poured a detachment of Spanish soldiers, veterans moving forward in an easy formation. They spilled over the Patriots with a ruthless impersonality. The shock of impact rocked back the men on the dike. They dropped picks and shovels and caught up their weapons. The musketeers fired into the Spanish ranks. A man fell here and there, but the wave rolled on and over.

Patrick dropped the bag of sand he'd been handing up. His sword scraped out of its scabbard. He was on guard without time for other thought than that he must not be driven too far to left or right into the waves beating at either side of this narrow slippery path. The blow of a sword jarred his arm to the shoulder. He struck and parried, moved a half foot forward against a huge berded man, was stopped, thrust relentlessly back while blade hammered on blade. The Spaniard lifted his sword, made a swift disengage to Patrick's throat. As Patrick felt the nick of the point, a musket ball struck the Spaniard and tore away half his head.

Now the Patriots were pushing back the wave, step by step. The ring of steel, the shattering explosion of the musket fire, the shouting of the soldiers, the shrill scream of the wounded crashed about them in a mad confusion of noise and movement. The Patriots again held the mile of dike between the two forts. Spades were caught up by eager hands. The breach in the dike widened. For three hours even the guns from St. George were silent. Spadeful after spadeful of earth was flung aside while carpenters cut at the timbers Parma had used to strengthen the barricade.

The dawn had come unnoticed, a faint lightening in

the eastern sky, then a rosy glow. The sea licked at the earthworks. As one man tired, another sprang to take his place. Incredibly the breach was completed. With a roar the sea leaped across the stretch of mud and crumbled it. A shout of triumph echoed across land and sea. One of the Zeeland barges maneuvered clumsily about in the small space among the hundred and sixty vessels that were being held off from the dike. It shot for the breach. Count Hohenlo stood on the deck, helmet raised high in a gesture of victory. Sainte-Aldegonde shouted from the dike above. The barge swung about. He leaped aboard it. He would be the first into Antwerp with the word to light bonfires and ring the bells.

Lightheartedly the Patriots cheered the two leaders on, turned to strike against the Fort of the Palisades which was held by so few Spanish soldiers that not even a sortie had been made. The advancing Dutch swarmed up to the entrance, battering rams in their arms. From somewhere came a warning cry. The huge iron-sheathed doors of the fort were thrown wide from inside. Spanish defenders poured out led by the Italian legion of Camilla Capizucca. The Patriots fell back, re-formed and held their position while the guns in the Zeeland vessels were trained on the new enemy forces. Shot after shot rounded high above the struggling lines to bury itself in the water beyond. One cannon ball ripped its way across the dike killing Dutch and Spanish.

The Patriots inched back to the half-completed breastworks they had erected earlier. "Save Antwerp or die!" The cry went from mouth to mouth. "Antwerp!" ... "Sainte-Aldegonde!"

The Italians made a brilliant thrust forward, but the sheer weight of Patriot numbers holding the breach in the dike rolled them back. The lines swayed back and forth. A hasty step, and a man was over the side, slithering down the steep bank, the weight of his armor dragging him under the water. "Antwerp or die!" Spanish and Italians were pushed back toward the fort. The Dutch guns spattered the length of the dike.

A cry sounded from the rear, was echoed by the Italians in front. "Parma!"

Parma had been at Beveren when the attack was launched. Impossible for him to get down from Beveren, across the bridge under fire from the Antwerp boats, across the dike being shattered under shot from the Zeeland ships. Impossible! The word echoed sickeningly through the Spanish madness. Impossible? Nothing was impossible to Parma.

Patrick felt a stinging along his left shoulder. His clothes were wet inside from blood or sweat, he did not know which, nor care at the moment. He stumbled over the bodies of dead men as the Patriots surged against the Italians. His sword swung like a scythe, echoing some crazy rhythm in his brain that broke and began again jaggedly as the blade struck armor or stabbed into flesh. His foot slipped. He caught himself, his hand against the open mouth of a writhing soldier. He retched.

They had almost reached the Fort of the Palisades. The tide began to turn against them as the Spanish and Italians held them there, started to push back. "Parma! Parma! Parma!"

"Sainte-Aldegonde!" But Sainte-Aldegonde was not here. He was celebrating their victory in Antwerp. Patrick had an insane desire to laugh. A big Spaniard in steel and leather leaped toward him. Patrick's sword ripped him cross the stomach. The man staggered, fell sideways, was kicked out of the way by a heavy foot and slid gently over the side of the dike.

Hemmed in by the Patriots, Patrick had a moment to catch his breath. A black mass of figures in the mile of dike fought for this narrow strip of land. An opening appeared before him. He lunged. A shot from St. George arched over the heads of the combatants, struck a Patriot ship. Torn planking rose into the air and fell among the soldiers. The tide was going out. One by one the Dutch vessels maneuvered away from the dike so as not to be stranded on the sands.

Someone shouted, "Retreat! The ships are retreating!" No rally cry of command answered the alarm. In twos and threes and then in tens, the Patriots

131

threw aside their weapons, jumped into the sea and swam for the boats. Spanish veterans, swords in their teeth, swam after them to massacre their victims in the water, while others turned to close the breach in the dike.

Panic ran like a live thing from man to man. A few Patriots with despairing courage fought on until the rush of Spaniards made their stand impossible and they followed the retreating army. Patrick, among the last, tossed sword and helmet aside and dived into the water. The crews of the ships threw out lines to help their comrades in, then jumped to the oars, the head wind making the sail useless.

Patrick sank to the deck. The cold gale bit into him through his wet clothes. He was not aware of it, nor of the throb of the wounds in shoulder and thigh. A numbness seemed to settle on both soldiers and seamen. As they went toward the city, the bells which had been pealing out suddenly clanged in discord. The ships landed at the pier. Without words the soldiers who could walk disembarked. Citizens who had streamed from the town lifted out the wounded and dying.

In the streets gay with streamers and bright hangings there was silence. A silence cleft by an angry voice that was taken up by others, a scream of rage against the leaders feasting even now at the Town Hall.

A woman shrieked as a man and boy picked up the dead body of a soldier. "To the Town Hall! Let Sainte-Aldegonde see his victory!" A roar of fury went up from all the streets as the citizens started to walk, broke into a run to converge on the hall. Some caught up stones to hurl through the windows.

Patrick went slowly toward the Dolphin. His feet seemed heavy, as though they belonged to someone else. Maurice turned from the window as Patrick entered. The dying clangor of the bells echoes through the room. Patrick leaned a shoulder against the jamb of the doorway, pushed his wet hair out of his eyes as though even that were an effort. His clothes were plastered to his body, and under his leather jacket his shirt was sticky with blood. He moved over to sit down

132

quickly as his legs were oddly shaky. He looked across at Maurice." Parma recaptured the dike."

"So I gathered. Are you hurt?"

"No!" Maurice's chill voice implied that Patrick had been out on some escapade—Patrick who could still feel the slime underfoot, hear the scream of wounded men.

Maurice said, "Antwerp will surrender now—on Spanish terms."

"But the city can still hold out! The defenses have not been breached!"

"The citizens lost heart after the fiasco of the fire ships. Will their failure last night stiffen their resistance?" Maurice looked down, adjusting the ruff at his wrist. That faint parallel occured to him. Antwerp! Antwerp! What is there in your fight against forces too strong for you that is like my struggle? Hold out longer? Yes. While men and women are slain and commerce is ruined. What would you win but the right to die in the faith that pleases you? Suicidal.

But he knew Antwerp's fate would lie forever cold on his heart. He shrugged. "What does it matter?" he said to Patrick. "Do we not have what we came to the Provinces for?"

8

Paris in the summer felt gay, lighthearted, lightheaded after the gloom of Antwerp. The pile of stone buildings from the Sainte-Chapelle to the Cathedral de Notre Dame cast a shadow across the bluish-green waters of the Seine, but the sunlight danced along the dark twisting streets, warming the gray stone, lighting the face of an old, old man dozing in a doorway, making pure gold of the curls of a baby who splashed happily in a shallow puddle formed between broken street stones.

Voices high and light rose and clashed, outcrying one another. They had an intensity in them as though all life were poured into selling this silver knife, that leg of pork. The odors of the street made the senses

133

reel until custom dulled them. Even under siege, Maurice remembered, Antwerp made war on dirt.

Odd how each country, like each person, had one attribute that stood out and was instantly capped by a less lovely trait—the Dutch with their cleanliness and grim stand for freedom made less attractive by their stolid lack of humor; the vital force of the Frenchman's passionate embrace of every aspect of life thinned by his grasp at first one emotion and then another, making a dizzying pattern to the eye and leaving a quicksand underfoot when you dealt with these people.

The bells of Notre Dame pealed out across the city, echoed by the bells of the smaller churches. The golden clangor filled the narrow streets. Maurice crossed the Street of the Three Angels to a tall building wedged between two smaller ones. A prentice standing outside almost fell over him in his eagerness to open the iron-studded door. The room within had a faintly greenish light from the thick panes of glass in the wide windows across the front of the shop.

A clerk came forward, a sallow young man with a toothy smile. On the shelves behind the wide counter, bales of velvet and serge, satins and silks, lengths of exquisite lace, linen, fine cambric and delicate batiste were like colored flames of green, brown, scarlet, white and gold. Maurice said, "I would like to speak with Monsieur Chapé."

Two other clerks were waiting on a gentleman and the young woman with him. Bale after bale was laid before her. Her selections were gaudy but had a certain flamboyant taste, Maurice noted idly.

"Monsieur Chapé? He is with an important customer, a very important customer. Perhaps I can help you?" The clerk's teeth gleamed under his small black mustache as he mentally added up the cost of Maurice's doublet and hose, the gold gorget at his neck, the velvet gloves with a pearl crest on each cuff.

Maurice shook his head while his eyes went over the merchandise thoughtfully. "I'll wait." He pushed back the damp hair from his forehead. It was too hot in the shop and no window was open to the summer breeze.

"Perhaps the assistant, Monsieur Florentin?"

"No." He said indolently, "You have rivals in the city, I hear, from the House of Gascony."

The clerk brushed off the mention of competitors with a flick of his long thin hand. "Rivals? That heathen house? Why, they're half infidels. One of the owners is from Turkey! M'sieu, you flatter them to say they rival us."

Behind the counter a door from an inner room opened. A short round Frenchman with a florid complexion came out. "You must see these samples, m'sieu! The finest lace, the most delicate. Félix!" Without looking up he called to the clerk who'd been speaking to Maurice. "The ruffs from Cambrai, the lace from Malines—quick!" He called back to the man in the room, "Fragile-looking as the web of a spider but strong as twined linen. Quick, Félix! He is ready to place an order of——"

The Frenchman glanced vaguely toward Maurice as Félix hurried to draw out the material demanded, looked again and went across the floor at a trot that had a ludicrous touch of dignity about it. "M'sieu! It can never be—Monsieur Quain! To have you standing out here waiting like the poorest customer. Why did you not tell us?" He almost felled his customers and the two clerks as he swung back the hinged plank that formed part of the counter to let Maurice through.

"I was waiting for you to be done with your customer, Monsieur Chapé."

Chapé waved both his hands eloquently. "You having to wait, it desolates me!" He jumped at a crash from the back of his shop. About Félix's feet swirled linen and lace. Chapé pulled his hair, named off the Sacred Heart, the Virgin and all the saints in Heaven in a shrill whisper as though he were praying violently. His voice broke. He wrung his hands.

Maurice stripped off his gloves as he waited. He had always found the Gallic temperament trying. From appearances a scene like this could go on all day. "Perhaps, Monsieur Chapé, your clerk will be good enough to repair the damage he has done, and your assistant

135

can show me to a room while you finish your business before your customer displays his better judgment by going elsewhere."

Chapé left off wringing his hands and said briskly, "M'sieu, it is done."

He came half an hour later into the room where Maurice was waiting. "Here are our accounts for the last three months, Monsieur Quain, for which we have not sent you a statement. Business is good . . . fair." He leafed through a pile of papers he had brought with him.

Maurice glanced down the list of figures. "These reports are reasonably satisfactory. But the profits are not keeping up with the expenses. Why?"

Chapé lifted his shoulders, rolled his eyes, turned out his hands, palms upward. "Times are bad, m'sieu. Terrible. All is desolation, ruin, Paris is a dead city. I could weep."

Maurice, wondering coldly if he would carry out his words, said shortly, "What do you know of the House of Gascony?"

Chapé looked hurt at Maurice's lack of interest in the economy of Paris. "The House of Gascony? Not much, m'sieu, and nothing to its credit. No one is quite sure who owns it. A Turk is rumored to control it— which goes to support the gossip that it's founded on the ruins of the Le Roux Company you may have heard about. They have a house in Constantinople, agents in London. Their profits seem high. They deal in goods smuggled in from the East and often undersell us. What we need, m'sieu, is a factor in Turkey for our exports and to send us silks, spices, drugs. Our trade with the Court would be doubled."

"You're right enough, but at the moment plans for the East can wait." Maurice paused, weighed Chapé a moment with his eyes. "I am interested in this House of Gascony. I have a bill of exchange on it—for seventeen thousand pounds."

"Seventeen thousand what? Pounds? M'sieu! It will ruin them if they pay it."

"I feel they will pay it. Perhaps you have a suggestion how we may move this money out of France?"

Chapé threw up his hands. "But it is impossible! Well—" he met Maurice's cold look—"I will think about it. There may be a way, perhaps shipping it down the Seine—— But seventeen thousand pounds! M'sieu, I would forget the matter. That is the way of wisdom. The House of Gascony won't honor the note, and if they do, they'll never let you out of the country with the silver."

"Well, if you cannot think, m'sieu, I want you to keep the money in your strong room until I find a way to move it out of Paris. Can you buy weapons or armor without question?"

Chapé said cautiously. "It would depend on their purpose, Monsieur Quain. Such purchases are eyed by the authorities."

"Be good enough to make inquiries, Monsieur Chapé. Good day!"

Maurice met Patrick and Webster outside the House of Gascony. He had gone alone to his own shop to attract the least possible notice to his comings and goings. He was indifferent, however, how much interested attention the House of Gascony did or did not receive.

Patrick said, "The master of the house is away, but his assistant is in the shop today. We told the clerk we'd return to place a large order—but we didn't say for what commodity."

The assistant, a middle-sized man with fierce mustachios, enormous feet and a limp handclasp, came forward at once to meet them as they entered. Maurice said abruptly, "I am Monsieur Quain. I have some business to transact. I had hoped to meet the owner of your house, but if you have full power to handle affairs in his absence, I can give you the details."

At the mention of his visitor's name, the assistant's face, which had been set in genial lines, tightened warily. "I will be glad to hear you on any subject, Monsieur Quain. But of course I cannot give you a final answer. My master must do that. Him," he added with whispered reverence, "no one sees. I will give him whatever information you wish. This way, m'sieu. Will your gentlemen come with you?"

Maurice waved to a form against the wall. "Wait here."

A minute later the Frenchman faced Maurice across a narrow counter in a room at the end of a long dark corridor. He watched Maurice warily, shrewdly, his hands clasped limply together. Maurice's mind cast about like quicksilver. Had he left any loophole, any unguarded joint in his armor? Somehow the shadowy figure of authority behind this man gave him an uneasy feeling. He considered, and rejected, refusing to do business with any but the owner. That would take time and mean possible defeat. He said smoothly, "I don't believe, m'sieu, I heard your name."

"They call me Monsieur Étienne." The mouth under the concealing hair smiled perfunctorily.

Maurice looked at him with open annoyance. "An odd house where the owner is invisible and the assistant has only a given name. However, that is neither here nor there. I met a mutual friend—or shall I say acquaintance?—in Antwerp. He gave me a bill of exchange on your house." Étienne's eyes flickered with interest but he said nothing. "His name at the moment—he's had several—is Joseph Strauss."

Étienne's mustachios seemed to quiver. He moved his limp hands about half an inch from their former position, then was as rigid as ever.

"A note for seventeen thousand pounds in gold or silver." Maurice said coldly and had a certain satisfaction in Étienne's quickly strangled exclamation.

Étienne swallowed at once. "May I see it, m'sieu?"

"Why not?" Maurice drew out a rolled paper from his doublet and tossed it across the desk.

Étienne's eyes went over it once and again. He looked up. "That is not Joseph Strauss's signature." He moved back in his chair, shaking his head rebukingly at his visitor's simplicity.

Maurice smiled. "I am pleased to observe you are so familiar with his writing, Monsieur Étienne, that you can tell instantly the genuine from a very good copy.

You will see the original note when the seventeen thousand pounds are in my hands."

Étienne leaned forward quick as a cat. "How can we be sure of that?" It was half a snarl. He bit his lips at the words, recovering himself slowly from Maurice's telling thrust.

"Because my word is good anywhere in Europe, which is more than can be said of the nameless men running a house of questionable foundation." The slow color crept up Étienne's face. "When may I expect payment, m'sieu?"

Étienne's flabby hands were clenched into fists. His whole body had the tenseness of controlled anger. Maurice could read in his face the desire to throw "Never!" in his teeth. "As I said, Monsieur Quain, I can but pass on your request to my master. Whether he will honor this note, or when, must be decided by him in his own time." His big feet moved back and forth on the planked floor.

Maurice rose. "Twenty-four hours is as long as I can give him for an answer, m'sieu, and forty-eight for the money to be in my hands." He started to reach for the paper he had tossed on the counter.

Étienne had his hand on it first. His thick jointless-seeming fingers looked like limpets clinging to the wood. "May I keep this, m'sieu?"

"Certainly! I can have a dozen copies as good as that made for me in an hour. Give my respects to your master."

Étienne did not stand up as Maurice moved away, but stared unbelievingly at the paper in his hands, started to reach for the bell when Maurice was at the door.

Maurice turned. "As you no doubt realize, you can dispatch a messenger to my shop in the Street of the Three Angels. To save you trouble of sending a man to follow me, I am staying at Auberge Perrichon."

Auberge Perrichon was a small inn that looked self-respecting and at the same time had an air of daring like a middle-aged matron who would coquette upon occasion. Vincent tried unsuccessfully to suppress a yawn as the three men entered the apartment on the top floor. The yawn changed to an exclamation of dismay at Maurice's first words.

"I want you to take one of the servingmen, Vincent—Joseph will do—and ride to Le Grand Andely where the *Falcon* is awaiting us."

Vincent said, "Andely? I'm . . . I'm a very poor rider, Master Quain."

"If practice will improve your ability, you'll be a better horseman before you're much older." Maurice went over to the table, drew out a map. "Here's a sketch of northern France. There will be a coach leaving Paris within the next three days. At these post stops—" he pointed to two circled in red on the map—"I want a change of horses ready day and night. Whatever is asked, pay half without haggling. Tell the innkeeper he'll have the other half when the horses are actually used. Wait for me aboard the *Falcon*. I want you to ride at once."

Vincent said, "Yes, sir!" and went out, not briskly, to call Joseph.

Webster said, "If I were Scottish and had the second sight, Master Quain, I'd say I foresee you are walking—no—leaping into trouble. Strauss and the House of Gascony. Being an unimaginative Englishman, I would look for a way to avoid the difficulty. Now in Turkey—but there a bride to an official would do anything but move the Seraglio."

"What the devil," asked Patrick, "is the Seraglio?"

"The Sultan's palace above the Golden Horn."

"That sounds like a song."

Webster said dreamily, "It is a song—the marble and ivory, the spires, the gold and mosaic, the gardens and courts and fountains, the beautiful veiled women. Of course no one but the Sultan ever enters the harem," he added practically. "It is death to look at his slaves. But one can always dream, and there are the Greek women. The slender minarets of Constantinople—but how can the drab Western world ever realize the exotic beauty of the East?"

Maurice said, "I have heard that the pariah dogs of

140

Constantinople make the streets almost unlivable to the foreigner."

"Your memories of Constantinople depend, Master Quain, on whether you look up or down."

Maurice lifted his brows in faint amusement. "We'll never get there, or anywhere else, unless first we move this silver out of France." He contemplated the furniture in the crowded room as though he might find an answer in the overdecorated chairs, the huge bed with its woolen curtains, dyed scarlet once, now showing faded streaks where the light struck through the casement window.

"Master Webster, find where we can exchange the full amount of the silver for jewels, or gold if that is not possible, and where it can be done quickly. Seventeen thousand pounds' worth of jewels will be easy to transport. The silver is too heavy. Patrick, I want you to check Chapé's figures and see that his inquiries for arms are answered and an order placed for several suits of armor—whatever you can get, swords and so on, none of it good. Today is Tuesday. I would like to leave Paris Thrusday night, at the latest Friday. One matter more, Master Webster: Hire a boat and a sturdy crew of at least four men."

Webster's face screwed up in thought. "That sounds as though you intend to smuggle the money down the Seine. Unless you know the right boatman to go to, anyone familiar with the city can easily follow a stranger's tracks."

Maurice looked at him coldly. "I think if you'll just carry out your instructions, I'll be more than satisfied with your services."

Jacques entered as the others left. Maurice barely controlled a start at the sound of a footstep and turned swiftly. He eyes his valet with annoyance. This affair was making him nervy. He wished he had seen the owner of the House of Gascony. "Yes?"

"I was just bringing your hot water, monsoor—Master Quain."

"What's the matter? Have you changed your nationality again?"

Jacques looked offended. "Those ridiculous oafs say

I have not the accent, Master Quain. And after seeing them, mon Doo—I mean, by God—I'm glad I'm not French! You can call me James until we're back in England."

"It's hardly worth my trouble to remember. We're leaving Paris soon."

"It won't be an hour too quick for me, Master Quain. I——"

Maurice paid no attention. He might facilitate the transport of the loan if he asked help of the English ambassador. But to see him would take time, and, if the ambassador were in a delicate position because Elizabeth Tudor was encouraging the Huguenot faction, it was not certain he could do much. No government in Europe liked to see silver going out of the country, even so wealthy a nation as France. Maurice decided he would take his own chances. If the reward were his, the gamble also was his.

Maurice opened his eyes slowly the next morning, stretched lazily and yawned losing in the naturalness of his movement the dark vagaries that had disturbed his sleep. The door opened and closed again. Maurice waited, expecting the rattle of a jug being placed on the stand, the metallic clank of the bronze basin. There was only silence. That was odd. Now if the loan should be paid today——

There was a soft footstep near him. He reached up, pulled the bedcord to open the curtains. His eyes widened and then narrowed. He half sat up, leaning on one elbow. A big man stood there, a Turk, softly fat under loose Eastern robes. Under his turban he had a round face, dark and oily, thick lips. He gave the *témena*, the Turkish salutation, the right hand nearly touching the ground, then his knee, heart, mouth and forehead. As he bowed, Maurice could see behind him a thin man, a servant probably, who repeated his master's silent greeting like an automation.

Maurice neither moved nor spoke. The Turk's face creased into a smile. What had seemed passively sinister looked now actively evil. "I am Ali Bey," he said in careful English, "of the House of Gascony. You are Effendi Quain?"

142

Maurice bowed slightly, reached for the crimson velvet robe at the foot of the bed and stood up. His eyes seemed to take on a deeper blue. He moved a chair out from the wall, swung it about so that his visitor would be facing the light, and sat down, his own back to the window. Where were his attendants? In particular, where was Jacques?"

"I have been informed—" Ali Bey spoke in a soft voice startling in so large a man—"that you honored our humble shop with your presence yesterday." He held back his immaculate robes so that they would not be soiled by a touch of this infidel Englishman.

"I was at the House of Gascony, sir."

"You have a letter of credit for seventeen thousand pounds?" Ali Bey smiled again.

"A letter of credit payable on demand, yes. The money can be sent to my shop in the Street of Three Angels any time today. Or if immediate payment would inconvenience you, tomorrow."

"Inconvenience? I smile at the thought, effendi. I but hesitate over one or two small matters. While I admire you most sincerely, we must first protect our clients. A false note was given to the man you spoke to yesterday. Admittedly false, yes. But you can understand I must see the original before I can go further into this. I know you are above petty dealings. But you are a merchant. You understand one cannot be too certain in such matters. Then say you convince me of the genuineness of the letter—I am assured you will so convince me—have you thought of the difficulties of moving so large a shipment of money across a war-torn country? It is a difficulty."

"Well?"

"I would suggest a simple solution. You give me Strauss's letter. I will in exchange give you a bill of exchange on a business house in London."

"What assurance have I it will pay the note?" As he spoke Maurice stood up to cross to the table, took the sheet of parchment lying carelessly on the top, and brought it to the Turk.

"When I name the house, effendi, your doubts will be settled." Ali Bey looked at the document, handed it

143

back unwillingly. "That is Strauss's signature. I was sure it would be."

"What assurance have I——" Maurice did not change his tone—"that I will reach London to claim the money?"

Ali Bey's eyes almost disappeared as he laughed silently. "You will have your jest, effendi. Then we can consider the matter closed? I will have my letter made out within the hour."

Maurice shook his head. "Thank you, sir, but no."

Ali Bey leaned his monstrously fat body forward. "Why, Effendi Quain, should I honor this letter of yours at all? Antwerp is an open city. Strauss no longer resides there."

"Doesn't he? It is of little moment. I had audience with the Prince of Parma for a safe conduct out of the Netherlands. If Strauss has left Antwerp, His Highness will have no difficulty finding him for me. Does that answer you?" He watched Ali Bey, trying to penetrate what was going on behind those folds of skin.

The Turk did not speak for a long time. Maurice waited while the silence pressed heavily about them. Ali Bey said finally, "If I should tell you, effendi, that we cannot pay this letter of credit on sight without possible ruin, you would say——"

Maurice looked at him coldly. He did not believe payment would ruin the house. "I cannot see what possible interest you expect me to have in your business affairs, sir. You can honor the letter or not. But if the loan is not in my hands by the ringing of the Angelus tomorrow evening, I have but one course open to me. Which naturally," he added, "I will take."

Ali Bey lifted himself to his feet with the help of his silent servant, his voluminous white robes swelling out over his huge body. He bowed his turbaned head. "At the moment the victory is in your hands, effendi. The silver will be at your shop today before the sun is in the western sky." He looked at Maurice silently, carefully, as though he wished to remember his face. He said softly, "The curse of Allah will come upon you, effendi. You will die and your seed with you."

Maurice smiled, eyebrows raised. "You are fortunate to know the secrets of Allah."

The smile or the words touched off the servant as a flash touches off powder in a musket pan. Maurice lifted his head in surprise at the little man's shrill voice. He'd thought the servant a mute. "Dog of an infidel! May you one day be in our country! You will be remembered! Your flesh will rot from your bones, you will die the death of a thousand——"

Maurice looked at Ali Bey with fastidious disapproval as he too rose. "My dear sir, must we listen to such chatter from your servant before breakfast? It hardly fits this early hour."

Ali Bey said, "He is not my servant, effendi, but my friend."

"I would still prefer to discuss something more pleasant to the ear. The scarlet silk from China that you were displaying yesterday was exquisite."

Ali Bey's eyes opened, a gleam in them. "Exquisite! A tawdry word to describe that sheer luminous beauty, delicate as a cobweb, the hue exhilarating as spilled blood, and the price—it is giving it away. A mere fifty francs for a——" He called himself with an effort. "But you are not interested in making a purchase, effendi. And if you were—— You will hear from me today on this Strauss matter." He gave the Turkish salutation again, knee, heart, lips, and forehead, and rolled out softly on slippered feet, his servant or friend following him as silently as they had entered.

Maurice, coldly angry, rang for Jacques. There was no answer. He felt a momentary disquiet under his annoyance. Where Ali Bey's full robes had passed, they might leave some unimaginable desolation behind! Maurice's mouth thinned. He rang again. Flying footsteps sounded outside. Then the door was flung open and Jacques came in, broad face and figure quivering with indignation. Behind him was Tom. Maurice said, "How did I have a visitor unannounced?"

At the noise Patrick and Webster came in from their rooms at the end of the suite.

Jacques spluttered. "Visitor! A son of the devil! He locked us in, Tom and me. Three of them came up be-

145

hind us, put a gag over our mouths and threw us into a room under the steps. Next time I see those heathenish bastards . . ." His voice went off into an indistinguishable growl.

Patrick asked, "What happened, Master Quain?"

"Nothing of consequence. Master Webster, when you have completed arrangements about a boat, hire a coach that will leave the city any hour, night or day. Probably tonight. Buy a permit that gives us leave through the gates after curfew. Your coach owner should be familiar with such details."

Ali Bey of the House of Gascony. His coming had been a tactical error. Ali Bey invisible had a menacing quality about him. But once seen, if somewhat sinister, he was still only another man, Maurice told himself, a merchant worried over his business. But the assurance lacked conviction.

The silver, in long bars and coins, was in open chests along the wall of the strong room. The armor and weapons were stacked neatly beside it. The glitter of silver and steel hurt the eyes. Chapé said with satisfaction, "Everything is here to the last ounce, m'sieu. This chest—" he waved toward a small brassbound box—"contains the jewels, which are worth the full seventeen thousand pounds. I gave the goldsmith who brought them a bill of exchange for the silver, though he is not pleased that Monsieur Webster insists he wait three days before it is delivered to him."

Maurice said, "Good! Until we are well out of Paris we do not want the silver transported from here for the House of Gascony to see. And now where will you have it put? I want the chests emptied out for the armor."

Webster, who had long before jumped to Maurice's plan, began to lift out the metal. Patrick moved forward to help him. There was only the sound of silver clanging against silver, then the sharper sound of steel on steel.

Webster said, "I realize, Master Quain, I need only follow your instructions, but I'd like to put in one word."

"Well?"

"I assume this armor is to be smuggled out of the city by boat so that the officials of the House of Gascony will think the weapons are their silver and follow the boat down the Seine."

"Well?"

"You had the silver exchanged for the jewels so that the chest can be carried out of the city by coach?"

"Yes."

"You of course will go by coach, but you need a good man in charge of the boat. Now I—as you know, Master Quain, I'm a modest man—but who could do so well?"

"The task is yours then. Let its carrying out be half as good as your boast and we will speak further on a post in the East."

"It shall be. We're—almost—as good as in London now."

Maurice smiled faintly, but he did not feel he had heard the last of Ali Bey.

Night over Paris. Silence and unlighted streets, the cry of the watch, an occasional figure slipping through the lane, a darker shadow among shadows. Down the Street of the Three Angels men walked, two at a time, heavily, groping their way, a creak or rattle giving evidence of the burden they were carrying. Maurice waited for the last chest to be carried toward the river, then an hour longer, before he and Jacques and Patrick and Tom made their way with Félix as guide through the seemingly empty city. Half a dozen streets away a coach was drawn up in the darkness. The pawing horses struck sparks from the cobblestones. The brass-bound chest was put on the floor and the riders stepped in.

The coachman flicked his whip, the wheels turned grindingly, and the coach jolted off. The wind cut through the open windows. They were stopped once at the gates. There was a brief exchange of words between guard and coachman before they drove on. Maurice settled back against the cushions, his cloak muffled about his face to protect him from the chill night air.

147

At the best it would be noon before they could reach Le Grand Andely. The murmur of Patrick's and Jacques' voices became indistinguishable, merged into the background, formed an undertone to his snatches of sleep.

The sun was high overhead, beginning to slide down the western sky before they could see in the distance the little town of Le Grand Andely, roofs and church tower dark against the clear blue sky. The stretch of wooded slopes on either side of the winding road began now to give way to meadows and harvested fields, the stubble of the grain withering against the earth.

An uneventful ride, Maurice thought idly, for a warring land. But it was the south that was being torn apart at the moment by the armies of the royal Houses of the Valois and Navarre and the ducal house of Guise in savagely shifting patterns of blood and intrigue and changing loyalties. The coach crashed into a hole, swayed, righted itself precariously.

Patrick voiced Maurice's thought. "A quiet journey for——" The coach was pulled to a halt with a harrowing yell from the coachman; the spatter of hoofs on the dry earth. Patrick put his head out the window. In the quiet could be heard the sound of pounding hoofs coming toward them. Patrick said, "God's cross!" kicked the door open and jumped out. Maurice followed him deliberately.

A horse galloped toward them. The bloody figure of a man reeled in the saddle. Patrick caught the bridle. The horse started to rear, then quieted. The sunlight caught on the tangle of the rider's sandy hair. No one but Vincent had hair just that shade. There was blood on his face, on his torn clothes. "Master Quain, don't go into the town! They set on me, tried to make me tell when you were coming, but I got away. They hit me here—— God!" He put one hand to his side.

Maurice's eyes swept the countryside. There was no sign of any moving figure in front or behind them. Patrick and Tom loosened Vincet's grip on the saddle, laid him on a cloak Tom spread on the ground. Vincent pushed them aside feebly. "I want to tell . . . Master Quain . . ."

Maurice said, "Take off your shirt, Tom, and tear it into strips. Give him some wine, Jacques. Who did this to you, Vincent?"

Vincent shook his head. "I don't know." His voice was thick. "They followed me from Paris—it was at the Sign of the Lily. Joseph got away. Get across the Seine quick—have the *Falcon* take you on board there." He began to mutter incoherently as though he'd held his wits together for one supreme effort and now was done.

Maurice put a hand to the faint pulse, looked at the ragged flesh wound below the floating rib. Jacques poured wine on the strips of cloth and started to bandage the wound deftly. Maurice said, "Patrick, have the coachman go with you and see if you can get a boat." He looked toward the town, his eyes glints of blue light between narrowed lids. He was in a cold fury to think anyone had touched a man of his. But an Englishman in a French town looking for French ruffians—— He would have little chance finding them, and he had jewels to get to England.

Patrick and the coachman came back in a wide flatboat with two men at the oars. Vincent was placed in the bottom on a cloak, the chest of jewels under a rough seat. Maurice, paying off the coachman, advised him to drive the horses hard back to Paris. The suggestion was not needed. Maurice watched the coach careening down the road. Sooner or later Vincent's attackers would pick up his trail and the flying coach would draw them for a time.

As he stepped into the boat, everyone stiffened at a new sound. Was that distant pounding of hoofs still from the coach horses or mounted men from Le Grand Andely? Maurice turned to one of the oarsmen. "See if you can get up there and observe how many men there are without your being seen."

The man spoken to crawled up the bank to hide in a hollow between the roots of a great oak. The horses' hoofs swept past. The Frenchman sprang back into the boat. "Six riders, monsieur."

149

Maurice nodded. "Push off! I'm meeting a ship down the Seine. Do you know if the *Falcon* is in port above Andely?"

The rowers put their hands on the oars. "Yes, monsieur. She came in three days ago, but she weighed anchor and sailed toward Le Havre this morning."

Maurice started to say "Impossible!" and stopped. He knew it was true. He looked at the strange and hostile country about them, the leaky river boat, the chest of jewels at his feet, the wounded man who was beginning to groan softly, then at the others waiting for him to speak.

Patrick said, "May the devil fly off with Fox's soul and the plague smite his body!" As Maurice eyed him coldly, he added, "I have a more helpful suggestion than that to offer, Master Quain. These boatmen should know a place for all of you to wait. Then they could take me across the river and I could go up to Le Havre. If Fox isn't there, I could hire another ship."

"No. I doubt if you'd get to Le Havre alive."

Patrick shrugged. "I'd rather be killed trying than stay here to be found by a band of brigands."

Maurice shook his head. "Vincent is moving. Try to force some wine down his throat. He must know something more than he told us."

Tom loosened the dagger at his waist. "When they catch up with the coach and find it empty, Master Quain, they'll come back."

Maurice said, "It is not unlikely." He watched Vincent as Jacques placed a wet cloth on the injured man's head, put the bottie of wine to his lips. Vincent twisted, moaned. He opened blank eyes. The sun beat down, the wind stirred acorss hot perspiring faces, and the boat reeked of the smell of fish and of blood.

Vincent's incoherencies broke off abruptly. He said, "Master Quain!"

Maurice leaned toward him, his eyes holding the wounded man's. Vincent's face looked puzzled as though he did not quite believe there could be so much pain in the world as tore at his flesh. Maurice spoke carefully. "The *Falcon* has left, Vincent. Do you know if there is another English ship in the river?"

Vincent started to move his head, stopped with an oath that was twisted from him. "No . . . I don't know. English . . . there was a grand . . . English . . . gentleman at the inn. I would . . . have begged his help . . . but they set on me . . . too soon."

"An English gentleman. Who is he?"

"I . . . don't know, Master Quain. Saint Swithin . . . those bastards!" His hand groped toward his bandaged side. "I . . . don't know . . . but I saw him once in . . . Paris. A great gentleman, I think." He writhed in pain.

Maurice bit his underlip absently, then turned to the boatmen in quick decision. "Could you bring us to a place where this man would be safe, messieurs?"

The two men exchanged glances. One said, "Yes, monsieur. We have a hut down the river. It's not worthy of a fine lord like you, but your man will be safe."

"Take us there." He turned to Patrick. "You'll all stay with Vincent. I'm going into town to the Sign of the Lily. If I'm not back by dawn, try for Le Havre."

The houses of Le Grande Andely huddled together as though shrinking from the next blow fate would inevitably deal them. Maurice walked slowly up the one street of the village. A large painted lily swung out on an iron rod just beyond the church. He had a feeling of unreality. The dust underfoot, rising at every breath of wind, every footfall, danced in the slanting rays from the sun sinking in the west.

He went up the low step to the inn door, threw it open. His eyes narrowed against the darkness within after the hard brightness of the light outside. It was two steps down to the hard clay floor of the common room. He stood a moment in the entrance, his figure silhouetted against the light, the crown of his wide-brimmed hat almost touching the lintel. He stepped down as his eyes grew accustomed to the dimness and objects in the room took shape—tables and benches, the blackened hearth, a gleam of copper. The room was empty except for one man. The feeling of unreality grew starkly tense.

151

The man crossed the floor, blue satin doublet laced with silver shining in the half light. "I was rather expecting you, Maurice." He glanced toward the door. "You know I hoped you would come—or be brought. You're not in trouble, I trust?"

"Why should I be?" Maurice did not even feel surprised, as though he had known "the great English gentleman" would be Blount. It was all of a piece with Ali Bey, and a man of his being hurt and his ship gone.

Blount pulled out a bench from a near-by table, sat down and waved to Maurice to be seated. Maurice, with a day's growth of beard on his face, doublet and hose crushed from the night's ride in the coach, surveyed him coldly.

Blount smiled charmingly. "I thought perhaps since you were alone and appear, if I may say so, rather like a fugitive, you might want assistance."

Maurice looked uninterested. "Where's the tapster?" The man came in at his rap on the table. "Bring me some bread and beef and a red wine."

"You don't need help?" Blount watched Maurice through half-closed eyes as the servingman scurried out. "You know, I was just remembering the last time we ate together, Maurice. In Blyth."

Maurice wondered how long it would be before the horsemen they had heard would overtake the coach, find it empty and either beat up and down the river or return for further orders from Blount. "A pleasant dinner if I recall it right. But I have no complaint about any meals in Paris. The French are excellent at preparing food."

Blount shrugged. "I like my food plain and unadorned. I'd trade all the fancy sauces and garnishes they use to conceal bad meat for one piece of good English mutton."

Maurice drew back as a platter was placed before him with beef swimming in half-congealed grease, barley bread and a mug of pale wine. "Not quite in the best Parisian tradition this, Sir Edward. But one must put up with some inconveniences in traveling, I suppose."

"You aren't accustomed to inconveniences, Maurice?" Blount made an impatient movement. "Or I should say, you weren't? You're in rather an inconvenient position at the moment, I'd think."

"I am?"

Blount's voice rose. "Yes! Perhaps you wonder what I'm doing here?"

"Really, Sir Edward, I haven't been interested enough to question your presence."

Blount said, "I have a share in a French business in Paris, the House of Gascony. I heard from . . . a friend in Antwerp you were going to that city."

"Ah, yes. Someone mentioned you were in Paris."

Blount's eyes opened at that. "I had your man followed out while the House of Gascony pursued a boat that slipped down the Seine." He watched Maurice. He hadn't heard whether the money had been in the boat or not, but he felt that where Maurice was the seventeen thousand pounds also would be. "Well, Maurice?" He tried to keep himself from smiling, but he knew that finally he had Maurice in a position he could not hope to better, would not change if he had dreamed it.

Maurice also knew the bitter truth.

Blount said, "Your ship was in here until this morning. The captain—Fox, isn't it?—was persuaded that your plans were changed unexpectedly that you wished him to meet you at another port. Since I am English he supposed I was a friend of yours. Which of course I am. In fact I have passage for us both to London. As I have friends in Andely, however, need I mention that you cannot buy a passage—except from me?"

Maurice said quietly, "And what is the price of the voyage, Sir Edward?" Blount laughed, savoring to the full the sweet and heady taste of victory. Maurice looked at him, a bored expression on his face. "Don't make it too high. It's worth only a limited amount to me."

Outside, hoofs pounded, came to a stop at the door. Maurice thought he had heard rather too many horses today. Four men came in a moment later, crossed to Blount. The noise of their boots was dulled by the clay floor. Blount glanced up at the leader, a thick-shouldered man with a bearded face, a long scar on one cheek where the flesh had been torn from eye to mouth. "Your ride was for nothing, lads. I have the man we want." He waved his hand toward Maurice. A ring on his index finger sparkled.

There was a growl. The four men moved closer. The leader looked at Blount, let the lid droop over one eye and made a gesture with his thumb toward the door. Blount shook his head. "No, lads. Our friend's going to be reasonable."

Maurice did not turn to look at the newcomers. Blount thought it was his infernal misfortune that Maurice feared neither man nor devil. If he would so much as wince, Blount could wring a princely sum out of him. But he could not see Maurice paying a shilling for his personal safety, and he would pay only so much and no more to save the seventeen thousand pounds, which they might or might not be able to find by themselves if Maurice should be stubborn. There was always the chance too that if anything should happen to the Queen's financial agent, questions would be asked. His triumph was beginning to sour.

He said, "Since you are willing to be agreeable, Maurice, I can do nothing less than match you. Passage will cost you—"

He pondered a moment. He could hold Maurice till he sent back to Paris to Ali Bey. But in the meantime the loan might be on its way to London. And if it were not—— For his help in this he could not expect over two thousand pounds. Ali Bey had said as much. The business, the Turk had given him to understand, had more need of the money than Blount. But didn't Elizabeth Tudor have the greatest need?

"Well, let us say, it will cost you three thousand pounds. I would make it higher—I am tempted to, Maurice—but my honor bids me be moderate since you are on business for Her Majesty. The welfare of Gloriana is dearer to me even than my own." He thought suddenly of a point that had not come to mind. "Three thousand pounds, Maurice, and your pledge of silence on this incident in England."

Maurice looked at Blount consideringly. The sick taste of defeat was in his mouth, the smell of it in his nostrils. "That includes of course my retinue and all baggage?"

"Of course."

"Very well. When do we sail?"

9

Katherine Perrot unlatched the casement window, leaned out to watch Debbie. The little girl was four, with wide blue eyes and a mop of golden hair. She had on a long dress of gray silk, but in spite of the impeding skirts she moved so lightly she looked as though the wind were blowing her across the grass.

Katherine smiled and turned back into the small room of the Stepney cottage. "Debbie looks well and happy, Elly. But you—"

Her dark brows drew together as she gazed at the older woman sitting on a chair between hearth and table, a woolen blanket over her knees, hands crippled with rheumatism lying idly in her lap. The idleness stabbed Katherine. Her earliest memories of Elly had been of an untiring and cheerful briskness. A distant relative of Sir John Perrot, Elly had been his housekeeper in the years he'd been on the Welsh marches. When Katherine had left the barren castle at a summons from Court and Sir John had moved to another post, Elly had come to London too. She had said placidly that she was tired of country life and wanted to see the world before she died. As a good needlewoman could always support herself, why shouldn't she indulge her whims? Katherine had laughed and agreed with her.

Elly smiled at Katherine's anxious expression now. Her wrinkled face was soft, though there were fine interlacing lines of pain about eyes and mouth that made her appear older than her fifty-odd years. "I? I'm happy—which is better than being healthy, my dear! Has Hannah left, Kit?"

"Yes. She went down to the market half an hour ago. I gave her some money." She smiled across at Elly. "We learned a new measure yesterday for the

155

next ball at Richmond. Would you like to see it? It's the pavan, but it has new variations from the French Court."

She hummed a melody softly to herself, stepped forward, curtsied and whirled into the dance, a beautiful and exotic creature against the whitewashed walls of the cottage, the roughly made furniture. She made a final pirouette on her toes and dipped into a curtsy again, the blue velvet skirt with its gold embroidery coming to rest about her. There was a wild rose color in her cheeks.

"That's lovely, and not one of the dancers, I know, will be so lovely or so light on her feet as you."

"Thank you, Elly!" Katherine pulled out a three-legged stool and sat down. The anxiety in her eyes was at variance with her bright face and rich dress. She glanced down at it. A gown was so expensive, and this was beginning to look worn. She folded the hem of the skirt back unostentatiously so that Elly would not notice the frayed edge, then leaned forward impulsively, one slim hand on the old woman's crippled knee. "You don't look so well as you did last time I was here, Elly. You know what I shall do? Ask the Court physician to come out to see you. I'm sure he can help you."

Elly said quickly, "No, oh, no, Kit! A Court physician here!" Her blue eyes twinkled. "Why, he'd soil the soles of his feet even coming out from London. Don't do that, Kit!"

"We must think of something," Katherine answered firmly. "If you're worried about the payment, I'll manage that easily."

Elly closed her eyes a moment to hide a twinge of pain. "You must not, darling. Too many people know their way here now."

"Too many?" Katherine said lightly. "Who?"

"A young man named Anthony Babington."

"No!" Katherine came to her feet. "He can't know. I'd never tell him."

Elly looked up. "You know who he is, Kit?"

The girl twisted her fingers together. "Yes, oh, yes. He's the one I mentioned to you months ago, the leader of that group pledged to free Mary of Scotland."

She glanced nervously about as though someone might be listening. "I gave him some money once to help smuggle a friend of his out of the country."

"Oh, Kit!"

"I suppose it was rash, but he was desperate. And I find 'no' a hard word to say!"

Elly shook her head. "I'm not worried about that—it's what I've done. When Master Babington was here a week ago, he said you were in agreement with him. I didn't know who he was, and I let him stay overnight."

"He will ruin himself and all of us who have been near to him." Katherine wanted to speak lightly but her voice had a soft huskiness in it. "Elly, listen. If you hear that anything has happened to me, you must get Debbie away at once. I'll not rest till I know she's safe. Nothing will go wrong, but I want to be sure about her anyway. After all, just being alive is a continual gamble!"

"Of course, dear, you can trust me to do that, Hannah and me. She's devoted to the child, too."

Katherine laughed, bent to kiss Elly on her cheek. "I'll forget my worries then, and I've not another trouble in the world. All the same," she added thoughtfully, "I wish Master Babington would turn from his plans. I feel now they can end in nothing but tragedy. What is it in men that drives them to disaster?"

Elly said, "Do you know, Kit, I wondered when he was talking, if he would not like to forget this too. He seemed worried and said if he fails, not only is his head endangered but the Scottish Queen's as well. Sir Francis Walsingham seems to be encouraging him."

Katherine looked at Elly with horror. "Oh, no! Because if Walsingham is, it's for one reason only—to carry this conspiracy so far that through it Mary Stuart can be brought to trial once again. If that is true, Babington is as good as a dead man now. I must warn him. I have not seen him for a long time. I didn't answer their last appeal for aid."

She remembered the evening she had received it. She had burned the paper in the candle flame with Patrick North standing across the room from her. Perhaps if life had gone differently, she might have cared for

157

someone like him. She had been too young when she'd gone to Court, heartbreakingly young, and more afraid of the glitter than wooed by it. It was hard to remember the taming of her wild spirit to Court decorum, the poignancy of her first love affair, the cold fear when she'd discovered she was pregnant—the sort of ill luck that happens to others, but never, never to oneself. Her lover had become suddenly interested in petitioning the Queen to send him to the Welsh border. In her scorn of him she had added her voice to his to help him on his way. Even now she could not think of him without a momentary reliving of her anguish and her panic at the desertion.

Fortune had been kindlier when Elly had begged to have the child Deborah remain with her—that was before her hands had been crippled—and at Court again she had met Edward Blount. Ned had given her to herself again somehow. He had loved her when she needed someone desperately. Whatever he did or said or was, she would always be grateful to him. Out of all the pain and the storms had come a polished and suave young woman who had learned everything she need know about how to advance herself—except not to follow her heart.

"Elly, I wonder. Did Babington mention a Master Quain?"

"Quain? No, he didn't, Kit."

Katherine took a deep breath. "No matter. If there is anyone in this world who does not need a word of warning about imprudent plots, Quain's your man!"

Why did she think of him? He had been back in London for months, but she had seen him only briefly when he had audience with the Queen on some appointment. She had believed that after all the months of his absence on the Continent, she would have forgotten him. She had almost forgotten him—his slow way of looking at you as though before he even spoke to you he drew back into himself while he held you off. She couldn't remember any other man who had not at least tried to flirt with her. She felt a careless annoyance with him for that, a deeper anger because under his dull manner she sensed in him a need of friendship.

158

He was not a man who had so many friends he could reject one and not be the loser.

She glanced up with a wry smile. She was forgetting Babington. Her quick impulse of pity for him would not let her rest until she had done something. She dared not ask about him except of a sympathizer or she would harm him or herself. Who were his sympathizers? Ned could find out since he often worked for Walsingham, but she knew him too well to think he would even hint at a government secret. Perhaps this conspiracy was necessary to the welfare of the State. The world of men was harsh. Maurice Quain might know about Babington if Walsingham had tried to involve him in this. Fear that was a stab of pain suddenly assailed her. Who had told Babington of her daughter here?

A thin dry suspense swept through her. She must leave quickly. She felt as though her presence would bring danger on those within. She called Mattie, who was in the garden with Deborah. Elly said, "Shall I have your daughter brought in, too?"

Katherine shook her head as she threw on her cloak, fastened it about her shoulders and pulled on her gloves. "No. I saw her earlier and she's well. She's a sweet little mite and hard to leave, Elly."

Mattie looked uncomfortably about her as the horses trotted down the rutted road toward London. "I don't like this, two women traveling alone. It isn't seemly, mistress."

Katherine laughed, put up a hand to catch at a loosened strand of hair and adjusted the small half mask of velvet. A haphazard childhood had given her a sturdy independence under her outward softness and flexibility. She began to wonder, though, as they turned into the main London road. She had expected to be lost in the usual stream of people going into the city, but there were fewer riders and wagons than usual. They must have stayed later than she realized. She glanced at the western sky. The sun was low, and dark-edged clouds drifted across the clear bluish green, serene and far away. There was the feel of storm in the air. She flicked her whip against the horse's flank, then reined up to wait for Mattie who was jogging behind her.

As she half-turned in her saddle, she noticed idly three young men coming up behind them. They were not savory-looking. The horses they rode were of a better quality than their clothes and grooming would lead one to expect. They stared at her as they passed and slowed not to get too far ahead.

Katherine turned toward Mattie. "I heard someone else from the Court was out this way, perhaps looking for us. Did you chance to mention Stepney to anyone of late?"

Mattie, eying the three riders nervously, said, "No, of course I didn't mention it to anyone, my lady, except once to Master—what's his name?—Poley?"

Katherine stared at her waiting woman. "Oh, no!" Poley. Poley was Walsingham's man. She felt a nausea mount within her. She put the back of her gloved hand hard against her mouth so that her teeth cut into her fingers. What did she fear? Walsingham's man knew where her daughter was. Anthony Babington had been there. Well? An odd coincidence, yes. An unpleasant one, but nothing more. And yet fear wove a net about her. She knew how gossamerlike a web was thrown about a victim, so sheer one was unaware of the tightening strands until too late.

The houses were clustered more closely as they neared London. The wind was beginning to rise. Mattie looked about. The sky was darkening. She was afraid of storms. "If only, mistress, you had taken a retainer with us!" She cast another glance ahead. The young men had neither shortened nor lengthened the distance between them.

Here and there a window showed chinks of light through the shutters. The massive stone wall encircling London ahead of them was grim and forbidding. They slowed to a walk as the stream of people from the road narrowed to go through Aldgate under the eyes of the guards. Mattie muttered, "I hope they arrest those rowdies ahead of us. I'm sure they've stolen the horses they're riding."

"Poor Mattie! I shouldn't take you with me to these wild places."

Mattie bristled at that. "Who better to go with you? Only, we should have a manservant." They rode in under the gate. "Can we wait someplace, mistress? It's too far to Whitehall. I'm sure those terrible young men mean us ill as soon as it grows dark." She folded her lips together primly. Lightning streaked across the western sky. The sound of the horses trotting on the stones was swallowed up in the roll of thunder.

Katherine laughed. "I do know of an inn, Mattie, the Saracen's Head. I've been there with Ned."

An oil lamp flickered over the sign of the Saracen's Head. Katherine hesitated one moment before dismounting. It was the only inn in the city she was acquainted with, but she remembered the scene when Ned had Maurice Quain arrested. She was rather afraid Maurice might again be staying here, and she wasn't sure she wanted to chance meeting him.

Mattie caught her breath with a sob of fear as she looked over her shoulder and saw three figures coming toward them out of the night. The men had dismounted so that there had been no sound of warning hoofbeats. No one else was about, the threatening storm having driven everyone within doors.

Katherine glanced around quickly. Mattie tugged at her sleeve. "Let us go inside, mistress. The landlord will—"

The words were choked off as a big hand was clapped over her mouth. Mattie's teeth sank viciously into the assailant's fingers. He yelped but did not let go. Another growled, "Get their purses and let's be off."

Katherine felt more incredulous than angry for a moment as she also was seized. She jabbed her elbow savagely into the stomach of the man behind her, tried to twist herself out of his powerful grasp. He gasped but did not ease his grip. The third one of the group was near Mattie. Katherine could hear him muttering as he felt for her waiting woman's purse, then the sound of a loud kiss. "Your purse is thin, mistress, but for this we'll forgive it."

The man holding Katherine cried out at her silent struggle. "Quick over here, you! Someone will be along any minute." He strangled a curse as Katherine's heel came down hard on his foot.

The door of the Saracen's Head opened. The figure of a man was black against the diffused glow of light. The hand on Mattie's mouth was loosened. Mattie took advantage of it to shriek piercingly. A shout sounded from the doorway. The man from the inn dashed forward, plucking a dagger from his belt. There was an instant of uproar, a scream as the dagger found a mark. The three assailants scattered lightly. Katherine brushed off her skirts with one hand, clinging to her purse with the other.

The rescuer said, "You must come in a moment, mistress, and rest. Are you all right?"

His voice was vaguely familiar. A nice voice, Katherine thought, as she and Mattie went up the steps and into the light. "Master North! Though I don't know why I should be surprised. I know you used to stay here."

"Lady Katherine! It can't be—— Did those villains hurt you?"

Katherine said lightly. "Cutpurses, Master North, and not too adept at their work."

"You are sure you were not injured? Those swine— to touch you!"

"It was nothing, sir, though without your assistance it would have been an unpleasant affair. Do you suppose we could impose further on you and ask you to secure us an escort to Whitehall?"

Her light delicate tones created a live warm circle about them as though they were alone in the world. Patrick was hardly aware of what she said, only of the sound of her voice, liquid, drowning his senses. Her quick amused glance recalled to him that he stood there staring at her. "Of course, mistress. You must allow me to accompany you."

"You are very kind, Master North." She looked at him expectantly, waiting for him to order a horse.

162

A wild thought shot through Patrick's mind. No. That would be mad. Out of the night and back into it? He could not let her slip from him so easily. A graceful invitation given casually. No more was needed. He tried to make his voice sound casual. "Our apartment is above, madam. If you'd care to refresh yourself before we ride farther—"

Katherine's brows lifted. She glanced at Mattie, who scowled at the suggestion, and back at Patrick. "It is very thoughtful, Master North. We will indeed." She wondered why she accepted his invitation, but he had looked at her persuasively, as though so small a favor on her part meant much to him.

A trifling affair, he thought with a wry humor. It had taken no courage to chase these unarmed men. Yet he experienced a possessive tenderness toward Katherine. He said, "This way, mistress," and guided the two women up the stairs and down the corridor.

When his hand was on the latch to their apartment, his heart sank. What in the name of God would Maurice say? Maurice had sent him out to take some late dispatches to Bowyer's. He would not like this delay. Maurice's chill courtesy could be more cutting than another's anger. He looked at Katherine, at her tender determined profile, straight nose, rounded chin, the clean line of her jaw above the slim throat. At the feel of his eyes on her, she turned her head toward him and smiled, and he had no further doubts. He flung open the door and ushered her in. Mattie followed reluctantly.

Maurice, who was seated at his desk, lifted his head at the sound of their entrance, came slowly to his feet, his eyes on Katherine unbelievingly. Katherine here? How many times had he dreamed of her so? Perhaps—no, she was real enough. Her hair was disordered and the small jeweled cap awry.

Katherine, her mask in her hand, looked at Maurice with a quizzical amusement as he came forward, dropped him a curtsy that had a hint of mockery in it. "Master Quain!"

He kissed her hand. "Your servant, Lady Katherine."

163

Patrick swung a chair about for her. The first moment had not been too bad. Katherine moved across the room with an easy grace, her skirt swaying. She smiled a thank-you at Patrick before turning to Maurice. "Master North was very brave. We were set upon by three cutpurses and he rescued us swiftly and competently."

Patrick disclaimed any credit. "Such riffraff frighten easily, my lady. So would I in their place," he added, "since being caught means hanging. But enough of them. Will you have a glass of wine?"

Maurice said, "The Canary is on the lowest shelf of the cabinet. Or would you prefer a Greek wine, Lady Katherine?"

"No, Canary will be very pleasant indeed, Master Quain. I am sure your judgment is better than mine." She laughed. "That is, in such matters." She looked about the room appreciatively. "This mat is from Turkey, is it not? I should like to go there someday. Ned has even promised to take me." The name of Edward Blount hung unpleasantly in the air. She changed the subject hastily. "You two have been traveling on the Continent. Tell me about it. That's next best to going oneself."

Maurice shrugged. "A dull journey, Lady Katherine, which kept us too long from business."

"You went to Antwerp, didn't you? A cool way to speak of the fall of a city, Master Quain, and that a stronghold of our ally."

"Patrick shares your fine sentiments, Lady Katherine. He fought for Antwerp."

"You must be kind enough to give us the story, Master North."

Patrick said, "It was nothing, my lady. Besides, we lost."

"One never knows when one is the loser and when the victor," she retorted cryptically, "and I am sure that it was a gallant fight. Do tell me."

Patrick said briefly, "We sailed down to the Kowenstyn dike, took it, and Parma recaptured it." He added with a smile, "There were other details, but they are not essential."

164

Katherine laughed. "Anyway, I'm sure you were very brave, Master North. I would never have such courage."

Maurice lifted his brows sardonically. "Nor I, Lady Katherine. You can always hire mercenaries."

Katherine looked at Maurice with quick anger, but she waited a second before replying suavely, "Yes. You can hire a man to protect your property, Master Quain, but whom can you hire to save your soul?" She sipped the last of her wine daintily.

Maurice smiled without warmth. "It is much too late for that, Lady Katherine. Will you have another glass?"

"Thank you." Her eyes were on Maurice as he poured the wine. She could feel her words had gone home too bitterly. Her voice trembled a little. "Forgive me. I did not mean to say that."

"It's of no consequence."

Katherine looked away. She must get back to White-hall. She was already gone too long. She felt reluctant to leave. There were currents and crosscurrents here, disturbing and unresolved and magnetic. She remembered abruptly her fears earlier in the day for Anthony Babington. If she should ask Maurice Quain, she knew he would not betray her. Whatever his faults—and God knew he made them easier to find than his virtues!—she did not think he would hurt a woman in that way. But particularly she believed—since who knew really of what such a man was capable?—that he would not trouble to leave his business long enough to do her any idle harm. She said briskly, "Master Quain, I wonder if you could help me."

His expression became blandly cynical. "Yes?"

Patrick said, "Could I?"

"Master North, I like you! It is only information I want. About Anthony Babington."

The cynicism deepened on Maurice's face. "Why come to me, Lady Katherine? I'm sure any of your friends at Court could tell you more. I saw him once, and that was too often. What did you want to know?"

"Perhaps if I tell you my interest in him, your suspicions will lie down and die, Master Quain. I put my

165

safety in your hands in saying this to you. I had correspondence once with Master Babington. But later I withdrew, if one can ever take a step back. Now I'm afraid he has been led further than he wishes to go, not by his own will but by Walsingham's."

"And what has that, madam, to do with you or with me?"

She leaned forward, hands clasped lightly together. "Nothing. But it has much to do with our common humanity. You perhaps do not see how far-reaching this is. I think the final goal in Walsingham's mind is to lead this young Babington on, keep him hot to the plan when he might begin to falter. Not to ruin Babington. That would not be worth the trouble expended. But perhaps I weary you?"

"On the contrary," Maurice said, politely bland.

"This plot reaches farther than Babington and his friends. It will be used as a weapon against Mary Stuart herself. Anthony Babington," she said sadly, "a blind Samson toppling ancient structures to destroy his friends and Walsingham's enemies."

"Not a pleasant picture," Maurice agreed. "Still, so reckless a young man as Babington appears to be will never die peacefully in bed. If I were you I should stay as far from him as the limits of England allow." He added ironically, "You have a rare kind of beauty which it would be a pity to ruin in so fantastic a cause."

Katherine smiled impishly and unexpectedly. "If you're trying to anger me into leaving without involving you further, Master Quain, don't put yourself to so much labor. I wanted to learn if you had any knowledge how I might reach Babington. He must leave the country. That will both save him and put an end to his treason."

Maurice said, "I'm sorry I can't help you. If I were you I'd forget the matter. But tell me why you came to me?"

"I didn't exactly come to you," Katherine retorted good-humoredly. "I am here on your secretary's invitation. However, I thought you might at least have met

166

with Babington because—— Well, I don't know why I thought it."

She could not really believe Ned had sent Babington to Maurice. Ned was ambitious. He was not treacherous. His unguarded words that he would have Maurice in the Tower had been only a foolish and unfounded threat. "There was no need, I'm sure, to warn you about him? No."

"No."

Katherine eyed him thoughtfully. "I hoped you might help me, but my thanks anyway." Her brows puckered. She felt she should rise to leave, and yet there was something holding her. From the corner where her waiting woman sat she could hear Mattie's foot tapping, the rustle of her skirt as she moved impatiently. Katherine glanced at Patrick, whose gaze had hardly left her, at Maurice who was looking not at her but into his wine. "I trust that your business abroad prospered, Master Quain."

He lifted his head sharply. Was that another stab, random conversation or an interest in his work? He was not sure. "It was much more successful than I deserved, Lady Katherine."

"What your deserts are, I, of course, would not know, but you have won the Queen's favor. It will be of no small value to you in your commerce at home or abroad."

"To say I've won the royal favor overstates the case. I have finally received an appointment as a Crown member of the Turkey Company. I've long wanted this. The profit has been thinned a bit by almost a year's wait between the service to Her Majesty and her reward to me for it. But I can now establish a branch of my own house in Constantinople. Perhaps I can even reach out to Persia if peace holds long enough between Turkey and Persia." He stopped abruptly. Her warmth and interested air had urged him to speak more fully than he had intended. "But of course a lady of the Court has little taste for such matters."

"You mean a lady has little chance to acquire such a taste. Tell me more. What sort of place will you set up in Constantinople? Whom do you hire, Turk or Chris-

167

tian?" She colored slightly at her use of the word "hire," hoping he wouldn't remember in what way she had used it earlier.

His chill expression told her he did remember. "Hire? I am really not far enough along in the business to have further plans myself."

Katherine came lightly to her feet. His voice had shut firmly the hardly opened door between them. "I must be going, Master Quain. Thank you for your hospitality. And you, Master North, have done me a great service. I am grateful."

Patrick smiled. "If it were not such an inconvenience to you, mistress, I'd be pleased to be of like assistance every day of the year!"

Maurice bowed over her hand. The soft feel of her flesh, the fragile bones, flamed through him, lighting up the aching emptiness within him, twisting and hurting. But Katherine thought only that the latent hostility he always set up between them was now alive past hope.

Maurice handed cloak and plumed hat to the attendant in the anteroom and walked into the huge paneled chamber in the upper story of the Royal Exchange. Over a dozen men sat about a table, in doublets of every color from sober black or dark blue to crimson and gold, collars ranging from the plain flat linen of the Puritans to the wide, deeply pleated ruffs with lace edging of the more fashionable merchants.

Maurice walked across the room, had his hand on the back of an unoccupied chair before anyone glanced up from a heated discussion. A voice said sharply, "Master Quain, this is a meeting of the directors of the Turkey Company. Should you have business with any of us, we will be pleased to hear you later. I beg you will take no offense, but we must first finish our meeting. Will you wait in the anteroom?"

Maurice looked at the speaker, a faint surprise on his face. "Her Majesty, Master Osborne, did me the favor, no doubt undeserved, of bestowing on me a Crown membership in the Company. I thought you would have been apprised of this."

Edward Osborne's genial face suffused with color.

His eyes snapped. "This is the first I have heard of this . . . this highhanded . . . of this appointment."

Maurice said indifferently, "Is that indeed so?" His eyes swept the astonished faces of the members, outrage on Osborne's, a friendly smile from Dick Staper.

Staper stroked down his graying hair as he said briskly, "We're glad to welcome you among us, Master Quain. The talk just now was on our next shipment. Spain is building a larger fleet, making the entrance to the Straits of Gibraltar precarious. But to move our wares overland across France, Italy and Greece runs up the expenses inordinately. It is three to five times slower with France none too friendly to us English merchants."

Osborne forgot Maurice. "I was about to suggest the route through Navarre to Marseille. We would thus avoid both Gibraltar and the long overland roads. We will send an agent ahead to see which ways are the most passable."

Staper nodded. "An excellent suggestion."

Another merchant said, "The Huguenots in Navarre have to love England if they hope for more money from us. But if you go overland, I'd think Venice might be a better port. We'd avoid the sea trip about Italy where one is too near the Moors and pirates of Tripoli."

Osborne shook his head. "No. Our rivalry with Venice in the East would make it dangerous to send so much of our wealth through that door to Islam. The Doge might seize it, and the duties, as you know, are outrageous." He turned to Maurice with a chill courtesy. "Our next shipment will be in three weeks. Can you gather within that time the supplies you'd like to send? We can delay a few days, but we like to keep as closely as possible to our promised schedule."

"I am sure I can manage, thank you."

"If I were you, I'd consign whatever goods you send directly to Sir William Harborne. He's the ambassador as you no doubt know, but our Company pays all his expenses and he will handle anything shipped to him. Of course for more flexibility you should establish your own factor in Turkey as soon as possible." He glanced around the table. "That's all the business for today, I believe, sirs."

Staper said, "We were going to bring up the import question too, Osborne. Harborne says the usual cargo is being shipped—silks, camlets, rhubarb, oil, galls for dyeing, raw cotton, spices. But he has a new Turkish product, new to us at least, that he inquires if he should export. It's coffee. He says it's a hot drink, black-colored and supposed to be very good for expelling poisons from raw meats and herbs. They have houses in Constantinople where it is sold the way we sell ale and wine. I'd like to have some sent for my personal use out of curiosity, but whether it would be worth shipping on a large scale as a novelty I don't know. I rather doubt its being worth the price."

"Not for me," Osborne put in. "We have enough imports on which we're certain of good profits without bothering about such fantasies as coffee. Shall we forget the suggestion? Is there any further matter for discussion?"

Maurice said thoughtfully, "You mentioned that the Turkey Company pays the full expenses of Harborne as ambassador to the Porte of the Sultan, Master Osborne."

"Yes."

"I cannot understand in that case why the members should have so much expense in shipping their goods to Turkey."

"You would say—"

"That Harborne with his well-known diplomatic gifts could save us that expense and, incidentally, do his country a good turn as well by suggesting to Sultan Amurath some sort of an alliance. Instead of sending his corsairs out haphazardly against the merchant ships in the Mediterranean, the Turks could fling them against Spain. They have an old score to settle with Philip Hapsburg—Lepanto."

There was a sharp intake of breath. "Lepanto! There all Christendom held the heathen from pouring across Europe."

"Ally ourselves with Infidel against Christian! What devil's prompting is this?"

"England would be the scandal of the world."

"Of what use," Maurice asked idly, "is a good reputation to a pauper? And of what need to a rich man?"

Staper laughed. "You put it well, Master Quain, but cold-bloodedly."

Maurice started to adjust the ruff at his wrist meticulously, then stopped. A foolish mannerism. "If you would have the same suggestion put more acceptably, gentlemen, you might remember that France has long encouraged Turkish aggressions against the Hapsburgs in Spain and in Austria. Or you might dwell on the picture of the Armada riding victoriously at anchor below us in the Thames, of England as a satellite of Spain, an estate to be disposed of by Hapsburg hands. Does this thought please you more than using to our advantage Turkey's jealousy of the Spaniard? Where is your patriotism?" His glance went mockingly about the table.

Osborne's expression was not friendly, but he said, "We will think about this and then make our suggestion to the Queen and Privy Council."

"Perhaps it is good advice," a merchant said. "Such a word from us might increase our prestige with the Council. They are not always too friendly. I can assure you they will hear of it from a most promising source."

Maurice looked up. "No doubt we could not do better, but pray I ask who is this 'most promising source' you mention?"

The man cleared his throat, "Well, to tell you the truth, Master Quain, it's a . . . well, an influential friend of mine."

Osborne said with a touch of impatience, "The man who often presents our business to the Crown or Council, Master Quain, is Sir Edward Blount, a well-wisher of ours who has given us much aid at Court. While keeping this an association of merchants has its advantages in many ways, often we need a friend in higher circles. A dispute over an appointment or some such matter may have the Council threatening to close down the Company till it be settled."

171

Maurice looked contemptuous. "Edward Blount? You might do worse, but I doubt it."

Osborne said sharply, "Very well, Master Quain. You are in the royal favor. See to it yourself. The suggestion is yours. You are more than welcome to the credit. Such an alliance may be a necessity. Most of us at least recognize it as an evil too."

"I shall be happy to see Her Majesty."

"Then if there is nothing more, sirs?"

The meeting broke off into small groups. As the members came to their feet, Maurice heard a chance remark from a merchant standing near him. ". . . last night at Bellamy's house."

"They were all taken?"

"One may have escaped. I'm not sure. But Babington himself was captured and one or two with him, as I heard the story. Well, so perish all enemies of the Queen! I'll see you at the 'Change tomorrow at noon."

Babington taken? A young fool like him, Maurice thought, wasn't born to die quietly. What of Katherine? Had she stayed away from him? He checked his thoughts as Staper came up.

"Are you sending a factor to Constantinople, or will you go there yourself, Master Quain?"

Maurice smiled. "I'm going as soon as all my affairs in England are in order."

"Excellent! You can see my agent Sanderson when you arrive in Turkey. He will give you any help you need."

"Thank you." Maurice felt again the magnetic pull toward the East, the sensing that somehow his own destiny was there. Or was it in him the last faint flicker of the romantic spirit which had flamed so destructively bright in his first youth, lighting easily the way to ruin? Abruptly with the thought, he felt a momentary chill, a shadow of uneasiness. For the first time the East repelled as well as drew him.

10

Katherine and Blount let out their horses for a final gallop along the banks of the Thames, then across the grassy slope toward the cobblestoned courtyard of Hampton Court. Katherine thought she loved this above all the palaces. Hampton had graciousness and warmth. The red-brick walls glowed in the misty light. The tall windows were pleasantly wide and inviting, open to the wind that stirred lazily across the August fields and lifted the branches of the immense oaks and tall, clean-limbed beech trees. Blount slid off his horse in the yard, threw his reins to a groom and helped Katherine dismount. She turned her ankle on an uneven stone, caught at his arm to regain her balance.

Blount smiled charmingly. "May I always be there, Kit, when you need my support!"

She answered his smile with her eyes as she reached up to take off her riding hat, swung it in her gloved hand. The heron's feather swept the ground. "You look pleased with yourself today, Ned." She turned to walk under the great arched entrance, the edge of her gray skirt looped over her arm to escape the dirt.

Blount matched his long stride to her step. "I am, my dear. A delightful gallop in the morning, preceded by an even more delightful night." His glance slid sideways to meet hers. He hadn't been sure of her last night. She had seemed distrait, remote. There had been some lack in her response, a certain generous abandon missing. Well, at best, women were capricious creatures. "And I attend Walsingham today at an audience with Her Majesty." He stripped off his gauntlets as they went across the square inner courtyard.

"You and the Queen are so often together, Ned, that I grow jealous." She looked amused.

Blount said roughly, "I wish to God you were jealous of me for any reason. Then you'd know what hell I suffer because of you. Robert Dudley smiles oftener at you than he does at Elizabeth."

Katherine laughed outright. "Ned, if you stoop to
173

jealousy of the Earl of Leicester, I'll never speak to you again. Do you know what I think? I think you're pretending anger so that I won't guess you have taken a new and wealthy mistress. Your tailor must be working twenty-four hours a day with the fine fashions you've been wearing of late. And this ring you gave me—" she drew off her glove to admire an amethyst set in a circle of diamonds—"are you sure it's not a bribe so that I won't ask you too many questions after you've been away? Once you were gone a fortnight. But it's a beautiful piece of jewelry, so I'll forgive you your infidelities."

He did not laugh with her. He said, "Perhaps it is I who must forgive you yours. Quain—"

Katherine looked wearily away. Mattie must have been talking as usual. She never had the sense not to answer questions.

"—whom you've seen again in spite of my feelings about that traitor—" He broke off abruptly. "Well, no matter. You'll see your merchant again today. He also has audience with the Queen, Sir Francis mentioned. But today, I promise you, you'll see him in his true colors."

Katherine glanced up at the great astronomical clock that Cardinal Welsey had made for Henry the Eighth before presenting the King with the forced gift of Hampton Court Palace. The golden numbers were ashine in the light. "It's late. I must hurry, Ned." She felt annoyed with her lover for spoiling her pleasure in their ride this morning. "I hope I do see him in his true colors, as you put it, because I don't know what they are, and I doubt if Master Quain does."

She smiled at the guard at the door, ran lightly up the square staircase in the hall within. She would see Maurice Quain today. She didn't know if she were glad or sorry. If his hostility had not lessened since their last meeting, to see him might hurt too deeply.

Maurice had not even glanced in her direction since he'd come in. It was a small audience, the Queen's ministers, Burghley and Walsingham, Blount and Maurice, and only three women attending the Queen. He

174

must have seen her, but he gave no sign of having noticed her presence. Patrick, however, had improved upon his master. He had come with Maurice, stood waiting by the door. His eyes were on Katherine. She glanced at him once and away. There was some trait in him that went to her heart—more than his devotion, something enduring, an integrity of character. She drew a thread through her cloth, looped it about to fill in the golden heart for a Tudor rose.

Lord Burghley, sitting just behind Elizabeth, moved his gouty foot tenderly. His thin parchmentlike hands, the veins, blue cords under the skin, were clasped about his silver-headed cane. A still figure, fatherly-looking with his long white beard, his watchful attitude, his shrewd considering eyes. A quiet man, soft-spoken, unassuming—and deadly. He had lifted his head as Maurice finished speaking of an alliance with the Sultan of Turkey against Philip Hapsburg of Spain.

Elizabeth bit her lower lip absently. Some of the paint from her mouth made a streak of scarlet on her yellowed teeth. "There would be a lot of unpleasant talk in the Courts of Europe."

Maurice said sardonically, "Since when has chatter troubled Your Majesty? Beauty is born to be gossiped about."

Elizabeth laughed and tapped the merchant's shoulder with her fan. "Come, come, Master Quain! Do not try our patience." But she was not displeased.

Burghley said sharply, "Such an act of overt aggression is tantamount to a declaration of war, Madam. We cannot afford a war with Spain. We dare not."

Elizabeth snorted. "Dare not, my Lord Burghley!"

He repeated firmly, "Dare not!" His thin hands opened and closed. "The House of Guise in France is negotiating with Philip. Madam, if there is peace between France and Spain, you know how that peace will be used—for the House of Guise to put their kinswoman Mary Stuart in your place. We must pacify Spain, not anger her."

Blount hesitated, feeling for Elizabeth's mood. "That is all true, Your Lordship." He balanced delicately between his need for the good will of both Elizabeth and Burghley. "But it is doubtful if Guise is strong enough in France to conclude such an alliance with Spain. Henry of Valois is still King. He will not want a kinswoman of the Guises on the English throne. Even more, he would not be moved to take up arms against the fair princess he once wooed though he did not win her." He bowed slightly toward Elizabeth. The padding of his new crimson doublet made his movement stiff.

Elizabeth smiled fatuously, remembering the portrait of Henry the Third, the handsomest prince in Europe, and not remembering how he had refused her before she could refuse him. He had refused her not gracefully, diplomatically, as a man who was then only brother to the French King, but with the petulant insult that he'd not be mated to the whore of Europe. Well, she could afford to forget. Henry was between the fires of the ultra-Catholic Guise, backed by the city of Paris, and the Huguenots under Henry of Navarre, while she herself had never sat so securely on the throne of England—except for those small creeping fears of plots and conspiracies like grass fires licking at one's feet. She forgot the suggestion to urge that Turkey attack Spain, forgot the Spanish menace. "You have taken into custody every man who was in this horrible plot, Burghley. Every man?"

"The leaders, Your Majesty. We will soon have the names of all the rest to the very limits of the conspiracy. You may sleep easily, Madam—until Mary Stuart's adherents move again."

Walsingham said, "That, Your Majesty, will be soon. Let your servants close their eyes for one moment—"

Elizabeth glared at them. "You will not bully me, my lords, into signing Mary's death warrant. But Anthony Babington—" Her long fine fingers were clenched convulsively and her voice was edged, vindictive. "That murderer! Make his death as slow and painful as it is in the power of the executioner. Let him suffer as no man has suffered before."

Burghley said deprecatingly, "Your Majesty, it is hardly possible to increase the agony a criminal suffers

176

in hanging and drawing, but I will give the executioner your order."

Elizabeth did not hear him. Her green eyes seemed to be turned inward. She had been only three when her mother, Anne Boleyn, was sent to the block. She remembered the years of her adolescence when she had lived in the shadow of the Tower, the plots since she had come to the throne to replace her with that whey-faced cousin of hers, Mary Stuart, and now this, the most far-flung net of conspiracy yet thrown into international waters, reaching to Paris and Madrid. She felt cold, unbearably alone and old. She whispered, "Do not forget to speak to the executioner, Burghley."

Burghley bowed his head as he smoothed his long, carefully combed beard. Walsingham and Blount exchanged glances. Blount said, "Your Majesty, now is the time to move not only against the avowed leaders of this accursed plot, but against fair-weather friends, potential enemies." He turned his head to look directly at Maurice, and the expression on his fair face, the intensity of hatred, suited oddly with his usual easy charm.

Maurice glanced at Blount and away without interest. Walsingham turned his gaze not on Maurice but on Katherine.

The Queen's eyes followed Walsingham's. The vindictiveness was still in her face. Walsingham said, "One cannot put trust even in those closest to the royal person, raised by Majesty's favor to peaks beyond their desserts."

Katherine put the needle through the cloth on her lap carefully. The small sound was loud in the silent room. Elizabeth's voice was sharp. "You seem indifferent, my girl, to strong charges."

Katherine said quietly, "I did not think, Your Majesty, that Sir Francis could possibly be speaking of me." She started to unsnarl her thread, stopped, put one hand lightly over the other so that it would not be noticed how they were trembling.

Elizabeth sneered, "Treason mighty run in a family. Let your father go on as he has been doing, and he will

177

come home to the Tower. He might well be lonesome."
How cold Elizabeth felt under her heavy robes!

Blount opened his mouth to speak, hesitated, then
struck. "But what, Your Majesty, of a man who is no
better than Babington, a man who would have rocked
England with his traitorous plots, a man who has been
convicted of treason once in his lifetime?"

Maurice read into his words that Blount was a fool
to turn against one who had been of assistance to the
Queen. He did not read into them that Blount was so
high in favor himself he dared speak openly against
Maurice and get in return no more than a mild rebuke.

Elizabeth straightened her red wig, put a hand to the
matched pearls about her throat. The necklace was a
recent gift from Blount. "If I have pardoned a man, Sir
Edward, it is with reason. So if you speak, as I would
judge, of Master Quain, I would like to remind you I
have heard enough from you against him. He has
earned my trust."

Walsingham's brows came together as he glanced at
Blount. He did not believe in allowing private ambitions and antagonisms to clog the smooth working of
the State. "The loan from Antwerp was well done. Sir
Thomas Gresham himself could not have done better
in his day."

Maurice looked at Walsingham sharply, suspecting
that he spoke well of him only to use his approbation
as a weapon. Walsingham's next words confirmed his
thought. "Master Quain has given excellent service, but
what proof have others of loyalty? A lady, for instance,
whom we have all heard speak of our glorious Queen's
greatest enemy in words of sympathy, perhaps more
than sympathy—perhaps devotion. It does not sound
well. Nor the efforts she made to get in touch with Babington—for what reason we do not know." His hostility toward the Queen of Scots tightened his dark
features.

Katherine said suavely, "Sir Francis, you speak of
me? As you know, as Her Majesty knows in her heart,
there is no one here more loyal to her who has been
my benefactress. But would not anyone with a heart
sympathize with that most unfortunate lady, the puppet

178

of Spain and the Guises?" Her dark head was a little to one side, her voice pleasant.

Blount caught his breath audibly. Men had been sent to the Tower for less. Fear, living and poignant, leaped to his eyes.

Sir Francis glanced from Blount to Katherine. "Pity, my lady, which is admirable in a woman, is not always even safe for one close to Majesty. It is particularly dangerous when it is coupled with more than sympathy—when, Lady Katherine, it is coupled with knowledge of guilt."

Patrick moved unconsciously toward Katherine, then stood rigidly alert. The air seemed full of bright pain. He could feel in himself the sickness of panic in Katherine—the same shivering terror that ran along the nerves of a hare before a fox, a fox scented by the hounds, the same shattering sense of helplessness before a strong and pitiless force because in the very nature of the world this man must be her enemy, as hare and fox and hound must forever be pursuer and pursued. His supple young body was taut as a bowstring.

Elizabeth turned her head toward Katherine. The cords of her neck stood out under her filmy ruff, and her profile was sharply etched against the stiffened upright collar of her short mantle of gold cloth. "You knew of this plot, Katherine?" Her eyes were the eyes of her father, the Eighth Henry, merciless.

Katherine rose to her feet to face her accusers. "Of what use, Madam, to deny knowledge when no one will believe my word?" Her hands were clasped loosely in front of her, and she stood tall and proud as though she were not aware how alone she was. There was not one beside her. The maids of honor had moved back. Walsingham had risen too and stood like a judge before her. Blount was beside the Queen's Secretary, afraid for her so that the veins stood out on his forehead and he wiped his right hand unconsciously up and down the left sleeve of his expensive doublet, crumpling the silver cloth. He said nothing. He did not even look at her.

179

Walsingham said briskly and impersonally, "There are ways to find out the truth."

Patrick strangled a cry in his throat. Blount turned to look at him. Patrick shivered, while one hand felt for the dagger at his belt. He didn't know what he would do, but he knew what he would not do and that was to let her go without raising a hand in her defense.

Katherine slipped a ring off and on her finger over and over again. It was the ring Ned had given her. The amethyst glowed purple against her gray velvet skirt and the diamonds made hard sharp splinters of light. Horror drenched her. In a moment, she thought, I'll be at Elizabeth's feet begging for mercy. I must not break so far. That would be as good as signing my own warrant. It would give Elizabeth exquisite pleasure to strike. She will be sorry later, unstrung with quick pity for me, but it will be too late. Sir Francis will see to that.

I thought I was here among my friends. Not one dares speak for me. Ned will fight for me when Elizabeth's anger has paled. But now I am alone. Elly, Elly, take care of Debbie for me! There is nothing I can say, only wait, and not let them know, never let them know that what hurts beyond anything they can do later is what they have done already—stripped me of every friend I thought I might turn to.

The ring slipped from her nerveless fingers to the floor, rattling in the silence. No one moved.

Walsingham, watching her, repeated, "There are ways to find out the truth. But I think with Lady Katherine we need not resort to them. Perhaps she is ready to confess her part, the part any friends of hers have taken."

The deadly excitement of the hunt was in the air. That the hunted was a woman made the atmosphere dank, as though something unclean out of the earth and dangerous for the nameless depths from which it came smirched the room with brutality.

Maurice moved back a step, wiped his hands with his handkerchief as though they had been soiled and turned to look at the speaker with chill dislike. "It is little wonder, Sir Francis, a plot climbs so close to success when the Principal Secretary of England can find nothing more profitable to do with his time than threaten gentlewomen." He put the handkerchief back into his sleeve, walked deliberately across the carpet, picked up Katherine's ring and returned it to her. He hardly glanced at her, but he stayed at her side, his tall lean figure in black Venetian velvet setting off her own white slenderness.

Elizabeth snapped, "Master Quain, you go too far!" She looked at Walsingham then, a slow fire in her green eyes.

Walsingham's hands shook with fury. "That conspiracy had never a chance of success. We, my Lord Burghley and I, have been on the trail of the plotters since they first took oath to form their association years ago."

"In short," Maurice said contemptuously, "you had more knowledge of the whole affair than you say the Lady Katherine had. You will forgive me, but it sounds like a most strange accusation and one Lady Katherine would hurl in turn at you but for her gentle breeding." He turned his back on Walsingham. "As you were saying, Your Majesty, on this Turkish problem—"

Katherine's knees gave way. She sat down on the settee from which she had risen. She whispered, "Of all men—you!"

"—if the Turkish Navy does no more than divert Spain's attention, it is worth the effort, the cost of official gifts. If their Navy does more and actually harries Spanish shipping, England can well put up with a few hard names. In a struggle for survival a good reputation is of little use to a dead man or a conquered nation."

Elizabeth looked at Maurice, cynical smile matching cynical smile. "Perhaps you're right, Master Quain. And Sir Edward who also urged this move." She gave Blount a fleeting arch glance, then turned back to Maurice. "The Turkey Company," she said graciously, "has our permission to carry out this diplomatic service in any manner it should find fitting."

There was not a word, not a hint, that it would cost

181

money. If the members of the Turkey Company wanted to help save England, let them pay for it. She was thrifty, she was downright stingy. Yet, Maurice thought, because she used every weapon at her command, husbanded each small strength of England not for her life but for her country's, there was no mean and petty action that failed to carry obversely a definite grandeur about it.

Lord Burghley spoke with a cold passion. "Madam, you do not know the risks you are taking. You are plunging into an undeclared war with the greatest empire on earth. The only outcome of such a war—I need not say it—is disaster. Spain, Austria, the Netherlands, all under the Hapsburgs. We cannot look to the King of France, who should be our natural ally against Spain because the House of Guise controls Paris at the moment. Our only hope of survival is to withdraw into ourselves, giving no offense. I have no faith in military ways."

Walsingham said, "With all respect to your judgment, my lord, there is not room in the world for Spanish idol worshipers and those of us of the true religion. The Turkish alliance can do us no harm."

"It can do us the greatest harm—precipitate us into war!" Burghley shook his head, hunched his shoulders. "I'm old and the only sane man in the kingdom."

"There is nothing," Maurice said coldly, "more unpalatable to a merchant that involving his own country in war. We see eye to eye on that. On the other hand, London will not inherit the commercial mantle of Antwerp if we are alone and defenseless against the launching of the Armada at the will, or whim, of King Philip."

"The will of King Philip," Burghley repeated thoughtfully. "That resolve can be weakened, Your Majesty, one way: the armada will not sail to put a dead queen on the throne."

Elizabeth turned to Burghley, her open hand striking the arm of her chair. "I know what you would say, my lord, I'm sick to death of your harping on it. I will not sign my cousin's death warrant. How would I appear in

182

the eyes of Europe if I should have the head of a sister queen, and she one who fled to me for protection?"

Maurice looked at Elizabeth. On his lips was the desire to say lightly and venomously that perhaps Mary Stuart had had enough of her protection. There was a time, given such an opportunity, when he would have said it. Elizabeth's gaze caught his. He could see in her at that moment the core of solitude in every person deepened and darkened by the ice-cold inescapable loneliness of a spinster queen. In that chill hard light of understanding, the arrogance, the brutal cruelties that nature and necessity forced on her seemed to be something apart from the essential woman—the woman in Elizabeth that must, when refusing to come to terms with the queen, be overridden. In that passing moment of understanding Maurice inwardly stood up and saluted her, even while he thought how hollowly rang her words "cousin" and "sister queen" and "protection."

Burghley caught up Elizabeth's last word. "Protection! The tiger seeks protection of the lion? Your Majesty, shrink from it as you will, you know, as we all know, that there can be but one queen in a kingdom. These plots and conspiracies stretch from your most faintly disaffected subject to the King of Spain. Until their source is cut off you cannot rest easily one night in your bed. You know it, Madam."

"At that," Elizabeth said ironically, "I can sleep more peacefully than you, my good Burghley. Some of my subjects love me." She looked directly at Maurice. "Is that not true, Master Quain?"

"All of your subjects who know you, Madam. Rebellion springs from ignorance."

"Ignorance? Yes. But of me or of the penalty of rebellion?" She sighed. "Let us hear no more of this 'source of conspiracies,' my lord. I will not sign the death warrant for Mary Stuart."

Burghley inclined his head. "Your word, Madam, is law. You will hear no further word from me of the dangers surrounding you. I am silent. Let your enemy live, let Mary Stuart reign in your place. We who stand beside you can but go down in blood. If we cannot

183

save you from the next assassination plot, we can have the great joy of dying with you and for you."

Maurice looked at Burghley with distaste. Burghley die for anyone but himself! Burghley, a Protestant under Elizabeth's brother, Edward the Sixth, an aide in Northumberland's attempt to put Lady Jane Grey on the throne, a deserter to Mary Tudor's side, going piously to Mass, carrying the largest rosary in England until Mary's day faded out. Burghley, the first at Elizabeth's feet, with rosary and Mass discarded and the Common Prayer Book clutched in his hands, and Catholic estates soon swelling his properties. Burghley would serve Elizabeth while Elizabeth served him, and not one hour longer! He thought with contempt that Burghley would land on his feet catlike if Philip were King of England tomorrow.

He turned his head at the sound of Blount's voice. "You have the opinions of your friends, Your Majesty, on Mary Stuart. I wonder if it would not be valuable to have the judgment of your——" He stopped as though hunting diligently for a more courtierlike word to use than "enemy" and changed the end of his sentence to "the judgment of a merchant."

Maurice smiled. For Blount that was not a badly directed blow. He glanced at Walsingham who was leaning forward lynx-eyed watching to see if Elizabeth might turn on Maurice or with equal readiness on Blount. Elizabeth did neither. She laughed. "You do not like your old neighbor, Sir Edward?" It was the first time she had shown she remembered their relationship. Her voice was neutral, giving no hint how she might feel.

Edward Blount bowed his head slightly, then looked up with a charming smile. "Your Majesty, it is only that I am jealous of the life and good health of the most admired princess in Europe, my Sovereign Queen."

Elizabeth said sharply, "No dross in the gold of your love for me?" She glanced back.

For one moment Blount was tempted to reject Katherine. Instead he turned the opportunity to account. "None. Could I care for anyone who served near you if

184

that one were sullied by the least breath of treason? No, Your Majesty. Just as I fear to trust as yet one who has been so sullied."

Elizabeth's fingers tapped relentlessly on the chair arm. "I am not completely satisfied there," she murmured, a trace of vengefulness still in her voice as she thought of Katherine. She turned her gaze on Maurice. He knew the weight of a feather either way could decide his future now, his very life. "My loyal servants Master Quain, urge me to a deed I shrink from. What is your advice?"

Every twist and turn a man could make, the despising of old loyalties, contempt for lost causes—he had been guilty of all, if it were guilt and not wisdom. With a word he could accomplish his final ultimate rejection. It would make no difference in Mary Stuart's fate, which was probably as good as sealed already. Policy bade him say unequivocally that if Elizabeth would reign unfettered, her rival, powerful in her very helplessness, a pawn ready for the hand of any invader, must be put out of the way. The very forces of nature demanded it. Such a statement would silence Blount would silence Walsingham. But never—and now he realized why he was searching so desperately for just the right words—would it put a quietus on Katherine's unspoken condemnation of an easy betrayal of himself. If Katherine prevented him from betraying his past, he had equally no intention of betraying his future.

He said smoothly, "Your Majesty, what does a merchant know of statecraft? A loan in Antwerp, investment in Europe or the East—in such matters I am honored to serve you. But what would I know of policy?"

Blount trapped out, "You had enough to say on a Turkish alliance."

Maurice said contemptuously, "So I did, Sir Edward. The Turkish alliance has some small bearing on my commercial transactions. The domestic situation has not. To be brief, I gave up politics some time back."

Blount looked at Elizabeth, waiting for her to take up that gage. Elizabeth veered again. "As you would

185

point out, your deeds have spoken loudly enough for you, Master Quain. Let them continue to do so."

Walsingham said softly, "There is another here whose loyalty has been questioned."

Elizabeth said, "Yes. Maybe, my girl—" she spoke directly to Katherine—"you would do well to see your friend in his last moments. An excellent lesson."

"Yes, Your Majesty." Katherine's face was paper-white.

Maurice looked at Blount for a word from him. Blount's eyes were on Walsingham, then swerved to the open window framing the topmost branches of oak and beech trees and the high clouds drifting across the sky. Maurice stepped back from Katherine. The girl's mouth trembled. He said, "If you have no better escort, Lady Katherine, I'm at your command."

The tavern host said, "I'm sorry, sir, madam, but the best windows in the inn are gone. They were taken days ago and paid for in advance. It isn't every day, my lady—" he turned to Katherine—"that one sees a young gentleman hang for treason. The mob's out for blood."

There was a distant sound like the humming of a giant bee, the shrillness of a woman's voice, the deep growling undertone of a restless crowd. "And they'll get it," the host added. "There will be a fine execution. All the galleries around the scaffold are sold. A devilish villain. May all traitors to the Queen come to the same end!" He finished on a sonorous note, wiped his hands on his soiled apron and shook his head sadly. "I'm sorry not to put you up, sir. I am indeed. But the road is all that's left, though I'm feared your ladyship will be sorely crumpled there."

Maurice waited coldly for the landlord to finish, then repeated his request for an upper room for the party of four, Katherine and her waiting woman, himself and Patrick. "But I told you, sir——" Patrick drew out two gold pieces. The host did not complete his refusal. "Well, perhaps . . . yes, I will find you a place, sir."

"And without a dozen fools idling around us."

The landlord lifted his shoulders resignedly, sent two

servingmen flying upstairs, and a few minutes later ushered Maurice into a small room that was being rapidly cleared of empty tankards, the remains from recent occupants. Maurice turned to look at Katherine. Her face was pale above the wine-red riding habit she wore, paler than the falling band at her throat, and her dark eyes were wide with a touch of panic. Her glance darted about the room as though this were a prison cell that she feared to enter.

Maurice said, "Why do you go through with this, Lady Katherine? We'll stay long enough for you to refresh yourself and then leave."

Katherine whispered, "No. You are most kind to come with me, Master Quain. But if I were to go now, the Queen would know and be angry. Besides I owe it to Anthony Babington. I could not give him warning in time. The ports were closed when he tried to get a passport. Perhaps the fault was not mine, but I'll always feel that maybe if I'd tried harder——" Her voice thinned and broke. "I owe him this. You do not. You have already——" She turned her head away. "You have done far more for me than I can repay. I wonder why."

Maurice said, "I rather wonder myself, my dear. It is not a weakness, however, that is apt to become a habit."

"Ned didn't like it."

Maurice said indifferently, "Blount? Didn't he?"

A breeze blew capriciously through the window, stirring the tendrils of dark hair about her face. She tucked the loose curls back absently under the small arched velvet hood that made her face heart-shaped.

The growling of the mob had been so steady it had hardly been noticed in the last few minutes. Now there was a nervous rustle outside, a heightening of tension, so that every breath of emotion twanged discordantly on the crowd like a touch on the overstrained strings of a lute.

Patrick moved toward Katherine protectingly. She looked at him over her shoulder and smiled faintly, appealingly. He put out his hand to touch hers in quick

187

sympathy. Her fingers closed on his, and her clinging to his was headier than wine, sweeter than musk.

Even here within the inn one could sense the surging of the crowd. The prisoners were coming. The shouts of the guard rose in staccato above the growling, demanding a path for the victims drawn behind them on a hurdle. Maurice turned to the window, flinched from the crowd's atavistic roar of fury as the condemned men came into sight. He could see over the mass of heads the opening wedge the guards were making for the grim procession. Mounted men were on either side of the hurdles on which the prisoners were drawn, watching keenly, ready hands on pikes, for any sign of an outbreak. But against that immense wave of blind hatred any sympathizer would have been trampled to death or torn apart.

Two figures were on the hurdles, broken hulks, caricatures of manhood. Which one of those ragged and broken bodies was Master Anthony Babington, once young and fashionable and reckless? The crowd parted grudgingly for the prisoners, closed in again behind them like beasts padding after the prey.

Maurice looked down. "An unpleasant sight, mankind en masse." For one fleeting moment he remembered another crowd—a rabble that had been an army fleeing before the victorious royal troops. His heart contracted at the memory of the blind panic, the sobbing for breath, hares run to earth by hounds. Beast of prey or cowering victim, for each one of them Christ had died—if after seeing a mob one could believe in Christ! The unexpected thought of Christ's sacrifice shivered through him.

The first prisoner was helped by the guards up to the scaffold. The muffled roar, the unleashed bellow of hate subsided with an unwilling ferocity as a guardsman stood forth to cry out the penalty proclaimed against the prisoners.

"The awful sentence that the law has pronounced against your crime is that each one of you should be taken to the place from whence you came and thence you were to be drawn on hurdles to this place of execution where you are to be hanged by the neck, but not until you are dead. While you are still living your bodies are to be taken down, your bowels torn out and burned before your faces, your heads are to be cut off and your bodies divided each into four quarters, and your head and quarters to be then at the Queen's disposal, and may the Almighty God have mercy on your souls!"

Anthony Babington was given his last chance to speak. His words, faint and broken, did not reach so far as Maurice. Then the noose was slipped over Babington's head, tightened about his neck. His body swung for one moment in the air. He was cut down. This prisoner was not to die too soon. There was a terrible thick silence. The planks in the galleries creaked as every man and woman strained forward to watch. The hangman's knife plunged slowly into flesh. The prisoner's bloody entrails were in his hands, the heart plucked out of the body. Through that scarlet mist of quiet, the man who should have been dead cried out in a voice not of the earth, out of some hell of agony, "Jesus! Jesus! Jesus!"

The words were not loud, but the shrill thin tones seemed as though they would spread across all England. The entrails were thrown into the waiting fire. The acrid smell scorched the nostrils, caught in the throat. The blade swung again. The limbs were thrown into boiling water, the severed head was held high.

A sigh went up from the crowd, long-drawn and piercing.

"So die all traitors to the Queen!"

A roar answered the guardsman. The other conspirator was thrust forward, the noose drawn tight about his neck. The line twisted and grew taut before it was cut; the victim was secured while the blade slashed into skin. Blood spurted out, trickled down the prisoner's leg, lay in a pool on the planks of the scaffoled. The entrails were drawn, the limbs struck off.

Now the yells were only an echo of the earlier savagery. Its thirst for blood satiated, the beast was ready to slink back to its den until it grew restless and cruel again. It was breaking apart, back into men again, except for those who pushed up to the scaffold to wet handkerchiefs or rags with blood to sell to the curious.

Maurice looked out with cold eyes. No matter how they had suffered, they were dead men now. And they had had something they'd thought was worth living for and dying for, though he had heard Babington had not stood up well under examination, while the friends he had drawn into the net had shown an unwavering loyalty to one another.

He turned sharply from the window, the abrupt movement oddly forceful in the too-quiet room. Mattie was standing to one side, completely indifferent to the spectacle, neither the fierce huntress nor the pitying woman. Katherine's face was so white it seemed blood would never warm her cheeks again. She said, "Are they . . . are they . . ." She gave it up. Her dark eyes were wide with horror and her skin was taut. It gave her a look of fragile somberness, a fine-drawn nervous grief.

Maurice said, "We are done here, Lady Katherine. Will you have a glass of wine before we escort you home?"

Katherine looked at him, her mouth twisted in an effort to keep her lips steady. "Home? No, thank you. I will return to Hampton alone. You have been kind, and I cannot trespass further on your good will."

Maurice bowed, glanced toward Patrick. "My secretary will insist on accompanying you, Lady Katherine. If I should not see you again, my best wishes for your future!"

Katherine's hand went to her throat. "Not see you again, Master Quain? You are going away?"

He inclined his head. He did not want to talk to her. Her provocative and troubling beauty somehow brought out in bitter tragic relief the image of young Anthony Babington swaggering into his apartment that evening long ago. And his quartered body was now not two hundred feet away.

Katherine said, "Then I must bid you Godspeed on your journey, Master Quain. You go, I'll swear, to Constantinople."

"Yes."

"It would be ridiculous to try to thank you. May I hope instead that the East brings to you all that you desire?" She curtsied to him deeply, her red skirt dipping in soft folds to the floor.

Maurice said, "Thank you," coldly and looked at Patrick, waiting for him to take this wench and go. Maurice watched them leave, then glanced about him at the empty room. How quiet it was! Outside the mob had thinned out. The raucous cries, a voice raised in anger, the sound of a blow, drifted through the open window. There was the feel of autumn in the air today, a tang in the wind, but in his nostrils was only the odor of dead flesh.

Jacques opened the door of the apartment for him. "You have a visitor, monsoor. Do you want to see him? He gives his name as Sir Edward Blount. He's in the anteroom."

Maurice handed Jacques his hat and gauntlets. "Bid him in."

Blount entered, a gay figure in crimson doublet, sewn with seed pearls, sleeves puffed and slashed. and at his throat a falling band embroidered with silver. "Good day, Maurice."

Maurice's brows lifted. Even three thousand pounds wouldn't last long if Blount bought a new suit for every day of the year. He must have invested a large share of the money in gifts for the Queen, to judge by his rising status at Court.

Blount smiled agreeably, ignoring Maurice's lack of response. "You're perhaps surprised to see me here, Maurice?"

"Not at all, Sir Edward." He sat down, waving to Blount to do the same. "I have a few minutes to spare you." He glanced up at the silver clock on the wall.

"I came to see you, Maurice, about your journey to Constantinople. You leave—when?"

Maurice did not trouble to answer a question he considered impertinent. "You had business with me?"

Blount crossed his legs, said irrelevantly, "You saw

191

Babington executed today? But of course. I heard he shrieked 'Jesus' three times when his heart was in the hangman's hands. Rather interesting, wasn't it?"

"I didn't hear him. You had business?"

"Ah, yes, I did, Maurice. It concerns Constantinople." He lifted his eyes to Maurice's. "Her Majesty has done me the inestimable honor of suggesting that I accompany you to Turkey with letters to Sultan Amurath. For one of no ranking like you to bear the royal greetings and offer of an alliance would be to court rebuff before we were heard. Since you are traveling east, it seems better that we go together." He smiled again.

Maurice felt as though he'd received a violent blow under his ribs, but his face remained expressionless except for the look of slightly bored interest. "That would be a matter I would have to take up with the Turkey Company, Sir Edward. They will have no objections, I am sure, but Osborne must confirm your passage, since Her Majesty intends no doubt the Company to pay all expenses."

Blount shrugged. "I would not know the business details. You plan to leave soon?"

"I plan to sail at my convenience, Sir Edward. Should you be in haste, there is a shipment leaving London for Turkey in about a week's time."

"You do not accompany it, Maurice?"

"No."

Blount murmured, "It was Sir Francis Walsingham's suggestion that I go with you. The Queen agreed."

Maurice began to understand the antipathy of the merchants of London to having the Court's finger in any commercial pie. He stood up in dismissal. "I will send you word, Sir Edward, of the time of my departure."

Blount rose reluctantly. He had been enjoying himself. "I am sure it will be a delightful experience." He bowed slightly to Maurice, took the narrow-brimmed, high-crowned hat that Jacques had brought him, and gave the final thrust. "You will hear from Sir Francis when we are to sail. Your servant, sir!"

At the open door he turned suddenly and walked

back to Maurice, who was still standing beside his chair. "I forgot one small matter. It was . . . ah . . . kind of you to speak for Lady Katherine to the Queen the other day. It was also of course quite unnecessary. May I hope that in the future you do not concern yourself with the fortunes of my mistress?"

"Hope, Sir Edward? Why not? That's one of the few privileges Parliament has left us. Though no doubt, like faith and charity, it will also be taxed when a way has been found to put a collectible price on the virtue."

Blount's face matched his crimson doublet. "I will be more blunt, Maurice. I am warning you to stay away from Katherine Perrot."

"If you insist on being so wearisome every time we meet, Sir Edward, I'll have to beg Her Majesty to permit us to sail separately. One can be expected to suffer only so much in the service of one's country. Good day!" He turned. "Jacques!"

"Yes, monsoor?"

Blount repeated lamely, "I have warned you, Maurice." He clapped his hat on his head and swaggered out.

Maurice did not hear him. "Were there any dispatches today, Jacques?"

"Yes, monsoor. A letter from Master Bowyer. It is here on the table."

Maurice picked it up, broke the seal. It was a brief note concerning the property Maurice held as collateral from Bernardino de Mendoza, the former Spanish ambassador, for a shipment of supplies to Madrid. As the doors of the Spanish embassy were closed behind him, Mendoza having been involved in one too many plots against Elizabeth, the Spaniard had preferred to give up to Maurice the manor house in Sussex rather than make payment.

Bowyer wished to know if Maurice wanted to keep the property for his own use or preferred to sell it. Maurice tossed the paper to one side. What would he do with a manor house in Sussex? He had a home in Blyth. Still, he rather liked the thought. Perhaps he'd keep it for the time being. He was wealthy enough to

193

indulge some of his whims. If there was a picture in his heart of a black-haired wench at an open doorway, it was so obscure he need neither acknowledge nor shut it away.

Part III

THE SHADOW OF ALLAH

11

Mary Howard, the Queen's diminutive maid of honor, opened the drawer of the small writing desk with its ivory and gold inlaid top and pulled out a pack of cards. "Her Majesty would be alone with her Christopher, girls. I've a new game I learned from Tom last night to pass the time."

Bess Throckmorton looked up. She drawled, "Not to pass the time last night, Molly?" She eyed her fingernails critically.

Mary smiled mischievously. "We don't all have a Walter Raleigh who will found colonies in a New World, plant potatoes and tobacco one day, write love sonnets the next, go out privateering the third, suffer the Queen's frown the fourth, and love us in his idle moments between. We must take the dull men who are left."

Katherine laughed, ruffled the cards absently. "Show us the game, Molly. We'll probably have to wait until midnight." She yawned, put her hands about her slim waist, arched her back. "Doesn't Her Majesty ever get tired? She's worse than Raleigh. What he does in a week, she crowds into a day. Hunt in the morning, meet with the Lords of the Council all afternoon, the French ambassador at dinner and now Sir Christopher Hatton importuning her for God knows what—probably the Lord Chancellorship."

Bess stretched her slender body with a feline grace. "If Sir Christopher begged me as he petitions the Queen, well, I'd never say him nay." She made a moue. Raleigh was out of favor with the Queen at the moment and forbidden the Court. Elizabeth Tudor had heard repeated Raleigh's scandalous hints that the lovers of the Queen were forced to shameful tricks and devices to give her pleasure. The remark made at the end of a night of drinking started again the old questions and rumors that had kept the Court gossiping for almost twoscore years, since Elizabeth was a girl in her teens. Was the Virgin Queen so made she could not bear a child? Raleigh, Bess thought, under his brilliant glitter was really rather stupid. She intended, however, to marry him when his mind came out of his fanciful clouds long enough. She'd see he kept out of trouble then.

Mary Howard swept up the cards with her small jeweled hands, dealt around, turning up the king, queen, chevalier and valet. Katherine only half listened to the explanation of the play. The warmth and lights made her pleasantly sleepy, so relaxed her body seemed to be dissolving and floating off into space. Both young women called to her to play. She drew the unnumbered card, the fou, took another.

The square pieces of painted vellum cut into her flesh as she started at the opening of the door. She looked up. It was the Viscountess Rochford, a large amiable woman. She was panting for breath from her haste. "Oh, there you are, Katherine!" She sank down on a chair, waving a plump hand in front of her for air. "I have been looking all over for you, my dear."

Katherine pretended to study the cards in her hand before she lifted her eyes again to the viscountess. "Nothing serious, I hope, Lady Rochford?" The viscountess could be equally in a turmoil over the loss of a pair of gloves or the desertion of a husband. Katherine felt a sickness of suspense rising in her, and her tired body seemed pricked with a thousand needles of pain. She was always overwary of late, she scoffed to herself.

The viscountess, breathing normally now, crossed to the settee, sat down beside Katherine and took her hand. "My dear child, I'm sorry to be the one to tell you, but Her Majesty——"

Mary Howard and Bess Throckmorton dropped the cards onto the table with a clatter. Mary said, "Merciful God, Lady Rochford, tell us what the trouble is!"

Lady Rochford said soothingly, "Nothing so very bad. Nothing time will not mend. Her Majesty commanded me to tell you, my dear, that you are to leave Court."

Bess laughed. "Well, I see my Raleigh is not the only one to lose favor."

Mary said, "Ah, Kit, it's a shame! We'll all miss you. The Queen's anger never lasts long, though, and she'll be asking for you soon again."

Katherine rose unsteadily to her feet, but she forced a smile to her mouth. "Thank you, Molly. Her Majesty will not see me, Lady Rochford?"

"No, my dear."

Katherine remembered the cold way Elizabeth had looked at her tonight, but she'd thought it was only that the Queen was tired or out of humor. She slid out from behind the table, shook out the heavy folds of her skirts and shrugged. "We all have our share of ill luck. I'll learn your game, Molly, when I come back." She bowed to Lady Rochford. "You were kind, madam."

She went out of the lighted chamber into the half-darkness of the room beyond, past the guard, up the stairs and through the narrow shadowy corridor. She walked slowly with an easy lithe grace. In her own room she would not be able to hold off longer the naked fear that was all about her. Elizabeth had dismissed her. That had been Walsingham's doing. While Maurice had turned the Queen's anger at its height so that she was not arrested, she should have known Walsingham would not stop there.

Would he move further against her? No. She'd be sent for again probably. She wasn't the first or the last maid of honor to lose favor. Where would she go now? Her father Sir John Perrot was in Ireland. Though at best he was not a staff to lean on, his presence here might have helped her. Never would she let Debbie be so alone as she herself was now. She began to run. She pressed the back of her hand against her mouth to hold back a sob. The door to her room was locked. She pounded on it.

Mattie opened it sleepily, peered at her. "It's you, mistress? I thought you were to sleep in the Queen's

197

apartments tonight." She stood back to let Katherine
enter. The candle she carried in her hand lighted up
her face in an odd chiaroscuro.

"Mattie, oh, Mattie!" Katherine wiped the tears
from her eyes with the tips of her fingers. "Have the
page find Ned for me. I must see him now."

"Mistress, you're mad! Go running through the
palace for a man at this hour. Impossible! Have him
seen coming to your door—"

Katherine pushed Mattie toward the entrance. "You
heard me, Mattie. I want him. Now."

"Very well, mistress. You will have your way. But
your willfulness will ruin you." She went out angrily.

Katherine twisted her hands together, walked up and
down the floor from wall to bed, from bed to window,
back again. She put her knuckles against her teeth as
though physical pain could dull her anguish. This won't
do, she thought. I must be calm. I'll be all right when
Ned comes. He'll know what's to be done. When others of the Queen's ladies are dismissed they have some
place to go, but I—Pity of God!

There was a quick knock, Ned's signal. The latch
was lifted. Katherine went across the room to him.
"Oh, Ned, I need you." She put her face against his
padded silken shoulder.

Blount's hand ruffled her hair. He stepped back.
lifted her head with a finger under her chin. "Whatever
is the matter, sweetheart?"

He looked so handsome and confident standing there
that she smiled shakily. "It's all right, Ned, Now you're
here."

"But what—? Kit, you look ill."

She put her hand in his to feel his comforting
warmth and strength. "Ned, the Queen has bidden me
leave Court."

Blount stepped back from her. "No! Kit, you would
not jest with me? But darling, that's—— What will you
do?"

His words sent a shiver through her. She whispered,
"I hoped you could tell me that. I can't think. Oh,
Ned!"

"But why? What have you done to anger Her

198

Majesty? Kit, I've warned you a thousand times to be more discreet."

"It's a little late for a warning now, Ned! There's little Debbie too. What shall I do?"

"We'll think of something, sweetheart. Only, why did it have to happen now? I'm leaving the country soon."

"No!"

There was a touch of impatience in his voice. "Of all times for you to be out of favor, Kit! I didn't tell you before, and you must say nothing of it. I'm being sent to the Sultan with messages from Her Majesty."

"Oh, Ned, that's why I'm being dismissed, so that I'll have no friend at Court who would dare to remind Her Majesty of me." She lifted her head slowly. "Would you dare, Ned?"

"Of course, of course. When I return—but you'll be all right by then. Only naturally it would be madness for me to petition Her Majesty's clemency now. After all, Kit, you know as well as I that if you had rejected Babington's first appeal to you, gone with it directly to Sir Francis, you would not be in this awkward position."

Katherine caught her lower lip in her teeth, wiped the blood from her mouth absently. "With you gone, I wouldn't dare stay alone in England. Ned, my mother's people are in France at Limoges. Perhaps they'd take me in. I don't know. They sent word to me once long ago to come to them. If I could only get Debbie there! They wouldn't refuse to help a child. Ned, could you stop at a French port on your way to the East?"

Blount stared at her. "My dear girl, do you know what you're suggesting? That the Queen's agent smuggle you out of England. We're crossing France to take ship at Marseille, I'm told, but I wouldn't dare take you with me. It's selfish of you even to mention it."

"Perhaps it is, I can't seem to think of anyone but Debbie. If anything happened to me—— Ned, could you get me a passport from Sir Francis? I'll manage the passage somehow if you can just get us leave out of the country."

Blount tried not to show his annoyance, though his pale-blue eyes narrowed. "No, sweetheart, you know I can't. There isn't a possibility of your getting a passport. Sir Francis would refuse, and he'd be right when every friend of Mary Stuart is making a desperate effort to save her. He'd think you were going to Paris or Madrid to carry information to the conspirators there. You'll be all right in England, dear. Sir Francis feels that until the Queen of Scots' trial is completed and the death warrant finally signed, he cannot have Stuart sympathizers about Her Majesty. That's all. Women are so damned unreasonable."

Katherine turned away from him, her hands beating together softly. "I know, I know. Only I'm afraid to stay here if you're gone. How will we live?"

He laughed pleasantly. "There, darling, I can help you. As you know, my fortunes have taken a better turn of late, and while this embassy of mine will be a little expensive, I'll bring you fifty pounds in the morning."

"Ned, can you afford that? It's too much."

"Not at all, dear. You're smiling a little now, Kit. You'll be quite all right."

She nodded. But she hadn't smiled because of the money. Fifty pounds would stretch far, but it would not last if Ned were gone long. The smile had been sheer and heady relief that he intended to help her. The sickness of his refusal to aid her to France had been for one instant unbearable, the feeling that he too was deserting her.

He said, "I'll be here in the morning, Kit. I have to leave you now. We—Phillipps, you know, Sir Francis' secretary and I—were just discussing this journey. I can't tell you more about it except that I travel with the Turkey Company officials who are bringing a shipment to Constantinople. One of them is your friend Quain." He laughed lightly to show her how little he cared for Maurice Quain's rivalry. He need not worry tonight over Katherine's thoughts straying toward another lover. He bent his fair head, kissed her on the mouth.

Katherine said, "You are sweet to me, Ned," and
200

smiled at him as he left with a brisk and businesslike step. She was unreasonable. She had expected more of him.

Mattie was packing her gowns in the morning when Blount came. He said abruptly, "Kit, perhaps you were right last night. You should leave England for a while."

Katherine, who was washing her hands in a pewter basin, turned to him. The water spattered from her fingers onto the floor until Mattie caught up a towel and brought it to her. "You said it was impossible."

"Yes. Only last night Phillipps said Sir Francis would find you lodgings." They stared at each other across the room, both remembering that Anthony Babington, when he had been attempting to get a passport to France, had been offered lodgings at Walsingham's home. All Blount's love was in his eyes as he looked at the girl, slim and fragile in a white satin night rail that hung straight and childlike from her shoulders to the floor. "I thought of a way it might be managed."

She crossed to him, her loosened hair a soft cloud about her shoulders. "For Debbie too?"

"Well——" He made an impatient gesture with his hand. "Perhaps. I could not smuggle you aboard the *Judith,* the ship I sail on to Bordeaux, but as I mentioned last night, Maurice Quain also is going on this convoy. Only he's sailing in his own vessel which he—" Blount flushed angrily—"declares cannot accommodate me. He says we'll meet later in the journey. While I'm supposed to accompany him, it hardly seemed worth a quarrel for so short a distance. So, my dear, if he sails alone, I thought—well, he's so full of chivalrous desires to help you, let him aid you again."

Katherine looked at Blount, a little frown between her brows. "I couldn't ask him, Ned. He helped me once. It would be a strange way to show gratitude to ask him to endanger himself by trying to get me out of the country without a passport. No."

"He wouldn't be in any danger. There will be others aboard the *Judith* who would know you, but he'll be sailing with only his own attendants and crew. He would have nothing to fear."

201

"I couldn't, Ned. He has done too much for me already. I couldn't ask him."

"You were hot enough to get yourself and your brat out of the country when it was just my skin at stake. Now it's Maurice Quain's, oh, no! Well, do as you like."

Katherine thought of Debbie, the tiny hands, her sparkle, the soft golden curls and sweet rounded face. "Oh, Ned I don't know."

"What's the name of Maurice's secretary, Kit? Do you know the man I mean? He was at Hampton the day I had audience with Her Majesty, and he was looking at you in a way I cannot say I liked. Yet we might find him useful."

"Patrick North. But I cannot see—"

"Never mind that. Only tell me—if I get you passage on Maurice Quain's ship, will you sail?"

Katherine laughed, though she'd thought she would never laugh again. "Ned, if you can persuade Master Quain to take me to France, I'll certainly accept. He'll refuse." Her face whitened. She wasn't laughing now. "I'll be at Stepney, Ned."

Blount grimaced. He didn't like to think of Katherine there. Their affair would have more dignity if she had, if not a wealthy, at least a more genteel background. He felt a momentary impatience with her, but he said kindly, "Well, make yourself ready, because we'll get you safely to your kinsmen in France, sweetheart."

Blount didn't go to Maurice. He ordered a private dining room at the Saracen's Head and sent for Patrick. Patrick's expression of faint surprise deepened to hostility when he saw who had summoned him. Blount smiled. "Come in, Master North." He sat at the side of the table, hat and gloves beside his tall goblet of silver and glass.

Patrick went slowly into the room. Copper plates on a shelf about the wall winked in the gray light. "You wanted to see me, Sir Edward?"

Blount nodded agreeably. He did not, however, suggest that Patrick be seated or offer him wine. "Yes, my good man." He changed his tone slightly as Patrick eyed him. "I did not want to trouble Master Quain—Maurice. I thought I'd mention the business to you and you can tell him or not as you like. It concerns a friend of mine and Maurice's." He twirled his goblet in his fingers. "The Lady Katherine Perrot."

Patrick's hostility changed to astonishment. "Lady Katherine! She's not in any danger?"

Blount put his hands together, leaned forward, his face grave. "She is in great danger. The only man who can help her is Maurice. He came to her aid once. I was most grateful, as I've told him." His eyes flickered away from Patrick's for a moment. No, Maurice was not apt to have repeated that or any other personal conversation to his secretary. He repeated firmly, "I have told him how grateful we were."

Patrick brushed Blount's gratitude aside. "What trouble is she in?"

"She was dismissed last night from Court. That may mean Her Majesty was annoyed and wishes to show her displeasure and will recall her when she feels a lesson has been learned. But I fear that Sir Francis has further evidence of her connection with Babington and that she's being removed for some serious reason. I don't know. In any case, she is fearful. As you may have heard, I'm leaving for Constantinople when you do. She will be friendless here and would like to go to her mother's family in Limoges. In the circumstances, she will never be able to get a passport out of the country."

"You are suggesting, Sir Edward, she go with you as far as France?"

"To take her with me is of course what I would most like to do, what my heart urges me to do. But for me to smuggle a woman on board a strange ship—well, Lady Katherine would be far worse off if she were found trying to leave without a passport than if she stayed here. Maurice, I understand, is sailing on his own ship."

Patrick said eagerly, "You think she'd sail with us?"

Blount suppressed his smile. "I'm sure she would be in your debt forever, Master North. I understand the convoy is to meet at Bordeaux, then go overland to Marseille to take a galley across the Mediterranean."

"Yes."

"A simple matter, as you can see. From Bordeaux Lady Katherine can be sent with attendants to Limoges while we go on."

Patrick thought of sailing down the Thames to the Channel and out into the Atlantic with Katherine beside him at the rail of the ship. For that little time she would not be the great Court lady but a young woman who needed him. "I'll speak to Master Quain, Sir Edward. He'll be delighted to be of service."

Blount drained off his wine, came to his feet. "Good! I see I came to the right man." He put on his hat, pulled on his soft leather gloves as he went out the door that Patrick held open for him. "You can send me word of arrangements at Whitehall."

Maurice was not delighted. Patrick had waited until the younger Bowyer and two clerks from his house had finished their business with Maurice and left staggering under armloads of documents, ledgers and instructions for the first shares of the Eastern Company. Maurice's moment of unguarded pleasure was shattered. He turned to stare coldly at his secretary. "I'm sure I do not understand you correctly, Patrick. You suggest we take Katherine Perrot to France with us?"

"She's in trouble. How else can she get out of the country?"

"Patrick, I don't know whether Lady Katherine should leave England, and I don't care if she does. It's not our affair. Where are those dispatches from Blyth? This sending of Blount to Constantinople is the devil's own luck. The shipment for the Turkey Company is delayed until we can make ready, and we have to hurry our preparations. I wanted to go up to Blyth before we leave. Roberts seems to be doing well enough there, but I preferred to see for myself. Thank you." Patrick had searched through the neat piles of papers on the table and brought out the one Maurice had asked for.

"With a good wind, it wouldn't take us above two days to get to Bordeaux. It's so small a favor, and a woman's life, Katherine's—Lady Katherine's—is hanging in the balance."

Maurice said, "Let's hear no more about it, Patrick." He looked around at the furnishings in the apartment. "We'll have to store these or—" He smiled lightly. "I now have a house in Sussex. Perhaps I'll have Bowyer ship them down there." It pleased him to think of owning a manor which he had never seen.

Patrick mentally consigned the furniture to hell and said, "You cannot refuse her."

"If I hear more about it, you can stay in London to comfort the lady. In the meantime should you be able to keep your thoughts on the business of the day long enough, will you write out a letter to Roberts?"

Patrick looked at Maurice with opaque eyes while his young face hardened. The first quill broke under his fingers. He tossed it aside and picked up another. He thought of Babington's execution. Maurice's chill voice flowed on, while Patrick's mind raced ahead, overriding the sense of disloyalty that was heavy within him.

Blount detached himself from the group of courtiers bowling on the green in St. James's Park when a page came up to announce Patrick. A mature elegant figure even against those birds of paradise, Patrick noted absently.

"As I told you, I'll be pleased to be of service to Lady Katherine."

Blount frowned, not liking Patrick's tone. "Yesterday you sais it was Maurice who would be pleased."

"Yesterday, Sir Edward, I was as precipitate as you. On second thought I can see no reason at all for involving Master Quain in an affair that does not concern him."

Blount's eyes widened in dismay. "We must help Katherine! There's no other way. Would I ask for so great a favor if I had anywhere else to turn?"

Patrick snapped, "Yes. This situation couldn't fit you better if ordered from your tailor. Should Katherine be smuggled out, the success is to your liking. If she's discovered, you think the guilt will be on Quain's shoulders."

Blount started to snarl, "You grow insol——" He stopped. "You said you would be of service."

"I will put Lady Katherine aboard the *Falcon* at dawn Thursday. We sail on the evening tide. It's unfortunate she'll have to stay in the cabin for the day while the ship lies at anchor, but there'll be too many people around later. Would you ask her to be at the Unicorn? If Lady Katherine is the reason for my making a fool of myself, Sir Edward, she's also my safeguard. You aren't likely to betray her."

Blount said petulantly, "I don't like this. If Maurice should find she's on board—I don't like it. I'd prefer you had his consent."

Patrick said grimly, "Would you? Get it then."

"Perhaps you know best, Master North." Blount's smile was strained. "Kit will be at the Unicorn. We're both in your debt for your assistance." He turned away.

"One more thing, Sir Edward."

Blount swung back indifferently at Patrick's words. "Yes?"

"If anything should go amiss, the responsibility of this affair is mine. Don't try to throw the brunt of any failure on Master Quain."

Blount laughed. Patrick went on levelly. "I don't know what happened at Le Grand Andely last year, Sir Edward. But I do know it cost us three thousand pounds to get passage through you to London. As we had just raised a royal loan, Her Majesty might inquire further into the matter if I found it necessary to bring it to her attention."

Blount stood looking at Patrick for an instant. His expression was murderous. Prudence stopped the words on his tongue.

Maurice stood on the quay at Billingsgate as the last bales and boxes were swung aboard the *Falcon* before she was warped out into the river. The tide was running up the Thames, freeing the keel that had sunk into the mud, and bringing with it the oppressive penetrating stench of London tidewater. The hurrying ripples slapped lightly against the sides of the *Falcon*. The curses of sweating crews were mingled with the creak of the boom and the squeal of the line in the block, as a huge bale of wool was lifted laboriously from the dock.

Patrick rolled up the paper in his hand, said, "That's all, Master Quain. When the rest of this wool is loaded, you'll be ready to sail."

"Good! Tell the customs man, the one standing near the water cask, that he can go aboard now."

Patrick swung about to face Maurice unbelieving. "On board? Why?"

Maurice shrugged. "You know some of these men and their petty officialism. They like to search every ship before it leaves port. What's the trouble?"

Patrick shook his head and went toward the customs man.

It had not been too difficult to get Katherine past Captain Fox this morning. After the captain's first shock of surprise at having a woman aboard he'd laughed at Maurice's infatuation, tried to get a glimpse of Katherine's face under her mask, straightened his lace collar, smoothed his black beard and let her have the master's quarters with fair grace. No, that hadn't been so bad, though it had taken awhile to convince Fox that Maurice did not want to discuss the woman with anyone. Fox had said, "Quain has queer ways and that's the truth. You're sure she isn't your light o'love?"

Patrick said boldly he wished she were, and the captain had dropped the matter. If anyone knew Maurice's wishes, Patrick was the man. No, that had not been so bad. But when a child had been lifted onto the deck, the captain's mouth dropped open so far one could see the stumps of all his teeth. Patrick thought how the captain felt wasn't a shadow of his own sensations! If he lived to be a hundred years old Patrick knew he would never forget the moment when he'd seen Katherine waiting for him with a little girl, hardly more than a baby, clinging to her skirts. He'd been sick down to his boots.

Captain Fox had grimaced. "All right. If Quain says so." He'd looked again at the child as though she were some curious fish just hauled out of the sea. "All right. But if the crew makes trouble, they'll both be put off at the first port we touch."

"They're just going to France, Captain."

"France?" Fox's eyes opened. "France?"

"Of course. Bordeaux. Where we meet with the *Judith* and the *Enterprise.*"

"Ah, yes, of course, Bordeaux." But Fox had given Patrick an odd look.

Patrick stopped in front of the customs man. "You can go aboard now, sir. The shipment is complete." He followed the official up the planks to the main deck of the *Falcon,* ignoring Maurice's call.

The official lowered himself clumsily down the rope ladder into the hold, went rapidly over the cargo, glanced through the forecastle and then turned his attention aft, clambering up the half deck and stooping to enter the captain's quarters under the poop. Going below he moved through the main cabin with lowered head to avoid the half-deck beams, opened the door to the small starboard cabin littered with Fox's trunks and effects.

He turned to the master's cabin. "No passengers, Captain, except this—what's his name?—Quain and his immediate attendants?"

Fox had his mouth open to answer. Patrick's heel came down hard on his toes. Fox yelped. Patrick said, "Your pardon, Captain, for my awkwardness." He turned to the official. "No one except my wife and daughter. They're in here. My wife has been very ill, sir, and her physician ordered a sea trip for her."

Captain Fox gulped. "Yes, yes, she—Mistress North is quite ill. But if you want to put your head in to be sure your duty is done—" He stood aside.

The official stepped into the cabin and out again quickly. "Quite all right, Captain. Quite all right."

Patrick, after following him off the ship to the quay,

went over to Maurice. "Everything has passed in-spection, Master Quain."

Maurice said curtly, "Why wouldn't it? I told you to send the official on board. I didn't say he needed your valuable company." He turned as Webster came up, followed by a porter leading a horse on which were piled a trunk and a number of boxes. "Afraid I might be late, Master Quain, and I wasn't sure how long you'd delay the sailing time just for me."

"I was about to send Patrick for you. The *Falcon* will be warped out into mid-channel and we hope to sail with the tide. Will you two make a final check to see that all supplies are in order, and the staff too? The last I saw of Vincent he was going into the tavern up the lane. See that he's sober before he embarks."

Webster said, "Yes, sir. He has a head easily turned by wine or women. He used to drink for pleasure, but since he was injured at Andely last summer, he says ale is a great salve for old wounds, though the worst he suffered was a bit of bloodletting which he could well afford. But we'll sober him if we have to throw him into the Thames. Patrick doesn't need sobering. He looks like a mother hen brooding over her chicks."

Patrick turned his head in startled anger. He could feel Maurice's eyes on him questioningly. He said sharp-ly, "We'll see to the supplies first, Master Webster." He caught his companion's arm, swung him around be-fore they boarded. "Any more remarks like that last one, and it won't be Vincent who's swimming in the Thames."

Webster laughed with malicious humor. "Can this be our unfailingly courteous Master North of the House of Quain? Why, Patrick, there must be a woman in this. They do the damnedest things. Don't hit me, Patrick. I'm just a sour old man." His thin wiry body pretended to flinch.

Patrick turned without a word and went up the gangplank. A gibe like Webster's would be just the sort of fool thing that would betray him. He did not breathe easily again until the anchor was tripped, the fore and main topsails were sheeted home to the evening breeze, and the *Falcon* slipped quietly down the river toward the Channel.

The ship seemed ghostly in the half-darkness and attended by ghosts, the *Judith,* ahead of them and the *Enterprise* astern, its spread of sail darkly silhouetted agaisnt the evening sky. On the main deck the crew manned the sheets and braces while forward a boatswain and three of his mates stood over the anchors and cable ready to let go if the eddying current of the tide should draw the *Falcon* into shoal water. The ship moved diagonally downstream, pulled by the tide, with the wind giving her so little way that she scarcely answered her helm.

Webster shivered in the chill wind, looked at Vincent, who was regarding everything through a vague and happy mist, and then at Patrick. "Well, my lads, let's get a pot of ale to warm us up, then into our cabin to drink and to bed. Many's the night I've had no better crossing than these poor devils out here. I like this traveling better." He moved toward the master's cabin.

Patrick stood in front of the two men. "It just happens, Master Webster, that an unfortunate error was made. The cabin is being used by someone else, I understand. We'll have to sleep out here or we can go below in the 'tween-decks."

Webster said, "We don't sleep in there, Patrick? I warrant you, I will!" He clutched at the rail as the ship swung unexpectedly about. "We get a bed or I'll see Quain."

Patrick let go of an iron stanchion to catch Webster's arm. "God-a-mercy, it won't hurt you to sleep out one night!"

The urgency in his voice made Webster peer at him again. He shrugged. "All right," he conceded grudgingly. "But tomorrow we move in or I'll know why, and it'll be Master Quain who'll tell me."

"Tomorrow," Patrick agreed cordially, "you can see God or the devil about your quarters."

By morning the mist had thickened so that England was but a dark blue line on the gray horizon. The *Fal-*

con was cutting through the waves, flinging up spray from her bows as she heeled over gracefully before the wind, and overhead the sails bellied out. The big lateen had been set on the mizzen together with the main and the fore mainsail. Forward the little square spritsail swelled like the pounting cheeks of a cherub as it led the ship in its long sweep over the swells.

Patrick climbed to the half deck, knocked at the door of Maurice's cabin. His mouth felt dry. The next half hour would not be pleasant. But Katherine was safe. He lurched as he entered, caught at a chair and almost fell into it before he regained his balance. "I think, Master Quain, I'll be glad to set foot on the fair land of France."

Maurice, standing at the stern window watching the waves rolling past, turned. "Don't put too much heart into the anticipation, Patrick. We sailed from London without Blount for more reasons than his lack of personal appeal. He expects to meet us at Bordeaux. The factors of the Turkey Company have been told of my change of plans. The *Falcon* is bound for Almería in south Spain where I have arranged to meet our factor from Madrid. Blount would be rather a nuisance at our proceedings. From there we'll take a galley to join the convoy at Naples."

Patrick looked at Maurice for a stunned moment. "We aren't sailing for France?"

"No. Does it matter?"

"Why wasn't I told? Did Captain Fox know?"

"Yes." Maurice spoke indifferently as he moved toward the chart table built against the forward bulkhead.

"But you didn't see fit to tell me of your change of plans, Master Quain?"

Maurice brows lifted at Patrick's tone. "It seemed unimportant, especially with your head so full of the Perrot woman's plight. Now that it's no longer necessary to keep our destination secret, I want these bills of lading changed to Señor Huércal in Madrid, and the price averaged out into Spanish reals."

Patrick made no move to pick up the papers. He felt a clear flame of anger that made him forget his care-

211

fully chosen words for breaking the news of Katherine to Maurice. "I'm not alone in being concerned over Lady Katherine's plight, Master Quain." He flung the words at Maurice like a challenge. "She's in the master's cabin."

Maurice eyed Patrick unbelievingly. The silence was brittle as thin ice. "Call Captain Fox!" The *Falcon* heeled over as Patrick went to the door, sent a seaman for the captain. Neither spoke until Fox swaggered in, glanced from Patrick's set face to Maurice's cold one.

Maurice said, "What's this I hear, Captain, about your taking a passenger aboard?"

The captain leered, smoothed out his rumpled clothes that looked as though he'd slept in them for a fortnight, caressed his pointed black beard with a callused hand. "Oh, we're taking excellent care of your . . . ah, friend, Master Quain. Food, hot water, bedding—better than I get."

"My friend?"

The captain, his mouth half-open, looked at Maurice again. His teeth clicked shut. "*Madre de Dios!* So it was your secretary's light o'love! If that young puppy has made a fool out of me——" He swung on Patrick truculently.

Patrick said, "Oh, I'm not proud of that, Captain. It isn't a difficult task at any time."

"Why, you whoreson swagbelly knave!" He turned back to Maurice. "He brought the woman on board yesterday and said you wanted her well cared for. That——"

Maurice interrupted the tirade. "And you believed him,"

Fox snarled, "Why wouldn't I? You've sent me queerer orders than that."

"Such as the time I told you to wait for me below Andely? It seems, Captain, that you're anxious for a new master when you spend so much time listening to commands that aren't from me."

The captain's face turned from red to white to purple. "*Mille tonnerres du diable!* How would I know that the fine English gentleman in France wasn't the friend he said he was? How am I supposed to guess

212

that this songbird of yours would betray you for a woman?"

Patrick said, "No!" Betray had an ugly sound. "Choose your words with more care, Captain, or use your whetstone on your sword where it will be needed instead of your tongue."

"I'll take care of Patrick later, Captain Fox. We'll forget the French affair which cost me a small fortune and should have cost you your ship. But if you cast your thoughts back, you may recall that I was either on the wharf or on the ship all day yesterday before we sailed. You did not so much as breathe a word of this harlot you took aboard. Why were you silent?"

The captain looked at Patrick, his big hands opening and closing, his face murderous. "By God, I don't know!"

Patrick murmured, "I told him, Master Quain, that you wanted to hear nothing about her."

"I should have known you were a liar when you spoke of putting in at Bordeaux to get rid of that slut."

Patrick took two steps around the table to face the captain. "Don't say that word again, Fox!"

"What do you want to call the hussy, Patrick? I don't like women on the sea. They bring bad luck. I'll have her thrown overboard if you give the word, Master Quain." He had recovered his usual blustering assurance. He remembered the customs man. "And you having me tell lies to Her Majesty's official for your wench!"

"What's that?"

Fox told Maurice about Patrick's "sick wife." He added with a touch of admiration, "The devil sure was at his elbow prompting him yesterday and me standing there and agreeing with him."

Maurice eyed Fox. "Of course you understand that if this Perrot woman had been found aboard without a passport you'd be looking at the sky now through iron bars? So would I."

Patrick said, "No——"

He was overridden by the captain. "For a woman I'd be flung into gaol? Master Quain, could I step outside for a minute with Patrick? I'll throw him to my crew—what's left of him."

"Your crew? Just how long, Captain Fox, do you expect to be in command of this ship?" Maurice moved away from the door. "You may go."

Patrick turned on Maurice as Fox left. "Do you think I'd have let the guilt fall on you if Katherine had been discovered?"

"You would have confessed? Who would have believed Katherine was on the *Falcon* without my consent?"

"Anyone. Why not? If there had been any other possible way, I would have taken it. I could not leave Katherine alone and in danger. No man could." He stopped before he added what he thought of Maurice for deserting Katherine.

"I need not inquire how she bought your promise of aid." Maurice's voice was acid. "But you haven't helped her much by taking her out of England to leave her in Spain."

"No! You can't do that, Master Quain! You couldn't—for no better reason than because we owe her an obligation. Without her assistance at Court, this whole Eastern venture would have been impossible."

"As you'll probably use neither to profit, Patrick, they may both be unimportant to you, but I can do better without the venture than without my head. I might have forgiven Katherine somewhat, but not that she went to you to trick me into a risk like this when I can least afford a mischance. And I was idiot enough to stand her protector once."

"Trick? She didn't come to me. I didn't see Lady Katherine until yesterday. I had the story from Edward Blount." Maurice lifted his head at that. Patrick added shortly, "Don't think I save Katherine's reputation to the damage of my own. Blount will never move against her. If this had failed, he couldn't shift the responsibilty to you instead of me. I let him know if he tried he would have some explaining to do about the three thousand pounds paid him after we were in France. Whatever the truth of the transaction, I doubt if it's to his credit. You can't leave Katherine at Almería," Patrick ended breathlessly.

Maurice's brows rose. "No? You may go. Send Katherine in. I'll let her know her destination has been changed. I hope she'll profit by the lesson, but I doubt it."

Patrick made no move to leave. "You don't want to take time to change your course to Bordeaux, Master Quain. But Captain Fox can stop there on his return to England. It won't interfere with your plans and you'll be dealing fairly with Katherine."

Maurice pulled around a chair to sit down at the table, ruffled the bills of lading with an idle hand. "Do you know, Patrick, I can think of nothing that concerns me less than doing justice to Katherine Perrot? Quite aside from that, Fox is sailing from Almería down the west coast of Africa. But he won't be lonely. You'll be on the *Falcon*. I feel I can do better without your services in Constantinople than with them. Will you send Lady Katherine here?"

Patrick had expected dismissal. It seemed the penalty whether at Court or in commerce for giving a thought to any but oneself. He said grimly, "Yes, sir. But if Katherine is to be put off at Almería, I'm going ashore with her." He turned at the door. "I don't think it would have fallen out that way, but perhaps I did risk your life, Master Quain."

Maurice said coldly, "Thanks for conceding so much. I had the impression you felt you'd done me a favor."

"But it just happens that while I'm nothing to Katherine, she's worth the hazard of both our necks to me!" Patrick went out.

Maurice came to his feet as Katherine opened the door a few minutes later. Her face was pale and tired-looking, but she smiled at Maurice with eyes and mouth. The smile denying her fatigue stabbed for a blinding moment of pain through the icy wall of anger about him. She held to the latch to steady herself at the rolling of the deck underfoot, then glanced behind her as she came in.

Maurice's eyes followed hers. "God's wounds! What's that?"

"Debbie. I didn't want to leave her alone. You don't mind?" She moved across the cabin as though she felt herself a welcome visitor and sat down on the bed that was near Maurice. Her dark woolen dress molded shoulders and breast and waist, fell over her hips in heavy folds to the floor. Without a farthingale her body looked slight and breakable. Her hands with narrow ruffs at the wrist had a helplessness about them as they lay idly in her lap. The child, a miniature of Katherine except that her hair was a golden mop in contrast to Katherine's black waves, watched Maurice shyly while she clung to Katherine's sleeve.

Maurice felt behind him for the arm of his chair and sat down slowly. Katherine smiled. "Did you expect her to be more of a baby?" She leaned forward impulsively. "I seem to be ever at a loss with you, Master Quain. You've been kind to me past words. I didn't dream you'd consent. But even though you did, I wouldn't have let you take this risk if it hadn't been for Deborah."

Maurice felt like striking her across her lovely treacherous face. "Let's forgo the gratitude, Lady Katherine. I only wanted to tell you that the *Falcon* is not putting in at Bordeaux. We're bound for the southern coast of Spain. You can disembark at Almería. You may find the distance a little farther to Limoges across Spain and the Pyrenees than you'd expected, but I feel, Lady Katherine, you'll experience no great difficulty. Do you speak Spanish?"

Katherine stared at him. Her lips parted a little. She shook her head.

"That will present a slight problem, but it won't trouble you for long. The language you know best can be interpreted by any man in any country."

Katherine stood up, face white with the hurt he had done her. She said, bewildered, "I can't understand, Master Quain, what I could have done since we sailed that you should turn against me now. Whatever harsh things I've heard of you I did not believe you could stoop so low as this." Her breath came in a sob. "What

216

do you gain by turning a woman and a child into a strange country?"

"Don't misunderstand me. I'd be happy to put you ashore in France, Lady Katherine. The sooner the better. It just happens that we aren't touching land before we reach Almería, and we aren't changing our course for a—for you."

"Why did you take us with you?" She put one hand protectingly on the child's shoulder.

Maurice said coldly, "As you well know, Lady Katherine, I would have blown the *Falcon* to hell before I'd have allowed you on board." He did not look at her.

"Oh, no! You didn't know I was to sail with you?" Her eyes were enormous.

"Do I look as though I'd taken leave of my senses?"

The color was creeping back into her face. She put out her hand toward him helplessly, dropped it to her side. "I told Ned you'd never take me to Bordeaux, but he said he'd spoken to you and you'd consented. Patrick brought me into the cabin yesterday. Even at the last moment I wondered if I were not mad to leave. But I was afraid. I thought Debbie would be safer with my mother's kinsmen. It's the first time I've been desperate enough to ask them."

Deborah, hearing her name, began to cry softly. Katherine dropped to her knees beside the child. "Oh, darling, what have I done? What will I do for you now?" The golden hair was soft under her touch and the round little face was wet with frightened tears. "You'll be all right, sweetheart. I'll take care of you."

Katherine rose lightly to her feet. "We'll not interrupt you longer. We have been too much trouble to you already, Master Quain. There's no use my saying I'm sorry that my friends were too devoted. I can't undo the harm. At least we'll cause you no further bother once you've reached Almería."

Maurice could not doubt the honesty of her words. Whatever he might think of her judgment, she had acted in good faith. He said, "I'm meeting my agent in Spain, Señor Huércal. He'll no doubt help you to travel across the country into France. He speaks English." He stopped abruptly. He had not meant to remind her of his slur that she did not need to know Spanish.

Katherine's chin was high above her ruff. Her slim shoulders were very straight. "You're kind, Master Quain. Come along, Debbie." She took the child's hand in hers.

Maurice watched her go. It would take more than his provision of an escort across Spain and half of France to wipe out for her the memory of his bitter words. That was just as well perhaps. In knowing that she had not planned with Blount for his possible undoing, he might have softened toward her, might have remembered again that manor house in Sussex, might have idled away this sea voyage in impossible dreams.

From the first moment they had met he had felt a bond between them. Now he had cut it through. She would go back to Blount when the knight returned from the East and could have her reinstated at Court. Or perhaps she would go to another man. What did it matter? He could find as good a wench in any whorehouse in Europe. Only not one, not ever again, who through all his defenses could stab him so heartbreakingly that when most he wanted to suppose her any man's mistress, he thought instead of her tenderness, her sympathy, her gay spirit, the proud and indomitable will under her softness. Oh, Katherine, my darling!

Desire for her tingled through him. He could rise and follow her to her cabin and there was not one on the ship could stop him. He could tear the dark clothes shielding her beautiful pliant body, slake his thirst for the whiteness of her flesh, the curves of her long slim legs, for her hips and breasts. This woman at his mercy. He stared down at the half circles of red in his palm where his fingernails had cut into the skin. The thought of her unwilling surrender had itself a dark and terrible compulsion. God in heaven! If she did not ruin him with love, she would through lust.

Señor Huércal was a middle-aged man, tall, spare-boned and dark-skinned. His alert black eyes gave him a look of youth that was denied by the way he dragged his right foot when he walked. He had come out to the *Falcon* in the gig Maurice had sent to shore for him.

The harbor was filled with ships, from Portuguese caravels, looking like broken wine casks with the ends slightly raised, shoelike carracks from Genoa, towering Spanish galleons to fishing boats, pinnaces and the long low-lying galleys. The town of Almería lay in a white heat under the noonday sun. The Castillo de San Cristóbal with its four Morrish towers crouched above the city like an enormous lion, the houses looking like its prey between its paws. Behind town and fortress, hills ringed the valley like a protecting wall.

Huércal finished up his business with a dispatch Maurice had not expected of a South-European. He was sending marble from the Sierra Nevada—some of the newly wealthy in England wanted to build houses that made the old manors look like dark prisons. Wine from the white grapes of Almería he had exported a month ago. Spain needed to import grain. The rainfall had been tragically light again. Grain would bring a high price. It had been a bad season for the crops, and so large a share was taken by the royal purveyors to store for the Armada and to be sent to the armies in the Netherlands, that there was little left.

Maurice looked at Huércal sardonically. "The Armada, Señor Huércal? Are the plans still going forward?"

Huércal said in surprise, "Yes, Señor Quain. But the people are apathetic about it. The building of the ships is delayed—green timber is sent to the yards instead of seasoned, often the cordage is rotten, the guns are not properly cast. But of one thing you can be sure, señor: The plans will go forward, the Armada will sail."

Maurice wiped his face with his handkerchief, stood up to give a tug at the stern window in an annoyed effort to provide more exit for the oppressive heat of the cabin. Through the open door forward streamed the hot damp air, laden with the odor of tar from the sizzling deck. He said abruptly, "You have hired a galley for us, señor?"

"Yes. You can go aboard her in the morning. Captain Melzi is a friend of mine. He will not cheat you unreasonably, although you are aware, of course, that galleys are not the usual choice of a merchant. They are fast and gave you an excellent chance of escaping the pirates who plague our Mediterranean shipping, but you must pay for the advantage."

Maurice nodded. "You can send the bulk of our cargo on the next convoy east. There's one more matter. I have an Englishwoman on board. She wants to go to France. Limoges to be exact. Unfortunately she has with her—" Maurice grimaced—a child of four, five, six years. They all look alike to me. There will be also a young man to accompany her. Will you hire coach and guard for them?"

Huércal started back at the suggestion, dismay on his face. "Señor! Across Spain? You cannot mean it!"

"Why not? The expense is not important."

"No, Señor Quain. It is not safe for them. Even if it were, I would not touch the affair. Indeed I beg you will not allow them on shore."

Maurice looked at the Spaniard coldly. "We have had a long and pleasant association. I hope it will not be necessary to bring our mutually profitable alliance to a conclusion."

Huércal, who had started to rise, lowered himself into the chair again. "Señor, if it were a question of your traveling across the country, I might risk it. For two English people whom I do not even know—I cannot attempt so foolhardy a venture." He glanced down at his crippled leg and up at Maurice. "I was taken once by the Inquisition. I was released." His lips came together firmly. "Your ship here is already attracting comment. While I have distributed a few gifts to the officals, I cannot guarantee the safety of an English ship for more than a day or two."

Maurice shrugged. He would not jeopardize the head of his Spanish house to help Katherine to Limoges. "What do you suggest I do with the lady?"

Huércal looked up toward heaven for guidance. These mad foreigners who would take a woman on a sea voyage and discovered too late they had better have sailed with the devil! "Could you send her back on the *Falcon?*"

"No." Maurice saw no reason to explain that even if Fox were returning to London he would hesitate to leave Katherine and her daughter on the ship. A woman at sea was bound to bring trouble with the best disciplined crew. Since Fox was sailing for the African coast, it was impossible.

"The only way left then is to take her to Naples with you, señor. Though what you will do with her there, I would not know."

All the anger Maurice had ever felt toward Katherine surged up in him, tingled to his finger tips. That slut! She had caused him more trouble than all the rest of this voyage to the East. He would like to throw her to the Spanish or the crew, and Patrick after her.

Then he smiled unexpectedly with a grim humor. "You have hit it right, Señor Huércal. I will take her to Naples. I am meeting a gentleman there who will undoubtedly be as delighted to have this responsibility as I am to rid myself of it."

12

A cool breath of wind stirred across the Mediterranean. It ruffled the blue glass surface of the sea, sent the long gold and scarlet pennon fluttering away from the mainmast and dispelled the haze of heat above the deck.

The *Ascención* drove forward over the scarcely perciptible swells, long curls of white foam whirling away from the oars. The slow rhythmic beat of the timing drum accompanied by the crunch of the shafts against the tholes made a monotonous undertone to the sounds of the ship—the gurgle of water under her stern, the clatter of spars and gear as the crew bent the big lateen sails to the yards, the incongruous squealing of pigs kept for slaughtering.

Maurice stood under the awning on the afterdeck. Barefooted sailors brushed past him with powder and case shot for the small breechloaders mounted on swivels at the forward rail of the aftercastle. As they worked they glanced apprehensively to starboard where a small black triangle far to the south marked the approach of another gallery.

Webster, coming up at that moment, waved a hand toward the distant sail. "Corsairs," he said laconically, "from Tripoli. Now that we're well away from Spain, Captain Melzi tells me he has only half his usual complement of slaves so we can't outrow the galley. We're hoisting sail to save the slaves for later in the day." He turned to watch the seamen hauling up ammunition, removing tampions, checking gun priming, opening chests and distributing arms. He added grudgingly, "Our men are moving with more dispatch than those clapperdudgeons usually do. I suppose it's the thought of rowing out their lives on Turkish galleys."

Maurice said indifferently, "Huércal mentioned pirates, but I didn't expect to meet them so soon."

The wind was freshening, rolling up masses of ominous black clouds behind them. The sailing master walked forward rapidly, giving orders in quick Italian. Sailors tailed onto the main halyards raising the great main yard and spreading the dirty green lateen sail to the breeze. With the canvas sheeted home the crew turned to the foremast and then aft to the mizzen, hoisting the last of the three sails. The ship heeled slightly, and Maurice was aware of a great speed through the water. Oars were lashed. The slaves sprawled on the main deck, resting from the long morning pull.

Katherine at the rail caught sight of Maurice. She smiled at him casually. The color in her cheeks was high with excitement, darkening her eyes, accentuating the fairness of her skin that had been protected from the sun by the heart-shaped slip of velvet mask she held in her hand. Maurice noted mechanically that for once she didn't have the child with her. He went toward her, hardly aware of Patrick at her side.

He thought she had never been so beautiful. The look of strain that had been so habitual he had hardly noticed it was gone from her face. Her warm quick smile put behind them forever his angry words on the

222

Falcon, the bitter hurt he had given her, the wrong she had done him. It was as though they were meeting on a new plane where they could be friends without anger or bitterness or chill reserve here on the *Ascención* cut off by the sea from ties to the past and to the future. It would not last, but how sweet it was!

Katherine said, "Master Quain, I'm trying to be very sorry for the trouble I've been, trying at least to regret you could not put me ashore in Spain. But I must ask your pardon because instead I'm enjoying myself very much indeed."

The Court seemed incredibly far away. Elizabeth Tudor, Walsingham, Leicester, Mary Howard and Bess Throckmorton all held an unreality about them. She would return, she knew, to the highly complicated existence that was at once soft and harsh with always a menace under the routine of glittering days and nights. The wrong word, a frown when one should smile, a word of sympathy where one should condemn—she winced at the thousand small fears that paid for each moment of pleasure.

It was difficult to remember that day when Walsingham had turned on her and Maurice had stood her friend, that night of pain when she'd been dismissed by the Queen on Walsingham's insistence. Here she felt young in a way she had never had a chance to be young, and lighthearted without a dozen pair of eyes watching her in the closed world of the Court, a dozen tongues to chatter with unthinking malice about every move she made, of whether Leicester looked at her oftener than at the Queen that morning, of whether Edward Blount—

Her lips parted in surprise. She had almost forgotten Ned. Her heart went down sickly at the thought of meeting him in Naples. He would be in a vicious temper, ready to call out Maurice Quain. He would have reason to be jealous, she thought honestly. But not of Maurice. Every word Patrick spoke to her, every glance or gesture, showed wittingly or unwittingly his devotion, wooing her in a disciplined and self-denying way that went to her heart. She was not used to men who gave more than they wanted to take. The

223

sweetness of his naked and unshamed love could make her believe, just for this short while and only as a pastime, how dear he might become to her.

Maurice said coldly, "I am pleased you do not find the voyage monotonous, Lady Katherine. We will be in Naples in a few days. There you will be with your friends again."

Katherine laughed. "I refuse to believe, Master Quain, that any friend would have done more than you and Master North have undertaken for me." Maurice, Maurice, be kinder to me! It is for only a little while.

She looked away, caught her breath as she saw the ship bearing down upon them. The *Ascención* had turned south and was again under oars. The sails had been furled and the yards securely lashed, leaving bare poles sweeping against the darkened sky. Ahead of them on the starboard bow across a narrow expanse of tumbling green waves was the pirate vessel, a long single-masted galley. Its sail seemed to speed toward them of itself with the ship beneath something incidental to the movement of the great black triangle.

Katherine said, "I must go to Debbie. She may waken and be frightened." She lingered a moment.

Patrick smiled at her. "There's nothing to fear, Lady Katherine. If there should be a battle, stay in your cabin. Perhaps it is just another merchant ship."

Katherine smiled. "I'm sure of it, Master North."

Maurice watched her leave, glanced toward the approaching ship. Patrick said, "I thought, Master Quain, that Webster and Vincent and I would stay here near Lady Katherine's cabin if they should board."

"I see you insist on being heroic."

Patrick's brows lifted wryly. "I really prefer to hide in the bilge, but as I'd be no safer there than on deck, I may as well appear brave."

Maurice looked coldly amused. He was not sorry he had changed his mind about sending Patrick back to England. A good secretary was hard to replace. He felt too a faint respect for Patrick's refusal to desert Katherine. His thoughts were interrupted by a sudden shock from the recoil and an echoing explosion as the *Ascención's* main battery was fired. The rhythmic vi-

224

bration of the oars increased in tempo. The two galleys were driving toward each other, rapidly narrowing the gap between them, now only a quarter of a mile wide.

The timing drum thumped loudly as the overseer of the slaves steadily advanced the tempo and the rise and fall of the flashing oars sent the galley racing ahead. Spray flew over the bow, and a long line of foam rolled out from the prow as she knifed through each succeeding wave. The main deck of the galley was only a foot or two above the water line, and the sea poured through the scuppers, tumbling about the feet of the rowers.

Quartermasters carrying whips moved along the raised center gangways as bread soaked in wine was placed in the mouths of the slaves toiling at the oars. They gulped it avidly, then sank back, each man into his own private hell. Gunners stood at the fowling pieces that were trained on the rowing benches to prevent mutiny. Slave on pirate ship or merchant galley, where was the difference? The whip was no softer, the hours were no shorter, the food was no more ample on the one than on the other.

The crash of the forward battery again jarred the *Ascención,* throwing a sudden pall of smoke over the forecastle. Maurice noticed how the galley's main guns were secured to stationary mountings in the prow so that they could be trained only by the movement of the vessel itself, the gunner watched the rise and fall of the ship and signaling the helmsman as he selected the moment to fire.

Maurice understood now the need for changing the vessel's course with the approach of danger. Except for a few small port pieces there was no armament that could be trained astern and little that would be of use for broadside firing. The low freeboard and narrow beam, together with the use of all main-deck space for working the oars, made it impossible to mount heavy guns anywhere except in the bow, leaving the galley helpless against a flank attack and incapable of defending itself against a pursuer.

The corsairs, continuing to drive on under both sail and oars, were firing their forward battery harmlessly

225

into the sea. The pressure of the big sail depressed the bow too much to give the guns an effective range.

The *Ascención* turned rapidly to starboard and rowed directly into the wind. The steady precision of the slaves—rising from their benches as they moved the shaft aft, the careful feathering, the dip and the pull as they heaved with their full weight, sending the oars grating sharply against the tholes—seemed like the movement of a huge loom shuttling back and forth to send the galley ahead against wind and sea.

Following the *Ascención's* lead, the pirates swung around to head off their intended victim, but in doing so brought the wind directly abeam, heeling their vessel hard over. The starboard oars could not clear the water, and for a moment the vessel pivoted back on her original course. Sheets were let fly, the black sail swept free, and the oars were again sweeping rhythmically, but headway and time had been lost, enabling the *Ascención* to reduce the priates' wind advantage.

Maurice grasped the rail as the vessel lurched forward through the rising waves. Tumbling clouds streamed up from the black mass in the western sky. He could see the corsair clearly now, oars flashing against the red and black topsides, bow and sterncastles packed with turbaned men. If the galley succeeded in closing, the *Ascención* would be overrun in a few minutes, her fighting personnel outnumbered five to one.

Bow chasers on the Barbary vessel were firing steadily, small puffs of smoke issuing from the gun ports, followed momentarily by the sharp explosions. On the *Ascención* the culverins on the forecastle were answering, guns leaping in their carriages as they warmed to the constant firing.

A ball crashed through the main-deck bulwark, showering splinters among the rowers, smashing an oar and plowing along the port benches. One slave collapsed in a pool of blood, neatly decapitated, while another stared stupidly at the mangled remnant of his hand. The oars hesitated, missed a beat. Quartermasters ran to the benches, pulled the bodies out, hurled the shattered oars into the sea, cleared the jammed tholes and forced the terrified rowers back into position. Whips cut into flesh and the flaltering oars worked back into the stroke. The entire bank moved forward again as a single unit.

Splinters sang through the air about Maurice as another ball plowed a furrow in the aftercastle deck, sending two sailors into a bloody heap against the rail. Maurice's eyes smarted from the acrid smell of powder and the sickening sweet ordor of blood. The air vibrated from the steady cannonading.

Only a ship's length away and pounding straight for the *Ascención's* larboard beam was the corsair galley, oars shuttling relentlessly, water cascading from her prow, the massive beak reaching out toward them. Maurice thought of that ram plowing into them, snapping oars, crushing through the bulwarks, embedding itself in the deck while the pirates swarmed aboard.

Smoke covered the oncoming prow. Shot whined overhead, crashed into the vessel beneath him. But they were unmistakably pulling clear of the pirates. The slaves on the Barbary galley, exhausted from their long chase, were no match for the comparatively fresh men who manned the oars of the *Ascención*. Overhead the cloud mass was piling higher. A yellowish unreal light settled over the sea. The wind was rising, singing through the rigging with a high thin note. The sea which had changed to short choppy waves in the late afternoon was now a waste of tumbling waters.

Webster, coming up to stand beside Maurice, looked at sea and sky with an experienced eye. "Never been across the Mediterranean yet, Master Quain, that I didn't have a brush with pirates or a storm. It seems a plentitude of riches to have both in the same afternoon."

Maurice shrugged. "They add variety to a monotonous passage."

Webster looked back at the pirate ship which was dropping rapidly astern. "Even the robbers of the sea are changed these days. Used to be they'd pursue a ship until hell closed over them. Now the dash out, growl and show their teeth, and if your cannon barks at them, they're only too willing to slink home and wait for easier prey. An extremely poor lot, sneak thieves instead of robbers."

"I'd be sorrier for your disappointment, Master Webster, if ransoms were not so expensive. And with this storm coming up. I don't believe we can accuse them of breaking off the engagement only because they're afraid of us."

They both caught at the railing as the galley lurched under a sudden gust of wind. Lightning streaked across the sky. There was a long reverberating roll of thunder. Clouds pressed lower, leaving the world in a sinister half-darkness. The galley was rapidly becoming unmanageable with the main deck awash and seas burying the oars, sweeping the rowers from their benches. The vessel rolled wildly in the heavy waves, her long narrow hull having little stability.

Veering to starboard, the *Ascención* slid for a moment into the trough of the sea, heeling far over until it seemed to Maurice she must capsize. Then she began to fall off before the wind. The foresail was hoisted and sheeted down. The madly cracking canvas sent the vessel careening headlong, threatening as she coasted down each succeeding wave to drive her under. Oars were shipped and lashed, guns secured and hatch covers checked. Cold rain drove in sheets across the sea. The foremast trembled and whipped under the pressure of the straining canvas.

As sailors began to run life lines across the deck, Webster shouted above the uproar, "I'm going below, Master Quain!"

Maurice followed Webster indifferently. He thought for one moment of going to Katherine's cabin. No, Patrick would be there. And the captain and master too no doubt if she wanted them. Patrick however was below with Jacques and Vincent and Tom. The table had fallen over. Broken glass was scattered on the floor and wine was flowing from a jug that rolled crazily on a shelf.

Maurice held to the bulkhead as he went in. Webster started to stumble, caught himself against the overturned table. As the ship listed heavily the glass slithered across the floor with a tinkling sound. The jug

228

crashed onto the bench below. Maurice said coldly, "Clean up the cabin, Jacques, Tom! There's no excuse for shambles like this."

Jacques gave him a dying look. Maurice turned to Patrick. "I thought you were with Katherine."

"I didn't know if. she'd want someone—though the storm seems to be getting worse. She ought to have a woman with her, Master Quain."

Maurice glanced at Jacques and Tom and Vincent as the ship plunged forward from under their feet. "I think we have enough women here without asking for more. I'll go up."

"If she should want me——" Patrick damned himself. He had been too much afraid of taking advantage of her.

Maurice said, "No!" shortly and went out, crashed against the bulkhead, almost lost his balance as he climbed up the ladder. Why hadn't Patrick gone to the girl earlier? He would have sent him now if the seas had not been so heavy. He reached the deck. It was completely black. The noise was unbelievable. The wind shrilled through the rigging. The seas crashed against the bow, washed over the bulwarks.

A sailor running on bare feet brushed against him in passing. He felt cautiously in the darkness, stumbled forward faster than he expected as the ship tumbled into the trough of a wave, swayed and righted herself. His shoulder smashed into a bulkhead. He stayed there a moment in wordless agony, moving his arm to feel if a bone were broken while he wished Patrick's soul to the devil. Then he moved his hands along the wall, came to the door of Katherine's cabin and pounded on it. He could hear the latch drawn back, the creak of the hinges as the door opened. There was the sound of crying, a low frightened whimper. He said, "Katherine?"

Her voice was breathless. "Oh Maurice. It's dark . . . the light went out, and Debbie's afraid and . . . and so am I." She moved to him naturally as though they had always been friends. He put his arms about her. He could feel the wild beating of her heart against his. One hand slid protectingly along her shoulder. He

229

had no aching desire to tear this brief peace. She stepped back quickly toward the low wooden pallet in the corner of the cabin. He groped his way after her. "Here, Maurice, sit down on the bed. At least it's nailed to the deck! Everything is all right now, Debbie. Master Quain is here to take care of us."

The galley plunged on. Debbie cried, fell asleep shortly from sheer exhaustion. Maurice thought that when there was nothing else between them, there was always this damned child around. He reached over to put his hand on Katherine's. She turned her palm upward so that her fingers clung to his. The sweetness of her need for him here in the darkness with the pounding waves filling their ears, the fragrance of the perfume she used exotic above the dankness, stirred through him poignantly. He braced himself as the galley seemed to hold itself motionless, dropped away into space. Katherine fell against him. He put an arm about her. They felt like helpless pawns flung about in a mad game of sea and sky and wind.

It was almost dawn before the waves began to quiet. The rise and plunge forward and the fall of the ship eased so that one could stand upright without being flung against the bulkhead. The gray light seeped through the square latticed window of the cabin. Katherine looked at him. Her face was wan, and there were dark circles of fatigue under her eyes, but she smiled whimsically. "You were very kind again, Maurice!"

He glanced about the cabin, picked up her cloak that had fallen across an overturned settle. "You lie down now, Katherine." She started to protest, instead moved over beside her small daughter. Maurice spread the mantle over her, smiling sardonically at himself.

Katherine put her hand between her face and the pillow, her dark eyelashes lying fanlike against her cheeks. She looked a young girl, virginal, unaware and defenseless. He was not in the habit, he thought, of leaving a wench at dawn after spending the dark hours of the night holding her hand! He reached over to pull up a cover about Deborah's shoulders. She opened her

230

eyes, smiled at him sleepily and turned to fling an arm over her mother.

Maurice did not notice that Patrick was still awake when he went below, nor if he had, would he have been aware of the insistent unspoken question in the young man's eyes. He felt bruised and sore as he undressed, but under his aching body he knew a releasing of his spirit. The steadily rising tide of passion for Katherine Perrot must reach the crest of completion naturally, inevitably, now in this magic interlude that cut them off from the past and from the future. The Court and Edward Blount were far away. Even the Turkey Company, his plans for his Eastern house, seemed distant, detached. When they reached Naples——But they were still far from Naples.

Maurice did not see Katherine again until late the next evening. She was just coming out of her cabin, closing the door softly behind her. Her dark blue dress blended into the paneled wood. Her hands and face had a pale cameolike quality about them as though they were carved from ivory. She smiled as she saw him. He said, "You shouldn't go out on deck alone, Katherine." He dropped her title unthinkingly.

She put her hand on his sleeve, moved across the deck to the rail with him, lifted her free hand to Patrick, who was lounging near the companionway where he had been half the day waiting for her to come out. Patrick's smile answering hers was strained. They would be in Naples soon and after that—— Well, he'd outstay Maurice and see her if only for a moment. He turned his head away. He had tried never to be importunate, but, oh God, how his body demanded hers! How thin and meaningless words like honor and marriage and selfless devotion were, thinkling like false silver, useless when you needed them most!

Maurice said, "Katherine——" again and stopped.

She looked up at him, her dark eyes questioning him mockingly, but her mouth soft for kissing. The smooth firm skin was delicately tinted as the blood came and went in her cheeks. He put his hand over hers. The ring of amethyst and diamonds which Blount had given

231

her cut into his hand. Katherine's eyes went down to it, then up to Maurice's. Always it brought back to her not Ned but that moment at Hampton when she had been alone, with the Queen and her ministers against her, and only Maurice had come to her side.

There was no need for words. The sky darkening into night was streaked in the west with gold and crimson. A crescent moon glimmered palely overhead, and the long rolling waves broke into foam as they curled up against the bow. The air seemed washed after the storm and palely blue in the distance. Her skirt just brushed against him. He could feel the need of her warm and living flesh mounting within him intolerably. He did not know how long they stood there before he turned toward her. She looked at him a moment weighing him with her eyes, her head a little to one side. She put her hand on his, half hesitatingly at first, then in a gesture of surrender.

They went into her cabin. He remembered Deborah abruptly and grimaced. Katherine said, "She's in the adjoining room asleep," and laughed at him.

Maurice pushed home the bolt in the outer door and turned to face Katherine, shoulders flat against the carved panels. His eyes were luminous and the chill hard lines of his face were smoothed out. And then he was across the cabin. His lips were on her mouth, her eyes, the hollow in her throat where her white collar sloped to a point. He unclasped the fastening of her wide loose outer gown of blue velvet, let it fall to the floor, unbuttoned the long-waisted bodice with the rolling piccadill at the shoulders. Her arms round and curved gleamed white against the dark cloth as she slipped off bodice and skirt. Her linen chemise, padded and ruffled and embroidered, clung to her small bosom, her flat stomach, the gentle curve of her hips.

They could hear the waves slapping against the ship, the shout of a sailor, a chanty someone was singing. Here they were alone in their own world. The last light of day slanted through the latticed window, painting the girl's delicate skin with gold, her arms, her long slimly rounded legs, and touching her hair outspread on the pillow. The black waves were silky under his

232

hand, and her flesh was warm and firm. The chemise still fragrant from her body was tossed to the side of the bed. Katherine's eyes were softly alight in her piquant face. She smiled to herself.

Maurice said, "What are you thinking about, sweetheart?"

Her brows lifted. "Of many things, Maurice. And of you." Her smile deepened. There was something delicate and airy about her as though she might vanish in a breath.

All his defenses against her were down. His thought that had at first urged him to take her at once, quickly, because this fortune might not last, now seemed ungallantly cautious, tawdry. He would hold himself in leash, not hurrying her, woo her until her passion would match his, that remote coolness about her would finally be set aflame, and she would surrender all of herself to his love.

Patrick moved unbelievingly across the deck to the starboard bulkwarks as the cabin door closed behind Katherine and Maurice. He put his hands on the rail to steady them, scraping his palms across the wood back and forth. A splinter cut his skin. He did not notice the pain. He shivered. The blood pounded through him dangerously.

That Maurice should have Katherine seared him like a whitehot iron. On the other side of that door was paradise, and out here a cold limbo of despair. He loved Katherine. He had wanted her until the repression of his desire had been a torment in the night. To know that Maurice must be possessing her now released in him a lust for her perfect body, a lust in which the gentleness of neither love nor devotion had a part. He flung away from the bulwarks while he could still leave the anguish of his vigil.

Katherine turned her head toward Maurice, her dark eyes on him thoughtfully. She had not realized it could be like this—to lose herself in her lover's embrace, give herself to him as she had never been able to do with Blount. There were no dark disturbances under the rise

233

of passion. She'd had no doubts of Maurice as she had at times of Ned, no feeling of withholding herself from the final demands of love.

Maurice slipped his hand through her hair, down the slim column of her throat to her shoulder. His fingers tightened about her upper arm. In all his life he had not known the sweetness of a woman's body until tonight. Not a quick slaking of one's thirst, but the slow seeping through him of a golden liquor of delight which was as headily satisfying in fullfillment as in promise, which stayed with him so that the pleasure of her still swam in his senses. The harlots he had disciplined himself to be satisfied with—it seemed now impossible he had ever even needed them. Even Lucy—— He sat up. Pain stabbed him remorselessly.

Katherine said, "What is it, Maurice?" She shivered, reached for the quilted silken coverlet on the bed.

Maurice rose, pulled on his body linen, hose and doublet. He did not answer or look at her. Lucy. Lucy had been a virgin when he married her, and she had betrayed him. And he was now putting his heart again into a woman's hands. Into Katherine's—and she was the mistress of Edward Blount. What complete madness had possessed him to deliver himself again to the rack? He must leave her quickly. He had known long ago he should not see her again. The curse of God on Patrick, who had brought her to the ship, on Katherine who—— No. The fault was all his.

Katherine's brows came together in bewilderment at his averted face. "Maurice!"

He fastened the ruffs at his wrist, turned his head toward her. "Yes?"

Her lips parted in wonder. "Maurice, what is it?" She shook her head. From the lover to this icy stranger—it was some bad dream. "What has happened?"

Maurice said coldly, "Nothing, my dear. A delightful hour." He unpinned the brooch on his doublet, a ruby that looked like spilled blood on a golden field, put it on the shelf at the foot of the bed.

Katherine stared incredulously at the jewel and then at Maurice. Before she could feel the hurt he had dealt

234

her, anger flamed so that there was a blackness before her eyes. "Take that with you, Maurice, or throw it in the sea. I'll not touch it."

He left the brooch, drew back the bolt, went out, closed the door behind him. He stayed there with his hand on the latch, staring unseeingly across the dark waters. Oh, Katherine, my darling, what have I done?

And then he felt harshly that he'd done what he'd had to do before it was too late. To be betrayed twice—no, not that again! She had been unbelievably beautiful and the sweetness of her yielding he could never forget or embitter. Better to cut her off now that when she was so much a part of him that her inevitable desertion would be past enduring.

The galley with a brisk wind still blowing out of the west was continuing under sail. It was strangely quiet without the steady drumbeat, the oars creaking against the tholes, the sound of the whip on naked backs. They had no refinement of torture here. The last turn of the rack, the flaying of flesh beyond bearing, could be done only by a woman.

Patrick went below to the cabin in the morning. He did not want to see Maurice, not ever again. Maurice, eating breakfast at the table, glanced briefly at him. "Good morning, Patrick."

Whatever Patrick had anticipated he did not know, but he had not expected this chill tone, the impenetrable face, the cold reserved eyes. He felt a vast sense of relief. Whatever had happened behind that closed door last night, could Maurice have had Katherine? To possess her and then show this masked face to the world in the morning? Hardly. Perhaps she had refused him. No man could reject her.

He colored slightly as Maurice looked up from the bread he was breaking to say. "We'll be in Naples soon. Please see that all our papers are in order and the captain satisfied. We'll not be going ashore in Italy. Naples is more Spanish than Almería these days. We'll transfer at once to whatever galley in the convoy has been held for us. They've probably been delayed if the journey across France was uneventful."

235

The mention of France brought the same thought to both their minds. Patrick said, "If we do not go ashore, what of Lady Katherine?"

Maurice continued to break the bread until it crumbled in his hands. He dropped the pieces on his plate. "Katherine Perrot? What about her?"

"Are you going to throw her into the sea?"

"You know, Patrick, that's one of the most reasonable suggestions you've yet made about that lady. The only reasonable one. However, before you start to smuggle her from frying pan to fire, perhaps I should mention that the moment we anchor I'm sending her to Blount's galley. How her lover chooses to take care of things is not of the slightest interest to me. If it is to you, you came to so good an understanding with Sir Edward before we sailed that if you think it would continue, you can go with her."

Patrick moved his head back sharply as though he'd received a blow. He said nothing, but his mouth was a thin line. Maurice could always find the exact words that hurt the most. He went across to unlock and fling back the lid of the chest holding their papers, tossed the sheets out onto the bed and sat down to glance through them.

Maurice looked at him. "I hope you're more aware of what you're doing than it seems to the naked eye. Certain women don't blend well with business, Patrick. When we get back to England, find yourself a young girl. Perhaps marriage will remake you into the steady and dependable person you were before you had the misfortune to meet that black-haired wench in the sterncastle."

Patrick crumpled the sheet of paper under his hand. "Do you know, Master Quain, the trouble with me is that I've always been so damned steady and dependable I didn't have time to live."

"Do you mean live or love? If you haven't won the lady's easy favors yet, I doubt that you'll find yourself more lucky in the next few days. But I suppose it is always worth the try. After all, what difference does it make if her thoughts are on Edward Blount, just so she's in your arms?"

Patrick stood up and walked out without a word. Maurice wondered at his own bitterness. To taste of heaven and then to retreat quickly to purgatory lest you be flung into hell—— God, how long before they would be in Naples? He felt he had been on this galley forever.

The *Ascención* nosed its way into the Neapolitan harbor past the lighthouse at the end of the Molo Grande and into the vast concourse of ships swaying at anchor. Maurice looked at the incredible beauty of the scene with jaundiced eyes—the bay from the Capo di Miseno on the northwest to the Punta della Campanella and Capri in the southesast; at the houses crawling up the volcanic hills; at the castle dominating the city, and beyond them all to Vesuvius.

The sun shone with a hard brilliance in the cloudless arch of sky. Maurice narrowed his eyes against the light as he watched a tender work its way toward them in and out among the ships. As it came closer he recognized Blount and Hall, the factor traveling to Constantinople for the Turkey Company, in the stern. He thought it rather likely they had been scanning every ship that came into the harbor for days.

Patrick, also catching sight of them, went over to Maurice. "Will you see them here, Master Quain, or shall I have them sent down to your cabin?" The galley rocked gently in the swells.

"The cabin would be best. When you speak to the gentlemen, don't sound quite so much as though they were bales of wool to be thrown about, Patrick. Of course if Blount were cargo he'd be serving a useful purpose in life."

He went below, called Jacques to put out wine and glasses. Beads of moisture stood on his forehead. He wiped them off with his handkerchief, looked up as the door opened and Blount came in followed by Hall, an elderly trader with a good-humored but slightly anxious expression as though he were a nursemaid with an overlively charge. Patrick came in and closed the door behind them.

Blount took the first three minutes to express himself

237

with profanity. Hall's distress deepened. "Really, Sir Edward, it was just a slight misunderstanding. Here we are all friends together again and ready to sail east. No harm done." Hall looked anxiously at Maurice. "It seems, Master Quain, that Sir Edward was expecting to meet you in Bordeaux, and when you didn't arrive and I mentioned our meeting place was Naples, he was a little upset. Natural, no doubt, in the circumstances, but it has been rather a strain waiting for you this last week." He smiled hopefully.

Maurice said, "I trust your journey across France was pleasant. Did you ship out of Marseille?"

"We did, sir. We have the cargo from Naples in the hold and we are indeed ready to leave at your pleasure."

Blount's fair face changed from crimson to white. "At Maurice's pleasure? The whole damned voyage has been for his convenience." He turned to Maurice. The veins stood out on his forehead. "You knew, Maurice, we were to make this passage together, that I was ordered to accompany you the whole way."

Maurice turned to Hall. "Won't you sit down, sir? And you, Sir Edward? Patrick, will you give them wine? From Gascony or Alsace?" Hall sat down gingerly and took the wine Patrick poured for him. "I'll have the cargo we're carrying on the *Ascención* transferred at once if you'll give us the name of the galley to be loaded, Master Hall. You wish to sail on the evening tide?"

Hall nodded, Blount said, "You're taking passage on the *Isabelle-Marie* with me. You don't escape my vigilance again."

Maurice's brows rose. "No doubt an oversight on my part, Sir Edward, but I have not till now chanced to be aware of your vigilance. Won't you be seated? There may be a matter or two to discuss before you leave."

Blount sat down belligerently. "Maurice, I trust the first word will be an explanation of the change of route you took to Naples."

"Change? I'd never planned to go to Bordeaux, as Master Hall of course knew."

Blount's mouth dropped open. He sat up straight,

the seed pearls on his blue doublet gleaming in the light through the porthole. "You didn't even touch at Bordeaux?" He shot a look at Patrick. Patrick's face was a blank.

Maurice watched with cold satisfaction as Blount's eyes went from him to Hall and back again. Maurice said, "But you wanted a word on my passage? We had a brush with a corsair, a few hours of storm, no further inconveniences that I recall."

Blount snarled, "All right, Maurice!" At his tone Hall raised a deprecatory hand. Blount didn't notice him. "What about Katherine Perrot?"

"Master Hall will have more wine, Patrick," Maurice turned to Blount. "Katherine Perrot Perhaps it's you who could do the talking there."

"The last I saw of her—she was aboard the *Falcon,* wasn't she?"

Maurice was abruptly filled up to his teeth with Blount. "She was aboard the *Falcon,* Sir Edward. She is now above us in the first cabin on the *Ascención.* Whether you wish to put her ashore in Naples, ship her to Marseille or take her with you to the East, I don't care. She's in your hands."

"You can't do this, Maurice. What would I do with her? You promised to take her to Bordeaux."

Maurice said silkily, "I'm sorry if there was some slight misunderstanding between you and my secretary over our destination. I can't assume responsibility for it. As a matter of fact, I rather expected a show of pleasure on your part to have your mistress rejoin you where you least expected such a delightful surprise."

"It will be pleasant to see her," Blount admitted. "I have missed her. If I could take her with me—— She's a charming companion for a man weary with traveling." He remembered suddenly that Maurice had had more than enough time to discover this for himself. He came to his feet. "If you've taken advantage of her while she was with you, I'll not rest night nor day till I have your life's blood for it!"

Hall stammered, "Gentlemen! I beg of you, gentlemen! We're all friends here together. I'm sure . . . any difficulty . . . we can smooth it out. Let us be calm, let's not become angry, distort our vision."

Maurice smiled. "You're quite right, Master Hall. Perhaps, while we discuss the cargo, Patrick could show Sir Edward to the lady's cabin. It should be a merry meeting, especially—" he spoke directly to Blount—"if the child is yours."

"Child? You don't mean Deborah? She took that whelp with her?"

Maurice said, "She's rather a pretty little thing, but the sea is not the place for a wench of any age." He turned to Hall. "I took on a cargo of Spanish wine at Almería. Do you want it in the hold of the *Isabelle-Marie,* or will it ship better in one of the other galleys?"

Edward Blount felt torn between two outrages—the proof that Maurice had stopped in Spain and the knowledge that he had not only Katherine but Deborah on his hands. He chose the latter as a more immediate way to vent his fury and turned on Patrick. "You young fool! Were you completely out of your senses that you allowed Katherine to bring that brat with her?"

Patrick shrugged. "If you wanted the affair handled more skillfully, Sir Edward, why didn't you see to it yourself?"

Maurice looked up. "It's of no consequence now. Please show Sir Edward to Lady Katherine's cabin, Patrick."

Blount changed to another tack. He said graciously, "Perhaps I was too hasty, Maurice. In a difficult situation like this, with the Queen's own maid of honor dependent on us, we might do better if we all considered the best course to take. As I am with the royal Embassy, as I practically am the royal Embassy, my liberty is more restricted than yours or Halls."

Hall started back. "Gentlemen, I know nothing about this. I want to know nothing about it. My duties are to the Turkey Company. I'm out of place, quite out of place, with great ladies of the Court."

"If it were only the lady—but a girl child!" Blount gave Patrick a venomous look.

240

Maurice said, "I fear I must join Master Hall in washing my hands of the matter. Perhaps you and Patrick can find a solution." He unrolled a paper on the table and handed it to the factor. "Here's the shipment I have on board. You can judge for yourself where you'd like it placed. Is there any Company business to be cared for?"

Hall stood up. He did not like the tension in the air. He wiped his forehead with his sleeve. "Not at the moment. We'll return now, Master Quain. I'm also on the *Isabelle-Marie,* so we'll have ample time to make any plans for the Company between here and Constantinople. I'm leaving two of our crew to show you where we're anchored. As for your cargo, I'd like to speak to the captain of our galley before we go farther into that. I bought extra food and bedding for you and your attendants before we left Marseille and made arrangements with the captain for fresh water, so you need have no worries over provisions for the voyage."

Maurice also came to his feet. "Thank you, Master Hall. You were most thoughtful."

"Just my duty, only my duty to the members of the Company, Master Quain." He looked nervously at Blount. Should he suggest they go together or was the knight supposed to stay with the lady who appeared— dear heaven, how these great men lived!—to be Blount's mistress. There was a child, too. He saw the glimmering of a solution. He said hesitantly, "Sir Edward, I wondered if no better plan comes to mind, it would seem difficult to me to send a lady and child alone from here through France. I'd suggest she go with you to Constantinople. Sir William Harborne's wife is there, and some of the factors are married. She could stay in the Embassy until the Turkey Company's next shipment goes back to London. Often the factor who accompanies it has his wife with him. It would be quite respectable and safe if she wished to return with them."

Blount laughed. "I'm sure Lady Katherine will be relieved to find she can go home respectably anyway. It seems to me a long way round to Bordeaux, but if you see no better way, Maurice——"

Maurice said coldly, "So far as I'm concerned, Sir Edward, I don't intend to lift a finger whether you throw Katherine Perrot into the sea, marry her or sell her to the next corsair we meet." His voice intimated there was little to choose among the three proposals.

Blount turned to the factor. "We'll take your suggestion, Hall. Patrick, will you show me to the lady?" He had recovered his equanimity now that Katherine was provided for without his shouldering the responsibility. As Maurice said, it was a delightful surprise to have her with him in the long months ahead.

At Patrick's knock Katherine slid back the bolt, swung open the door. How tired she looked! Patrick thought remorsefully. Those men wrangling over her as though she were a bone, while she had to wait helplessly for their judgment! Katherine smiled at him whimsically as though she read his thoughts, then looked beyond him as Blount stepped into the cabin. She said, "Ned!" and for an instant seemed poised as though for flight. Patrick put out his hand toward her, dropped it to his side as she recovered herself. She repeated his name: "Oh, Ned!"

Blount crossed the distance between them in two steps, gathered her in his arms. "Sweetheart, I have so longed for you."

"Oh Ned!" Katherine put her face against his silkclad shoulder, soft against him in the safe familiarity of his embrace. Whatever his weaknesses, his selfishness, always he was there when things looked darkest. She had never needed him as she needed him now—to find her footing again in a world where she had lost herself. If Ned veered from devotion to false promises, still it was always within known and human limits. He did not, as Maurice had done, betray her into surrender of her innermost self and then turn to wound quivering flesh that she had stripped naked of defense.

Her head went back as she looked at her lover searchingly, his pale-blue eyes warmly glad to be here, his face familiar and loving, unclouded with thought of past or future. "What would I do without you, Ned?"

Katherine noticed Patrick as he moved toward the

242

door. She started to say a word of gratitude to him and stopped. She thought, It is best that we part now or he'll fancy himself in love with me again. There should be some way to say good-by so that I will be a pleasant memory in his heart and yet let him close the door between us. If only he were experienced enough to kiss me lightly and go quickly!

And then she knew she didn't want him to go, to leave her here with Ned. She had been glad to see Ned. She felt him a refuge. No. Ned needed her now, but when he no longer needed her, when he was married to his heiress—— Well, that was the risk she had to take with the life she must lead, and the best she could hope for was to accept gallantly whatever came. To be beautiful and have no dowry—— She smiled mockingly. One could always find some excuse with just a little searching. She put her hand on Patrick's in a swift gesture. Always he made her want to excuse herself.

The door to the connecting room opened. Deborah came out sleepily in a long night rail that trailed the floor. Her mouth made a small oval as she yawned. Her blue eyes rounded at the sight of the two men who seemed to fill the cabin. She sidled over to Katherine. Katherine laughed, knelt down beside the child. Ned looked at the mop of golden curls, the small face, the skin moist and pink, the lips set firmly together in too old and too quiet an expression for so tiny a girl. "Why in the name of God you had to take that whelp with you, Kit, is beyond my understanding."

Katherine said pleasantly, "But I did, Ned, and it seems now you must put up with the both of us." Her mouth trembled.

Blount's eyes turned to Patrick still at the door. "I thought you were leaving us." The look on his face implied he would like to express himself in stronger terms.

Katherine's glance caught Patrick's. They smiled unexpectedly as though they had some private understanding which Blount did not share. She said, "We will probably not meet again, Patrick. God go with you!"

Patrick looked at Blount and at Deborah and then at Katherine. He said challengingly, "I think, Lady Katherine, we will meet again!"

13

From Marmora to the Bosporus Constantinople rose in terraced grandeur up the broken pattern of its seven hills. The grim many-towered wall held the city cupped like a jewel. Palaces and gardens, tall cypresses and slender minarets stabbing the sky gave a lightness, a spacious quality to the city, exotic after the dark towns of the West where houses huddled shoulder to shoulder behind walls that ringed them too closely. Maurice's eyes swept the checkered brilliance of color against the vine-clad slopes across the Golden Horn.

Webster wiped his hot face with his sleeve, narrowed his eyes against the glare of sunlight on the water. "There are only two kinds of weather in Constantinople," he grumbled. "Summer when the wind's from the south even though it's December now in any Christian country, and winter if it's out of the north. Tomorrow we'll be freezing or drowned in the rains."

The *Isabelle-Marie* had dropped her anchor, and the sweating slaves, exhausted after the long pull through the Dardanelles and the Sea of Marmora, sprawled on the main deck. Sailors moved along the center gangway and over the thwarts—dropping the oars overside, lowering and securing the large booms that carried the galley's lateen sails and rigging harbor awnings to provide some shelter from the sun.

Maurice turned. "What are those buildings, Master Webster?"

"Now that, Master Quain, depends on which way you're looking." Webster spoke with a shade of patronage. "Down there to the left is the Castle of the Seven Towers. Stories of prisoners come out from the dungeons, but the prisoners never do. I could tell you tales of torture, of how they kill men by pieces with knife or saw, of eyes plucked out, of white-hot pincers to tear flesh from bone, of——" He noticed Maurice's expression. "But that doesn't interest you? The Hippodrome is just within the walls here—that's an arena where they have all their spectacles, races, you know. Those palaces and towers reaching down to the water front form the Seraglio of the Sultan, and the great dome on the hill is the mosque of Hagia Sophia——"

His words were interrupted by Edward Blount, who came over from the larboard side of the deck. He smiled with an easy charm. "When you're established in your quarters, Maurice, you must call at the Embassy. I'm sure Sir William can help you in your mercantile ventures, though of course we may have little time to spare from our royal duties."

He felt he could be blandly complacent. Had Katherine not been his for these three weeks, with both Maurice and Patrick staying well in the background, so impressed by his presence they'd hardly spoken to her? Was he not becoming a person of international importance? And in Constantinople were the headquarters for the House of Gascony. The smile continued to play about his lips as he eyed Maurice. After all these years he would have this man exactly where he wanted him.

Maurice looked at Blount indifferently. "I shall see Sir William in a day or two." He turned to watch the arrival of the first shore tender that would carry the passengers and their light baggage to their pier. Blount did not lose his smile as he moved back to Katherine.

"Dionesupulos has good quarters across the Horn where the foreigners live in Galata," Webster said reflectively. "I couldn't afford to stay in his house when I was in the East before, but now, why not?"

The narrow twisting streets of Galata were hot under the brilliant sun as they rode up from the Golden Horn. The gray and purple houses of the foreign quarter reflected the light in muted tones. Beggars huddled in the shade of doorways and alleys. Pariah dogs came slinking after them—emaciated, masterless creatures that growled and snapped at rider and pedestrain, fought with one another in a snarling ferocity. The heat pressed down on them, motes of dust dancing in the haze. Their dark Western garments matted to their bodies.

245

Dionesupulos' house was unpretentious from without, but inside the rooms were high and the walls hung with bright curtains of Persian cotton. Divans, cushions and low single-footed tables were scattered about in brilliant colorful profusion. From outside could be heard the splashing of water in a marble fountain.

Maurice said, "This will do very well. As soon as our belongings are brought up, Patrick, you and Webster put our papers in order. We need new lists for the customs officers of the shipment when it comes, and we must see about the purchase or leasing of a warehouse."

Webster looked at Maurice resignedly. If Quain thought that you dispatched your business in the East, if he hoped even faintly to put through his own ventures and an alliance with Turkey in the same brisk manner that he had raised the royal loan in Antwerp and Paris, he would be woefully disappointed. His staff, however, wouldn't be disappointed. They'd all be dead from overwork under the Levantine sun.

Harborne was of the same opinion when Maurice went up to the Embassy on the slopes of Pera. The ambassador was a burly Englishman just past middle age, with a gray spade-cut beard, and hair curled across the back of his neck while the thinning strands on top were combed carefully forward to conceal a balding spot. The long white robe he wore gave him the incongruous appearance of having united East and West by the drastic measure of grafting a British head onto an Oriental body.

He laughed and threw up his hands at Maurice's request for the name of a Turkish firm with which he could do business, what warehouses to lease, a word of how much demand there was for English products. "Not so fast, I beg of you, Master Quain! To begin with, it would be useless for me to recommend a Turkish firm. They would never deal with a Christian dog. But some English house——"

He stopped as Maurice shook his head. "No, thank you, Sir William. Wherever I establish my house, I em-

246

ploy natives of the country. My factor should be English, but after only three days in Constantinople I am convinced a Turkish firm would be the best to deal with. The officals would know not only the language, of course, but the devious methods necessary to move merchandise across frontiers, through hostile regions and around local customs and barriers. While too many English—well, to put it briefly, go to hell in the East."

Harborne said, "You're right of course in the last, but I would not even know to what firm I should direct you. I'll send you a letter of introduction to the Grand Vizier. He might help, though he's antagonistic toward all Englishmen."

"I'll appreciate your aid, Sir William. If we can be of assistance to you at any time, please call on us." Maurice stood up.

Harborne glanced up at Patrick and Webster who had accompanied Maurice, then back at Patrick. "My dear young man, is that a green lining to your cape?"

Patrick looked surprised. "Yes, sir. It's of taffeta." The material had been recommended as excellent protection against the fleas which infested everything in the East.

"If I were you, I'd take it off before you leave the house. Green is to be worn only by the descendants of the Prophet. I've seen Europeans beaten by mobs if they have so much as a green lace in their shoes. You have to walk warily here, and I hope you will since I feel responsible for your welfare."

"As you suggest, sir. We had hoped that Master Webster, who *says* he has been East before, might act as a guide." He grinned as Webster looked mortified at the oversight. He wondered if he could inquire about Katherine. No, not since Maurice had forgotten or, more likely, ignored her. Perhaps he could return to the Embassy. He put in quickly, "Shall I call for the letter of introduction tomorrow, Sir William?"

"Tomorrow!" Harborne looked at Patrick with a smile. "You merchants! I'll have it brought down to you when it's ready." He stood up to see them to the door and send for their horses.

247

The wind veered to the north, bringing cold wet days. No word came from Harborne about the Grand Vizier or Turkish firms. Maurice was not used to waiting on other men's convenience. He sent a coldly civil note to the Embassy, but the letter of introduction, when it came, accomplished less than nothing.

Maurice turned his eyes toward the Seraglio and sent Webster to the palace with their interpreter, an Armenian eunuch. He was softly fat, silent unless spoken to and then listening with his arms folded across his breast, his head bowed. There was something pathetic about this big man—his body warped from its natural function, his high singsong voice that never charged except when money, the eunuch's one passion, was mentioned. He knew that in the ways of the Seraglio the barber was one of the Grand Viziers' most valued advisors. Webster brought the barber a chest of beaten gold, accompanied by a letter requesting that he intercede for them to obtain an audience with the Vizier.

They waited again while the rains came down and the wind blew coldly out of the north. The days dragged monotonously. The Grand Vizier's barber accepted the gift, but he had not sent even an acknowledgment.

At Maurice's remarking of this, Webster shrugged. "The officals are so arrogant here, Master Quain, they never thank a Christian for a present. But in his own good time the barber will say the right word at the right time to the right person." He smiled, feeling in his element. It was a long way from the old days in London's Royal Exchange where he had had to seek temporary employment during the intervals when the African Company was not operating. He turned to Patrick. "I've some entertainment for us today. A lovely lady asked to see you."

Patrick looked up. "Who?"

"I've been renewing an acquaintance with Monsieur Lemaire in the foreign quarter, and I strained my conscience so far giving you a good character that his wife asked to meet you. Make yourself handsome, my lad, and we'll see her today."

Maurice turned. "Who is Monsieur Lemaire?"

"One of the factors for a French house, Master Quain. I knew him years ago when I was out here. He's a sober man of business, but his wife adds a little pleasure to the lives of factors and clerks by opening her house to them afternoons. A delightful young woman."

"Why does a Frenchwoman trouble with English clerks and secretaries?"

Webster shrugged. "I imagine, Master Quain, because she likes visitors and excitement. It's quite an international meeting place. Coming, Patrick?"

Maurice looked thoughtful but he said nothing more.

Thérèse Lemaire was a small vivacious young woman with hazel eyes and golden hair that she wore piled on top of her head and secured with turquoise pins. Her gown of rose satin fitted tightly over her full breasts and plump figure.

Webster grinned as he brought Patrick forward to present him. Thérèse held Patrick's fingers a moment as he bowed over her hand. "Monsieur Nort'?" Her voice was high and sweet. "You mus' seet down, I mus' know you." She waved her hand to the men about her dismissing them with a torrent of French. The soberly gowned clerks and factors looked out of place against the gold and white of the long room.

Patrick, who had taken a place beside her, felt a momentary annoyance especially when he caught Webster's malicious smile. Thérèse moved closer to him, so that he could feel the warmth and softness of her flesh through his heavy silken hose. "You are so sweet, Monsieur Nort', to come to my poor 'ome. You mus' convairse with these men. You will not be then so lonesome for the 'ome in your gray England." She gazed at him searchingly, then smiled and called to one of the servitors to bring him a goblet of cordial from a silver bowl.

Patrick took a long drink and returned her smile. It was a cold amber liquid with essence of roses, thinner than wine and more intoxicating. He felt a little thrill of danger in Thérèse's touch, in the whiteness of her bosom where the dress was cut so low it showed the

249

first swell of her breasts, in her perfumed hair that was, at closer sight, obviously bleached. He was less aware of what she was chattering about then of her light pleasant voice until she made a move to leave.

"I will have your glass refilled, *mon cher*. You must come often to my poor 'ome when we can talk. But now—" she sighed as though she were sorry to leave him—"I mus' see to my other frien's." She stood up, straightened her gown over her hips with long slow strokes.

As Patrick rose with her he found himself not quite steady on his feet. He watched her move off to the group which immediately closed about her, and shook his head to dispel a hazy feeling that was creeping over him a little too delightfully. He looked twice at the sparkling amber liquid in the goblet the servant brought up, then moved over to pour the contents surreptitiously into a tall Chinese vase. He turned at a sound behind him to see Webster watching him with a grin.

"You 'ave more of the common sense, Monsieur Nort'," he mimicked his hostess, "than I t'ink." In his normal voice he went on: "Come along and I'll introduce you to some of the men present. Not important people, you will notice, but they might be someday. In any case you often pick up more of the rumors going about the city and the foreign quarter and the plans of the different houses than you'll hear any other way, even in the Exchange. I suppose Madame Lemaire also has that in mind."

Patrick said pleasantly, "Don't insult me now, Master Webster, by suggesting that I should imitate the merchant who hears all and says nothing. Besides, Madame Lemaire does not give one overmuch opportunity to talk."

"When your turn comes, my lad, she will. Now this Venetian over here——"

Patrick did not heed description or introduction of the Venetian or any of the other half-dozen men of all ages and nations he met. He was glad he had come, and he would certainly make use of Thérèse's invitation to return.

Maurice looked his disapproval but said nothing about the Lemaires when they returned to the apartment. He was standing by the tall window facing to the east, an enormous roll of paper dangling with seals in his hands. He tossed it onto his desk. "This came while you were gone. The Grand Vizier will see us in a fortnight. After that perhaps we can begin to do business here, I'd like to be established before we're involved in this political alliance. It might complicate the way to our goals."

He didn't like to be entangled in political maneuvers. And he had no intention of making matters difficult for himself by putting forward any suggestion to Harborne than he discuss the alliance as well as his own needs now that the elusive Grand Vizier had finally consented to an audience. He was in Constantinople for the House of Quain.

The Grand Vizier Othman watched his visitor out of hooded eyes. His face was dark and lean under his high headdress of white muslin with its wide horizontal bands of gold lace. The flowing white robes of sable-trimmed satin seemed sculptured on him as he sat motionless in his great chair of bronze and jade. The long room was shadowy with windows curtained in blue damask, walls hung with cloth of gold, and a score of slaves near the dais looking ghostly in their pale robes and rigidly humble posture.

Maurice, the only Western European in the chamber, stood with his interpreter before the Grand Vizier. He was beginning to feel a chill annoyance, not lessened by the fact that every word spoken had to be translated, sometimes more than once when the Grand Vizier pretended a diffluclty in hearing.

"You are from Londro?" The Vizier's voice had a note of contempt.

"We call it London, Excellency."

"Am I to understand you wish to deal with a Turkish firm instead of through your own foreign quarter?"

"Yes, Excellency." Maurice had been under the impression that both points had seen settled long before. He wondered if Othman were not trying to antagonize him. "I feel my business in Constantinople would be cared for more efficiently by your countrymen—adopted countrymen."

He had forgotten for the moment that the Sultan's ministers were never chosen from his Turkish subjects but from Christian slaves, forced converts to Islam. As Othman stared beyond him with impassive features, Maurice wondered at the diabolical system which turned the children of the hated Christians through years of careful training into fanatical Moslems. He'd heard that these selected slaves were educated in the Seraglio itself, some passing into the ranks of the Janizaries, the most formidable infantry in Europe and Asia; others becoming clerks in the Treasury and mixers of the Sultan's cordials; while the most highly educated changed their plain clothes to satin brocade and gold cloth and became servers of the Sultan's person. From among these personal attendants would be chosen ministers of state, governors of provinces, pashas.

As the Grand Vizier stirred in his chair, Maurice continued, "We could supply you with Western products of use to your state."

The Grand Vizier looked scornful. What could the West send that the East did not produce more abundantly and in more refined form?

Maurice said, "Tin and copper from Cornwall for cannon for the Persian war, Excellency, as well as cordage for your ships. And naturally we will be honored if you will accept a humble share of each cargo that moves through your domain." The share Maurice resolved, would get humbler every day the Grand Vizier kept him waiting. It was worth only so much to him to get higher profits by dealing through a Turkish merchant.

Either Othman read his thoughts in his face or the mention of a percentage made him more affiable. He lifted his hand from the arm of the bronze chair in a gracious gesture. "Our Moslem-born are reluctant to deal with Christian dogs, but we have one large house in Constantinople which has connections in the West. I will send them word of your desire to be honored

252

by an interview with the head of the house, Mustafa Rahmi. They will inform you in due time regarding their willingness to give you so great a privilege." He bowed in dismissal.

Maurice's interpreter went down on his knees before the dais, bowed four times to the Grand Vizier as he backed out. Maurice followed the eunuch, not dissatisfied with the short audience. Mustafa Rahmi. He could speak to Harborne about the firm.

In answer to Maurice's questions the next day, Sir William said, "Mustafa Rahmi? He has a good reputation in the city, I understand. We have had no direct dealings with him since we believe in having our own factors and keeping our business completely English. Perhaps the French and Italians have more flexibility of mind than we. You have something of their international outlook, Master Quain. The danger in that is that you may be unwittingly helping the enemies of your country."

Maurice shrugged. Harborne smoothed his thinning hair across the top of his head. "I have been trying to think where I'd heard the name Mustafa Rahmi recently. I remember now. Sir Edward inquired about the firm."

Maurice said bluntly, "Why?"

"He wanted to make some purchase, I believe, for Lady Katherine."

"Lady Katherine? I suppose she's returning when the next cargo is shipped to England." Maurice's voice was indifferent.

"There was mention of that, but I'd certainly not recommend a sea voyage for another five or six months at the least unless for some impelling motive. The winter storms in the Mediterranean are only for hardened sailors."

Maurice changed the subject abruptly. "I'm sending dispatches to Osborne when the cargo goes out, Sir William. Could I give him any word about the alliance with Turkey? Osborne mentioned to me before I left that he did not have overmuch confidence in the royal courier after he'd spoken to him on the treaty."

Maurice made a deprecatory gesture with one hand. "Of course you know the London merchants. Possibly they are too wary of couriers."

"The alliance . . . ah . . . Perhaps I should send Osborne my own report." Harborne shifted in his chair, adjusted a cushion under his elbow. "Or perhaps, Master Quain, I should speak openly to you."

Maurice glanced at him coldly. "Not if it's more a matter of State than of the Turkey Company. The treaty or any other political affair is of no interest to me at all."

"I heard differently. I heard in fact that you were much interested, but not for England's sake."

Maurice laughed. "For whom do I work then—besides myself, which is obvious?"

"To be blunt, for Spain instead of against her. I heard you stopped at Almería on your way to Constantinople. Before that you were one of Mary Stuart's adherents. You sell supplies to Philip Hapsburg, and you are one man who never suffers from Spain's ill will toward English merchants. Now you ask me how this alliance against Spain is going while disclaiming all interest."

"My dear Sir William, I won't waste your time or mine discussing my loyalty. But I beg you will hold a better opinion of my intelligence than to think that I'd trouble to give secrets to the Spanish government or that I'd work for Philip. As you must know since you're a businessman, the bribes would never make up for the profit I'd lose if I were on any man's side either for or against England." He looked at Harborne mockingly. "You wouldn't have 'heard' all this from Sir Edward? He's rather a trying companion and not one I'd have chosen for the post he was given. But his patriotism, I'm sure, can't be called into question."

There was a glint in Harborne's eyes. "No, it can't Master Quain. To my mind his loyalty and integrity are virtues that more than balance any of the aspersions you cast on him. I'll admit he's not the best man for diplomatic work, but since we have our usual channels to the Sultan, it hardly matters. I suppose his remarks about you were an excess of zeal. It's difficult to understand an attitude like yours. Since Osborne and Staper do seem to have confidence in you, perhaps I took Sir Edward too seriously."

An uneasy look crossed his face. "I'm not too satisfied with the way the treaty is being delayed. Our connections in the Seraglio are with the Sultan Saifé. But of late Janfreda Kadein, who is the head of the palace women, has been superseding Saifé and we've not been able yet to buy her friendship. As you know, while the Grand Vizier holds the country together, it's really governed by the harem. If Roxane could oust Suleyman's favorite Sultana, the Rose of the World, have his friend and Grand Vizier assassinated, sway him to have his only capable sons murdered to make room for hers on the throne, you can understand that this Amurath is wax in the hands of a favorite. Since I went to Saifé first, I'm not in Janfreda's good graces."

Maurice stood up to leave. "Let's hope, Sir William, that, like the Queen, time also is your friend and your affairs mend soon."

There was a quick knock at the door and Edward Blount came in without waiting for Harborne's voice to bid him enter. He looked at Harborne and then at Maurice, a flame of hostility in his pale-blue eyes. "I didn't expect to see you at the Embassy, Maurice."

"No?" Maurice turned to Harborne. "If I can be of any service, Sir William, you know where I lodge."

Blount smiled. "Do you know, Maurice, I rather think the need may be yours, not Sir William's."

Maurice said smoothly, "We'll hope so, Sir Edward since Sir William is important to the welfare of so many."

Harborne murmured graciously, "We'll be glad to see you again, Master Quain, whenever you have time to spare, and we'd like to hear how your connections with Mustafa Rahmi go forward."

Blout said nothing, but he turned to watch Maurice's tall figure until the door closed behind him.

Maurice glanced about for Webster as he went into the lofty hall. A page detached himself leisurely from the wall which he'd been leaning against and offered his services. It was almost ominiously still. Outside

Maurice could hear the wind shrilling about the corner of the house, a loud voice, the sound of a horse's hoofs, but within it was as though he were in a house of the dead. The scarlet curtains on the wall fluttered in an occasional draft. The Turkish mat underfoot gleamed red, blue and yellow in the cool light. The silence seemed deeper for the color that fed the eye.

There was a flurry of voices at the outer door just beyond his sight, the sound of footsteps soft on the thick piling of the rug. He stood where he was unwillingly because he had heard a woman's laughter. A small group of men and women came into the hall. He saw only Katherine.

She came forward simply and naturally as though between them there were not an hour of golden intimacy and a bitter hurt that must scar, as he had meant it to scar, past healing. "Master Quain! I had not seen you. . . . I wondered if you were . . . But of course you are never ill. That wouldn't be at all becoming to your dignity." She laughed as she held out her hand for him to kiss. Then she turned her head.

Maurice, following her gaze, saw that there were only another woman, middle-aged and of an overpowering presence, and two gentlemen attendants, probably of the household staff from the way they drew back. Katherine said, "Lady Harborne, this is an English friend of mine, Master Quain. He's of the Turkey Company, so no doubt you'll be seeing him again."

Lady Harborne came up, magnificent in a cloak of crimson velvet with the leopards of England embroidered in gold thread. At every gesture the sleek animals seemed to move gracefully down the front and about the hem of the garment. She had on a wide-brimmed hat with a sweeping plume that touched her shoulder.

Maurice bowed, acknowledging the introduction in a chill voice.

Lady Harborne graciously extended the tips of her fingers. "We shall expect you to come up soon to renew your friendship with Lady Katherine and to allow me to meet one of my husband's associates in the Company." She paused as though she would say more, then mercifully gathered Katherine and the two gentlemen attendants to her with a nod and swept on.

Katherine, still smiling, curtsied to him before she followed the others. She thought whimsically, Good heavens, my smile is so fixed maybe it will never come off! She stopped a moment to ask about Patrick.

Maurice said coldly that he was well, and did not turn his head to watch her go down the hall toward the room he had just left. A shadow passed between him and the light, and Webster came in from the corridor, the page with him. Maurice said curtly, "You were long enough on whatever business you were attending, Master Webster. Are the horses ordered out?"

Webster, who had been asleep, suppressed a yawn. "Yes, Master Quain. I didn't expect you to be finished so quickly." He patted the purse hanging at his belt. "I helped reduce some of the surplus riches that drive young men to ruin, though the gentlemen were so unmannerly as not to let me use my own dice."

As they rode down the slope toward Galata, Maurice was inattentive to the now too-familiar streets. He should hear soon from Mustafa Rahmi and then he could begin to tap the wealth of the East. He looked up as Webster reined in his horse on the edge of an open square. Maurice had been only vaguely aware of the people filling the space, crowding about in their turbans and flowing robes.

Webster said, "I heard there was a raid into Russian territory. These must be the captives." He edged his horse into the fringes of the crowd with a lively interest. Two enormous Russians, dark and bearded, were being brought down for the prospective buyers to examine while the seller intoned their merits in a high singsong voice. There were a few scattered calls, a spatter of halfhearted bids, then an angry altercation that was settled by the ring of gold coins paid into the auctioneer's hands.

The seller motioned the captives off the dais impatiently, signaled for the next. Three girls were led out, tall and well made, with strong almost masculine features. Webster murmured, "The best of the lot were sent to the harem. These men have to take what's left them by the Shadow of Allah. You should see one of the really big markets when there's a war with Persia. Even the harem can't accommodate all the beauties, and the ordinary man gets a chance for a pretty little thing in his own home."

Maurice turned to look from the mart to Webster with a slight shock. He felt he'd never seen Webster before. The wiry middle-aged man sat hunched up in his saddle, while his eyes regarded the scene neither lasciviously as Maurice had expected, nor with a sadistic enjoyment, but with curiosity about the way of the world.

An old woman waddled out after the captives. She had dyed, black hair coiled thinly about her head, a wide face, small eyes peering out from rolls of fat, and an immensely heavy body. She started to strip the girls slowly like one displaying her treasures, showing first the strong straight back, the firm breasts, then the wide hips and long-thighed legs. The bidding grew more lively. There was in the attitude of the first girl a hunted submission. The muscles of her neck were rigid as she turned her head from the crowd, and she crossed her arms to hide her breasts. The old woman, noting the concealing gesture, jerked her hands down.

In his own aching flesh Maurice could feel momentarily the horror and despair of these Christian girls. A man could go mad trying to right a vicious world! He lifted the reins of his horse to go on. These captives were of no consequence to him. He was a rich man. If it pleased him, he could send Webster to buy one of these young women as his slave, use her as the victim of his savage impulses. There was a darkness in him like the stirring of muddy water. If he could not right the world, he could use it to the bitter end.

Webster followed him down the street reluctantly. He said above the clatter of hoofs, "They were just beginning the selling, Master Quain. The best of the captives won't be brought out for some time. Don't you want to watch?"

Maurice, his gauntleted hands tight on the reins, said shortly. "No. I may be overly fastidious, Master

Webster, but bartering human flesh like cattle at a fair doesn't appeal to me this morning."

And yet perhaps this too was part of the spell of the East, one of the darker shadows that by its very brutality brought out more strongly in relief the amazing luxury of gold and marble and silver and jade, the exquisite architecture, the slender minarets, the strange languages, fragrant perfumes, the veiled women behind latticed windows.

The horses started to canter as they turned down the sloping street leading to Dionesupulos' house. They dismounted at the heavy iron-barred door that always gave the illusion of leading into a dreary prison instead of the airy spaciousness of the Greek's dwelling with its high rooms, rich carpets and colorful hangings.

Patrick came forward as they entered. "A messenger from Mustafa Rahmi just left, Master Quain. He came to say his matter would be honored to see you—though it's an honor he's been obviously in no haste to enjoy."

Maurice stripped off his gloves and handed them with hat and cloak to Jacques. "Good! We'll send an answer in three days, not to show too much haste or waste too much time. Perhaps our affairs will begin to move now." He smiled. It was for this he had come to Turkey.

14

Maurice returned somewhat ruffled from his first interview with the Turkish firm. He said with annoyance, "Mustafa Rahmi is in Bodajoz, and there's no one here who cares to take the responsibility of so unorthodox an arrangement as I'm interested in. The best I could do was to make plans with his official, Ali Efessis, to ride north and see Mustafa in a few days."

Webster said, "Good! When do we go?"

"Master Webster, you leave tomorrow for Gallipoli where there's a factor from the Turkey Company. Have him send a message to my house in Rome for a shipment of tin and copper for the Grand Vizier. Too many questions are asked if I send the message from here. Time enough to discuss a matter when it's accomplished. The reason for the haste is that Hall also is traveling to Gallipoli tomorrow, so we need not worry about an escort for you. For myself, I'll leave Thursday. Ali Efessis suggested that since I have the time, I go up with him to their warehouses along the Bosporus to see the caravans and meet some of the inland traders."

He pulled open the carved drawer of his desk, drew out a map. "Here are the warehouses, Patrick, about ten miles up the straits. Instead of my coming back to Constantinople, I'll return with Ali Efessis as far as this crossroad which leads back to the city or on to Bodajoz. There's an inn there called Le Cocq. I'll meet you there at high noon on Monday. Kyrion Dionesupulos has already said he'll hire a guard."

"Meet me there!" Patrick's eyes opened wide. "Am I not going with you?"

"No. I'll take Jacques. The fewer Christians in a party, the easier it is to do business with a Turk, especially the natives from the inner provinces."

Webster said, "That's true. I know travelers who'll never go in a party where there's another European. It takes so little to antagonize these Orientals, and if one Christian annoys them, they retaliate on the whole group."

Patrick frowned. "All the same I don't like your going alone."

Maurice looked at him in amused surprise. He did not, however, change his mind.

By Sunday Patrick liked Maurice's plans no better. Maurice might be shrewd but he had no sense of personal danger. The Grand Vizier had recommended the firm, Harborne had given it a good reputation; still Patrick intended to leave early the next day with the guard and be at Le Cocq long before Maurice could possible arrive. He pulled back the curtain from the window. On the near-by rooftops there was a rime disappearing now under the afternoon sun. It seemed oddly quiet in spite of the street noises. At home the clangor of bells marked every hour, every occasion, while here bells were considered of Christian origin and prohibited by the Moslems.

He turned as Vincent came in yawning. He said restlessly, "I'm going out. Do you want to come?"

"Not me! When Master Quain's away, I sleep." Vincent stretched lazily and dropped onto a bronze couch.

Patrick laughed. "I should insist you come to Le Cocq with me just for the exercise. You'll forget how to move entirely." He caught up his cloak. "Well, if I break my neck or get drowned in the Golden Horn, you'll have to go. And a good thing, too," he added heartlessly as Vincent, who was no horseman, shuddered at the suggestion of the long ride.

Patrick walked aimlessly down the street toward the bridge between Galata and Stamboul. There was a sound of footsteps behind him. He was vaguely aware they had been behind him for some time. He turned. A small Frenchman sauntered up, bowed cheerfully, ignoring Patrick's suspicious glance.

"Good day, Monsieur North! I was wondering whether it was you or not." At Patrick's blank look, he went on, "I was introduced to you at Madame Lemaire's a few weeks ago, but I fear you don't remember me."

"I'm sorry but I don't." He eyed the Frenchman thoughtfully. There was nothing to distinguish him from a dozen clerks Patrick had met the several times he had been at Lemaire's.

The Frenchman nodded. "The name's Rougier. We'll meet again no doubt." He started to move on, stopped. "Are you on your way to see the Sultan and his troops?"

Patrick grinned slightly. "That would depend on whether they're nearer Constantinople or Persia."

"They're marching through the city up this way." Rougier fell back to match his steps to Patrick's. "The Sultan appears with the army. At the end of the review he returns to the Seraglio and the soliders go to Persia."

They crossed the bridge, went past a white Moslem mosque and turned into a wide street that was lined with noblemen, traders, merchants and slaves. Pariah dogs darted back and forth, snarling at one another. Well-fed cats with tails curled high moved sleekly down the street as though the people were there only to watch them, the favored of the Prophet.

A stir of excitement swept through the crowd as the sounds of horses' hoofs and marching men could be heard in the distance, thundered closer. Heralds appeared swinging around the curve. They were chanting a veritable litany, "*Padishahin chok tasha!* Allah give long life to our lord the Padishah! The Sultan of the Ottomans, Allah's Deputy on Earth, Lord of the Lords of This World, King of Kings, Emperor of the East and West, Prince and Lord of the Most Happy Constellation, Seal of Victory, Refuge of All the People in the World, the Shadow of the Almighty Dispensing Quiet in the Earth."

Rougier interpreted the cries, added as the first detachment came into view, "That's the royal bodyguard, the *solaks*." Tall men in plumed and gilded helmets marched by, and after them huge soldiers, artifical braids hanging down their bronzed cheeks, scimitars glittering at their sides. "The *peyks*. In that litter, as you would know without my telling you, Monsieur North, is the Shadow of Allah himself."

Like a wind sweeping across grass in a field, every man in the street bowed before the magnificent litter of bronze inset with jewels, lined with white satin curtains and embroidered with pearls. The Sultan was staring straight ahead, though his small sleepy eyes were almost lost behind rolls of flesh. His large body scintillated with the mass of emeralds and rubies and diamonds on his robe of gold. Not even his eyes moved, and the three heron plumes attached to his dazzlingly white turban trembled only from the movement of the black eunuchs carrying the litter.

Patrick shivered. A repulsive-looking creature, and yet at the lift of that fat hand, armies were flung against the East or the West, Persia or Hungary, hammer and saw heard in the imperial shipyards. For his smile women from Europe and Asia would be enslaved by the victorious army, would be presented from beglerbegs of the chief cities, would be sent as hostages from tributary countries.

Behind the litter of the Sultan rode the Master of the Turban who carried an exact replica of the headdress on the Sultan's brow. As the crowd cheered, he inclined the turban to right and left in acknowledgment of their loyal applause.

There was the sound of iron-spiked shoes on the stones. The Frenchman said, "Here come the *yenitcheri*, the New Soldiers—Janizaries you probably call them."

They marched in steady ranks, blue cloaks swinging, each tall conical hat decorated with plumes from the bird of paradise and a copper spoon thrust through the crown. A white banner with a text from the Koran embroidered in gold floated over their ranks. Among the Asiatics moving before and after them the European faces of the Janizaries, those slaves with Christian parents, looked strange.

A disorderly throng of light horse swept by after tem. "The *akinji*." The Frenchman grimaced. "Locusts, vipers—they can't stand against the Christians, but they follow the army and fall on defenseless houses, burn fields, slay women and children—pah! Those horsemen behind them are the Madcaps."

A fitting name, Patrick thought. Their steeds were decorated with furs and feathers, their hair was matted under leopard caps, and mantles of lionskin were fastened about their shoulders. A few held pikes and scimitars but most had clubs in their hands.

"Of course you know the dervishes." The Frenchman waved toward men, naked except for tall hats of camel's hair and green aprons edged with ebony beads, who ran along beside the marchers shouting and blowing raucously on their horns.

"And here's the regular cavalry, the spahis." The spahis rode in order, rank after rank, under their flaming red banner, gem-studded weapons flashing in the sun. After them camels swayed by and then supply wagons loaded with grain.

Patrick watched the last of the army flow down the street, started to turn away. Rougier said, "It's Sunday, m'sieu, and nothing to do in the foreign quarter. Would you care to go over to Madame Lemaire's? After these Oriental hordes, Christian faces will look cheering to me."

Patrick hesitated, then shrugged. He had nothing to do until the next morning and Vincent was not an exciting companion. "If you think we would be welcome."

Thérèse Lemaire did not leave him in doubt about that. She was alone in the gold and white room where he had first met her, sitting pensively in a great chair. She stood up quickly to cross to him. *"Mon cher,* it is long since you were 'ere! I am so 'appy to see you! And you, Monsieur Rougier." She smiled at the little Frenchman.

Rougier dropped onto a couch like a man who felt at home. "I just happened to be near the bridge when Monsieur North was out walking, Thérèse. We watched the parade and then thought we'd stop to see you. A happy coincidence meeting, monsieur, was it not?"

Patrick looked sharply at Rougier at his insistence this was a chance meeting. He was sure now Rougier's steps had been behind him for some time before he'd turned. But what possible purpose would Rougier have in following him and bringing him here?

Patrick, not intending to delay his leave-taking for an answer to the question, said pleasantly, "Yes, a fortunate happening. It's a pity I'm not free today to enjoy my good luck. I came only to pay my respects and to ask when I might see you, madam, for a longer visit."

Thérèse's hazel eyes widened. "Monsieur Nort', please! You cannot go so quickly. Do sit down a moment." She drew him to a rose and gold divan under the curtained window. Patrick sat down reluctantly. Thérèse turned to her countryman. "Won't you have a glass of wine, Monsieur Rougier? And I'm sure Monsieur Nort' would like one before he's so unmannerly as to leave." She turned toward Patrick. The thin blue gown she wore accentuated her generous curves and her perfume was exotic.

Patrick looked away. The desire she stirred in him was overlaid with a suspicion of danger. He took the goblet Rougier brought over, murmured a thank-you, but made no move to drink the wine.

The Frenchman glanced at Thérèse. "Is your husband in his office, madam? If you'll excuse me, I'll go up to see him about the cargo to be shipped out tomorrow."

Thérèse gave her permission graciously. Patrick came to his feet as Rougier went out. "Perhaps I might see you next week, madame?"

She pouted a little. "I don't know why I should like you so much, Monsieur Nort', and you so unkin' as to leave me today. But come when you can, *mon cher*. I will be mos' pleased to see you any time."

He bowed over her hand, crossed the room, started to open the door. She gave a small scream. "Oh, Monsieur Nort', watch out!"

At her cry he swung back involuntarily. The latch was pulled out of his grasp, something crashed against his head. Blackness splintered as a thousand needles of light descended upon him.

Patrick struggled out of the darkness into an awareness of incredible agony. He opened his eyes slowly, looked blankly about the gold and white room, groping for remembrance. As he moved his head he heard a rustle of silk.

Thérèse Lemaire bent over him. "Oh, my poor Monsieur Nort'!" Her big eyes were limpid with sympathy. Patrick swung his feet over the side of the low couch and sat up. He swayed dizzily a moment. "M'sieu, you were so unfortunate! I called to you. There was a mace on the wall. When you opened the door, you must have dislodged it."

The whole affair came back in a rush. His eyes did not follow hers to the weapon suspended on the wall over the door, nor did he trouble to point out that however effective a mace might be in a quarrel, it could hardly pull open a door before striking a victim.

He put his hand to the swelling on the side of his head, said abruptly, "What is the hour?" The windows were curtained so that he could not see whether it was still afternoon or night.

Thérèse murmured soothingly, "It does not matter, Monsieur Nort'. I will send word to your friends where you are."

Steadying himself with one hand he got to his feet. The dizziness was beginning to subside. "I'm quite able to tell them myself, thank you, madam. What is the hour?"

"You will be mos' annoyed when I tell you. I am so sorry it 'appen in my 'ouse." She paused. "It is almost noon."

"I've been here overnight? Impossible!" He tried to keep the dismay out of his voice. She must be lying— but he knew she wasn't. At noon he was supposed to be at Le Cocq.

Thérèse shrugged. "You may see for——" Her words broke off as he moved swiftly across the room.

With his hand on the latch, Patrick stopped. "Would you care to go out first, madam? This time I'd like to leave."

"Monsieur Nort'!" Thérèse sputtered indignantly. "you do not think I——I do not like what you would say! You are free to go. I am sorry so 'orrible an acciden' 'appen 'ere. You cannot believe——" Then she smiled at him, her eyes wistful, one small hand touching his arm lightly. "But you are upset. When you res' you feel better. You not think such terrible things about poor Thérèse."

Patrick opened the door and stepped back unchivalrously for her to go first. It was agony to move, but one thought cut through his dizziness, the pain that made his head throb, and that was to get safely out of this house and to Le Cocq. Perhaps it was all right. It was just possible that when he had not returned yesterday, Vincent had had the sense to ride with the guard to Maurice.

Thérèse gazed up at him reproachfully. "If I meant you ill, m'sieu, why would I have let you wake up at all?"

Patrick said shortly, "That is only one of a number of questions that need answering, madam." The hall outside was empty except for an old porter who, at Thérèse's nod, opened the door for Patrick.

Tom, lounging on the divan in the deserted splendor of the apartment, sat up in surprise at Patrick's appearance. "Name of God, where have you been?"

"Never mind that. Where's Vincent?"

Tom said indolently, "He rode out an hour ago to meet Master Quain at some outlandish place."

"Only an hour ago? You're sure?"

"Maybe it was longer. He delayed, hoping you'd return. Where?—"

"Get your cloak and order out the two best horses Dionesupulos can acquire in a hurry." Patrick put one hand gingerly to his head. "Maybe Master Quain will be late at the meeting place. Or—— God's blood, hurry!"

Tom was halfway down the steps at the usual violence in Patrick's voice. Patrick had a sick sensation this was only the beginning of some evil adventure.

They were maddeningly delayed in the press of wagons and people moving aimlessly through the streets of the city, went more swiftly as they passed through the north gate and up the slow curve of road beyond. Far to the left the Sea of Marmora crashed along the shore, and ahead of them the mountains rose darkly against the blue sky and with its wide scudding clouds. The wind from the east was cutting. Patrick muffled his cloak about his throat. There was a singing in his ears. He turned his head painfully as Tom called to him above the pounding of the hoofs on the rutted road.

"Do as you like, Master North, but you'll kill the horses if you don't slacken rein, and we'll be walking the rest of the way."

Patrick, as he took Tom's advice mechanically, looked ahead. Seven men were rounding a curve on the long slope below them, one rider lagging behind. That must be Vincent. Patrick spurred his horse cruelly. The tired animal's head jerked up at the pain, then mane and hoofs were flying as they went down the half mile

267

of road before Patrick reined in. It was Vincent and the Greek guard. "Where's Quain? Why are you returning alone?"

Vincent, grateful for the chance to rest, sat a moment in his saddle gasping for breath. "He w-wasn't at Le Cocq, Patrick. He left word he had to go on. We were too late. Here's a message for you." He searched frantically in his doublet, pulled out a torn piece of paper.

Patrick took it sickly, just glanced at it. "You idiot! This isn't in Quain's hand!"

"No. The innkeeper said he wrote it for him."

Patrick read the message. It said only that Maurice could wait no longer and had gone on to Bodajoz alone. He would return to Constantinople in a few days. Patrick shook his head. "No innkeeper wrote that. What did the man say? Who was at the inn?"

Vincent looked at Patrick in dull surprise as he wiped his forehead with the back of his glove. "No one. The innkeeper said he knew nothing more than is on that paper."

Patrick thought if Maurice hadn't written the message, it was because he'd refused to write it. He turned to the Greek captian who had ridden up. "Did you inquire in the yard or the stables if there were others than Master Quain at Le Cocq?"

"I did so, Kyrion North. Perhaps I'm overly suspicious of these Turks, but it is not without reason. When the man I'm sent to escort is gone, I think at once it's because he cannot help himself. Anybody can write a message." He dismissed the paper with contempt. "But the stableboys, the kitchen workers, all swore there had been no one at Le Cocq today except an English gentleman and his servant, and that he'd ordered a coach and gone north to Bodajoz. They were all paid to lie of course."

Patrick said, "Ride back to Bodajoz. Master Quain was to see Mustafa Rahmi at the house of the customs officer. There isn't a chance in a thousand he'll be there, but it would be ridiculous not to inquire."

Vincent's mouth dropped open. "Me? Ride to
268

Bodajoz? I can't do it, Patrick. I'd like to. But it can't be done. The spirit is willing, but not the body."

Patrick, not troubling to answer, knowing Vincent would go, swung his horse's head about to return to Constantinople.

Patrick went to Mustafa Rahmi's establishment. He was shown at once to one of the inner chambers, a long light room filled so high with bales of merchandise that it was a moment before he saw an elderly Turk behind boxes of cramoisy velvet and damask and boxes of pungent spices.

The man peered around the corner of the stacked bales, came out as he saw Patrick. *"Entrez, monsieur! Entrez!"* His accent was worse than Patrick's. The Turk, seeing his perplexity, sent for an interpreter.

Patrick listened impatiently to the translation of Ali Efessis' greeting, his gratitude for Patrick's hororing his humble roof, his hope for a long and happy life, and his desire to assist Patrick in any matter at all. On and on. Patrick broke in; "Thank you. I'd like only to know where Master Quain is."

"Quain? When I left him this morning he was at Le Cocq waiting for his attendants. We were there early, and the man he was expecting had not arrived, effendi. I was in haste and could not wait, but he said he was sure he'd be joined at any moment by his guard."

Patrick said, "When the guard arrived, sir, Master Quain was not at Le Cocq."

Ali Efessis shrugged. "He must have gone on alone to Bodajoz. I know he was impatient to leave."

"I sent a man to inquire about that, though I'm certain Master Quain would not have left, especially as a message given me was not in his handwriting."

Ali Efessis looked bland. "I am sure you're disturbing yourself unnecessarily, young man. He'll be found at Bodajoz. If he is not, I regret I cannot assist you. All I know of Effendi Quain is that we parted in a friendly fashion at Le Cocq and I came on to Constantinople. I would not worry. Effendi Quain seems well able to take care of himself." A rueful expression flashed across his face.

Patrick gathered that Maurice had made some profitable agreement—profitable for Maurice—with the Turk. He hesitated, eying the impenetrable face of Ali Efessis, wondering how to get behind his mask. Webster might know, but Webster was not in Constantinople. He started to turn away, caught sight of the word "France" on one of the bales of merchandise and looked again at the cipher. It was addressed to the House of Gascony in Paris. He swung back impetuously.

Ali Efessis said in surprise, "Gascony? Of course, that is the branch of our house in Paris. Are you acquainted with it? A fine establishment with an excellent trade."

Patrick said, "I have heard the name, that is all. It has a good reputation, I understand." He bowed. "Thank you, sir, for your time."

He went out. The House of Gascony? The sky was darkening and the streets were almost deserted. He became aware that he felt exhausted. He started toward the Embassy, then changed his mind abruptly. Sir William Harborne would give little credence to his story unless he could say with assurance that Maurice was not at Bodajoz. He must wait until Vincent returned and he had something besides his own inner knowledge to fortify his demand for action.

He turned down the street toward their quarters. He was unbelievably tired as he went up the steps. His fatigue intensified the pain from the blow on his head last night. He longed to have his hands about Thérèse Lemaire's throat to choke the truth, or the life, out of her. He felt capable, and willing to strangle her if there were the slightest chance the violence would accomplish anything besides putting him behind bars.

He tried to keep himself from speculating on where Maurice might be and who his captors were. He remembered irrelevantly one of Webster's careless stories about the Eastern king who, annoyed because a messenger would not remove his turban, gave orders to have the headdress nailed to the unfortunate man's head. He shivered.

He must see Harborne the moment Vincent returned. If the ambassador could or would do nothing, there was the Grand Vizier. He had recommended the House of Mustafa Rahmi. Patrick had a vague unsatisfactory feeling that something essential was just beyond his grasp. Maurice had raised money from the House of Gascony in Paris. At Le Grand Andely he'd had to pay Blount to get the royal loan out of the country. Edward Blount.

Vincent and the Greek captain returned in the early afternoon. Vincent fell into a chair, declaring pathetically he was but the poor ruined remains of a man, stopped his complaints at Patrick's impatient questions. "Master Quain isn't in Bodajoz, Patrick, and no one from the House of Mustafa Rahmi has been at the customs officer's or even in the town."

Patrick turned to the Greek. "Captain Leonidas, will you start from Le Cocq again and comb the entire countryside. I can't tell you what to do because I'm entirely unfamiliar with this country, but you'll• know. Follow any scent you can dig up. Here are fifty ducats. If you need more money you'll have it. If you find Master Quain, you can name your own price."

The captain's teeth flashed in a smile. "I'll do my best, Kyrion." He took the purse, started to weigh it consideringly in his hand, changed his mind about questioning Patrick's claim of the amount he'd given him, and thrust the purse into the leather pouch at his belt. He saluted smartly and went out.

Patrick sent for Tom. Tom looked around in surprise as he came in. "Where's Master Quain? The guard's below in the courtyard, just returned. I thought he was with them."

Patrick brushed the question aside. "I want you to get a letter to the Grand Vizier Othman. Here's gold. Bribe everyone you have to. We want an audience tomorrow."

Tom, tall and fair-haired, grinned at Patrick. "You're beginning to sound just a little like Master Quain."

Patrick's lean anxious face relaxed into a smile. But his fingers drummed on the table while he looked about for a gift. No Turkish official would defile his

271

eyes reading a missive from a Christian dog if it did not look profitable. His gaze caught the silver chest Maurice used for letters, the sides and top of which were patterned with mother-of-pearl. He emptied out papers and parchments unceremoniously, dusted it off. "Take this with the letter. I'm riding over to Pera to the Embassy."

The first unpleasant word he had was that Harborne was out of the city and would not be back for several days. Patrick asked for Katherine. She sent word at once for him to come up. He followed the page up the wide steps. He must remember he was seeing Katherine for but one reason—not for his sake, but Maurice's.

She smiled at him as he entered, and vivid as he thought he'd kept the picture of her in his heart, her flesh-and-blood loveliness struck him anew with realization of how lonely he had been for her. The color had come into her cheeks. It faded, leaving her face white, and lines drawn faintly about her eyes. Instead of detracting from her beauty, it seemed only to give it a delicate charm. A robe of heavy blue damask fell loosely from her shoulders. As he went forward he noticed there was something different about her. Her body had lost some of its slim lines, or was it the gown she was wearing? Whatever the difference, it was becoming.

It was not until he bowed over her hand that he was aware of someone else in the room. He straightened up to see Edward Blount standing near the window. Blount looked at Katherine and then at Patrick, and there was a smoldering murderous fire in his eyes. It was only a flash and then was gone.

Blount said graciously, "We are happy to see you so soon again, Master North." His voice implied that Patrick spent most of his time at the Embassy. "You are well?"

"Yes, thank you."

Blount moved a little forward so that he could watch Katherine's face. "I thought I'd heard—but you know how rumors and gossip are forever flying about in the

272

foreign quarter. It's too small a world here, with too much time to spread unfounded tales."

Katherine looked across at Blount and there was some emotion in her eyes that hit Patrick like a blow. Was it fear? She said carelessly, "What sort of tales, Ned?"

Blount shrugged. "Your friend Master Quain is gone for a few days and immediately there are wild stories he has met with foul play."

At the first word Patrick moved as though by chance between Katherine and Blount on an impulse of protection. He was not quite sure why, except that she seemed defenseless before Blount's probing gaze. Patrick said, "Is that right? Ridiculous how rumors start, isn't it? Master Quain's away on business." He was sure now that Blount knew where Maurice was. He glanced at Katherine. He must see her alone.

She said, "Do sit down, Master North," and smiled at him.

Thank you." He stood waiting as Blount neither seated himself nor made ary more move to leave, but watched him, pale eyes narrowed. The silence hung heavy. Patrick thought he had to find something to say. When he spoke, his voice was deferential. "We were wondering how your ambassadorial duties—" that should please Blount!—"were advancing, Sir Edward. We find that for the smallest detail of business here there are a dozen obstructions. For statecraft no doubt there are difficulties which we would not even imagine."

"True indeed, Master North! Sir William tells me I've done extremely well to obtain a personal interview with the Sultan, and that I made an excellent impression on the Grand Seigneur." He eyed the floor modestly for a moment. "Though all we receive in answer to our suggested terms is the report that the war with Persia isn't going well, the treasury is exhausted, Turkey cannot afford to have a new enemy, and a dozen like excuses which mean nothing."

Patrick thought, Why the devil doesn't Blount take himself off to his maneuverings? He smiled and said, "I suppose you're in haste to have it done and return to

England. Whereas I——" He tried to look embarrassed.

Blount paid no attention. Katherine, womanlike, took up his words immediately. "Whereas you?—"

Patrick said confidentially, "—am in no hurry at all to go home. That was what I came to see you about, Lady Katherine. I don't know why it's easy to tell a woman how you've made a fool of yourself over a golden-haired wench, but to tell another man—no. Perhaps you'll be good enough to let me see you another time?"

Blount yawned, obviously waiting for Patrick to leave. There was a knock at the door. He glanced at Patrick to answer it. Patrick lifed his brows in wry amusement and went across the room. A page outside asked for Sir Edward. Barton, Harborne's secretary, wanted to see him.

Blount shrugged and came to his feet. "I'm sorry, sweetheart, I must leave you, but I'll not be gone long." He glanced across at Patrick and said graciously, "If Lady Katherine is willing to see you, why not talk with her now?"

Patrick hesitated. "You're very kind, Sir Edward. I'm just in an entanglement—I thought Lady Katherine might give me some much-needed advice. God knows I could use it."

Blount nodded. "I've been in enough scrapes to give you better counsel than Katherine, though not so gentle probably."

The door clicked to behind him. Katherine did not watch him go. Her eyes were on Patrick as he crossed the floor to her. So Patrick was in love? She smiled at him, but now that she thought he was gone from her forever, she knew how much she had depended on him, just on the knowledge he was alive and near. There had been too many dark hours in Constantinople. She was afraid of Ned sometimes, and the thought of Patrick had been an unacknowledged balm. How kind he had been always!

She said, "I hope, Patrick, your golden-haired sweetheart loves you as much as you deserve." She touched his arm in casual affection.

274

He put his hand on hers in a quick gesture, then grinned like a mischievous boy. "She rid me of Sir Edward anyway, and that's more than I ever expected of her. You know whom——— But I did not come here to tell you I love you."

Katherine looked up at him, strong and young and supple. "I want to wish you loved someone else. It would be much better for you. Yet to give you up— that would be very hard, Patrick!" She shouldn't have said it. Every such silken word bound him more tightly, and someday she must send him away for his own good.

He thought he'd remember every intonation later, but now he had no time even for the incredible sweetness of her words. "I came to you today, Lady Katherine, though I don't know just what you can do. Master Quain is not a man, as you know, to make friends and he needs them now."

Katherine's fingers crept up toward her throat. "Ned has been hinting, but I didn't know how much of it was true and how much he wanted to hurt me. You said Master Quain was away on business?"

"He was. He hasn't come back. I may be wrong, but I'm sure Sir Edward has some hand in his disappearance. I'd thought you might persuade him to tell you where Quain is. But since I've seen him, I wonder."

Katherine shook her head. "If Ned were sure I wanted to know, nothing would ever persuade him to tell me." She said simply and unhappily, "Sometimes Ned hates me. I'm not very lucky in my men, am I? Except in you." She murmured the last phrase more to herself than to him as she rested her head on her hand, shading her eyes. She looked up with an impishly amused smile. "There may be a way with Ned. I'll try it. I wish I could do something more. If you find out where Maurice is, that's hardly enough, is it?"

Patrick looked at her tight-lipped. "If you can discover his prison—I don't know that he's been seized of course, but there seems little else to think—we'll find some way to get him out, Lady Katherine."

"I wish you'd call me Katherine and sound less formal! But go now and I'll see what I can do."

"I've a small plan of my own, Lady—Katherine then! But it might help if I could say for a certainly what has happened to Master Quain. Shall I come back or will you send me word?"

"If you were near by too often, Ned would be—well, it doesn't matter." She had to hold from herself now any thought of Maurice in the hands of his enemies. She knew how savage Ned could be and how long he wanted to ruin Maurice. "I'll send a page down to you tomorrow, Patrick."

Patrick went out, ran down the steps to the lower hall. Blount was waiting below. Patrick stopped dead. Blount said, "I am rather disturbed about Maurice, Master North. You're sure he's only away on business?"

Patrick looked at him with a faint stirring of hope while the shadows in the hall seemed to draw in about them. He answered cautiously. "That's my belief, Sir Edward. Have you reason to think otherwise?"

Blount held out his hand to admire a diamond ring on his index finger. "No, not really. Except that Englishmen have disappeared before this in Turkey. While questions are asked about them, they are seldom answered. I would not like to have anything happen to our friend. I've spoken to Sir William but he scoffs at any danger."

Patrick looked at Blount's light-blue eyes which seemed masked, at his face cruel under the facile charm. If Blount had spoken to Harborne it was only to implant the idea that Maurice Quain's disappearance looked like a business journey he had not confided to his subordinates. Without proof Patrick would not easily persuade Sir William to start the tedious procedure of filing official inquiries through the government.

He had nothing to bargain with, because if Blount and the House of Gascony had Maurice under their hands, what could he give them that they couldn't force from Maurice? Except for this—that they'd be damned lucky if they got a shilling out of Maurice by the usual methods of persuasion. How long would they take to find that out? Too late for Maurice? He thought, Be careful, my lad. If you try to tear the truth out of Blount we'll have no chance at all. I'll be in gaol, and there'll be no one then to protect Maurice's interests—if any interests are left.

Blount watched him with a lazy smile. "Did Kit give you the advice you needed?"

"Yes, thank you, Sir Edward. Better than I'd hoped. Women are the very devil—the trouble they get you into." He shook his head. "I rather hope Quain doesn't return until I get out of this affair somehow."

"He probably won't come back too soon for your convenience, Master North."

Blount's proud he had his hand in this, Patrick thought. He doesn't care if I know because what can I do against a knight and the Queen's courier? He said, "You know it's rather curious, Sir Edward, you seem so assured that Quain has fallen on ill fortune." He waited to see if Blount would pick up that gage.

Blount lifted his shoulders, his satin doublet gleaming in the half-light. "No doubt I see the dark side of things too easily, Master North. Still, if anything should happen to him and you need another employer, come up to the Embassy. I think I could use your services. I expect to acquire some property and I, of course, have no trader's knowledge of business."

The day he acquired that property, Patrick thought, Blount wouldn't need a secretary, but a priest to bury him. He bowed to leave. Blount was not interested in bargaining after all. "I suppose now that spring is upon us, Lady Katherine will be returning to England or France."

Blount's affable indifference dropped like a cloak. His face went red. "Kit? Does she look, Master North, like a woman going on a sea voyage?" Patrick stared at him blankly. "I thought for a time the child might be yours but not now." His fingers dug into Patrick's arm.

Patrick understood suddenly a number of things, the way Katherine looked and how Blount veered from calm to passion worse than any woman could.

Blount whispered, "It might be mine, but, God, I don't know! If the child were, why wouldn't we have had one before? If it's Maurice Quain's———"

"No!"

Blount's head jutted forward so that his face was close to Patrick's. "But you don't know, do you? If I were sure it is Maurice's, what he is suffering now I would double, I'd treble——" He stopped, knowing from Patrick's face he had said too much. He added abruptly, "If I but knew where to reach him."

Patrick eyed him levelly in a way Blount did not like. Blount said, "But we have spent too much time on this profitless discussion already. Good day, Master North!"

There was no answer from the Grand Vizier the next day, but Thursday morning there was a curt message explaining that because of the urgency of the appeal, Othman would grant an audience in the afternoon. Patrick thought he must have written better than he'd hoped, or more likely the silver chest was convincing.

He looked over his ruffs. He missed Jacques' starching and ironing. The Greek downstairs could never do the work as expertly as a Western valet. He tossed the ruffs aside, pulled out a falling band which would wilt less quickly. He would be sitting in the first chamber for two hours at least with braziers in every corner, another hour in the next room which would probably feel like the Russian plains, and perhaps before nightfall he might arrive in the anteroom of the Grand Vizier's audience hall.

He started to fasten the collar at the neck of his blue velvet doublet, turned as someone knocked, opened the door. "Webster! How did you get back from Gallipoli so soon?"

Webster came in looking as brisk and cheerful as though he'd just risen from a sound sleep. "Me? On the contrary, my lad, I wasn't expecting you to be returned from Bodajoz yet. Thought I'd have the apartment to myself for a few days and be able to invite in all my debauched friends and——"

Patrick interrupted him. "We didn't go to Bodajoz. At least I didn't. Where Quain went, I wouldn't know."

Webster sat down on the side of the bed, tossed a

cushion behind him and lay back. "I thought he was going up the Bosporus and from there to Bodajoz. Why the change in plan? Do the Turks take longer to pound into an agreeable state of mind than the English or French?"

Patrick said shortly, "It just happens, Master Webster, that I didn't meet him at Le Cocq. I was delayed."

Webster grinned maliciously. "I'm surprised to find you in one piece in those circumstances. I'll wager Master Quain was not pleased."

Patrick said in exasperation. "If you'll hold your tongue for five minutes, I'll tell you what happened. I'm on my way to the Seraglio now to see the Grand Vizier."

"You? Well, well, how you've come up in the world, young man! Don't forget to say a kind word for me when you're a great merchant and—— All right, Patrick, I'm silent. I'm all ears. But I do hope you'll try to be entertaining."

"Vincent and the guard went on to Le Cocq without me, but they left later than I'd orginally planned. At the inn they were given a note from Quain that said he was going on to Bodajoz without waiting longer. But the writing was not his. And to be brief, he has not been seen since in Bodajoz or any place else."

Webster sat up straight. Patrick could not complain he had not finally been impressed. "What in the name of Allah and his Prophet could have happened?" He got to his feet. "We'd better start to work on this."

"How do you think I've been spending my time— waiting for you to return to advise me?"

"To be frank, Patrick, yes. Only someone who has lived in Constantinople would have any notion of the labyrinthine ways there are to follow in the East."

"Well, in any case, Master Webster, it will take everybody's head, including yours."

Webster grinned. "You mean that Quain will take everybody's head, and especially yours. I'm sorry. I didn't mean to interrupt. I'll not say another word. But I'm sure now I'm back we'll have no trouble running this down. Some bandit probably out for money.

Though it's odd, when you think of it, that you haven't had a demand for ransom."

Patrick said, "No, it isn't odd. I think I know what the ransom is. Edward Blount has a hand in this and he'll want half the Quain fortune if I know him." He'll look for more than that. Patrick thought; he'll want physical revenge too.

Webster's mouth dropped open. "What did you say?"

"Since Master Quain would have to sign that much money over himself, no one is going to trouble to get in touch with us. Of course, he won't do it. I don't think he'll do it. Though there are ways of forcing——" He stopped cold. "Anyway, when I tell you that the French outlet for Mustafa Rahmi is the House of Gascony in Paris, that I was held overnight at the Lemaire house——" He grimaced as he rubbed the side of his head which was still acutely sensitive.

"Lemaire?"

"Yes. By the way, I don't care for your choice of friends. Anyway, as I was saying, with the House of Gascony, Lemaire and Blount in the affair, you can see it's not the chance work of your usual bandits who waylay unwary travelers." Patrick finished fastening his collar. "You placed the orders for copper and tin, didn't you?"

Webster nodded. "Now if we only had some idea where Quain is——"

"I had word this morning from——" Patrick hesitated—"from Katherine Perrot that he's in the north tower across the Bosporus at Scutari. I don't like the sound of it."

"Shall I go over there?"

"Not yet. We'll see the Grand Vizier first. There are few locks that will not open at his command."

Patrick felt that he was some particularly distasteful sort of an insect the way the Grand Vizier looked at him, not turning his hooded eyes away even while he spoke to the interpreter. The latter said briefly. "His Excellency was willing to honor Effendi Quain with an audience. He is not pleased that the Effendi saw fit to send an attendant instead."

Patrick had a sense of being smothered in the Oriental splendor about him, the high room, the hanging of cloth of gold, the blue-draped windows, the Grand Vizier himself in his long white robe of satin trimmed with sable, his towering white muslin headdress trimmed with wide bands of gold lace, the enormous emerald on his right hand that looked like green fire, and the slaves standing white-robed and motionless in a half-moon about him. He disliked being awed. "We came, Your Excellency, in regard to the shipment of tin and copper which Master Quain ordered for you from Cornwall."

The Grand Vizier looked contemptuously inquiring.

Patrick said, "We regret that we cannot deliver the cargo to your government."

When this was interpreted, two lines deepened between Othman's brows. "What does the Christian dog mean? Has the shipment not been ordered?"

Patrick said, "Tell His Excellency the order has been placed, but there can be no delivery until a certain difficulty has been adjusted."

"What troubles this Christian dog?"

"Master Quain has disappeared." Having every remark translated in the high emotionless tones of the eunuch made Patrick feel as though he were talking through an opaque screen.

"His Excellency considers that interesting, but fails to see what it has to do with the shipment for casting the guns."

"Master Quain was abducted by or through the House of Mustafa Rahmi, a firm recommended by His Excellency. Before we can complete arrangements, he must be here to sign the supplies over to you."

The Grand Vizier's face was expressionless as he answered. The eunuch repeated his words. "His Excellency feels that no doubt Effendi Quain has his own reasons for not confiding his movements to his attendants. As for the shipment, that is unimportant. His Excellency is ordering out his own galleys to watch for the cargo. The customs officials will send the tin and copper directly to the government ironworks when the ship is brought into port. His Excellency gives you leave to retire."

Patrick checked an outraged retort at the banditry. He wanted to glance at Webster to see if between them they could not find an answer, but he did not take his eyes from Othman's face, nor give any indication of having heard the dismissal. He found himself saying with a cold desperation, "Tell His Excellency we have placed the order as I said, but we sent messengers abroad with the command to keep the shipment out of Turkish waters until Master Quain is returned to his own apartments alive and well." He could feel Webster's slight movement and astonishment behind him.

The Grand Vizier said in a bored voice, "What is this about Mustafa Rahmi? We know nothing but good of him."

"We have no doubt he has an excellent house of business. But we feel it is shortsighted to let Mustafa Rahmi hold Master Quain for ransom. How can the government receive its proper dues on our commerical dealings here? And in particular the metal for casting guns?"

The emerald flashed on the Grand Vizier's finger as he lifted his hand. "We are sure Mustafa Rahmi will have no knowledge of this ridiculous accusation."

If the Grand Vizier refused to do anything, Patrick knew their last chance had gone. It was well enough to say in bravado that he had only to know where Maurice was and he would do something! What was done must be done quickly.

He said, "Mustafa Rahmi himself may know nothing of the affair, Your Excellency. But if you would do us the inestimable honor of making inquiries at the Scutari Tower, we are sure Master Quain will be found—and your shipment delivered."

The Grand Vizier spoke briefly. The interpreter said, "His Excellency will consider the matter. If he should decide to move in this and Master Quain returns, he expects—in gratitude for busying himself about so tri-

282

fling a matter when affairs of state are pressing upon him—the full cargo as a gift."

Patrick knew this was only the first offer, and that Maurice, if he were there, would hammer it down until the gift would be only a quarter of the shipment. He was afraid to risk bargaining. "Master Quain will be delighted to have the tin and copper accepted as a small token of appreciation for His Excellency's good will in this matter."

"His Excellency would like a document signed to that effect."

Patrick said shortly, "I will sign if His Excellency will, but the word of the House of Quain is good anywhere in Europe."

The Grand Vizier's eyes closed and opened again. Through the interpreter he answered, "Very well. The Christian dogs have our permission to retire."

Patrick and Webster bowed and moved backward to the door. As they reached the anteroom, Webster said, "We should return to the foreign quarter before the Grand Vizier changes his mind and decides as long as they have the master they may as well have all his men too." His eyes twinkled. "You know, Patrick, if Quain isn't released soon and we have many more audiences, he may as well sign away his fortune before you do."

15

Maurice returned the next morning. His doublet was torn, his ruff gone, and his hose stained with slime. But he had evidently stopped at a public house for a bath and to be shaved, and he walked in as though it were any morning of the week.

Webster said, "Son of God! How did you get here?"

Maurice looked at him in chill surprise at his profanity. "A carriage."

Patrick, who had been standing at the window, whirled around in incredulous relief. "Master Quain!" He stopped abruptly as he noticed that though Maurice moved in his usual arrogant manner, he held his arms

283

oddly rigid. "What did they do to you?" His voice was strained.

Maurice spread out the fingers of his right hand, looked down at them. They were discolored and bruised and the thumb was swollen to enormous size Patrick's gaze went to Maurice's left hand. It was swathed with bandages that had once been white but were now dirty and caked with blood.

Maurice said, "There was a slight divergence of opinion. Would you send for a surgeon, Patrick?" Only the way his mouth was compressed into a white line showed the pain he was suffering. "Then I'd like to change my clothes." He fumbled at the throat of his doublet. "I'm afraid I need help."

Patrick whispered, "May their souls burn in hell!"

Webster at the door said, "I'll fetch the surgeon. I know of an Arabian but he may have to be persuaded to come to the aid of a Christian." They could hear his feet clattering on the stairs almost before he was finished speaking.

As Webster left, Tom came into the room. At the sound of a step behind him Maurice turned his head warily, then his face relaxed. His eyes were intensely blue in his pale face. He started to lift his hand again, let it drop. The pain was unbelievable. It wrung him dry inside, made a wall of flame about him cutting him off from everyone, leaving him so alone that he was held to life only by tenuous white-hot threads of agony. He had an insane desire to tear his hands from his wrists.

The look of wariness stabbed Patrick. He thought that one day he would meet Edward Blount and the knight would regret this with his last breath. In that moment he hoped Katherine's child was Maurice's. He was ashamed of every twinge of angry jealously he had ever felt.

Webster returned with a tiny wizened man whose face was brown and wrinkled under his white turban, and whose long thin hands with nails like talons reached out from wide sleeves. An attendant at least twice his size, and looking strong as a wrestler at the Hippodrome, followed them in. The surgeon touched one of Maurice's hands and then the other, nodded to himself, jabbered something sharply in Arabic. The attendant translated the command for the foreign dogs to leave the room.

Patrick scowled. "They look as though they would finish murdering Master Quain. I'm not leaving."

Webster said, "He's all right. But he won't do a thing if we're here, lest we steal his secrets for the West. These Arabs can work miracles in healing when they have a mind to."

The little surgeon came out two hours later. Unintelligible words streamed from his lips, and his hands gestured passionately. The attendant interpreted his words into an order that his patient be left undisturbed until their return the next morning.

Patrick eyed the Arab with distrust. "Before they go, I'll take one look at Quain." To his relief, Maurice lay on his bed with eyes closed, the deep-etched lines of pain on his face smoothed out, both hands swathed with fresh bandages.

The surgeon screeched and followed Patrick at a limping run. The attendant hardly had to translate the doctor's threat—if anyone touched his patient, he'd carve the criminal's heart out and throw it to the pariah dogs.

Patrick looked sheepish at his suspicions and offered payment, but the Arab's pride was touched. He would take no gold until his patient was recovered. And if Patrick ever got ill, he wouldn't life a finger to cure him though the unbeliever could make the heavens rain sequins.

Webster grinned as the two Arabs left. "You don't know how to handle these Eastern geniuses."

Even Patrick by the next morning had to admit to the surgeon's skill. Maurice sat up and fired questions like a volley of musketry. At the first one Webster look at Patrick, then back at Maurice. "Yes, I sent in the order for the shipment for the Turkish goverment."

"Good! We should make an excellent profit on the cargo. They're badly in need of the metal gun castings for the Persian wars."

Patrick said wryly, "Don't start making plans to invest the money, Master Quain. I was speaking to the Grand Vizier about the shipment." He stopped.

Maurice started to lift a bandaged hand, grimaced at the pain, though it was bearable now. "Don't tell me, Patrick, that you've agreed to a price! Well, we'll make expenses, and the lost profit we'll put on the debit side along with this whole misadventure."

"It's going to weight the debit side more than you think. You won't like this, Master Quain. The Grand Vizier demanded the cargo as the price for making representation to your captors. I agreed."

"The whole shipment? No!"

Webster put in casually, "I was with Patrick, and at the time it didn't seem too high."

Maurice smiled faintly at the implication that today the price was high. "I dislike throwing away money, though of course I'm grateful for your efforts. But they could hardly have held me forever."

The careless arrogance infuriated Patrick. "They couldn't? Well, how in Christ's name, did you intend to gain your freedom?"

Maurice said, "I'll tell you one way I didn't intend to gain it, and that was by giving those bastards one shilling. While an hour or two of hanging by your thumbs and losing your fingers joint by joint persuades you to reconsider the value of money, it also makes you rather determined that nothing in heaven or hell will force you to yield one inch to their demands."

Patrick whispered, "What did you say?"

"They started on the index finger of the left hand, a joint each day after our first discussions seemed unlikely to reach agreement. They didn't start on the next finger for lack of time. I knew that sooner or later they'd realize how foolhardy their scheme was and give it up."

Pity and anger twisted within Patrick. "Well, I wasn't blessed with your knowledge, Master Quain. I didn't guess that Providence was going to intercede for you by enlightening your captors. However, that might have been a little late."

Maurice's brows rose at Patrick's tone.

286

Patrick said shortly, "I'm sorry, but to hear you say you'd suffer anything rather than give up your fortune—— You can always get money again."

A slightly more human expression came into Maurice's face. "To say the truth, I knew that either they would find time and the goverment against them and have to release me, or if they meant to murder me they'd do so whether I signed away my money or not. So I dislike giving them satisfaction by turning over any gold."

Webster said, "And who are 'they'?"

Maurice shrugged. "I don't know. Three Turks and a Syrian. They must have had some connection with the House of Mustafa Rahmi or they wouldn't have known the exact time I planned to be at Le Cocq, and had everyone there bribed." He spoke in a detached voice as though discussing someone else's difficulties.

Patrick said bluntly, "The French outlet for Mustafa Rahmi is the House of Gascony."

"The House of Gascony?" Maurice's eyes had an odd light in them. "Write a letter today to our house in Paris. To Monsieur Chapé of course. Tell him to find out and report to the government about the smuggling activities of that house and bribe one of the French nobles to see that a fine is assessed aginst them—heavy enough to put them out of business."

Patrick's eyes opened in surprise. Maurice said in curt explanation, "Neither of you has troubled to ask about Jacques. He was with me when I was taken. While my hands were bound they strangled him before my eyes." His expression was impenetrable.

"No!" Patrick thought of Jacques with his broad Yorkshire face growing purple, hands clawing the air desperately, with a strangling cord about his neck. If Patrick had been at Le Cocq, that would not have happened. Yet what reason had he had to suspect that Thérèse Lamaire, or anyone else for that matter, would try to prevent his meeting Maurice?

Maurice was indifferently interested when Patrick explained why he had not met him. "If they hadn't captured me this time, they'd probably have been fools enough to attempt it another." He showed more animation when Patrick mentioned Blount's part and Katherine's efforts on his behalf. "So Blount was in on this. That man's an idiot. You'd think he'd forget his ridiculous ambitions and be satisfied with what he has."

Patrick recalled Blount's face when they'd spoken of Maurice, and he knew Blount would never be satisfied while Maurice lived. He said, "I don't know how intelligent Sir Edward is or is not, Master Quain, and you may dismiss him in contempt, but——"

Maurice interrupted. "Were there any dispatches while I was gone?"

"Yes, sir." Patrick hesitated, then went on. "One from Bowyer. Routine matters. The shares for your Eastern Company are selling well, and he's sending you a shipment of wool, furs, kersey and tin within the month."

Maurice's brows lifted in faint amusement. "I don't consider the success of the Eastern Company a routine matter, Patrick. Anything else?"

"There was a letter from Osborne reporting that the Queen has consented to have a consul established in Cairo. Also, speaking of Her Majesty, that she has decided this alliance with Turkey should be forgotten. A treaty would scandalize Christendom, and the aid given would not be of too much value compared with the damage England's reputation would suffer."

"This is not the first time. Her Majesty has been known to change her mind." Maurice's voice was ironical.

"No. In fact she has already returned to her original view——" Patrick stopped, went on slowly as Maurice eyed him with surprise. "There was also a dispatch to you from Her Majesty."

"To me?" Maurice said cynically. "What does she want?"

"It was written by Walsingham. He mentioned the rumors of the Armada grow worse each day, and Her Majesty begs you to bend every effort to aid Harborne in forwarding the alliance, not for her but for England who stands endangered. Do you want to see the dispatch?"

"Not particularly. Forward the alliance?" Maurice
288

thought Elizabeth always knew how to choose her men. He had suggetsed the treaty. She was throwing the responsibility of it back on him. He didn't think the Armada would sail. But if it should, England would need every friend she could make. Phillip Hapsburg's ships convoying the Price of Parma's veterans across the Channel to English soil? Parma, whose brilliant generalship could snatch victory out of the very verge of defeat; who could rebuild the shattered bridge which held Antwerp at his mercy, take back the Kowenstyn dike and be writing out his conditions for surrender while the burghers were celebrating their victory! Parma and his veterans drawing a tightening line about London?

When he had said that torture made you reconsider the value of money, it wasn't that gold was worth less to him, but that he wanted more value in what it purchased. This alliance would probably cost him money and time, and he had not meant to spend either on that or any other state affair. Yet if, in spite of Phillips's bungling, the Armada should sail—— He sighed and moved his shoulders uncomfortably.

"I'll see Harborne. This alliance should be carried through before Elizabeth reverses her policy again. And we must have another audience with the Grand Vizier for the name of a more reputable Turkish firm to act as our agent before the shipment comes. When I return to London. I'll have to leave one of you here." He looked at Patrick consideringly.

Patrick shook his head. "Not me!"

"No. I think you're very capable when it comes to rescuing either Court ladies or your employer, but I wouldn't like to have a continual crisis in our business just to keep you at your best. Besides, you wouldn't go to the same trouble to increase trade."

Patrick thought sometimes Maurice asked to be murdered! He glanced away, then back at Maurice. "There was more in Her Majesty's letter."

"Well?"

"Mary Stuart's trial was concluded," Patrick said evenly. "The Judges of the Queen's Bench and the Members of the Commission found her guilty of conspiring for the destruction of the State and murder of Queen Elizabeth."

Maurice leaned forward slightly. He said nothing for a moment. His voice broke the silence harshly. "What was the sentence?"

"There was a question whether it should be solitary confinement for life, but the death penalty was recommended. Her Majesty signed the warrant and Mary was beheaded at Fotheringay." He went on slowly, There was a postscript to your letter in Her Majesty's own hand. She swore the warrant for Mary Stuart's excution was never meant to be carried out. Walsingham had been sick, and Secretary Davison who brought the order to Fotheringay was, she said, in the Tower under her displeasure."

Maurice felt empty. Mary Stuart dead? She had been a living legend for so long it seemed she could not die, pass into tradition, without the sound of drums or of tears. In the magic words, Mary Queen of Scotland, one forgot that behind castle walls had been a living woman growing old and tired, losing her beauty but never her charm, a woman born to be a royal princess just as Elizabeth Tudor seemed born to be the thrifty chatelaine for a young lusty nation.

Mary—her greatest misfortune had been not her heritage of the divided Kingdom of Scotland but her nearness in blood to the House of Tudor. This had made her a constant threat to Elizabeth's peace. Maurice wondered how long she had known of the warrant before the executioner came, and how she had died. So much blood and ruin and waste transfigured by that fair name into a shadow of glory! He drew a deep breath to steady himself. Ridiculous how the hurt of her memory was a sharper pain than the fire running from finger ends to the aching joints of his shoulders.

But Mary, with all the warmly personal gifts of mind and heart that made men think it a small thing to die for her, always put her trust in the wrong adviser, turning on those who would have been friends to her and to Scotland. That was the flaw. Bred in rich and sunny France, yet given a dour and divided kingdom to reign over as a girl, how could Mary feel the intense flame of

meannesses, conveniently forgotten pledges, miser-
liness? If Elizabeth never forgot Elizabeth Tudor, she
patriotism that redeemed in Elizabeth her petty
didn't forget England either. And Mary Stuart remembered herself too often as the Queen and too seldom as
the servant of Scotland.

Politically it had been a shrewd stroke the executioner had given, for the Armada could no longer sail
under pretext of putting Mary Stuart on the throne. If
it sailed now to conquer England, it sailed only to add
the country to Spain's vast possessions. The men
there would have laid down their lives for Mary Stuart
would not lift a hand for Phillip Hapsburg. They would
remember their common English blood with Elizabeth
before their common religion with Philip. It was only
extremists like Francis Walsingham and Philip Hasburg
himself who would be trying now to take this of the
realm of national war into the scarlet insanity of a religious one.

Elizabeth wanted his help. She'd had the victory finally over Mary Stuart. Couldn't that content her without using the Scottish Queen's adherents in her own
schemes—?

His bitter thoughts were interrupted by the explosive
entrance of the little surgeon. The Arab glared at Patrick while a stream of what must have been obscene
disparagements fell from his lips.

Patrick looked at the big attendant behind the doctor. "Never mind translating. I think I have the gist of
your master's meaning. Is there anything you want,
Master Quain?"

Maurice said harshly, "No." He glanced at the attendant. "You tell the surgeon that if I have the use of
my hands by tomorrow, whatever his fee is, I'll double
it."

Upon interpretation, the little Arab snarled back he
could not work miracles. These Westerners—they must
always be up and working. Next week was the soonest
he'd promise—if it was the will of Allah to heal the in-
juries.

It was one day more than a week before the surgeon
unbandaged his hands and for the last time tested

muscles, bones and tendons. "Allah be praised! Your hands are as good as ever except for the loss of your finger, though after that hanging by your thumbs it may be months before you can wield a sword skillfully again. Or a pen."

Maurice said sardonically, "A small matter, sir. I cannot imagine the circumstances in which I would be interested in using any weapon. Not to use a pen of course is a handicap." He turned to Patrick. "We'll see Harborne this afternoon."

The small room at the Embassy facing toward the south was overheated with Braziers of charcoal about the floor and every window closed tightly against drafts when Maurice and Patrick were shown in to see the ambassador. Sir William Harborne coughed, sneezed violently, brought his face out of his handkerchief long enough to say, "Good morning, Master Quain! Master North!" He sneezed again, wiped his eyes. "When you get a cold in London, they say it's because we burn sea coal instead of wood like our ancestors." He smothered another sneeze. "I don't know how we get colds here." He looked at his wife appealingly. "Helen, order me some more wine."

Lady Harborne said severely, "You know what your physician said about gout, dear. Do you think it wise?"

Harborne glared at her. "No, I don't think it wise. I don't think it wise to have this damnable cold either."

Lady Harborne frowned at her husband's choice of words and then glanced toward the window. "Very well, dear. But just a small glass." She clapped her hands for an attendant.

Maurice following her glance caught his breath at the sight of Katherine on the wide window seat which was piled high with cushions. He had not expected to see her. Or rather he had hoped not to.

Lady Harborne shook her head at him. "I've been expecting you to call for months, Master Quain, to renew your friendship with Kit here, and you haven't darkened our door. And today you're here on business, I'll swear. Isn't that so?"

Maurice, who thought her a foolish goodhearted
292

woman, bowed. "I must plead guilty, madam. The news out of England seems to demand swift measures. But of course you know all about it."

Lady Harborne smiled. "Thank you, Master Quain. My husband will never credit me with knowing anything of State affairs, though I'm sure I'm at least as good an agent for him with the harem as the eunuchs he sometimes bribes."

Maurice turned his head toward her in a movement of surprise. "An excellent thought, Lady Harborne. I've been thinking of Janizaries and barbers and Grand Viziers, when of course the shortest way to the Sultan is through the palace women."

The attendant entered with the wine. Harborne gulped his glass down, coughed and said cheerfully, "Now, Master Quain, I feel more like discussing business. Sit down over here. I'm a little deaf from this cold. I heard from Sir Edward you were away on some commerical venture. Good heavens, what happened to your hand?"

Maurice drew back his left arm. He sat down in a great oaken chair that looked incongruous in the Oriental room with its braziers and cushioned divans and Eastern hangings. "I met with an accident. Of no great matter. We came up today to discuss this Turkish alliance. I'm beginning to get sick of the sound of the words, aren't you?"

Harborne waved a resigned hand. "We can forget it again. I heard from Osborne that Her Majesty does not wish to have the alliance formed."

"I had the same news from Osborne, Sir William. But I had a separate dispatch from Walsingham dated later. Do you have it, Patrick? It begs us to have a treaty ratified at once. Here it is." He handed the document to Harborne. "Knowing how soon we may get an order countermanding this, I think we should try to work swiftly. What is your opinion?"

Lady Harborne said, "Perhaps you men would like to discuss this privately?" She started to rise.

Maurice looked from Harborne to his wife. "Not if you are to take it to the palace women."

He could not see Katherine without turning but he

was aware of her in every fiber. The thought of her had sustained him in the dark hours at Scutari more than his pride had admitted. The feel of her gave warmth and light and color to this room.

Lady Harborne said over her shoulder, "Come over here, Kit! You're too far away."

Katherine slid down from the window seat and crossed the room to them, not with her usual quick grace. Patrick's eyes were on her, hoping for her smile. He remembered then he had not told Maurice that Katherine was with child. A difficult announcement to make at best and harder when you might add, "Furthermore, Master Quain, you are rather thought to be the father!"

Maurice looked at her with a slow and cynical smile. Edward Blount was no doubt happy.

Lady Harborne said, "If you are to discuss this treaty, should not the Queen's courier be here? Shall I send for Sir Edward, Will?" She did not notice the tension that followed her words.

Harborne shrugged. "Osborne wrote he thought Blount should not be given too free a hand, but I suppose he should hear any plans so that he may report to Her Majesty on his return to England. What do you think, Master Quain?"

Maurice's brows lifted. "My original opinion of Edward Blount is probably well known, Sir William. I've seen nothing of him since to modify or raise my judgment."

Harborne said ruefully, "This change in urging the alliance now—achoo—I beg your pardon!—this change in urging the alliance comes at a bad time, Master Quain. The crew of an English ship was captured and sold, and I sent in strong protestations to the Sultan only yesterday. It's a little difficult to beg him today to send out ships against Spain." He looked up as Blount came in. "We were just discussing the treaty, Sir Edward. Master Quain has word that it should be carried through."

Blount closed the door behind him and surveyed the group in the room. He bowed with vague condenscension to everyone and bent to kiss Katherine as he paused by the chair where she was sitting. She turned her head so that his lips just brushed against her cheek, but there was a casual possessiveness in the gesture that stabbed the two men watching them.

Blount sat down near Harborne and across from Maurice. He looked enviously at the diamond buttons down the front of Maurice's dark doublet, just glanced at his hand.

Maurice lifted cold contemptuous eyes to Blount before he turned back to Harborne. "Her Majesty feels that we should form an offensive-defensive alliance with the Grand Seigneur in which he unlooses his ships and those of the Bey of Tripoli against Spain. But we are not to promise help against Persia. Like all women she is a bargain hunter. But it would seem this time she wants almost too good a bargain."

Harborne said, "Of course it would be a labor of love so far as those pirates of Tripoli are concerned. The difficult part isn't to persuade them to loose their ships against Spain, but to loose them only against Spain and not against our vessels. The English ship they captured had over ten thousand pounds' worth of cargo in its hold. That is not given up easily."

"Will your protests bring results?"

Harborne shrugged. "They might free a few sailors just for the look of the thing. I've sent out four men to watch the slave markets and buy the crew when they're put up for sale. But we have to make any purchases through an Oriental or the price is out of all reason. Sometimes the man we hire lets the auctioneers know he's working for us, and then the Englishman is sold to a Moslem. Sometimes they force the crew to renounce Christianity. It's not a nice ceremony. One cannot blame a man, I suppose, if he turns renegade to escape slavery. But do you know, Master Quain, when I see some of those who are free but outcast from Christendom and despised by Moslems, I wonder if a physical slavery is not the lesser burden."

Katherine leaned forward impetuously, one hand toward him as though in appeal. "Can they not return to their own countries, Sir William, go back to their own faith?"

"Perhaps, Lady Katherine. But they don't. They become desperate men, knowing they have committed a crime in renouncing Christ and country that is unpardonable in this world and the next. We are beginning to make some headway in Turkey as our commercial relations improve, but there seems little hope in the Barbary States."

Katherine shivered. "Would this treaty help to set our sailors free, Sir William?"

"Yes, madam."

She made the loose folds of her skirt into little pleats with her fingers. "I've met Janfreda Kadein, the present favorite of the Sultan, you know. Perhaps she could be persuaded——" She stopped thoughtfully, then glanced up at Maurice who was watching her. "Janfreda is powerful and intelligent. She enjoys hearing stories of the English Court, and she mentioned she'd like me to bring Deborah sometime." A shadow crossed her face. "She said she misses her own child. It would give me an excuse to see her."

Maurice asked, "What is the price of the treaty if it's ratified through the palace women?"

Harborne said bluntly, "Gold. Jewels. The ladies of the harem are always saving against the day a new favorite will come in and they'll have no more influence and so no more gifts from the Sultan. If we can carry the alliance through them, you need have no worries about agreements for mutual aid. A word from the favorite and new ships are launched, the Janizaries march north, south, east or west, cities are razed. If Helen and Katherine will see Janfreda Kadein and can persuade her to speak to the Sultan, I'll beg a private audience with him and perhaps can carry it through. If he does no more than sign the treaty so that Spain fears the threat of Turkish power and there's a promise not to touch our ships, the price will be worth whatever we must pay."

Blount looked from the point of his Cordovan leather shoe to Harborne. "You say *we* shall have an audience?" he hinted gently.

Harborne murmured courteously, "It goes without saying that if I speak to the Sultan, the special envoy from the Queen will be the one most able to give the final messages from Her Majesty and her present state of mind toward her cousin in royalty."

Maurice said sardonically, "Surely you expect over-much of a plain knight? No mere man could hope to follow her labyrinthine turns of mind, her tacking to every wind, the tortuous bypaths of her policy."

Blount turned toward Maurice with a lazy insolence. "Your words come perilousy close to treason, Maurice. After escaping the rope once, don't you fear the feel of it again about your neck?" He added in explanation to Lady Harborne, "Maurice was found guilty of armed treason against the State. Her Majesty pardoned him. Such clemency would arouse in me lifelong gratitude and loyalty. But as Maurice says, I'm only a plain knight."

Maurice glanced at Blount with chill amusement. "I hope for the sake of the treaty, Sir William, that our rather heavy-footed envoy will learn the more subtle arts of diplomacy before he meets with the Sultan. Then his skill in Her Majesty's service will match his ardent devotion. Now as to the price of the gifts—Osborne said you're aware the Turkey Company will be ready to spend any reasonable amount."

Harborne said anxiously, "No trifles are accepted, you know. We sent the Sultana Saifé once a dozen bales of our finest wools. They were found spoiled from the sea voyage when they were unpacked and it took us months to regain favor."

Maurice adjusted the plain ruff at his wrist, looked up at Harborne. "I think the Turkey Company can bear a slight strain on its credit. If you need something more, I have six matched greyhounds that came in last week and a brace of mastiffs—" he flicked a glance at Blount—"with a better ancestry than some of our landed gentry."

Blount's color went from red to white. Katherine bit her lip, caught Patrick's eye unexpectedly and could not suppress a delighted laugh. Lady Harborne giggled, Sir William was uneasy at any breaking of the peace. "That will be most kind of you, Master Quain. It is not always money but something unusual in the way of gifts

297

that is expected. If all the promises are on Turkey's side, they'll expect to sell them at a good price."

"Of course you can use the argument that the Hapsburgs have always been the most determined enemy of Turkey, and if Spain's power is broken by England's Navy, Turkey has a better position in the Mediterranean."

Patrick leaned forward. Though Spain was England's enemy, the Hapsburgs in Austria and Spain had held the wall between East and West. Vienna had stopped the wave of Islam from breaking over western Europe, engulfing all the countries of Christendom. Spain at Lepanto sixteen years ago had broken the power of the Turkish Navy before which all Christian countries had trembled. He started to speak, then stopped. At Cadiz the Invincible Armada was gathering for the conquest of England. There seemed no choice. Strike against the nearest enemy first and trouble about the good or ill will of your ally later.

Maurice rose. "If there is anything more, Sir William, I am at your service. You can send a man down to see me about the hounds when you want them."

Harborne sneezed violently. "Perhaps Sir Edward— he is a good judge and a few more details may come up."

Maurice turned toward the ambassador with astonishment. "My suggestion was to send a man, Sir William." He moved to Katherine's side, bowed. He did not thank her for her help in releasing him lest it harm her with Blount, nor did he take her hand.

She looked up at him, tall and broad-shouldered in his dark doublet and hose, the white fluted ruff setting off his square impassive face, his cold blue eyes. His hand . . . what accident . . . Before all these people there seemed nothing to say to him. She wanted to cry out, "Don't trouble to thank me, Maurice, for my small aid! Why don't you leave now and leave forever? You want no woman to disturb your dreams. Go without words and go quickly."

And she wanted to put out her hand to him and say, "Maurice, cannot the ice melt enough to take me into

298

your heart? Have you not learned even yet how little your money can buy? Do you not know there is a bond between us that is bitter now because we both take the easier way of retreat instead of challenging life?—I to a lover and you to your golden gods. This child is yours, not Ned's. Would not this bitterness sweeten if we—?" She turned her head away. A fog of despair was in her throat.

He gazed down at her, the lift of dark brows against the pallor of her face, the sweet and tender mouth, the mass of black hair coiled loosely at the nape of her neck. A pity to leave a wench like this to Edward Blount! But better to leave her than to break his heart and his fortune taking her.

Patrick stood back. He thought, After all Katherine has helped Maurice. He might do more now than bow coldly and move away from her with that chill disapproval of his as though he had conferred the favor, not she. Except for the time when Maurice stepped in to turn the Queen's anger before it did fatal harm, he has always acted toward Katherine as though——

Patrick smiled then. Maurice bore himself toward her as he did toward the rest of the world, only it seemed more pointed here because who could know Katherine and not love her?

He thought of Blount's accusation. Maurice and Katherine lying together? He could not quite feel its reality. Yet when they were near each other, though there was not a word, not a smile, he felt excluded from some intimate understanding that was beyond speech or gesture or even perhaps the necessity of liking.

16

Janfreda Kadein's heavy-lidded eyes rested on the goblet in her hand. The glass was traced with fine lines of silver and so delicate it seemed that a breath would break it. The Sultan's favorite was a tall big-boned woman with a husky voice, black eyes and harsh features. "A gift from the Venetian ambassador, Lady

Katherine." She let her words drop one by one like pebbles into a pool of placid water.

A middle-aged woman, olive-skinned, face broad under a loose veil, sat on a striped cushion just behind Katherine and the Kadien to interpret for them. She never lifted her eyes from the linen she was embroidering and she never missed a word.

"The glass is beautiful," Katherine murmured. "Let us hope the Venetian friendship is not so fragile as the presents." Her expressive hands lay loosely in her lap, but she glanced toward a huge tray of silver with wine jugs, one of silver and one of beaten gold, and a dozen squat silver mugs rimmed with gold.

Janfreda's eyes did not follow hers. "Have you seen any of our Damascene silverwork, Lady Katherine? No? It's exquisite."

Katherine gathered that the gift from the Turkey Company did not come up to expectations. She smiled. "I'm sure it's lovely." She glanced with interest about the room. It was high-ceilinged and bathed in a warm glow from the sun streaming through the curtains of old-rose brocade at the window. Pale-blue hangings covered the walls, giving them a misty remote look, and on the floor of green veined marble were scattered rugs of Persian weave and bright cushions of red and blue and yellow finely embroidered.

Katherine's smile deepened at the picture of Lady Harborne's majestic figure perched on a scarlet cushion. Lady Harborne had had a headache and had not wanted to call so precipitately on the Sultan's ladies. But she was an Englishwoman and, since the Embassy needed her aid, she had come graciously enough, though the pucker between her brows bespoke the fact that her headache had not been bettered by her visit. Little Deborah, round-faced and solemn, sat beside the ambassador's wife. She accepted with grave pleasure the sweets and caresses of the beautiful women about her who acted as though she were some strange but winsome toy.

The Sultan's slaves with their red lips, brows darkened with kohl, fingernails stained with henna, looked like flowers in some brillant Eastern garden. Under-

300

vests of white damask embroidered with gold, crimson velvet caftans trimmed with ermine, and trousers of green, rose, blue and gold silk revealed more than they concealed of pearly flesh gleaming through the transparent cloth.

Janfreda said, "Your Western rulers have but one wife?"

Katherine thought of Elizabeth's father, Henry the Eighth. She said demurely, "They have but one at a time."

"A miserable way to live. Half the slaves here have hoped and intrigued and flaunted their charms so that they would be chosen for the royal harem. What chance would they have if there were but one queen?"

Katherine looked at the rare beauties from Russia, Greece, Hungary, the Balkans, dark-skinned girls from Arabia, Egypt and Algiers, pale women captured in the Persian wars. Their high strange voices rose and clashed pleasantly, their quick laughter was soft as music. The air was heavy with the fragrance of their perfume and glittered with the flash of jewels at breasts and ears and on small gem-encrusted caps. If their slavery was biting into their souls, they hid such bitterness well, except for one girl whose beautiful eyes were red-rimmed and whose small mouth was set sullenly.

Janfreda dismissed this girl with a wave of her hand. "She tried to escape, the little fool! I had her whipped. She does not yet realize her good fortune in being here. She should bear the Sultan a daughter, she will become a royal princess. Should she become the mother of a son as I am, she will be a Kadein. Or if, among all his treasures, she does not win his favor, she will be dowered at twenty-five and given in marriage to a high official of the Court. A bright future, Lady Katherine, for a girl Allah has seen fit to dower with beauty."

Her hard eyes went from the slave girl to the ruby brooch at the throat of Katherine's bodice where the ends of her open ruff met at a point. "A pretty bauble. Of Italian workmanship, isn't it?"

Katherine unfastened the pin. It was the first time she had worn the jewel since Maurice had given it to her on the *Ascención*. Too proud to use it and too

301

practical to throw it away, she had worn it today knowing how many doors in the Seraglio a bribe could open.

Janfrdea Kadein's hand closed over the brooch. Katherine recoiled from that hand. The fingers were broad at the base and tapered to narrow tips. A woman with hands like those must be as cruel, she thought, as every evidence pointed her to be.

Katherine smiled. "You must keep it as a trifle to remind you how well Turkey's interests sort with England's in this alliance Lady Harborne mentioned." She waited while the slave woman interpreted her words. She had the feeling that if she just talked loudly enough, she could cross the barriers of language without a translator.

Janfreda said, "I can tell the girl whom the Sultan next favors to whisper your request into his ear. But really, madam, why should she trouble herself over your difficulties?"

Katherine felt cold. Something was wrong. Janfreda Kadein had herself procured many slaves for the Sultan and ruled him through them. A word from her and the matter was halfway to succeess. Then Katherine realized what she had overlooked. She slipped off the ring of amethyst and diamonds Ned had given her so long ago at Hampton Court. Janfreda Kadein's voice was more gracious. "We will see what can be done, madam."

"When the treaty is signed, Sir William will beg you to honor him by accepting a finer gift than the silver set and these poor jewels."

Janfreda smiled thinly and nodded while her eyes went back to Deborah. "Will you have the child come here, Lady Katherine?"

For some reason Katherine's heart turned over as she called Deborah. Janfreda gave the little girl a long level look, said, "Have her turn around."

Deborah moved behind Katherine. Katherine, unwilling to offend the favorite, drew the child out to obey the curt order. Janfreda smiled. "A pretty child. Do you like it here?"

Deborah nodded solemnly. "They are very nice to

302

me. And I like all the shells in the garden paths and the fountains. But mostly I like him." She pointed a small finger toward the huge Soudanese Negro standing at the brassbound door.

Janfreda Kadein said, "That's the kislar aga, the Custodian of Felicity. He loves children."

Katherine looked toward the Negro who had saluted Deborah when they'd come in, though he had grumbled at the women with her. Curious and pathetic, she thought, the affection eunuchs have for children, overlaying their singlehearted passion for money.

Deborah asked with delight horror, "Does he eat children?"

There was a contemptuous twist on Janfreda Kadein's thin mouth. "No. Will you come to see us again?"

"If my mother will, madam."

Janfreda bowed her head. "I am sure she will. We must talk further on this alliance, Lady Katherine."

Katherine, taking the words as a dismissal, caught Lady Harborne's eyes and rose. Lady Harborne followed her example with alacrity. Katherine's fingers strayed over Deborah's golden curls. She wanted to get away from here with a terrible urgency. What corruption and blood and terror underlay the exquisite delicate structure of the harem? What savagery went forth from here when the largest bribe from any agent or any foreign power could sway this woman to work through the unleashed passions of the Sultan, and send the mailed fist of the Ottoman force crashing eastward against Persia or westward against Europe?

Janfreda Kadein smiled at Deborah, put a hand under the small chin. She spoke thoughtfully.

Katherine glanced with a wild leaping of her heart toward the interpreter. The woman who had neither risen nor looked up from the endless tracery of embroidery before her, translated, "Her Highness says the child is fresh and sweet and young, untouched by the world or by man, and she has the golden locks that the Lord of the Two Earths and the Two Seas honors with his favor." As Janfreda stood aside to let them move toward the great bronze door, the woman added,

"She says, madam, you will have other children to take her place. Janfreda Kadein will speak to you again."

Katherine smiled graciously, but there was a blackness before her eyes. She was exhausted. She tired so easily these days.

Maurice, Webster and Patrick watched the last of the bales and boxes from the Turkey Company warehouses being swung into the hold of the *Hercules* to be convoyed to England. The pungent odor of spices seemed to drench the salt air. There were bales of cotton from India, chests of uncut diamonds and of drugs, boxes of cloaks faced with Turkish grogram, carpets, silks from China, swords from Damascus that rivaled Toledo blades, tapestries from Persia.

Maurice said, "The Turkish House of Hamid, which Othman recommended, seems to be a satisfactory agent for us, Master Webster. Though it's a smaller house than Mustafa Rahmi's establishment, it's also more reliable. Now that we appear to have the Grand Vizier's favor I think they'll remain trustworthy."

He was hardly aware of the creaking of the boom, the shouts of the crew, the raucous voices of idlers about the wharf. Under the bright sun the dusty walks beside the quay shone like old silver. Long white robes whipping in the hot wind from the south seemed to reflect the light. Even the pariah dogs shrinking from he kicks and blows made a moving muted pattern of color. The cloudless sky was a hard intense blue overhead. But Maurice thought only that this venture was finally beginning to show a profit in spite of the outrageous demands of the Turkish officials. The cargo from his own house had sold well and the last shipment from his Eastern Company had come in.

Webster grinned. "I think they'll be trustworthy myself, Master Quain. I took the precaution of begging Sir William Harborne to hire the owner's youngest son for some official work he needed done by a native. A hostage is always valuable."

Patrick turned. "You were at the Embassy, Master Webster? How is Katherine—Lady Katherine?"

"Well I presume. I didn't see her. You know I also met Madam Lemaire on the street one day." He smiled maliciously. "Madam says she thought you were a such good frien' of hers, so—what you say?—*sympathique,* of the 'eart. But you 'ave not been to see 'er for lo! these many weeks. *Le bon Dieu* forgive her, but she t'inks perhaps you angry with 'er, Monsieur Nort'!"

Patrick said pleasantly, "To the devil with you!"

Maurice said, "Are you ready to start to Aleppo tomorrow, Master Webster? The agency of the Turkey Company is well established there now and it's time we found new markets. I understand that the Turks and some of the French and Italian houses use pigeons— carrier pigeons they call them—to send messages from one outlying city to another about prices of materials, supplies needed or ready to be shipped. A rather interesting novelty that we must look into."

Once well established in Turkey, he thought, he must go farther to the East—Arabia and Persia, India possibly. While they could now import Indian products, markets for England's expanding industries were even more important. The overland route was long and goods had to go through the hands of too many Oriental customs officials. A pity Spain ringed the world, making it impractical to send ships around Africa. If it became possible to avoid the Portuguese forts which Spain had taken over, another company could be formed, an East India Company. Well, he would put that aside for the moment. There was a commerical agency at Smyrna as well as at Aleppo. Webster could go there next.

He rubbed his left palm, kneading the muscles absently. His mutilated hands repelled him while a thin fire of pain like white-hot medal threads fanned out from wrist to finger tips. The sound of horses' hoofs caught his attention. He swung about to see Harborne and four blue-liveried attendants behind him coming up the narrow roadway to the wharf.

Harborne dismounted. "Good morning, Master Quain. I just came down to see that everything is in order before the ship sails, but I'm ahead of time. You have all your exports on board?" He nodded to Webster and Patrick.

"Yes, or ready to be put in the hold, Sir William. If the *Hercules* escapes storms and pirates, I'd say this will be one of the most valuable cargoes to London, won't it?"

Harborne nodded. "Fortunately trade increases very year. It was hard to get a charter for the Turkey trade monopoly from the Privy Council when we launched the enterprise a few years ago, and it will stay in force only so long as our shipments add up to five hundred pounds a year in English duties. The more valuable our commerce grows, the easier it should be to get the charter renewed."

"I'd think the final signing of this alliance would aid you, too."

Harborne shrugged. "The Privy Council remembers what it chooses and forgets what it will. If one did one's duty for the immediate reward, Master Quain, life would be a long disappointment. Incidentally, speaking of the treaty, the Sultan was gracious enough to say your greyhounds pleased him."

"Did your wife and Katherine have any luck in pushing the alliance with Janfreda Kadein?" Maurice asked the question without interest.

"Yes. But Katherine has been different since she went to the Seraglio. She's insistent on leaving Turkey, and of course no captain would take her as she is. My wife is worried she will make herself ill. She received a summons to return to the harem tomorrow, and I'm giving her instructions or suggestions to offer. At the moment the Sultan seems quite favorably impressed with signing an agreement."

Patrick said abruptly, "Why does Lady Katherine want to leave?"

Harborne lifted his shoulders expressively. "Why does any woman want to do anything? Perhaps now Mary Stuart is dead, she feels safe in England. I presume she will get a summons back to Court. But God-a-mercy, no woman can travel in the condition she's in?" He laughed. "Of course I'm a family man. You wouldn't notice those things. Well, she did us a lot of good with her persuasions to Janfreda Kadein, so we can allow her a few foibles, I suppose. Though to tell you the truth half the reason I'm here is to see that she doesn't try to go on shipboard. The moment she heard the *Hercules* was sailing she wanted to go on it. I feel responsible for her good health."

Webster looked at Patrick with a grin. "This looks like a task for you, Master North."

Patrick did not hear him. "Lady Katherine must have some good reason for this haste, Sir William."

"No doubt. Whatever it is, she feels it strongly enough. She was half crying, and I found it hard to deny her. She said if she told me why she must go, I wouldn't give her credence. We must remember women in her condition get notions it's impossible to dislodge. Well, I'll just go up and speak to the captain about it."

Maurice said, "That's an excellent thought. By the way, Webster is leaving for Aleppo tomorrow to see the consul there and discuss new markets. If there are any messages or dispatches, he'll be glad to take them."

"Good! I won't miss the opportunity. I'll send them down later today." He went on up the wharf.

Maurice thought sardonically that this time Katherine would have Blount right at hand to trouble about her. And she would have only Blount. It was a misfortune she had come to Constantinople at all. If he had it to do again, he would put in at Bordeaux at no matter what cost in time. He wondered for a moment if Blount had caused her tears. No. Was she not bearing his child! An inconvenience perhaps, but, if anyone would see the baby was cared for, Katherine was the wench to do it.

Harborne's dispatches came up to the apartment the next morning and with them a short note written in a round and childish hand and signed by Helen Harborne. Maurice, going over last-minute instructions to Webster, glanced at the signature and tossed the note aside until Webster had left. Then he picked up his gloves, said briefly, "I'll be down at the warehouse, Patrick, to see about renting space nearer the Golden Horn."

"Shall I go with you?"

"No. I'd rather have those reports written than the pleasure of your company. Call Tom."

Patrick started toward the door, then noticed the unread missive. "Did you want to see this, Master Quain?"

Maurice took the folded sheet of paper, expecting a dull but insistent invitation for him to call at the Embassy. He read:

Master Quain,
I feel there is some mistake, but Katherine begs me to ask you to come to the Embassy at once. She is very ill.

Helen Harborne

For the breadth of a moment he did not move. The wind stirred through the open window but the air seemed hot and oppressive. Fear caught fire from the very brevity of the note. Katherine was sick and asking for him. The thought, cold as steel against the flame of apprehension, twisted in him that if she must come to him for help, she was desperate. He crumpled the paper in his hand. "I'm going to the Embassy first."

The hoofs of the horses beat a rhythmic undertone to his fears. He had imagined many endings to his relationship with Katherine, but never that she might die. She was not robust. He should have seen that. They should have been aware before of the fevers and plagues in the East. If only she'd gone back on the first ship! But with winter coming on it had seemed an unnecessary danger when she was as safe in Constantinople with frineds as in Limoges with kinsmen. Friends? Who except the Harbornes had been her friends? Not Blount, who was incapable of caring for anyone but Blount. Not he himself, who had contemptuously tossed her to her lover like a bone to a dog. Only Patrick had given her the consideration that was, God knew, her due.

In the courtyard of Harborne's house he dismounted, tossed his reins to Tom and went into the great square hall and up the balustraded staircase to the floor above.

Helen Harborne came out of Katherine's room as he reached the top step. She dabbed at her eyes with a tiny piece of linen and lace. "Oh, Master Quain, I'm glad to see you!" She looked tired and wilted, unlike her usual majestic self.

"How is Katherine?"

"We don't know yet."

He put a hand to the latch of the door, said curtly, "May I go in now?" The woman sitting there moved to let him pass.

Lady Harborne sniffed, winked the tears from her eyes. "Maybe I'd better tell you first——"

"What is the matter with Katherine?"

"She had a . . . a slight shock yesterday and 1-lost the child she was carrying. We didn't think she'd live through it, but she seems better now, only very weak."

Maurice stared. "What in the name of God do I have to do with that?"

"I don't know, Master Quain. She wanted us to send for you last night but I couldn't do it. It wouldn't have been respectable. After all if she wanted anyone——" The color crept into her cheeks. "Well, Sir Edward was here."

He put his hand on the latch again. Lady Harborne said, "Wait a minute Master Quain. I wanted to tell you what caused it all." She wiped her eyes again. "I feel it's really my fault because I just blurted it out when I got the message from the eunuch at the Seraglio." Maurice looked at her impatiently. "Katherine was to go to the harem today, Master Quain. She was there before, you know, about this alliance, and Janfreda Kadien saw Deborah. The word we had last night was that the favorite intended to demand the child for the Sultan."

"Deborah? Ridiculous! She's not over five or six, is she?"

"I didn't believe it either, Master Quain, when Katherine first mentioned. It seemed preposterous. But do you know anything of the Sultan? He has perverted tastes, and Janfreda keeps her position as head of the palace women by pandering to them. With this word from our agent, I don't doubt the truth of it. Only of course it's a pity that Katherine took it so hard. We wouldn't give up the child—not without Katherine's consent."

Maurice's astounded look at the last words forced a further explanation from her. "In the East many think it an honor. The woman who reigned longest as Amurath's favorite wife is a Venetian—of the gentry, you know. There's a great deal of wealth and influence for anyone who holds the Sultan's love—a higher destiny, one would say, than awaits Deborah in England. Also, Master Quain, let's be realistic. If Sultan Amurath wants anything in Constantinople, he'll get it. If I had only told Katherine in the right way! But I was so astonished I just blurted out the news without thinking. Now she's lost one child and it looks as though she'll lose the other. While I don't approve of Katherine's way of life, she's rather sweet, I think. I wouldn't hurt her like this for anything."

"What does your husband say, madam?"

"He's furious that Katherine didn't speak to him before the *Hercules* sailed last night. He could have sent Deborah out on it. But you know he'd only have scoffed if she'd mentioned this. Now he's in a difficult position. If anyone in the Ottoman Empire but the Sultan wanted Deborah, Will could make a strong case for us. But to ask the Sultan to deny himself anything, especially in the middle of our negotiations——" She shook her head.

"Is this charming notion of Janfreda Kadein's known to the Sultan, or is Deborah to be a surprise for the Emperor of the World?"

"I don't know, Master Quain. Perhaps I'll find out something today. I'll have to go to the Seraglio in Katherine's place. I wish I didn't. Once the request is made, it will be a difficult situation for us here."

Maurice said coldly, "Will it?" and left Lady Harborne standing there with a frown of annoyance between her brows. She half regretted she had given in to Katherine's demands to send for him. Katherine must have been delirious and meant either Edward Blount or Patrick North, who seemed at least a pleasant gentleman. This merchant—she didn't wonder at Blount's

310

hostility toward him—icy, reserved, with a chill courteous manner and a way, of using razor-edged words
like weapons. She was sorry she had laughed at his slur
that the dogs' ancestry was better than Ned's. It didn't
seem funny any more.

Katherine turned her head on the pillow as Maurice
came into the room. A little attendant sat drowsily in a
chair beside the huge bed with its pale-green curtains.
There was the smell of blood in the air, overlaid with
scented water and some vile medical concoction. Katherine's eyes followed him as he came toward her. Her
face looked thin and her eyes enormous under her dark
brows. Her long hair, a black web against the white
linen, emphasized her pallor. Her figure hardly made a
curve under the quilted satin cover of the bed.

As Maurice's shadow fell between window and chair,
the attendant started up. "Did . . . what . . . did you
call, madam?"

"No. You go out and get some sleep. I'll ring when I
want someone again." Katherine closed her eyes. Even
those few words. exhausted her.

Maurice thought she looked as though she would
never come back to life. He wanted to pour into her all
the vigor of his body as he stood and gazed down at
her, afraid to move, she seemed so weak. He knew
now, when it might be too late, that all this time while
he had feared her betrayal of him, it was he who had
dealt treacherously with her.

She opened her eyes, looked up at Maurice. "Sit
down. You're too far away."

He drew the vacated chair to the side of the bed,
lowered himself into it. She slid her arm out from under the covers. The night rail of heavy blue satin had
long pleated sleeves edged with Flemish lace. He put
his hand on hers. She whispered, "That gives me courage," as though there were friendship between them
and not an almost savage indifference on his part.
"Don't look so long-faced like all the rest of them,
Maurice. I'm not going to die. Maurice, I want to ask
something of you." She waited, half expecting a cold
rejoinder. He said nothing. "I've asked Ned. But he—
well, he doesn't say yes and he doesn't say no."

Maurice smiled. "With all my faults, I've never been accused of being unable to state my mind. What is it?"

Color flooded Katherine's face, then drained away leaving her paler than before. "Did Helen tell you about Janfreda Kadein and Deborah?" She shivered.

"Yes, my dear."

"Oh, Maurice!" She wiped away tears. "I'm helpless here—I can do nothing." She but her lip not to cry out at a spasm of pain that shook her.

Maurice cursed Deborah to himself, the day she had been born and the night she had left England. "If that's your only worry, Katherine, you can rest. We'll find a way out."

"You're sure? Maurice, you promise me? And if you shouldn't—if they should be too strong and you can do nothing—will you swear to me that Deborah will not go alive into the Seraglio?" She remembered how afraid Deborah had been of the Sultan's favorite. She recalled the little slave girl who cried because she had been whipped for trying to escape. "If I had to think of her there among the palace women—— Maurice, you give me your word?" She raised herself on one elbow in her appeal.

"Yes, if it makes you feel happier. But we'll send her back to England."

"England! I'd like to go back to England. I'm afraid of the East. I want to go home with Deborah to Elly." Tears slipped down her cheeks. "I'm sorry. Only I'm so tired, Maurice, and so frightened. Tell me again Debbie will be all right."

Maurice said, "If you're well enough to travel in a week, you'll go home with Deborah. We'll get a woman to attend you and now that the winter storms are past, you'll have a fair voyage and be yourself again even before you're in London. You must stop troubling over anything but getting better." He did not think she could travel, but the hope of it had already put color into her cheeks.

"Oh, yes! I'll be all right. Yes, Maurice!"

He stood up quickly to leave. "I must not tire you." He did not want to stay least she ask him what he intended to do. He had no answer for that question. He bent to kiss her lightly.

She reached up to put her hands behind his head and to hold him a moment. "Maurice, I want to tell you—I didn't think I would, but I'd like to now. The child I lost was yours."

She didn't know what she expected of him—a disclaimer, a sharp disappointment because the child had been born too early that his immediate thought was just for her. "You have suffered this because of me? Oh, God, Katherine, why didn't you tell me? I thought——"

"Ned knew. That's one reason he hates you so much. What purpose would it have served to tell you?"

If he had known all this time in the East that Katherine was carrying his child—*his* child!—while he was coldly regretting having to leave her to Blount since he dared not love her—— But if he had known? Now it was only fear for her that battered at the prudent barricades he had erected about himself. He did not answer her, but drew the quilted silk up to her throat. "Think about nothing now but that soon you'll be well enough to go with Deborah."

She smiled, almost her old gay smile. "You're very kind, Maurice!" The anxious lines were smoothed from her face. "We're a lot of trouble, we Perrots! I think it's in our blood. Maurice, could I ask you one thing more? They won't let me see Deborah because they think it would upset me. But I'd be so happy just to know she's all right. Then I'll not worry about her."

Maurice went over to open the door, said briefly to the woman there to send for Deborah.

The attendant lifted her hands in horror. "No, sir! Lady Harborne said madam was not to be disturbed by the child. I don't think——"

"You don't have to think. Fetch the child."

Deborah came in a moment later, sidled past Maurice to Katherine. A lonely child, uprooted from the only home she'd known, brought across half the known world, set down in a strange house, and now frightened and bewildered with her mother ill and her own name whispered here and there, and then silence when she appeared. She moved noiselessly as a shadow, stood with her back against the bed. Her hand groped for Katherine's. She was a tiny child. Her mop of golden hair sorted oddly with the stiff silks and the ruff of her adult dress.

Maurice looked at her thoughtfully. "Katherine, before an actual request comes from the Seraglio, shouldn't she be out of the Embassy? It might save embarrassment and difficulties later. God knows what I'll do with her."

Katherine's eyes were alight. "Oh, yes! Oh, Maurice, if you had her there'd be nothing to trouble me. I'm so afraid a servant will be bribed, some danger will arise, that I can never quite forget my terror."

Maurice looked at the little girl much as he would have eyed a young greyhound or a foal that had to be shipped to market. He pulled on his gauntlets. "Come along!"

Katherine laughed. "She has feelings, you know. You go with Master Quain, darling, and he'll take care of you while I'm getting well."

Deborah's mouth trembled. "I'd rather stay with you."

"No—because—listen—don't tell anyone, but in just a few days you and I will go back to England together."

Deborah looked at Maurice. "Is he coming?"

"No, sweetheart."

"Just you and me?"

"And the captain and the crew."

Deborah's face brightened, then shadowed. "Is Sir Edward coming?"

Katherine stole a glance at Maurice. She looked almost her old self. "I don't think Sir Edward will be allowed to come."

Deborah said solemnly, "I'm glad. Because he doesn't like me."

"Well, Master Quain likes you. So you go with him now."

"Does he? He doesn't look as though he liked me. I wish he were Master North. He made me a doll once when we were on that boat. May I bring my doll?"

"Yes, darling. And Master North will be at the house where you're going."

"I'll go with this man then if I may just take my doll."

Maurice looked as though he were repressing a shudder. Good God, he thought, the Eastern sun has weakened my brain!

Patrick glanced up as Maurice came in, Tom after him with Deborah in his arms. Maurice said, "Give her to Patrick."

Patrick rose, white and shaken. "What does that mean? Is Katherine—?" He couldn't say it.

Maurice's brows lifted in surprise. He had not thought of that interpretation of the child's presence. "Katherine's not well, but I believe she'll be all right. You were so anxious to smuggle this child out of England, I thought you'd like to take care of her for a few days till we can send her back again. It's a duty for which you'll have no rivals."

Deborah, seeing only men around who looked at her with astonished curiosity as though she were something inhuman, started to cry. "I want to go back to my mother."

Maurice said, "I forgot. Katherine says she has feelings. Do something, Patrick!"

Patrick picked her up. "Is that the doll we made on the ship, darling? Well, we'll make you some more dolls and then you can go back."

"How many?"

"Three. Will you stay?"

Deborah nodded gravely. "But not for very long. We're going away."

Maurice dismissed Tom, told Patrick of Janfreda Kadein's order. Patrick said, "No! I'll tear the Sultan apart before he takes this child!"

"I think perhaps a little less violence might accomplish as much. Go down to the water front, see what ships are sailing and when. Have Dionesupulos hire a woman to take care of Deborah. Then get this child's hair cut and dyed and buy her boy's clothes. If Katherine can travel, they should not leave Constantinople together. Katherine may go overland to the nearest seaport town where the ship can stop to take her aboard." He looked at Patrick ironically. "But why should I tell you how to manage affairs like this?"

Maurice thought of Katherine lying on the bed, her face white and waxen. "Patrick, I want you to write out a deed today, for that manor house in Sussex—the one the Spanish ambassador released to us rather than give payment. Make it over to Katherine. If she's still out of the Queen's favor she won't starve in the streets. But don't give it to her until just before she goes aboard, or she'll refuse it. Send a letter to Bowyer by separate dispatch confirming the transaction."

He turned away sharply so that Patrick could say nothing. He didn't want gratitude from a man to whom nothing had weight against his love for Katherine. For himself, he was always generous enough with money he didn't need, but he had no generosity of the spirit. He'd gone farther along a dangerous road now than he expected when he offered to stake this much on the safety, not of Katherine, which might be understandable, but of Katherine's child. With a hammering of his heart he remembered that Katherine had staked her own life on his child. His prudence could not match her careless spirit, which gave without considering what she might get from life in return.

For all that, he intended to have nothing further to do with the venture beyond assuring himself of a reasonable chance of its success. He would not even see Katherine again. That would be best. He had the warehouses to inspect. He wanted to go into his plans further with the House of Hamid, and Patrick, he thought caustically, would be good for nothing but Katherine's affairs for the time. He'd take Vincent with him. What Vincent lacked in intelligence he would make up in single-mindedness. Webster had described it unkindly by saying it wasn't so much single-mindedness as inability to hold more than one thought at a time.

Hamid was a genial Mohammedan with the friendliness toward foreigners of some of the lower classes of Turks. He found that Maurice was less interested in

316

discussing new markets for wool than in discovering how reliable was a Venetian Company that shipped out of Constantinople to London.

Hamid said puzzled, "But I thought your stock went in the vessels of the Turkey Company?" He turned to signal a deaf-mute servitor to bring coffee.

Maurice answered shortly, "It does. But I want a report in a day or two on one of their ships, the *San Marco,* and on the honesty of its captain." He pulled himself together sharply. "Now you were saying that the provinces of Shirvan and Tiflis have not been touched yet as markets. Doesn't this war with Persia make trading uncertain there?"

He was pleased Hamid was one of the few merchants who had troubled to learn a European language. True, he spoke French with a Turkish accent and Maurice with an English, but conversation was possible without an interpreter.

"At the moment, effendi, the armies are moving far to the south and the country is untouched. The particular value of these markets is that you can tap the caravan routes from China and northern India before the goods cross the frontier. If supplies are shipped into Turkey under my name, the customs officials will demand a lower rate than they would of a Christian merchant. You can double, triple your profits. I have here a map of the country." Hamid unrolled a sheet of parchment showing the Ottoman Empire drawn with hair-fine lines. Their heads bent over it. Maurice forgot Venetian captains and Deborah and Katherine.

Hamid looked up. "Your part in this, effendi, will have to be kept secret from the authorities for the time."

"Why?" Maurice looked at the merchant with surprised arrogance.

"Because of this alliance against Spain that your English ambassador is negotiating now. As you no doubt know, the Grand Vizier goes into a fury at the very mention of such a treaty. That is more than half the reason why he started this Persian war—to divert all the military power of Turkey eastward instead of westward. He is well paid by Spain."

317

Maurice said coldly, "I'm sorry, sir, but I cannot see what that has to do with my trading plans."

"Not a thing if they aren't discovered. Such trade was a point of disagreement between Harborne and the Grand Vizier Othman. Because of the financial loss, the government has always objected to the English-man's tapping the spice trade before it reaches Turkish territory. Your Muscovite Company has attempted it several times, but usually without success as it is so far from the seat of their operations in Moscow. And to be brief, Othman refuses to sign until all such trading is stopped. Though the harem rules the Sultan, the Grand Vizier has much to say in foreign affairs. Now, effendi, how deeply do you wish to go into this venture?"

Maurice felt as though he had received a vicious body blow. Here was a chance exactly to his own taste—new markets farther to the east, an excellent se-lection of imports before they were handled and the choicest products taken by the Turkish goverment and merchants, an opportunity for novelties which counted so much in laying a sturdy foundation both for his own house and his Eastern Company. If he sent every bale of goods from the Eastern Company to Shirvan and Ti-flis in a gamble for highly profitable returns, and the shareholders got one hundred to two hundred percent return on their money, his Company would have more members than he'd care for, his own power and for-tune would begin to reach the dazzling goal he had set for himself—how many years ago?

He remembered the day long gone. The bodies of the Northern rebels had hardly been cut down from the trees where they had been hanged. The air was still fet-id from the odor of their rotting flesh. Mary Stuart was securely in prison. He himself had the taste of death in his mouth. His estates were gone. His wife was dead. He was betrayed in everything he had be-lieved in. On that day out of despair he had made for himself dispassionately a new faith to live by.

He remembered saying that he was like Elizabeth in that he was what it profited him to be. Elizabeth, a red-haired bitch who drove mad the men who served her, had appealed to him to help with this alliance.

318

How had she known it would be in his hands to aid or hinder? And if he helped and she changed her mind about the treaty, she was as capable of turning against him as she had turned against Davison for delivering Mary Stuart's death warrant to Fotheringay. He felt again the full shock of Queen Mary's death and recoiled from it with a savage desire to strike back at the woman who had signed the warrant.

He said, "I've had word that a cargo to the value of ten thousand pounds is being shipped out of London in the name of the Eastern Company. Have your markets and exchange products ready and we'll direct the full shipment to the provinces. But of course before it leaves Constantinople, I want assurance of the return that you promised."

Hamid nodded matter-of-factly. "There's no question of the profit, effendi." He gestured to the deaf-mute to give his visitor another cup of coffee.

Maurice looked at the coffee with raised brows. He had lost count after the sixth or seventh cup and the beverage did not appeal to him. He took it however with a murmured *"Ei-valé!"* What was the advice given travelers?—to have the back of an ass to bear all, a tongue like the tail of a dog to flatter all, the ear of a merchant to hear all and say nothing, and the mouth of a hog to eat what was set before one.

This was his moment of triumph. He knew with the sure knowledge which had never failed him that this would be successful, that it was the beginning of a company to rival the Turkey and Muscovy Companies. And then he knew with a deadly clarity that it did not matter. He did not need this added success, not now and not at so high a price. He'd had with Katherine an hour of golden pleasure which no money had ever bought for him; Katherine had carried his child; Katherine in her need had turned to him of all men in the world.

He finished the coffee, handed the cup back to the attendant and stood up. He said curtly, "On second thought, sir, I'd like the shipment I mentioned sold through the usual markets in Constantinople and

Aleppo, perhaps Cairo if the profits are higher there and would pay for the additional shipping costs."

Hamid made a startled movement. The steaming black coffee in his cup slopped over the edge, burning his fingers. He did not notice the pain. "But, effendi, the returns won't touch what we could do with that cargo in the outer provinces! I think your first decision was the wise one, in fact the only one for the enterprising merchant I took you for."

Maurice looked down at Hamid, his eyes intensely blue in his impassive face. "You know," he said coldly pleasant, "I find it highly annoying to have my agent attempt to do my thinking for me. If you limit yourself to carry out my commands, your work will be more than satisfactory. Good day!"

The honors, he thought, were all Elizabeth Tudor's. Or perhaps Katherine's? For the first time he could recall Katherine's words without flinching. "You can hire a man to protect your property, Master Quain, but whom can you hire to save your soul?" Today he had brought back some measure of his self-respect. But once the treaty was no longer needed, he intended to recover every shilling he was now giving up!

17

Katherine came into the apartment so early in the morning the candles on the tables were still lighted to dispel the gloom of the curtained chambers. Maurice, standing by the far window, turned at her entrance.

Katherine did not see him. She spoke to Patrick, cloaked and booted. "I feel I should have met you outside the city walls, Patrick. Should anyone have seen me, it would be too easy to trace your connection with my departure—and so with Deborah's yesterday. She's all right? But of course. If you and Master Quain undertake a matter, I'll swear it is carried through successfully." She laughed.

Maurice watched her, not moving. Her face was too pale but her smile lighted up her eyes, seemed to put a tinge of color in her cheeks. Her whole attitude was carelessly gay, expectant and alive at the hope of going home, of knowing Deborah safe.

She wore a dark-red riding dress of velvet that spread smoothly over her slim shoulders and her bosom, was laced in tightly at her waist. The wide skirt reached just below her ankles. Her plumed hat was held in her gloved hand. The golden light of the candles gleamed on the black hair held in a silken net at the nape of her neck, deepened her eyes, shadowed the incurve of flesh under her cheekbones and emphasized somehow the remote and passionless spirit which was as much a part of her as her dangerous beauty. Maurice thought she had never seemed so desirable, so worth the winning. But he knew at last that to win her for only an hour, a day, was not good enough for her.

Patrick bent to tighten his bootstrap, then turned toward Maurice. "Is there anything further before we leave, Master Quain?"

Katherine's gaze followed Patrick's. "Maurice!" Neither seemed to breathe as she and Maurice looked at each other. Her face was soft and winsome, heartbreakingly lovely. He came forward. Her eyes twinkled. "You're up early, Maurice. May I hope it is not just for business reasons?" She held out her hand to him.

Maurice frowned. "Are you well enough to travel?"

"Oh, yes. The ride will be nothing to the worry of staying and wondering if Debbie is all right. Not to mention I'll be glad to be away where I can receive no more summons from the Seraglio. I'd be afraid to meet Janfreda Kadein now." She shivered.

"You could stay here."

"No. I've brought you too far into this already, both of you." Her glance included Patrick.

Maurice's brows lifted. "They could hardly touch us."

"Don't say that! You're tempting the gods, Maurice." She laughed at herself, but for all that she meant the warning.

Patrick said, "We should go at once, Katherine, and get through the outer guard before any alarm can be raised. I don't see why there should be difficulty. You said Deborah was given until tomorrow to visit the Seraglio again, didn't you? But since you're under my care, I'd like to avoid even the shadow of trouble."

His young eyes watched her poignantly. This was the woman he'd hoped to win one day. He'd seen the look she and Maurice had exchanged, and though he could not read it, some deep understanding existed between those two. He put all thoughts aside but Katherine's departure. The only task before him was to see that she was aboard the *San Marco*. After that there would be time for his own concerns of joy or grief. But he prayed inwardly that Maurice would not kiss her. That would be unendurable.

Maurice only held her hand, bent to kiss it lightly and said, "Godspeed!" as though to make this a casual parting between friends.

Katherine smiled and curtsied. "I will see you in London, Master Quain!" She turned quickly and went blindly toward the door.

Patrick, one hand on the latch, said, "If all goes well, I'll be back in two or three days, four at the most, Master Quain." He followed Katherine out.

Maurice remembered he had not asked Katherine if Blount knew of her leaving. He shrugged and sent for Vincent. Since he was awake he might as well start early on the day. Money was not earned by late risers. If Vincent, who came in yawning at the call, did not see eye to eye with Maurice, he did not say so but changed into doublet and hose with dogged resignation.

Blount himself answered Maurice's question that evening. He smiled charmingly as he came into the apartment. "I was just riding by, Maurice, and thought I'd repay one of your many visits to the Embassy."

Maurice's cold look discouraged his smile. "It is kind of you, Sir Edward. Tom, take Sir Edward's hat and gloves." He eyed Blount consideringly. Had Blount discovered Katherine's flight and was he entertaining himself as he waited for the exact moment to tell Maurice he had stopped her? If he were holding Katherine, he had Patrick also. No, Blount didn't look pleased enough for that to be true. "Won't you sit down?"

"Thank you!" Blount accepted the glass of wine Maurice offered him. He made up his mind that he could be as impassive as Maurice, ask a few questions, and show as little interest in what had brought him here. He had one thing to find out tonight, and when he discovered that, he would in his own time unleash a power against Maurice for which there was no defense. The drink was sweetly heady. "This wine is excellent. Turkish, isn't it?"

"From Greece." Maurice thought contemptuously that Edward Blount had no discriminating palate at all.

Blount twisted the goblet in his fingers. "The Turks have strange wines and stranger customs," he said casually. "Speaking of customs, it was fortunate for Katherine, wasn't it, that she managed to have Deborah gone just when the child might have become a point of issue between the Seraglio and the Embassy?"

"Did she? I heard nothing of it."

Blount laughed. "Maybe you heard nothing, but I'm well assured you know something of her disappearance."

Maurice looked at his guest indifferently. Why did Blount watch him so tensely? Had he really hidden the child so well that the Embassy did not know Deborah had been here? "What would I know of Lady Katherine's movements?"

Blount dismissed Katherine carelessly. "Kit is in Constantinople. But Deborah vanished a fortnight ago. I'd been trying myself to think of a way out of the dilemma when you so kindly cut the Gordian knot for us."

Maurice sat back to eye Blount more carefully. He neither affirmed nor denied his part. "However it was accomplished, Sir Edward, I'm sure Katherine was pleased."

There was a touch of color in Blount's face. "Lady Katherine, if it please you, Maurice."

"What does it matter? I'm not apt to offend her or you, Sir Edward, by speaking to her for some time."

"What do you mean? Body of God, Maurice, what

do you mean?" He was out of his chair and standing over Maurice before he'd spoken the last word.

A Greek attendant moved between Maurice and Blount with the trained ease of one to whom assassination attempts were part of his daily work. Maurice waved him away impatiently. Odd how Blount who was so slow in many ways always seemed to have an instant perception where Katherine was concerned. "Just that I understood Lady Katherine was to be out of the city for a while."

"She said she was going riding early this morning." Blount stood there, his face haggard above his crimson doublet. "She would not go away without telling me." There was a bewildered pathos in his voice.

Maurice looked up at him coldly. Blount could change from bully to beggar in a breath. "I wouldn't know Lady Katherine's plans in detail of course, Sir Edward. But I suggest you do not try to have her followed. You might cause her trouble."

Blount moved back to sit down, a strange gleam in his eyes as he stared at Maurice. "She is on her way to England," he said with conviction. "I suppose with Deborah."

Maurice said, "Sometimes you show more intelligence than I expected." He didn't care whether Blount did or did not know about Katherine and Deborah or what he'd had to do with them.

"You fool! You think you've taken her from me. Do you know what you've really done?"

Maurice looked politely interested.

"You may think she'd be safe in England because Mary Stuart is out of the way. Katherine has never been safe there and now would be less than ever."

"You're rather unreasonable, Sir Edward. You objected when I put her into your hands at Naples. You sound out of humor now because she's off your hands again. As far as England's concerned, she seemed well enough in the Queen's graces up to the very last."

"Seemed is the word, Maurice." For the first time Maurice looked at him warily because Blount was neither swaggering nor plaintive. He was beginning to enjoy himself. "Do you know why she's always been at

324

Court under the Queen's eyes and Walsingham's rather than stagnating in some village? Do you know why her father Sir John Perrot is always away from Court at some troublesome outpost that will keep him busy?"

Maurice said curtly, "I can't say that the Perrot family has interested me enough to speculate on it."

"I'll tell you then. They're too near in blood to the throne."

Maurice laughed. "Perhaps in blood but not in law."

Blount shrugged his satin-clad shoulders. "As a merchant of course, Maurice, you wouldn't be aware how half England is gathering around the bone of succession to the Crown. Elizabeth will not allow Parliament to name her successor. Anyone with the slightest pretensions has followers—Huntington, for instance. Perhaps you remember how Catherine Grey was put into the Tower because she married a man who might eye the throne with the same interest her sister's husband showed when they made Jane Queen of England for nine days. And then there's this little Arabella Stuart to whom the Earl of Leicester's trying to betroth his son in case the succession should fall her way."

He paused. Maurice looked slightly bored. Blount went on patronizingly. "Nor must you forget that Henry the Eighth himself considered having his bastard son the Duke of Richmond named his heir, giving him precedence over the claims of his daughters Mary and Elizabeth. Fortunately for England," he added hastily, "the duke died and we were blessed with Mary's short reign and Elizabeth's long and prosperous rule. If one son born on the wrong side of the sheets could be considered successor, why not John Perrot as well? I merely tell you what the minister think. In short, I don't believe you were wise to send Katherine to England."

Maurice said, "Frankly it all has a rather unreal sound to me."

"It does? The Courtenays and the Countess of Salisbury—among other who had nothing against them but inherited claims to the throne—hardly contemplated the Tower or the headsman's ax with such fine detachment."

325

"I was under the impression Mary Stuart's son James had the best right to the Crown."

"He has the strongest claim, but whether our ministers will accept a Scottish ruler is another matter. I'm not speaking of who will or will not succeed Elizabeth, but of what a dangerous position Kit is in. You know, if I thought we might be together a year from now, I'd wager you any amount that John Perrot will be in the Tower by then."

He spoke with exquisite enjoyment. Everyone else feared Maurice, but he could bully or threaten him, knowing Maurice would not move against him. Maurice dared not touch the royal envoy. Blount remembered the three thousand pounds he'd made Maurice pay him once. The affair with Mustafa Rahmi had gone awry, but it would make his future success more enjoyable. He had shown Maurice he had power and could use it. His eyes went to Maurice's hands. A pity Maurice had been freed before he'd felt the real weight of their threats.

Maurice's fingers started to drum on the arm of his chair. He held his hand still. "You seem less concerned about Katherine now than at first mention."

"It has just occurred to me that as Katherine is no doubt with Deborah, she could not be persuaded to return." Blount waited, watching Maurice.

Maurice shrugged. "That might be true." It was too late to reach her anyway. He couldn't be sure how much there might be in Blount's talk.

"Besides, Maurice, I don't know that there is much to choose between Katherine in the Tower and in your arms." Blount smiled.

"Don't revenge yourself on Katherine for any mad dream you may have of her and me. How could any wench fit into my life? Would I send a woman I loved three thousand miles with a child and one attendant?"

Blount's breath went out in a little sigh. So Maurice did know what happened to Deborah! He spoke graciously. "Perhaps not, perhaps not."

"Will you have more wine, Sir Edward? So many humors are unhealthy!"

"No, thank you, Maurice. I must get back to the

Embassy." Maurice was none too clever. He had found out exactly what he wanted to know. The thought of Katherine disturbed him, but Walsingham would move no farther against her than to put her under surveillance. God knew he'd a thousand times rather have her in prison than with Maurice! He couldn't make this man out. On what had he really to base jealousy of Maurice Quain? Had the child indeed been Maurice's? If he only knew——

Well, he thought as he stood up, when Maurice is out of the way and I have the Quain fortune, I'll no longer care.

Maurice rose with him. "I'd suggest that in your next report to the Queen you give Lady Katherine full credit for her aid in this alliance. That might help if your fears have any foundation."

"A good suggestion, Maurice. I'll act on it. And if you should need our assistance in any matter, come up to the Embassy." Blount bowed, took hat and gloves which Tom brought him and went out.

Maurice did not go to the Embassy for a month and then only in answer to a summons from Harborne. The ambassador greeted him genially. "Our prestige will rise with the signing of the treaty, Master Quain. French influence seems to be on the wane, and it is the exact moment for the Tudors to step into the place the Valois have held for a century of domination." He said nothing of the reason for which he'd requested Maurice's presence.

Maurice looked up across his glass of Hullock wine. "You look well pleased with your progress, Sir William."

They were alone in the small room except for Harborne's secretary Barton who lounged on a couch under the window drinking cup after cup of hot black coffee. Barton put in sardonically. "He is pleased, Master Quain. However, it might be as much because we'll be relieved of our royal envoy as for the going forward of our negotiations." He held up one finger for the attendant at the door to refill his cup. His hand shook slightly as he raised the coffee to his lips.

Harborne said hastily, "Edward Blount has an excellent presence and I'm quite certain that he made a very fine impression on the Sultan. Only in the East you have to give a little here, a little there. He doesn't believe in bribing Turkish officals; he can't see why we allow gambling at the Embassy, have foreign women around, take up some of the customs here." His glance at Barton indicated the "customs" meant hashish. "With the Turkey Company charter coming up for renewal next year, we naturally prefer a more tolerant report to Her Majesty than I think we're apt to get. I'll be glad if I can end my duties here with something of value like this alliance, but we need a friendly word at Court too."

"You go home next year, Sir William?"

"Yes. Barton will take my place here to carry on the Company's business until a new charter is granted."

"When you're in London, Sir William," Barton murmured, "tell the Queen to keep her silken courtiers where they belong—at home."

Maurice looked at Barton's thin clever face with the deep-etched lines about his eyes and from nose to mouth. He rather suspected Barton had given Edward Blount a few uncomfortable moments. Barton smiled suddenly at Maurice. "I want to thank you for one thing. I enjoyed Sir Edward's face when he found out you had snatched Lady Katherine from the Embassy and sent her, I presume, to England. People like us have our faults, Master Quain," he added somewhat irrelevantly, "but hypocrisy is not one of them."

Harborne said peaceably, "We have enough quarrels with the French and Venetians, Barton. Let's not start among ourselves or we're undone. This latest news from home should make Englishmen of us all."

"What's that, Sir William?"

"Didn't you hear? The Spanish Navy was at Cadiz and Lisbon. Sir Francis Drake secured permission from Her Majesty to attack. The Dutch were convinced the Queen was ready to make peace with Spain over their heads and give up to Philip the towns we English have been holding for them. An outrage." Harborne added quickly, "a piece of treachery I know Her Majesty was incapable of contemplating. But to still such talk she let Drake sail against Spain."

Maurice said, "Don't tell me she didn't withdraw her commission!"

"Well, yes, she did send a message to recall him, but Drake had expected it and was on the high seas by the time the order not to attack got to Plymouth. He had thirty ships—six belonged to the Crown and the rest were all fitted out and supplied with crews by the merchants of London, so we can take some vicarious credit for the venture. He sailed into the harbor at Cadiz—I should say he ran in under the shore batteries—without difficulty, so great was the surprise. When he sank the first Spanish ship of war, the crews of the storeships fled to land, leaving Drake and his captains with command of the harbor. He tranferred Spanish provision to his own ships, set their vessels afire and cut the cables.

"The Spanish gentlemen admired Drake so much for the exploit that they said there was not his like in the world! He intended to strike at Santa Cruz himself in Lisbon, but this time the Queen's orders caught up with him and he was forbidden to go in. However, he set the Armada back a season at least. I think it will not sail this year."

Maurice said carelessly, "I doubt if it will sail any other year. Such a successful thrust at Spain should help you in your negotiations with the Sultan."

"Exactly." Harborne looked up at Maurice. "You aren't going home soon by any chance?"

Maurice's brows lifted. "No. Is that why you wanted to see me?"

Harborne said quickly, "We're not trying to rid ourselves of you, Master Quain. It's just—well, your presence might be even more valuable someplace else."

Barton laughed. "I'm the guilty man, Master Quain. The other night I happened to remember that your commercial connections in Madrid have survived the general breakage suffered by the other merchants. We had a very thorough report about you before you ever reached Constantinople," he explained offhandedly. "Anyway, the thought of your business in Spain made me wonder if you would possibly consider going home

329

by way of that country. You might get some valuable information about invasion plans—a few facts to balance the flood of unfounded rumor that is influencing the Court. A slight risk, perhaps. Perhaps not. But much less for you than for any other Englishman who might make the venture. You wouldn't have to look for a source of information. You'd have it in your own established representative. Undoubtedly he's in the good graces of the Spanish authorities."

"My dear sir, do you expect me to take your ridiculous proposal seriously?"

Barton said, "Sir William fears it too dangerous to ask of you. But in the guise of some business affair it doesn't seem too desperate a gamble. Of course you can throw it in my teeth that I'll be sitting here drinking coffee while you're running the fire of the Spanish Inquisition. A true rejoinder, but unavoidable in the circumstances." He flicked an imaginary fly from his wrist.

Maurice brushed the danger aside with a gesture of impatience. "What I object to, Master Barton, is your proposal that I drop my unfinished business here and thus lose half what I've put into it. You insult my intelligence. Why in the name of God do you think I came to Constantinople?"

Barton smiled. "That's a question, Master Quain, all of us ask ourselves sooner or later. You're still rather new here and can answer it by saying it was to make money. But after you've been here longer you may wonder. Some of us stay just because it takes less effort than to go home." His eyes followed the steam from the coffee rising toward the ceiling. "We know it would be good if there were anything in the world vital enough to draw us back before we die to the land that gave us birth. But in the East such magnets lose vitality."

Maurice eyed Barton coldly. "What I'd have to be convinced of before I'd even consider such a trip, is the possibility, however remote, of the Armada putting to sea."

Harborne said, "Doesn't the gathering of the Spanish Navy at Cadiz and in the Tagus convince you?"

330

"It convinces me, Sir William, that King Philip is thinking of an invasion. But for Philip Hapsburg from the thought to the deed is a long and weary road that loops backward oftener than forward."

Harborne pulled at his spade-cut beard. "I think you're wrong, Master Quain. As we know from our reports, John Hawkins is building up a Navy for England that has never been equaled. He's even trying out new ship designs to make his vessels faster and more maneuverable—lowering fore and sterncastles and lengthening the keel. Queen Elizabeth doesn't spend money on ships that won't be needed."

"Perhaps," Maurice agreed. "Still the complexion has changed with Mary Stuart's execution. Her sympathizers will not rise to put her son James on the throne. To the House of Guise in France it made no difference whether mother or son gained the Crown—both were their kin. But not one Spanish ship will leave the harbor to put the heretic James Stuart on the English throne in place of the heretic Elizabeth Tudor. The alternative that they'll sail out to crown Philip's daughter, the Infanta Isabella is possible, but this would lose them French and Scotch support—possibly the Pope's. France wouldn't dare let Spanish territory surround them farther. Pope Sixtus wouldn't wish Spain any more powerful than she is now."

Barton shifted himself slightly. "As you've pointed out, Master Quain, Philip of Spain travels a tortuous road. He may not realize that English Catholics won't take up arms for any puppet of Philip's merely because that puppet is Catholic. Until he does realize that, why won't the Armada sail—once it has recovered from this blow of Drake's?" He signaled for more coffee.

Maurice shrugged. "If you can convince me at any time, Master Barton, that the Armada will sail, I'll consider your suggestion to land in Spain on my way home—if it's no great inconvenience to me or my purse."

Barton looked at Maurice over the rim of his cup. "As I said, at least some of us aren't hypocrites."

331

Maurice felt tired when he opened his eyes to watch the golden light shining through the blue curtains at the window. He had left England a year ago and the weight of each day was heavy on his shoulders. Weariness crept through him. His eyes were tired. The muscles along his neck and his shoulders were stiff. He knew it was the aftermath of success. He had not allowed himself to feel tired until he reached the goal he had set his heart on.

Now with the Eastern Company expanding into new markets, with shares selling slowly but steadily at the Royal Exchange in London, with an agency set up in Aleppo under the Turkey Company consul there, he had a sound foundation on which to build a greater fortune without sacrificing his houses in western Europe. It was a temptation to make a large gesture and pour everything into the Eastern outlets. That would be unwise and against his fundamental business principles of scattering his fortunes as widely as he could to give him strength and independence. Let a ruler in one country—Elizabeth Tudor for instance—confiscate his holdings and he could take the loss with no great inconvenience.

He wished now to go on to Cairo. At the moment the Cairo duties were not so exorbitant as the Turkish, and the Sultan of Turkey listened graciously to English complaints; he did not want his official, the Egyptian Pasha, to grow too wealthy. From Cairo, Maurice thought he could send out travelers eastward to report on markets in Persia and India. He closed his eyes to rest them. It all seemed too much effort. One worked to reach a certain pinnacle, never satisfied until it was attained, and then on the crest of success remembered how brief a time life would give to enjoy the fruits. Contentment was to be found only in setting a new and distant goal to strive for.

Even the alliance with Turkey had been finally drawn up and signed. Edward Blount had gone home with the glory, and the pirates of Tripoli had been given the word to attack all Spanish shipping. Blount, he thought with a momentary enjoyment, would find his income reduced when he got home and discovered

332

the House of Gascony was no longer doing business. But Blount was home, and Katherine was in England. With all his interference, he could not have done better had he been Blount's greatest friend.

Pain was both the core of life and the rind. To hold oneself aloof was safest. He had grown wealthy. He had escaped intolerable hurt. And he had lost—Katherine.

He swung his feet over the side of the bed and reached for his furred dressing gown. He must shake off his lethargy of mind and spirit. Cairo—from there to India. He smothered a yawn. He felt so tired he ached with weariness. Katherine. He wondered about her. She had finally sent the briefest word through Bowyer that she was all right. Nothing more. Had she told the truth? She was too proud to tell him if she weren't. So all one could be sure of was that Deborah was all right. A pretty little thing but rather a nuisance.

He remembered how he'd felt drawn to the Orient because his destiny was here. Destiny? Perhaps. Only he'd not had the courage to grasp it. Well, heroics, as he'd said once, were a form of entertainment for the gods that he'd outgrown.

He didn't turn his head when Webster knocked and came in. Webster said, "I didn't know whether you'd want to be disturbed, Master Quain, but this dispatch just came from the Embassy."

Maurice looked at the sealed parchment without interest. "It's wiser not to open it. Probably some new prohibition the Sultan is pleased to put on commerce in Turkey. Or the Privy Council is making a forced loan before any ships in harbor can sail. Or the Turkey Company is being dissolved by special order of the Queen. No one sends a dispatch you want to read this early in the morning."

Webster grinned. "The messenger's waiting for an answer. Should I just tell him 'no'?"

Maurice was not amused. He broke the seal and unrolled the document. It was from Harborne's secretary, Barton.

Master Quain:

You may remember we discussed the Spanish situation some time ago and a part of you might have therein. You were rather reserved in speaking of the subject. Would your opinion change if I were to tell you that information from the Bey of Tripoli indicates that the damage Drake inflicted has been almost repaired? Our correspondent claims that the Armada sails in late March, though I question his reliability about the date. If correct, you would have sufficient time to dispose of essential business matters and still allow for the uncertain passage across the Mediterranean in the winter months.

Maurice could well imagine the sardonic enjoyment on Barton's face as he'd penned those words. An uncertain and damnably uncomfortable journey. He would not have half enough time to settle his affairs. He could leave Webster in Constantinople, but he'd have to forget Cairo, the push eastward to India. If, that is, he returned to England at Barton's request.

He stood up. He no longer felt tired. "On the contrary, Master Webster, we'll tell the messenger 'yes.' "

Part IV

AND HAZARD ALL HE HAS

18

Captain Fox, sitting across the broken table from Maurice and Señor Huércal, glanced uneasily about the dark interior of the lean-to adjoining the larger building of the inn. A tapster, with hair hanging over his eyes, thin oily face and out-at-elbow clothes, stood near the door, his sullen look giving the impression that he would be equally ready to serve his customers with wine or knife. Wax ran down the sides of the candles onto the table, making a melted pool on the boards. The unmistakable scratching of rats sounded from the corner. There was something about this place Captain Fox did not like. In particular he did not like its nearness to the Spanish mainland.

Maurice stretched out his long legs. He enjoyed the feel of the clay floor under his feet, the solidity of the earth—though, after all the months spent on shipboard, the ground still had an inclination to sway precariously at odd moments. By the time his affairs were in any semblance of order in Constantinople, Webster ensconced as his factor and the winds favorable enough to leave port, it had been well into January.

The Turkish galley on which passage had been arranged by Harborne had required over six weeks to make the trip to Tunis. It seemed to Maurice they had spent more time waiting for favorable winds or being blown back on their course than in going forward. He wondered if there were something in Leonardo da Vinci's complicated mechanical plans for moving a vessel through the water without sails or oars. A boon for commerce if a ship were not at the whim of winds and weather. But Da Vinci had been dead almost sev-

335

enty years, and no one else seemed likely to take up where he had left off.

At Tunis there had been another delay waiting for the rendezvous with the *Falcon* and obtaining the necessary clearance papers and safe-conduct pledges from the Bey before they could set sail for the island of Formentera.

Maurice turned to his companion. "I trust, Señor Huércal, it's not an inconvenience for you to meet us off the coast?"

Señor Huércal's dark face was more fine-drawn than ever tonight. He shifted his crippled leg. "Not at all, Señor Quain. Now I have here the reports about your company in Madrid. The business with private officials is almost at a standstill, but since you sell direct to the government your profits have not diminished too much. Your house has sent through few supplies of late from England, however."

Maurice dismissed that. "I still have doubts of the Armada sailing, but if it does, as I mentioned in my letter, I want to know how far Italy, France and the Prince of Parma will back King Philip, how many men Parma has under him in Flanders ready for the invasion, the make-up and command of the Armada."

Señor Huércal said nervously, "I can tell you what you can pick up in the streets of Cadiz or Madrid. The Armada is about one hundred and thirty sail. There are sixty or seventy large ships, the smallest of them of seven hundred tons, a number of galleys, for galleasses. As you know, this is not a Spanish Navy but is composed of provincial fleets operating under their own commanders."

Maurice said uninterestedly, "I'm sure Master Secretary Walsingham has had all that safely in his files for months. Is the Duc de Guise strongly enough in power in France to join with Spain?"

"Not at the moment, señor. When it came to the issue the Duc could not persuade France to help Philip add to his Spanish territories. Our Holy Father also seems to think Spain too powerful. He will aid Philip with a million crowns but only when the Spanish Army is on English soil. The Prince of Parma advises giving over this enterprise of England. He wants peace but will invade if the Armada effects a landing place. Whether his troops have recovered from the disease and famine of the autumn and early winter I do not know."

"Don't you?" Maurice sipped the wine before him. "This is vile-tasting liquid. If you're sending casks of it to England, you can expect your cargo back on the next ship."

Fox growled. "I wouldn't touch the stuff, Master Quain. Probably poisoned or drugged. I don't like this place."

Maurice smiled faintly. "I don't think there's anything wrong with this, Captain. I took the liberty of exchanging cups with Señor Huércal when the wine was brought in. But you were saying, señor?"

Huércal's lined face thinned and lengthened. The muscles of his throat worked as he pushed his battered pewter mug to one side. "Then you know, Señor Quain? Go now while you can."

The tarnished silver lace collar at the captain's thick neck fluttered at his abrupt movement. "What do you know, Master Quain?"

"That this is a trap, I presume. Your crew has the shore covered, Captain?" Maurice turned back to his agent.

Huércal had retired into his Spanish hauteur. "What did you expect, Señor Quain? In business I am at your service. But was I engaged to sell my country's secrets to the man who employs me? No, señor."

"Not if you would get a better price for selling me," Maurice agreed pleasantly.

Huércal said gravely, "This is war, Señor Quain. Private considerations, ordinary loyalties, commerce, must all be overriden by my duty to Spain and to His Most Catholic Majesty." He turned his head alertly as though he heard a sound.

Maurice's brows lifted. "I rather admire the sentiment. I might indeed go so far as to adopt it. It has always been one of my few principles, señor, to protect the men who work for me. But as you say, this is war. You have knowledge Admiral Howard might find of use. Could we persuade you to board the *Falcon* and accompany us to England?"

Before Maurice had finished speaking, Huércal was on his feet. A long dagger in his hand flashed coldly in the light. At his movement the tapster came to life across the narrow room. He lunged forward with a knife naked in his hand. Maurice swept the two candles from the table. They fell with a thud, blacked out on the clay floor. The room was impenetrable. There was silence but for the sound of heavy breathing. Then footsteps moved lightly across the floor.

Captain Fox grunted, "I have this one, Master Quain. Have him tell his bloodthirsty friend I'll put a knife through Hoorcal's ribs if he breathes too loud."

Maurice had not moved except to step back from the table. He repeated the order to Huércal, who spoke rapidly to the tapster. Fox said, "We're this far by God's blessed will. Now what do we do with these bully-rocks?"

Maurice made a grimace in the darkness. He disliked violence. There was a shrill whistle from far away, then a sound, though Maurice was not sure whether he felt or heard it. He said in rather bad Spanish to the tapster, "Two hundred reals, sirrah, to get us out of this to the shore."

The tapster's voice came out of the darkness, hesitant and rough. "Two hundred? How do I know you speak the truth?"

Maurice said shortly, "Half now when I hear the clatter of your knife on the table. The rest when we are at our own boat."

"Ah, yes, señor, I give up my knife—and then?"

"Bones of God! There's the bargain. Take it or Señor Huércal will be out of the way and the captain can turn his attention to you. Two hundred reals is more than you'll get again in your lifetime."

The whistle sounded again urgently. Now there was no mistaking the movement of men outside. In the room there was silence, then the clatter of steel on the boards. Maurice moved forward, fumbled for the knife, reached into his purse for money for the tapster, curtly instructed Fox to come with his prisoner. The tapster

338

grunted something unintelligible and opened a low door that led through a passage smelling chill and damp as though dug out of the earth.

Fox whispered, "How do we know he's not leading us right into a Spanish trap?" He pricked Huércal's buttocks with his dagger just to remind his prisoner he was there.

Maurice said, "Why should he? He'd have done better to leave us at the inn than to chance a stab in the back now. I rather think the two hundred reals impressed him more than Señor Huércal's life." He had to stoop as he walked. Each man felt his way in the blackness, the ground rough underfoot and along the walls. With his luck of recent months it was the wonder of God to Maurice that Katherine and Deborah weren't here with them.

There was the smell of fresher air, the taste of salt in it. They were coming out onto a sandy hillock near the sea. Brush was pushed aside at the entrance. The tapster stopped to replace it, then led them silently through tangled bushes and down a steep decline to the rocky shore. The ear was so accustomed to the noise of the waves breaking rhythmically on the stones that one was hardly aware of the unceasing sound until the eye caught the breaking crest of foam running into the land. There was a faint light from a quarter-moon in the sky.

The tapster said, "Your vessel is over here, señor," and turned to walk rapidly to the right, moving lightly across the rough ground. Huércal followed, dragging his lame foot painfully. They crossed a jut of land and almost fell into the arms of the waiting English crew who had lifted the wherry out of the water to conceal it under overhanging bushes.

Maurice said, "Where is the Spanish ship?"

"There's better anchorage up the shore, señor." The tapster's dark eyes darted from seamen to Maurice in uneasy question of the sort of shrift he'd get now.

Captain Fox said, "Call back our sentries and get that boat in the water, lads. We have an extra passenger." He pushed Huércal forward so hard that the Spaniard stumbled and almost fell.

Maurice's voice was sharp. "Be good enough to treat our passenger with respect, Captain. He's still the head of our Madrid house."

Fox grinned, the stumps of teeth gleaming yellow against his black beard. "Yes, sir! Yes, sir! What'll we do with this fellow who brought us here? Throw him into the sea?"

The sailors moved forward at that, a hard-bitten lot, muscles tensed for the word to turn on the hated Spaniard. Too many of the crew had brothers, kinsmen or friends who had been on captured English ships and were rowing out their lives in Spanish galleys.

Maurice counted out the value of the reals he'd promised, gave them to the tapster who took the money unbelievingly, turned to leave and was faced by the captain. "You'll wait right here, my lad, until we're out to sea. And just to be sure you don't go arunning to your friends—" he turned to his men with a sudden bellow—"bring a rope, one of you!"

A sailor trussed up the Spaniard so that he could neither move nor speak until he was released, while the rest launched the wherry. The night wind tore at their clothes, their hair, sent the spray flying into their faces. The waves crashing against the shore made a living sound about them. The *Falcon*, a dark hulk with bare masts was just visible against the night sky. Maurice splashed through the shallow water out to the boat held steady against the rolling surf. A cold trickle of water ran over the tops of his high boots, down his leg.

Huércal was already seated in the stern. He said bitterly, "No gag for me? Are you not afraid, señor, I will cry out and warn the soldiers of your escape?"

"They wouldn't hear you against wind and water, señor. Even if they could——" Maurice brushed the danger aside with a gesture of his maimed hand. "You know that would be the last sound you made on earth. And you value your life or you'd have called for help before we left the inn when your friends were approaching. No, señor, I do not think you need to be gagged."

340

Maurice looked eastward across the waste of water toward the blur of land that was Portugal. He was more than a little weary of the scene. He thought of Barton and cursed the ambassador's secretary. He should still be in Constantinople instead of dashing off as he had with his business but half-done there. Why in the name of God and all the devils of hell had he been in such haste? What had he gained but the loss of trade in the East and trouble with his house in Madrid. He'd have to establish a new agent in Spain, and in Turkey Webster could not push his business forward as far as he would have done himself. He hoped Barton would choke on the next cup of coffee.

He turned to Patrick who was standing silently beside him. "One more day of shuttling back and forth on this cursed ocean and then, Patrick, we set sail for England."

Patrick pulled at the edge of his wildly flying cloak. He'd been expecting Maurice to say this every day since the *Falcon* had arrived off the coast of Portugal. That was a week ago and since then nothing more formidable than a galley and a pinnace had been seen, though the *Falcon* had stood off and on in hope of sighting the Armada which Huércal swore would sail on the seventh of May.

Maurice said, "Señor Huércal has no doubt been amusing himself at our expense."

Patrick shook his head. "I don't think so, Master Quain. We have traveled all this distance for news of the Spanish fleet, and it would be a pity to go home without the most exact information—not when it's supposed to sail but the day it actually leaves port."

"I follow you only so far, Patrick, as to say it's a pity we've traveled this distance. Being hasty is a mistake I seldom make, but even once is rather too often."

He asked himself what precise madness had driven him on to this. He smiled ironically. Each time he forgot himself in a selfless deed he tarnished it with petty considerations, weighing an imponderable gain against a loss in profit. He knew exactly what had driven him on, why he'd grown so weary of Constantinople, why he had not been sorry at Barton's suggestion that he leave the East. Katherine was in England.

He watched the foam curl across the dark crest of a wave as it passed beneath them. Katherine always held him to the hard thing to do, without a word, making no demands on him, but just because she was Katherine and seemed to expect it of him. No—not expect. It was more subtle than that. She let him know that when he could forget his own interests for another's, it made her happy. Slowly, reluctantly, it was being forced on him that Katherine's happiness was his, that without Katherine life was arid.

Could he chance the hell of betrayal again? Wave after wave passed under the ship in a rhythm that seemed to deaden his faculties. Did he dare make himself so vulnerable again? Must he tear out his heart by denying his love, or give it to Katherine to trample on? Or perhaps—might he somehow have Katherine and yet keep himself impregnable behind the walls he had erected with so much care and at so high a price? He turned from the rail. Katherine had a shining courage about her that shamed the cold fortitude with which he faced life. Well, he could not put his faith in a woman and he had no confidence in the future.

Patrick said, "You don't really mean to sail for England tomorrow, Master Quain? After all this time, what's another day or two now?"

Maurice shrugged. What was another day or two? In London the distractions of business made him safer, strengthened his defenses. But to sail for home only to run away from himself was a weakness. He said grimly. "Three days then, Patrick, for you to sight this elusive Armada for us."

"We will! And when we reach England, Master Quain, I intend by your leave to have further sight of it from the deck of one of Lord Admiral Howard's ships." He grinned. "With all the experience we've had with the *Falcon* and Mediterranean galleys this last year, I wouldn't be surprised if the Admiral offered me a captaincy."

Four days later when Maurice was eating dinner a sailor pounded on his cabin door. Tom opened it. Maurice looked up from the salt beef on his plate. The sailor said deferentially, "Cap'n Fox sends his regards to Master Quain and asks that he join him on the poop deck. He has something he'd like to show him."

Tom turned back to repeat the message, getting hopelessly entangled in the "he's" and "him's." Maurice said, "Whatever the matter is, it can wait." He started to cut the beef, grimaced at its toughness, then stood up abruptly. "Hand me my cloak, Tom. This dinner looks none too appetizing."

He stepped out onto the half deck, followed the sailor up the stairs to the poop and across the deck to the weather rail. He'd been at sea so much in recent months he'd have to learn a landsman's life all over again if he ever reached England!

The *Falcon* was sailing close-hauled on the larboard tack, swooping easily over the long Atlantic swells. Maurice wrapped his heavy cloak about him as the cold northerly wind cut through him. Captain Fox turned, pulling at his beard with the conscious gesture of having done more than his duty.

"You wanted to see the Armada, Master Quain?" The captain pointed out to starboard. "There it is!" Fox waved his arm with the air of a magician who had produced the Spanish fleet out of the air solely for Maurice's benefit. "Too many big galleons to be anything else. Even the yearly plate fleet doesn't move with that much projection. I've seen it many times."

Maurice swung about to stare across the tumbling waste of water. Far out on the horizon an endless flotilla could be seen beating out to sea in a north-westerly direction on the opposite tack to the *Falcon's*.

The captain dropped his air of wizardry and said matter-of-factly, "You'll notice that there isn't much in the way of organization. They're out of some Portuguese port—Lisbon, I'd say—and trying to hold as close to the wind as they can. A lot of them are doing a pretty bad job of it, judging from the big gaps between 'em."

Maurice said briefly, "Send for Señor Huércal. He
343

might give us a few details." The Armada! He had never really believed the fleet would sail. A swift passion of excitement rose in him. He overlaid the sensation immediately and mechanically with the skeptical question: The Armada was leaving Spain, but would it arrive in English waters?

He turned idly to watch the sailing master and an assistant, who had been standing on the lee side of the poop deck, come up to the taffrail carrying a large astrolabe. The sailor suspended the instrument by its large brass ring, adjusted the movable arm. Fox stepped over to take the master's place at the peep sight.

Maurice turned his gaze upward, watching the tall spars sway in great arcs across the blue sky, the gray sails billow to starboard straining at yard and sheet, the long Tudor pennon trail out from the main against the fleecy white clouds. On the deck shadow patterns from the noonday sun were flung in an erratic fashion as the *Falcon* rode up on the white-topped crest of a great green swell, then raced down the long slope, rolling to starboard before the cold wind. The taut lines of the standing rigging whistled softly and yards creaked rhythmically against the constant swish and gurgle of the seas passing under the transom.

"Señor Quain, can I be of service?" Huércal, who had come up in response to the summons, looked haughtily at Maurice. He had the air of being a distinguished guest rather than a prisoner on the ship.

"Yes. What do you make of that?" Maurice pointed toward the southern horizon.

Huércal drew himself up proudly. "I told you the Armada would sail. With this wind they will be a long time in reaching England, but reach it, señor, they will."

Captain Fox looked up from the astrolabe. He glanced at the Spaniard contemptuously before speaking to Maurice. "We're thirty-eight degrees fifty minutes north latitude, Master Quain, about twenty miles north of the latitude of Lisbon. With all the cloudy weather, this is the first opportunity we've had to shoot sun or stars since leaving Gibraltar. You can

344

be sure of our latitude." He put a hand on his instrument like a man fondling his favorite dog. "This astrolabe was made by Humfray Cole and there isn't a finer one on any ship. Cole——"

Maurice said, "Spare us Humfray Cole, I beg you, Captain. How far west are we?"

"The longitude? Well now, Master Quain, that's another matter. No clock is any good on shipboard and without knowing the time the best we can do is guess at our longitude." Fox consulted the traverse board and looked at the sea for a moment. "I'd say we're about sixty miles off the Portuguese coast."

"If your guess is correct, the Armada must have been sailing out of Lisbon for the past day or two." Maurice turned to look again at the vessels on the horizon. "Can you identify the types and numbers, Captain Fox?"

"At least eighteen big galleons and fifty-six merchant ships." He added disdainfully, "And not one able to sail on the wind!"

Huércal said with pride, "That would be the main battle force, probably the Portuguese and Castilian squadrons, each with ten galleons and led personally by the Captain General, the Duke of Medina-Sidonia. The Duke may be inexperienced and reluctant to undertake this assignment as the rumors say, señor, but sailing with him on his flagship the *San Martin* as his principal nautical adviser is Don Diego de Valdes, commander of the Castilian squadron. He is a great gentleman and a fine sea captain who will make your Drake and Hawkins run before him."

Maurice looked coldly amused at Fox's angry growl, echoed by the master and sailor at the astrolabe. "You haven't chosen the most popular sentiment to voice at the moment, señor." He glanced at Fox. "You said the English fleet is waiting at Plymouth, Captain. We'll make that town our destination instead of London. I'd like to arrive ahead of the Armada."

"Change the course? Yes, sir! Plymouth it is, sir. The *Falcon* can outsail anything the Duke has. *Madre de Dios*. There never was a Spaniard who knew how to sail a ship on a wind."

"Just one hundred years ago, Captain Fox," Huércal retorted, "Bartolomeu Diaz sailed over these very waters on his return to Lisbon after rounding the tip of Africa, his Cabo Tormentoso, which his Prince saw fit to call the Cape of Good Hope. He met no English ships down there."

Maurice smiled. "Touché!"

Fox snorted. "Diaz was Portuguese, not Spanish, Master Hoorcal." He turned to the sailing master. "Call all hands, Master Hutton. I want her on the other tack, and keep her as close to the wind as she will lie."

The boatswain's whistle rang through the ship. I am going home, Maurice thought, home to England and to Katherine.

Maurice stood on the half deck of the *Ark,* Lord Howard's flagship. The wind howled out of the west with gale force, tearing at his boat cloak and driving the rain into his face in icy pellets. Patrick was beside him, leaning against the forward rail over the cobridgehead while they watched a group of men scrambling up the sea nettings over the main-deck bulwarks into the waist of the ship.

Only yesterday they had come over the side themselves in the same fashion, accompanied by Huércal who had missed his footing and had to be hauled dripping from the sea. The *Falcon,* driving past the Lizard in a southwesterly gale, had run into the English fleet and Howard of Effingham, Lord High Admiral of England, had received Maurice on the *Ark* to hear his reports on the Armada.

The ship was now hove to, and in the lee of her huge bulk three small gigs were maneuvering precariously close to her bulging topsides, the cox'ns waiting for just the right moment to pull in closely enough for the passengers to leap for the sea nettings and clamber aboard. With the ship's bottom slushed with grease and the topsides smeared with tar, agility was required. In this vicious weather, with Admiral Howard anxious to be under way again as soon as possible, there was no opportunity for a more ceremonious or comfortable entry for the English captains summoned to a council of war. Under the force of the wind the canvas whipped and slatted with pistol-like reports as it lay aback, sounding as if sails, rigging and spars must be torn from the vessel at any moment.

A slightly stooped man with heavy shoulders was helped first over the side. Patrick said, "That's Master John Hawkins, Treasurer of the Royal Navy. I saw him once at Whitehall."

Maurice eyed Hawkins with interest—Hawkins, one-time slaver and West Indian trader whose adventures had thrilled all of England until he'd been asked by the Queen to serve in the Navy. His more enduring but less spectacular exploits in achieving well-founded ships, soundly rigged and fitted, against the graft and apathy of the Navy board had not stirred the country, though his untiring work had made it possible for the English fleet to face the ships of the invader.

The next man climbing aboard Maurice knew was Captain Martin Frobisher, commander of the mighty *Triumph,* one of the two largest vessels in the English Navy. He'd seen once before on a London dockside the famed seeker for the Northwest Passage—the venture that had been defeated before it began by the insistence of his backers at Court that Frobisher bring back rock for assaying instead of going on to search for an opening north of the Americas to the Indies. Maurice would recognize anywhere that dumpy, squat figure which gave the captain the appearance more of a farmer than a sailor.

A tall very erect man bounded agilely over the side, disdaining the assistance of the sailors of the bulwarks. Sir Francis Drake, Vice-Admiral of the Queen's Navy, would be five or ten years younger than the captains who had preceded him, but from this vantage point Maurice thought he seemed twenty years their junior as he strode aft toward the main cabin. Drake looked the arrogant sailor who had circumnavigated the world, built a reputation as the terror of Spain and burned the supply ships of the Armada at Cadiz. Maurice felt an immediate and instinctive dislike for the Vice-Admiral. He didn't care for the type.

347

A command was shouted from the poop above. There was a flurry of activity on the main deck as the crew tailed off on braces and sheets, a moment of hesitation while the *Ark* slowly paid off, and then the ship rolled hard over as the wind caught the topsails. She crashed along now close-hauled, foaming water creaming along the topsides just beneath, the deck tilting sharply. Salt spray driving over the bow and whipping aft over the ship was added to the stinging pellets of rain. Maurice pulled his boat cloak more securely about his face.

"Master Quain, sir!" Maurice looked up as a young officer, standing spread-legged on the careening deck, saluted smartly. "The Lord Admiral sends his compliments and begs that you will attend him in the main cabin."

Patrick had been gazing to starboard. Over the bearded seas he could discern the dim rain-shrouded outline of the other galleons as the fleet drove past the Eddystone Rocks toward Plymouth Sound. He turned as Maurice started to leave. "Don't forget, Master Quain, I'd like a place, any kind of place, on any of these ships!"

Maurice shrugged. "I suppose you have a right to be an idiot if you want to. I'll speak to the Admiral."

He followed the officer down the stairs to the main deck, bent to step through the low doorway in the co-bridgehead. They walked past the two quartermasters, struggling with the whipstaff to keep the *Ark* on her course in the heavy seas, and passed into the carpeted luxury of the main cabin.

Maurice handed his boat cloak to the steward, mopped the spray from his face, adjusted the ruff at his throat and stepped forward toward the heavy oblong table with its gleaming candles and polished mahogany. The spaciousness of the *Ark* made him feel able to stretch out again after the weeks of dodging the low deck beams in the cramped cabin of the *Falcon*.

Lord Howard, sitting at the afterend of the table, said affably, "Gentlemen, Master Quain is the merchant I've been telling you about. He is a member of the Turkey Company and has been of personal service to Her Majesty on several occasions, among other matters raising a loan from the Dutch during the siege of Antwerp, and he has been instrumental in negotiating our alliance with Turkey." He turned to the man at his right. "Sir Francis Drake, Vice-Admiral."

Maurice returned Drake's stiff nod. Howard introduced Hawkins and Frobisher and motioned Maurice to a chair beside the latter. Polished wall panels gleamed in the guttering candlelight. The creaking of the ship's timbers beneath them could be felt rather than heard and the muffled wash of the water against the hull gave the voices of the men a faraway quality.

"A merchant? Name of God!" Drake blustered. "Of what earthly value are the opinions or observations of a landsman in the present undertaking?"

Maurice glanced across at the Vice-Admiral, liking him no better at close range than he'd cared for his appearance at a distance. Sea dog, freebooter, privateer, pirate—a brave man no doubt but with a rough and overbearing manner that, Maurice sensed, sat no better with the other captains, Hawkins and Frobisher, than with him. He said coldly, "I am here, Sir Francis, at Lord Howard's request. My own vessel the *Falcon* undoubtedly made port yesterday and I should at this moment be attending to other affairs."

Howard, a tall man with a thin face and easy controlled manner, interposed pacifically, "Master Quain, at the request of our ambassador in Turkey, and through his Spanish connections, has gone to considerable trouble to obtain for us information on the Armada. I want you gentlemen to hear his report firsthand as I've given the order to return to Plymouth because of his advices. Gentlemen, the Armada has sailed."

Even Drake was startled. He struck the table with his open hand. "Assuming our newly found observer would recognize the Armada if he saw it—which to my mind is doubtful—why are we beating back into our burrow so that we can be holed in like rats?"

Howard lifted his shoulders in a resigned way. "First, there is of course, as always, the question of supplies. Thanks to the victualing of our London ministry we do not have provisions for more than a few days at sea. Second, with this gale working unabated into the west, we would stand an excellent chance of being driven to the lee of Plymouth. I have no desire to leave this port defenseless against the Armada while we drift up the Channel beating futilely against the gale. And now, Master Quain, for your report."

Maurice put an elbow on the table, leaned forward slightly. The gold buttons on his doublet gleamed against black velvet. "We stood off and on near Lisbon for some eleven days waiting for the actual sailing of the fleet that, according to Señor Huércal, my agent in Spain, had been set for the seventh of May. On the eighteenth we saw Medina-Sidonia's ships streaming out in a disorderly line, sailing westward on a northerly wind—and in the opinion of the captain of the *Falcon,* making a very bad job of it. Captain Fox, who has sailed every trade route in the world for twenty years, identified the types and numbers of the vessels to such an extent we could be reasonably certain that Philip's invincible—or incredible, choose your own term—fleet was finally at sea.

"As to the organization of the Armada—rumors picked up in Tunis and Formentera by my men and checked with the details from a rather reluctant Huércal indicate that the main battle consists of ten Portuguese and ten Castilian galleons under Medina-Sidonia and his chief adviser, De Valdes. You no doubt are already aware that the Duc, although a man of some military reputation, has no knowledge of sea warfare, in short, Sir Francis, a mere landsman. It is common knowledge in Spanish naval circles that De Valdes for all practical purposes is the real commander of the flotilla. He's an expert in naval theory according to the Italian and Spanish Mediterranean schools, but his military record is questionable and he is jealous and quarrelsome by nature——"

"In other words," Howard interrupted, "the Spanish high command will be divided." He glanced at all of the captains in turn, let his eyes rest a breadth of a moment longer on Drake than on the others. "We can make an advantage out of that situation by maintaining the closest co-operation and liaison at all times among ourselves."

"In addition to the main battle there are four provincial squadrons composed of about ten armed merchantmen each," Maurice went on. "When a Spanish knight embarks on a campaign, his personal preparations are on such a scale that there is little possibility of secrecy. Don Pedro de Valdes, kinsman of Medina-Sidonia's adviser, heads the Andalusian squadron. He has been commander of the Indian squadron for a number of years and has had a number of brushes—shall we say—with English privateers.

"The Biscayan flotilla is headed by Don Juan Martinez de Recalde, by report of Captain Fox the finest seaman in Spain. We're probably fortunate Recalde was not appointed advisor to the Duc. Don Miguel de Oquendo, who has established a great reputation for personal bravery and ability, heads the Guipúzcoan squadron, and Don Martin de Bertendona leads the so-called Levant squadron. There is also a flotilla of four galleasses and a number of Lisbon galleys under Don Hugo de Monçada, Lieutenant General of the Galleys of Spain."

Drake drummed on the table with his fingers, blunt sinewy fingers that seemed as agile as his swift and supple mind. "According to your report, Master Quain, the Spaniards have twenty galleons, forty converted merchantmen and four galleasses, or about sixty-five effective fighting ships?"

"Yes, although there are another sixty or so hulks—we were able to count them with fair accuracy from the decks of the *Falcon*. They're victualing ships, transports, fighting pinnaces and so on, making an Armada of about one hundred and thirty vessels."

Howard said thoughtfully, "Our fleet will be rather evenly balanced against the Spaniards. Our galleons will equal theirs, and outsail them, and our merchantmen should match theirs in number and size. Now, Master Quain, what about armament and personnel?"

"A merchant, gentlemen, if he is to stay in business very long must have dependable sources of information on everything that effects shipping. That includes some knowledge of naval strength and operation. There is no evidence in any of the reports that have come to me that Spanish tradition has been changed in preparing the armament for the Armada. Philip's ships are gunned and manned for close action—short-range guns, boarding weapons and quick-firing pieces. There are about twenty thousand soldiers scattered through the fleet. As far as the crews are concerned, evidence is that far too high a proportion of the men are farmers and peasants recruited at the last minute."

Howard turned to his Vice-Admiral. "What do you think of the situation, Sir Francis?"

Drake said bluntly. "Of the report, my lord, I think little. Merchants and landsmen are better off at home than meddling with seamen's affairs. If you want my comment on the Armada as it has been presented to us, I'd say we are in an excellent position to smash Spanish sea power. We can match them ship for ship. We have heavier guns and we have manned our ships with experienced English sailors against their plow hands and soldiers."

Maurice smiled thinly. "It seems to me, Sir Francis, you are showing considerable enthusiasm over a report you believe worthless." He was filled up to his teeth with Drake even while he felt a grudging respect for the way the captain grasped immediately the essentials of his report and could vision it largely. "Of course there should be considerable booty, on the paymaster's ship especially, that can be plundered."

Drake stared at the merchant, started to rise. Howard's voice stopped him. "We have no time for bickering, gentlemen. We know the Armada sailed around the seventeenth with unfavorable northerly winds that continued almost a fortnight until this southerly gale began to blow which has prevented us from getting clear of the Channel. It's possible the same wind is bringing the Armada off the Scilly Islands right now."

John Hawkins said briskly, "We must revictual at once and get to sea as soon as possible. If the Spanish are not in the Channel by that time, we can attack them in whatever port they are sheltering themselves."

Howard looked grim. "Where will we get supplies?" He picked up a beribboned roll of paper and spread it before him. The Royal Seal glinted in the candlelight. "We have a communication from Her Majesty that will be of some interest to you. It was written by Walsingham after I'd sent word we meant to wait the Spanish fleet at the Isles of Bayona. Her Majesty forbids our doing so and demands that instead we ply up and down between the coast of Spain and England so that we may be able to answer any attempt which the Armada shall make against England, Scotland or Ireland!" He tossed the document aside.

The captains stared unbelievingly at the Admiral. Drake snapped furiously, but there was a certain awe in his voice. "How in the name of the Lord Jesus Christ can we guard England, Scotland and Ireland at the same time? Can't those fools at Whitehall understand that the only way to meet a threat like the Armada is to seek it out and destroy it before it can be organized to attack us?"

"Furthermore," Howard continued without a change in his level voice, "Her Majesty has ordered the decommissioning of our three largest vessels inasmuch as there have been no recent reports from Spain to indicate an immediate sailing of the Armada."

There was an ejaculation, a spatter of profanity, silence again. The swish of water could be heard along the side, the steady groaning of timbers, the rolling and plunging of the vessel. Drake said in wonder, "God's nails, I was on the other side of the world and had not the sense to stay there!"

Howard smiled. "Do not take the order too seriously. I have sent Her Majesty a dispatch even before meeting with Master Quain, refusing to follow her instructions to decommission the ships."

Maurice thought with chill amusement that birth could make one as impregnable as wealth. The Howards, as one of the oldest noble families in England, probably still looked on the Tudors as upstarts. Howard added the final thrust. "The pinnace with the Queen's dispatches brought word also that the promised supplies have not arrived."

353

Frobisher growled, "Mercy of Christ, that is too much! My men are lucky when they get half their rations, and most of the beer spoiled in the bargain."

"Men can't fight on empty stomachs," Hawkins echoed the other. "I've stretched my credit to the limit for the supplies we're using now."

Howard nodded. "I also. I might raise a hundred or a hundred and fifty pounds, but that won't be a tenth of what we need to put this fleet to sea on the most meager rations."

Drake brushed the matter of food aside. "All I demand is that the Queen give us a free hand in our strategy, allowing us to strike against the Armada when and as we see fit. Hell take the royal supplies! We'll capture a Spanish ship and eat Spanish provisions as I did after Cadiz." He had an overpowering presence that somehow gave everything he said an intensified meaning, making his words sing out boastfully.

Maurice glanced at Howard. "If it would aid you, my lord, I can place at your disposal a letter of credit for a thousand pounds which should be honored by the Plymouth merchants. Of course I want a receipt from you for the amount."

Howard's anxious face lighted up. "Excellent, Master Quain! It's hard to see our sailors failing for lack of food, to have fever sweep through ship after ship and the crews without the strength to throw off the sickness. Now we can at least get emergency rations together. Also, Master Quain, may we impose on your kindness to carry dispatches with you to London? Perhaps you could use your influence with Walsingham and the Queen, pointing out our need for supplies and a free hand in planning our strategy. English seamen stand ready to die for their country, but they cannot fight without food and powder."

Maurice thought he had business in London with his agent, not royalty, but he said shortly, "I will deliver your dispatches, my lord. By the way there's one request that I'd like to make."

Drake snorted. Maurice spoke pointedly to Howard. "My secretary begs to serve in the fleet, preferably on

354

a gun crew, I suppose, as he has been drilling for the past month on the *Falcon*."

Drake said truculently, "Your secretary? What in God's name would a clerk know about weapons? I won't have him on the *Revenge*."

Maurice's brows lifted. "No. He is interested in fighting for England, not going on some piratical foray. I want him in London while I straighten out my business affairs. He'll return in a few days."

Lord Howard smiled. "There'll be a place for him on the *Ark,* Master Quain. We'll need every brave man in the coming battle."

19

Elizabeth Tudor's long fingers drummed ceaselessly on the arm of her chair. In the early morning light diamond and emerald and ruby gleamed on her restless hands, at her thin throat, on her red wig. The glitter of jewels, Maurice thought, was no harder than her green eyes in the painted white mask of her face, but he could sense beneath the outward show her woman's shrinking from the harsh unpalatable demands of her ministers.

It was a small audience in the Queen's cabinet at Whitehall—Leicester, Burghley, Walsingham and two of the Queen's ladies, Katherine Perrot and Mary Howard. Maurice had only glanced at Katherine when he'd entered and had not looked at her again. He felt a blinding sense of relief at her presence. He had not believed Blount's assertions that she was in danger, and he had been certain her help with the Turkish treaty would restore her to favor now that Mary of Scotland was dead and Walsingham's enmity was no longer directed against Stuart sympathizers. But he knew now that his assurances had never convinced him, that to see her safe had been the most urgent reason of all for his leaving Constantinople. In the realization he felt a cool deliberate resolve had settled within him forever a turmoil of doubts.

Elizabeth looked past Maurice out the tall oriel win-

355

dow facing into the garden. The cypress trees bordering the walks bent under a vicious wind out of the northwest, their tops curved like bows against the white clouds that were scudding across the summer sky. Then she turned her head to smile fondly at Robert Dudley, Earl of Leicester, who was standing beside her. Leicester had been eying the charms of the two ladies in waiting, but from long practice he could sense when the royal attention was on him, and his answering smile to the Queen conveyed a feeling of amorous devotion.

They made a magnificent couple, the Queen of England and her favorite—Elizabeth in a gown of pale-yellow satin, the long-waisted bodice with pendants on her breast picked out with gold, the fluted ruff, jeweled stomacher and voluminous skirt looped with pearls over an enormous farthingale; and Leicester with jewels spangling his short-skirted doublet of scarlet velvet, belt studded with gems, long dagger with hilt of gold and diamonds. He wore high boots of perfumed Spanish leather with diamond buckles, and the plumed hat tossed carelessly aside had a rope of pearls about the high crown.

The staccato of the Queen's fingers on the arm of her chair did not stop, was loud in the stillness, seemed to echo back from paneled walls and molded plaster ceiling. Walsingham broke the silence finally. "God's wounds, Your Majesty, the seamen must have food and ammunition!"

Elizabeth looked at her Secretary coldly. "Why?"

"The followers of God and of Belial will be face to face, Madam, in a war for the survival of our country and the purer religion," he retorted sternly. "Starving men cannot fight nor empty guns fire against the enemy."

Elizabeth said shortly, "We gave them provisions a month ago. How much do our sailors eat, Master Secretary? As for ammunition—" her hand struck the arm of her chair angrily—"God-a-mercy, we sent Sir Francis Drake a week's supply and he used it for his gunners to practice, throwing good money into the

356

empty ocean! We'll keep him on shorter rations for a while till he learns good sense."

Burghley's thin blue-veined hand closed over his silver-headed cane. "In your father's time, Your Majesty, never was there a day when there were not victuals and ammunitions for six weeks at Portsmouth and Dover. If you do not awaken to the danger, it were better—with sorrow I say it—to sue for peace even at this late hour. A peace without honor, Madam, but better than defeat."

Elizabeth laughed harshly. "When you don't want peace, my good Burghley, we are in desperate straits. When the month is up, we'll send supplies."

Walsingham's face lengthened and darkened. "Madam, it takes a month to get the provisions together!"

"Let the seamen eat less then. They are but idling in harbor. Waste! Waste! Waste! That's all any of you can counsel. If you're so eager to throw money away, gentlemen, dip into your own purses."

Burghley, shoulders slightly stooped, silky white beard falling over the breast of his dark doublet, turned his head at that. "I have tried, Madam. But my personal credit is worth nothing when the Spaniards are on the high seas. That alone should convince you of the dangers we face."

Elizabeth looked at Walsingham. Walsingham in bitterness said nothing. His fortune had been drained when the creditors of his son-in-law, Sir Philip Sidney, killed at Zutphen, had demanded payment of him. The Queen had not turned over to him one estate, one monopoly, but had taken all confiscations of traitors for the Crown or given them lavishly to her favorites. Leicester, for all his glitter, had poured his wealth into unsuccessful commercial ventures and into his brief and unhappy generalship in the Netherlands.

Maurice murmured, "Lord Howard and Sir Francis Drake have strained their credit to the last ha'penny to hold off starvation until the royal supplies are shipped. As always, Madam, your devoted followers are ruining themselves in your behalf."

Elizabeth smiled cynically. "Except for you, Master Quain?"

"Except for me, Madam."

"My Lord Howard however says in the dispatch you brought," she conceded graciously, "that you did use your personal credit up to a thousand pounds for the needs of the Navy." Satin and jewels gleamed at her slightest movement.

Katherine looked up in surprise, a smile at the corners of her mouth. Maurice said, "I was buying a sea wall around England to protect my commerce. It wasn't a gift to the government, however, but a loan."

Elizabeth rapped out, "Master Quain, do you expect me to repay money you lend to a representative of mine, who had no power to authorize this business?"

"Perhaps 'expect' is too strong a word, Your Majesty? Let us say I hope." Maurice looked at her ironically.

Walsingham said dourly, "Starvation will drive our men from the seas, Madam. They are your first defense against invasion."

Maurice glanced at the Earl of Leicester's heavy mottled face with its weak mouth, his bloated body that a splendid costume and the veneer of grace and charm could not disguise. Leicester had been named Commander in Chief of the Land Forces. Leicester in a pitched battle against the Prince of Parma? The English Navy was the first defense against the invaders. It might be also the last.

Elizabeth leaned forward in annoyance. "You're all against me—always. Send supplies then, Master Walsingham, but for just a month. And only beer to drink. I see my Lord Howard has been pampering the sick with light wines—let him pay for that out of his own purse. And write him that he's been making too many new officers. Good God, doesn't he realize it all takes money, money, money? I'll not have it. As for the shot and powder they demand—we'll not send out one round until Admiral Howard tells us the exact amount he needs." She flung herself back in her chair.

Leicester said, "My dear Madam, I beg you that we'll not repeat the mad farce we played out in the

Netherlands. I made a fool of myself by your orders to help the Dutch in their fight against Spain with one hand, and with the other try to make peace with Spain at any price in honor. Now it's not Dutch against Spaniard, but England against Spain. The Armada is on the seas to clear a way for Parma's forces to land on our coast."

"You were raised by our royal favor, Robin," Elizabeth said furiously, "and by God we can cast you down! If you were all as wise as you'd like to seem, you'd long ago have found a way to stop Philip Hapsburg from launching his fleet!"

There was an indrawing of breath. No one reminded her how Drake had burned part of the Spanish Navy at Cadiz only because he'd slipped out of port before her orders could reach him forbidding him to sail. Nor did anyone mention how he had been ordered home before he could strike against Santa Cruz himself in Lisbon since she still hoped for peace. Elizabeth stared before her broodingly. "Parma. He's our only hope now. We must send to him."

Leicester said, "In the name of the Lord Jesus Christ, what for?"

"To bribe him not to land, Robin."

"Our promises, Madam, wouldn't bring in a farthing if put on the market," Walsingham interjected sourly. "Besides, the Prince of Parma has not been open to bribery. And he'd have no faith in any messenger you might send."

Elizabeth scowled, remembering how she had tried to tempt Parma to desert Spain and set himself up with her aid as the independent ruler of the Netherlands. All the while he talked with her representatives, he went forward with strengthening his army, striking against Sluys, which was held by the English, and capturing the town. He'd smiled and listened to her proposals and then spread them abroad in the Netherlands so that the Dutch lost the little faith they'd had in her, a faith shakily recovered when Drake struck against the Spanish fleet at Cadiz.

Elizabeth turned toward Maurice. "You have met the Prince of Parma, Master Quain?"

"Yes, Your Majesty, for a few minutes when I was leaving Antwerp after its surrender. I needed a pass through the Spanish lines to Paris."

Elizabeth said with a reminiscent half-smile, "I hear the Prince has been trying to raise a loan in Antwerp and had to pay above twenty-five percent interest. Perhaps we should lend you to him." She tapped her slippered foot. The Tudor rose embroidered in gold on the toe had a ruby heart that looked like a drop of blood against the leather. "I was about to say that we might use you as a messenger." She turned to Walsingham. "Sir Francis, do you not think the Prince would have faith in Master Quain?"

The Queen's Secretary eyed Maurice. "More than in most of the men you've sent him, Madam."

Aware how she disavowed her agents when their dealings might not sort with some change in policy, Maurice said curtly, "I care to be sent on no fool's errand, Your Majesty. If the Armada can hold the Channel, Parma will cross. What can you bribe him with—except England itself—that would deter him from the task for which he's been readying himself for years?"

"It is a task he's begged the King of Spain to give over as too dangerous," Walsingham said thoughtfully. "Perhaps just an appeal to his common sense, a word of how well armed our army and militia are, might do something. If Parma lands, it will be a bloody struggle that will drain Spain and England, but he cannot hope for ultimate victory."

Maurice looked skeptical at so thin an appeal. Elizabeth simpered. "Your suggestion, Master Quain, is admirable."

"My suggestion??"

"That only the promise of England itself will stay the Prince." Flakes of color appeared in her cheeks under her paint. One hand as though absently touched her low-cut bodice. "The Prince of Parma said once that if circumstances should demand that he marry our lamented cousin Mary Stuart, he would accept his fate. It would seem he was not adverse to becoming Prince Consort of England. Well?"

There was complete silence as Leicester, Burghley, Walsingham and Maurice stared at her in slow realization of her meaning. Maurice suppressed a laugh. Elizabeth for thirty years had kept all Europe guessing whom she'd choose for her husband. Austria, Spain and France had danced to her tune while she made promises, forgot them, had her ministers renew her proposals, broke her pledges as the balance of power swung one way or another. At the last, with the Duc d'Alençon's death, after having kept France on the qui vive for years, she had appeared to give over her thoughts of wedding. Her childbearing time—supposing against all evidence she could ever have borne children—was past beyond the fondest hope. Elizabeth was suggesting marriage again as the most gilded bribe, the only one left her to tempt Parma!

But it was rather late, even if Parma would not look with a jaundiced eye on any new offer of Elizabeth's. How often had she lived up to her bargains? But to be Elizabeth's Prince Consort—that was a goal worth a risk to some man. Would it be to Parma? Philip Hapsburg might once have regarded such a fantastic union benignly—wasn't Parma his nephew?—unless his heart was set past change on winning the throne of England for his favorite daughter Isabella. Besides, there was the inescapable hard fact that the Armada was even now on the seas.

Elizabeth said sharply, "Not a word, gentlemen? How of you, my Robin?" She turned toward Leicester.

His eyes were bloodshot. One hand clenched and unclenched about the jeweled hilt of his dagger. "You know my mind, Madam. Though it cost my life, better to see Parma in the field than at the altar!"

Burghley moved his gouty foot painfully. "Marry Parma? Better that, Your Majesty, perhaps, than to fight a war with no weapons in our hands." He fingered his white beard. Maurice thought, If anyone can change masters and not lose a shilling in the exchange, my Lord Treasurer is the man.

Walsingham said, "No, and a thousand times no, Your Majesty! Bow to Spain now? Never! Those idolators! Worshippers of Belial! Supply your ships, arm

361

your men, clap every Catholic in England in gaol, and the proud lords on the Armada will never see Spain again. But we must send our Navy ammunition and food now, today." He muttered with a touch of malice, "Though it would be almost worth it, were it any but a Spaniard, to see you married, so that we might deal with a man!"

Elizabeth laughed, her spiteful humor evaporating as she saw a familiar way out of England's dilemma, a circuitous path she had trod a score of times before, one that would cost no money, and that would give her time. She said aloud, "A delay would give us months more to prepare—and in the meantime," she added piously, "God might scatter our foe."

Walsingham groaned. "Time? And what use is time to us, Madam? We've had a year since Drake broke the strength of the Armada and we threw that year away. Our Navy has been commissioned and decommissioned so often that Master John Hawkins says he can't keep his records in order. Another month and you'd let all the sailors go back on the trade routes again."

Elizabeth said pettishly, "I've had enough of this whining and begging today, gentlemen. Master Secretary, write Admiral Howard for the exact amount of powder and shot he needs and order the supply of food, but not for a day more than a month. Master Quain, hold yourself in readiness to cross to Dunkirk to see His Highness the Prince of Parma. I'll speak further with you another day. Come, Robin!"

Elizabeth rose, majestic somehow in spite of her angular body, her limp and the pinched look of pain about her painted mouth. And then she smiled at them as she closed her jeweled fan with a click. "Gentlemen, we must all do our duty to England as we see it."

The indomitable fire that glowed under her avarice, her artifices, under her inability to see any situation in its larger aspects, flamed high enough for each man to catch a spark from it. While they cursed her, they were also ready to sacrifice lives and fortunes in her service. She swept out of the room on Leicester's arm.

Mary Howard and Katherine curtsied to the ministers and followed her. Katherine's eyes rested one moment on Maurice before she turned away. There was a certain gay bravado about her, he thought, her quick smile, the way she held her slim shoulders straight, her head poised proudly. Maurice bowed to Walsingham and Burghley and went out after her past the guards at the door. She heard his footsteps and turned, one hand at her throat, as he came up. Mary Howard glanced from one to the other, smiled mockingly and went on with a rustle of her silk skirts. Neither noticed her.

The corridor, lighted with a window at either end, was a background for a moving pattern of color. Two halberdiers went by, a page in scarlet doublet and hose, three young women in blue and green and rose, then a young knight, spurs clanking against the floor, sword perilously long. Katherine stood against the wall with its linen-fold paneling. She wore a dark gown that set off her white filmy ruff, her pale face, black brows and hair. Maurice came up to her, stood a little apart, not touching her.

Katherine smiled. "I've been wishing to thank you, Master Quain—Maurice then—for your last generosity. As you know I couldn't accept the manor house. I've been holding the deed to return it to you."

Maurice's voice was suddenly cold. "I'm sorry the place didn't come up to your expectations, Lady Katherine. I haven't seen it, so I cannot judge."

A slow angry color rose from her throat to her hairline. "If you willfully misunderstand——" She stopped, said gravely then, "I have not been there either, Maurice, lest the sight of the house and lands I could have should undermine my will. For I could not accept such a gift from you."

"Why not?" He smiled faintly. "You're the most difficult person I've ever met to give anything to." And the only one in the world, he thought, whom he wanted to give things to! He didn't say so aloud until she'd answered his question. Was her refusal because she and Edward Blount might finally be betrothed?

Katherine whispered, "Because of Ned." She put out her hand, set off by the narrow white ruff at the wrist. "Patrick told me at the last what had happened to you

363

at Scutari. Oh, Maurice! And Ned knew what they were going to do. Could I take a gift from one whom my lover had injured so bitterly?"

Maurice moved aside slightly as two grooms of the chamber came down the corridor. "When you put it so, perhaps not." He gazed down at her. There was so much to say, but he had no soft words at his command for this.

Under his eyes the blood drained from her face, though she smiled as she spoke. "You won't think my refusal ingratitude, Maurice?" Her voice trembled. "May I wish you every success with your mission to the Continent?" She curtsied formally before turning swiftly away.

Maurice felt a chill breath of fear at her move to leave. Too-familiar shadows closed in about him. He had desired her, he had felt she was necessary to his happiness. Now he knew she was essential to his very life. He was no longer invulnerable. Without her he could not face even the morrow. He whispered. "Katherine!" and stepped quickly forward. "I must speak with you now, before I go away."

"No, no. I'm in attendance on the Queen." She could not endure this. She had not wanted to see him at all. No, that was not true. The hope for his return to England had been a bright thread through every day since they had parted in Constantinople. And now her treacherous heart wanted each moment to be spun out, each word said twice if need be to lengthen this meeting. Only she thought that then the farewell between them would be almost impossible to say.

"The Queen has other ladies." Maurice glanced about in an agony of impatience lest they be interrupted. There was an open door across the corridor. He said questioningly, "Katherine?"

She nodded reluctantly, torn between her desire to stay and the prudence of leaving. "This is an anteroom for petitioners to the Queen to wait——" She broke off her sentence and stepped back as she saw from the doorway a tall angular man sitting in a despondent attitude on the wooden bench beneath the window.

Maurice scowled at the stranger. He would see

Katherine alone if he had to turn out the queen and all her ministers. He smoothed out his frown. "Sir, I am sure you are the gentleman whom the Chamberlain was mentioning to Her Majesty. If you will present yourself at once to Sir Christopher Hatton in the great hall——"

The angular man bounded to his feet, his dejection vanished. "At last! My benefactor! I have been waiting here day after day for four months and no one has even spoken to me. I feared—but Her Gracious Majesty will hear my plea, you say?"

Maurice murmured, "I could not be sure of course. I would speak to Sir Christopher if I were you." The petitioner was twenty feet away before his last word. Maurice bolted the door after him.

"Maurice!" Katherine's brows went up in amusement.

"Privacy at Whitehall is even rarer than innocence! Do you think what we have to say should be called out in front of every groom and page in the palace?"

Katherine turned her head away. The light gleamed coolly on a triangle of pearls in the silky darkness of her hair. "Don't say it!" She was sure he wanted only to insist arrogantly that she accept the house which she could never do. So this meeting would end with the old antagonism alive again between them, taking away the happiness she'd had of knowing he had been willing to risk much for her and Deborah. An intolerable silence followed her words. She looked up at him. There was no cold arrogance on his face, and his mouth was set in lines of pain. "Maurice, whether I take the manor or not cannot mean so much to you."

"Manor?" He spoke as though he'd never heard the word. "Katherine!"

She shivered, the tenderness in his voice stabbing her.

Maurice said, "There must be a better way to ask that you honor me by becoming my wife. I am too blunt and lack the art of persuasion, Katherine my darling. But I know now at last I want you more than anything in the world."

Katherine was white to the lips. "Wife? No, oh, no."

There was a stricken look on his face at her words, but he said only, "Blount? I wish for your sake, my dear, it could have been a better man who had your love."

Her mouth quivered as she tried to keep back the tears. "Oh, no, not Ned! Not ever Ned!" She added in so low a voice he could scarcely hear her, "I knew that was why you asked me."

Maurice said incredulously, "Marry you so that Blount would not have you? My dear Katherine!"

She whispered, "Out of pity then?"

He stared at her, winsome and infinitely desirable. His hands gripped her slim shoulders, hurting her, and his mouth was on hers savagely. He could feel the beating of her heart under the stiffened brocade of her bodice. She tried to turn away, but she was helpless in the strength of his embrace. And then she resisted no longer, her body molding into his arms, surrendering to his love. He released her at last with a smile. "Is that pity? I have come home. Now will you marry me, Katherine Perrot?"

Her eyes were ashine with unshed tears. "You and I together always? Yes, Maurice." A flicker of amusement crossed her mobile face even while she brushed at her eyelashes with her finger tips. "Of course, you know—Deborah would have to come with me. I couldn't desert her."

"Oh, of course, Deborah," Maurice agreed sardonically. "How could I feel natural without her clinging to your skirts? If you show half the devotion to your husband that you do to that—to Deborah——" He stopped, looking at her with a smile that faded as quickly as it came. Memory flowed between them of the cabin in the *Ascención,* of a golden hour torn across and across by his bitter denial of love or faith. He said, "Will you marry me as soon as I return? I'm afraid to trust my good fortune too long for fear you'll change your mind!"

"I've never changed my mind about you, Maurice!" She said unexpectedly, "But Patrick—what of him?"

Maurice stared at her. "Patrick?"

Katherine did not answer. Under her glow of hap-

366

piness, there was an ache in her heart thinking of Patrick, a small grief that dulled the brightness of the moment. Perhaps Patrick would find someone else? But she knew he wouldn't. Something of her reflections revealed itself in her face.

Maurice started to speak. There was the sound of running feet outside, a quick knock. Maurice unbolted and swung open the door. Mary Howard stood there. She looked from one to the other. "A pity and all, Kit," she said breathlessly, "but I've been searching everywhere for you. Her Majesty has asked for you twice and she's not in her best humor today to start with. So do come quickly."

"I must go, Maurice." Katherine glanced at him over her shoulder as she went out.

He thought, Katherine at the open door of a manor house in Sussex, waiting for him? That picture would come true. Katherine his wife? They would go up to Blyth together. Katherine in his house there, lighting it up with her beauty. No. He did not have faith in the future. A sense of apprehension chilled him as she disappeared.

Patrick glanced up and broke off a gay tune he was whistling when Maurice opened the door to their old apartment at the Saracen's Head. The young man was going rapidly through a sheath of documents on the desk. "These are from Master Bowyer. He'd like to see you at your convenience to discuss your plans and particularly your new markets in the East. By the way, shall we send for your furnishings, Master Quain, or take what the landlord has?"

Maurice's brows rose. "We'll take what's here, though I can't say much for the man or woman who hung those purple draperies on the wall and the orange curtains about the bed. I'll have to meet with Bowyer tomorrow. When are you leaving, Patrick?"

Patrick smiled. "I have one person to see, and after that as soon—to quote Bowyer—as suits your convenience."

Maurice turned his head sharply toward Patrick at those words. Then he moved slowly to the window, looked down at the stragglers on the street below. London seemed oddly deserted—not so oddly either perhaps, with half their young men dashing down to Plymouth or Dover and the other half out at Tilbury under Leicester or drilling in small bands of militia. Patrick and Katherine. The taste of victory was not so sweet, had a bitter quality in it. He turned abruptly. The kind thing would be to tell him now.

Patrick, catching Maurice's gaze, pitched his whistling in a lower key, then stopped. He said, "I really shouldn't be feeling quite this happy, Master Quain, when Katherine can't be too cheerful at the moment."

"What do you mean?"

"About her father."

Maurice's pulses quickened. "Yes?"

"Sir Edward was here today. . . . I don't know how he knew . . . oh, maybe he saw you at Whitehall. Anyway he was very pleasant, and well he might be for the privilege of still being alive. He said he wanted to know how our voyage home was, and then that he had news you might be interested in—Sir John Perrot was in the Tower, sent home from Dublin on the charge of treason. As I've met Sir John only once and under unfavorable conditions, I can't say the message means very much to me, aside from the fact he's Katherine's father. But what has he ever done for her?"

Maurice said, "No!" Blount in Constantinople saying, If I thought we'd be together a year from now—— And so his prediction had come true and Perrot was in the Tower for treason. The daughter next? Katherine hadn't known. Was the knowledge being kept from her or had it just not reached her yet? He said abruptly. "I must see Perrot."

From the courtyard below Sir John's cell Maurice could hear the knight's voice snarling at some unfortunate victim. He glanced out of the slits of windows as he went up the circular stone steps of the Constable Tower. He could see the outer wall of the fortress and then just a glimpse of the Thames and tall masts of boats swinging at anchor. The damp chill of the stone walls went through him.

The guard went up the last turning, across the stone floor and peered between the grated bars of the high door. A voice bellowed out. There was a crash and after that the door was swung open and another guard came through rubbing his shoulder. His tunic was dripping with beer. John Perrot, Maurice thought, had not changed a great deal since he'd met him four years ago.

His guide stepped in. Perrot roared, "Visitor? Who'd want to come to see me? Some carrion crow to gloat over my ill fortune! Throw him out!" The guard gave the name. "Quain? Never heard of him! Quain—maybe I do know the man. What's he want? All right, let him in."

As Maurice entered Perrot was tilting back in a rough wooden chair, his booted feet on the narrow table, a tankard of beer in one huge hand. His eyes were bloodshot, beard and hair uncut, and his soiled green doublet was open at the throat. "What do you want?"

Maurice said, "Good day, Sir John," and came all the way in.

Perrot jerked with his thumb toward the door. "Get out o' here before I throw you out!" He lifted his tankard threateningly. The guard glanced from one to the other, backed out and bolted the door behind him. Perrot chuckled. "Only place you can get any privacy is in the Tower. I remember you now. What do you want?"

Maurice sat down on the wooden bed. "As a matter of fact, I'm not quite sure, Sir John. It seems to me you did me a favor once and I promised to return it if you needed help. What do you lack?"

Perrot looked about his cramped quarters, the rough furnishings, the low door leading to the parapet where he was allowed to walk for one hour every afternoon, the narrow window from which he could see the life that went on in the inner courtyard of the fortress. "Don't need a thing, Master Quain. I'm finally freed from fools and spies and fortune hunters. What more would a sane man ask?"

They looked at each other, Maurice with a lift to his brow. Perrot with a leer. Maurice grimaced. "That beer

369

smells none too good. I'll send you in some wine. Any-thing else?"

Perrot glared up from under his brushy brows. "Why do you want to do me any favors? I'm no use to anybody. Always knew they'd get me in the end and they did."

Something in his voice brought back to Maurice that feeling he'd had when he'd met Perrot before, two doomed men staring at each other. He sensed the breath of it again like the shadow of a bird's wing be-tween himself and the sun, just touching him and away. "Why do I want to do you a favor? Frankly I'm not sure. Partly my promise—but that did not include seeking you out! Partly because you have a daughter, Sir John."

"Katherine? A lovely girl, Master Quain. Haven't seen her for years but I heard she's still at Court and still with that knight—what's his name?—Edward Blount. Not a man I'd trust. You wouldn't——" He sighed. He remembered he'd suggested Maurice marry-ing her once before and the proposal had not been taken kindly.

Maurice said sharply, "You haven't seen her for years? You swear to that?"

"Bones of God, why not?"

"And you've had no correspondence with her?"

"What of it? I'm no clerk to be writing letters all the time."

"I just wanted to be assured, Sir John, that for what-ever reason you're in here, it can't be enlarged on to draw Katherine into the same snare."

Perrot wiped his mouth with the back of his hairy hand. "I'm in the Tower because of my birth, of course. But the charges lodged against me are for bun-gling Irish affairs. Jesus Christ, Master Quain, nobody could bungle Irish affairs! They couldn't be in worse shape than I found them, not with the help of Satan and all the devils of hell. But what do you care?"

Maurice said briefly, "I intend to marry Katherine. And as I rather expect to be out of the country for a while I want to be certain she'll be in no danger while I'm gone."

Perrot threw back his head with a bellow of laughter. "You're going to marry Katherine! You must have seen the wench then. I remember you weren't to be talked into it before." He looked at Maurice with sudden suspicion. "But I'm a ruined man, Master Quain. You didn't come here to talk of a dowry."

"So that her dowry isn't a shared charge of treason, Sir John, I'm content."

"Ah?" Perrot ran his hand through his unkempt hair. "Well, as my future son-in-law, perhaps I could trouble you for a few odd pieces of gold. Gets damned cold in here and the food's vile. But with a little money the guards will do anything except leave your door unlocked." He leaned forward suddenly, a mocking expression on his unshaved face. "And of course all this talk of Katherine and Edward Blount—malicious gossip, nothing but malicious gossip, Quain. Katherine's a good girl, make a wonderful wife for you. How much did you say you could spare? These guards bleed a man worse than the moneylenders."

Maurice took out his purse, emptied it of ten ryals. "This is the poorest kind of investment it's possible to make, Sir John. I was wiser when I rejected your first suggestion to marry Katherine." But wisdom, he thought, did not always sort well with happiness. He smiled. Still he wanted to get away from here. A sense of oppression, caused not alone by the enormously thick walls, the slits of windows and the barred door, was heavy on his spirit.

The guard outside hammered on the planking. "Come along now, sir, come along. Time to leave."

Perrot slid the gold pieces inside his doublet, grunted "Thank you!" and poured more beer into his tankard. "I won't be drinking this sour stuff long! Master Quain, if you want to appreciate the peace here, get yourself appointed Viceroy of Ireland for a year and you'll embrace this life."

Maurice said, "We'll hope before you tire of it you'll get the Queen's pardon and a much more peaceful position. By the way, Sir John, I might be persuaded to make you a further advance through the House of Bowyer for your word that you'll not send to tell

Katherine of your imprisonment. It's just possible that for the while at least she'll not hear of it, and every day will add to her safety. But whatever amount you ask them for, make your reasons weighty. Bowyer isn't marrying your daughter."

He went out. He felt somehow shaken. He had everything in the world he desired. Katherine had promised to marry him. His blood surged through him at the thought of Katherine his forever, not for a brief poignant hour but in an enduring love. Only, her father was in prison, and Katherine—— He had forgotten how fear for the beloved was on the obverse side of the coin of love.

And there was Patrick. He would have to tell Patrick about Katherine and himself. He shrank from it. Perhaps he should wait.

When he returned he found that there was no need to tell him. Patrick was sitting at the table, a pewter mug of wine in his hand, a leather vessel of it at his elbow.

Patrick said, and his voice was thick, "Here's a dispatch from Her Majesty, Master Quain." He did not stand up to bring it over.

Maurice gave hat and gloves to Tom, crossed to the table, looked at Patrick sharply as he took up the parchment and broke the seal. The message was brief. To present himself at Whitehall the next day for final instructions and to be ready to leave London at once for Plymouth. God's wounds, wasn't that like the Queen! He'd have to see Bowyer early in the morning then and let the rest of his business wait for the time. And Katherine—if he saw her again it would be only in the presence of others.

He said, "Patrick, will you go at once to the Royal Exchange, tell Bowyer I must see him early as we'll be leaving London tomorrow. I'll want all his reports on hand so that I may go over them quickly."

Patrick drained off his cup of wine, stood up. There was a dull misery in his eyes. "Yes, sir." He steadied himself with one hand as he started to move away from his chair.

Maurice eyed him with a cold annoyance. "Never

372

mind. I'll send Vincent. But you'd better start sobering up if you expect to ride out of the city to Plymouth with me tomorrow."

Patrick sat down again and refilled his mug. It seemed a hundred years since his light words earlier today that he had one person to see before he left London. Well, he had seen her, and the pain of her refusal was an open wound that would never heal. He thought if he could spend his life for her, he would be happy. But she had no need of him. He looked up at Maurice. "I'll be able to ride with you to Plymouth or the devil tomorrow. But you have Katherine, Master Quain. Do you mind if I go to hell in my own way?"

There was a peremptory knock. Mattie muttered impatiently to herself as she crossed to open the door. Edward Blount entered, nodded to her. "You go out, Mattie. I want to see your mistress." There was a repressed violence in his voice, in the way he looked toward Katherine.

Katherine, sitting before her mirror, had one long braid over her shoulder which she was plaiting, the black hair silky against the white satin brocade of her dressing robe. Her skin was delicately flushed, her mouth soft. She had seen Maurice only briefly yesterday before he'd left London, but he had driven the last traitorous doubt of him from her mind. Maurice! Maurice! For her all his reserves had gone down. She thought she was safe with him forever. There would be no more fears of dismissal from Court, of not being able to take care of Deborah, of Leicester looking at her too often instead of at Elizabeth Tudor, of weighing each word and smile—no more fear of Ned, a fear which had been mounting steadily for months.

She turned to smile at him with sudden gaiety. She was free of him. He had not been her lover since he had returned to England with the Turkish treaty signed. But with his new prestige from his success he had been more sought after, and then he'd been given a lieutenancy in Leicester's army, and with her own return to favor she could always plead she must be at the Queen's service. So she was not sure whether he realized she had broken with him or if he thought that only circumstances had kept them apart. She must pluck up courage to tell him of Maurice, but she flinched from it.

He was dressed for riding, booted and spurred, with leather gauntlets and a leather jerkin over quilted satin doublet. The wide belt about his waist had his long sword laced to it with thongs. There was a touch of impatience in his voice when he spoke again. "May I see you alone, Kit?"

Katherine glanced at her waiting woman, who was still standing at the door. "You may go, Mattie. I'll ring when I need you."

As she left Blount crossed the room to Katherine, stood watching her a moment, thumb resting in his belt. "You look lovely, Kit." He smiled charmingly. "Were you expecting me?"

Katherine's fingers, securing the end of the braid with a gold clasp, suddenly shook. Her heart hammered with a slow suffocating panic. But she raised her eyes to his with an answering smile. "Well, no, I wasn't, Ned. I was just making myself ready to go out to Stepney."

"Yes. I knew you were not in attendance on the Queen today. I made sure of it."

Katherine's smile remained fixed, but she groped with one hand for the bell to summon Mattie. Blount caught her wrist, held it away. "I've said nothing yet of what I came to say, my sweet." His hands slid up her arms. He forced her to her feet. "And you haven't said you were glad to see me, Kit."

She tried to draw herself from the steel-like grip but she could not move. "Ned, what is it? What are you trying to do?"

He bent his fair head to kiss her on the mouth. She tried to turn away, but his mouth clung to hers. He released her but he stepped between her and the bell on the dressing table. "I was just showing you, my dear, that I still love you. I wonder—can you say the same to me?"

His eyes held hers. She felt a paralysis of terror creeping over her. She whispered, "Why do you ask?"

"Because I want you, my darling." He dropped his light tone. "You're beautiful, Kit!" His eyes went over her body, thinly clad in the white satin robe over rose-colored night rail.

She tried to smile again. "Thank you, Ned. But I think you'd better go now."

He drawled, "Why, darling? You can't be waiting for Maurice Quain. He's well on his way to Plymouth, or should be." He slid his hand under the silken material to touch her bare shoulder.

Katherine moved back quickly. "No!"

"You're growing overfine, aren't you, sweetheart? I was quite good enough for you once." His pale-blue eyes were luminous with desire. "There's been a change in you ever since we left London—separately. I don't like it."

She shook her head. "Not since then. It took me long to admit it, Ned, but when you left me to others it proved how little you cared for me. It doesn't matter. I'll always be grateful to you for what you've done for me."

He repeated, "Since we left London—and you on Maurice's ship."

"No." She put up her hand as though to hold him away. "Whatever was between you and me, Ned, was killed forever when I found out how you had Maurice tortured. And that was not because of your mercy he escaped further hurt. I did not think . . . you were . . . so cruel. Or perhaps I just hoped——" Her voice trembled.

"Maurice? Despite your protests I knew I had always reason to be jealous of him. I suppose you'll still say he's nothing to you." His tone was light again, but the airiness did not conceal the deadly quality beneath. He stood very still, and that too had something ominous in it.

He was waiting for an answer. Katherine lifted her head. "We are to be married, Ned, on Maurice's return."

"No!" Blount's head went back as though she'd struck him across the face. "No!" He just whispered the word, but it was all about her, filling the room,

375

echoing back from the wall. "By God, you'll not leave me for Maurice Quain!"

And now he moved. His arms were about her, his mouth was hard on her unyielding lips. He picked her up lightly, carried her to the bed. He stood looking down at her. "Call out if you like, my dear. I doubt if any will hear you, but if they do—would you have profane eyes gaze on your body?" He reached down, caught robe and night rail at her throat and ripped the garments downward. The sound of the rending cloth was like the cry of a person in pain. "Deny me your body, sweetheart, so you can save yourself for Maurice? No!"

She stared up at him, the back of her hand against her mouth, dumb with fear. She started to rise. He thrust her back, "Oh, no, my darling, not until I too have——" There was a madness in his eyes, in his hands as he broke her brittle resistance.

She drew away from him, her face still rigid with horror. And then the slow tears came. "Oh, Ned!"

He turned toward her petulantly, his passion satiated. "You made a lot of fuss over a small matter, Kit. One would think you a virgin. Good God!"

Katherine said, "You've had your way, Ned. Now go. I want never to see you again—not ever."

Blount murmured, "Your tears make a pretty picture, Kit. Had you used them before—— I'm sorry I was so rough with you, but I had to prove how mistaken you were to prefer Maurice to me. Now could you ever choose that ice when you might have my passion?"

She turned her head away and in that small gesture he knew she was indeed done with him forever. . . . But Maurice would not enjoy her beauty.

At the sound of the door closing behind him, Katherine stood up slowly, went over to the basin, filled it with cold water. She washed her face to hide the trace of tears and then her body that she might feel clean again. She must ride out to Stepney. She'd told Elly she'd come today. She couldn't face Elly. She couldn't face anyone. She wanted to cower in a corner and weep.

She dressed herself carefully, went over to her jewel box and drew out the deed to the manor that Maurice had given her. Then she rang for Mattie to have a page order horses for them. Mattie glanced at her carefully. Katherine's usually mobile face was stiff and masklike and did not change in the ride out to the village nor when they reached the cottage.

Elly, seeming older and thinner than the last time Katherine had seen her, looked up with a smile as she came in. Elly was sitting at the window, her crippled hands folded in her lap, watching Deborah pick a handful of daisies and sweet Williams in the garden outside—a pitiful handful in the tiny plot that was almost overrun with weeds.

Katherine thought, I mustn't disturb Elly with any troubles of mine. She remembered the deed then and smiled as she crossed to Elly, but she stood with her back to the window that the light should not fall on her face. She said, "Elly, you'll be glad to hear you will not have to stay out here another winter. Master Quain—Maurice—I'm going to marry him, Elly. He gave me this—I can say it's a betrothal gift, I suppose." She handed the older woman the parchment. "It's a manor house in Sussex. We can move there—any time." She winked rapidly as not to cry.

Elly looked up at her shrewdly. "Darling! Oh, Katherine! We're not in such need. Don't marry him if you're so unhappy over it."

At the sympathy in Elly's voice Katherine went down on her knees, put her head in the older woman's lap. She sobbed, "Oh, Elly!"

Elly's hand touched the girl's hair gently. "Can you tell me, darling?"

"It's nothing. I'm . . . perhaps I'm tired." She wiped her eyes with her handkerchief, then lifted her head, a smile showing through her tears. "I'm very happy about Maurice. This . . . it's something else."

"Master Quain's the merchant, isn't he?"

"Yes. Maybe you'll not like him when first you meet." Katherine sat back on her heels, her heavy skirt

377

billowing about her. The color crept up into her pale face. "But, Elly, after you know Maurice, promise me you'll love him!"

"That should be easy, dear, if you do." Elly was afraid to say too much lest Katherine not really care for this Maurice Quain and be marrying him because of her and Deborah. But she felt relief flooding through her that Katherine would be free finally from her burdens which were too heavy for her in spite of her gallant spirit. "You do love him, Kit?"

A rich merchant, Elly thought practically. She had always expected that if Katherine fell in love it would be with some obscure young man just able to make a living. She spoke her thought aloud absently.

Katherine laughed. "Do you know, Elly, sometimes I wonder myself why I fell in love with Maurice instead of Patrick North, and——" She stopped, remembering Patrick's pain, his white young face, when she had told him she was to marry Maurice. Blount he could have tried to rival, but not Maurice. Her heart twisted for him. Oh, Patrick, to have hurt you so when you have always been so kind to me!

There was a loud rap at the door. She shrank back instinctively. She thought of Ned and shivered. The maid Hannah hurried in from the tiny kitchen wiping her hands on her apron. The door opened before she reached it.

The entrance seemed filled with men, though there were only three: The first one, a sergeant, stepped in with a loud clanking of spurs; the other two more slowly. The sergeant glanced about the room, from the maid with her flour-streaked face and fingers twisted in her apron to the white-haired woman sitting in the chair, and finally to Katherine, who rose to her feet, hands clasped loosely in front of her. Nothing more could happen, she thought—not today.

The sergeant said, "Katherine Perrot? You are charged with conspiring against the Queen's person, I hereby place you under arrest during the Queen's pleasure. He walked across the room, put a hand on her shoulder.

Katherine looked at him unbelievingly, then about

378

the quiet room that was suddenly unreal, hostile. Elly said, "No! You've made some mistake."

The sergeant said, "I regret, madam, if this is Katherine Perrot there is no mistake. A charge of treason has been placed against her. Until she prove herself innocent she will be lodged in the Tower of London. She is to have communication with no one. Come, madam!"

Katherine knew as well as though the charge were written in Ned's hand that it was he who had done this to her. "She's to have communication with no one." The sentence hung in the air, cold and glittering, and deadly past pain. Maurice, Maurice, where are you? Ned, could you have had no pity in memory of kinder days together?

She gazed at Elly, then out the window at Deborah, who glanced up and waved to her. Her golden curls were alight in the sun. Katherine turned her head away. "Gentlemen, let us go quickly."

20

Maurice leaned back on one elbow as he watched the game of bowls on the greensward at Plymouth Hoe. The warm sun beating down on his dark doublet softened the chill in the light sea breeze blowing in from the southwest. A bowl rolled across the grass, stopped a yard from the jack. A groan went up from a knot of seamen as Frobisher, squat figure looking ponderous and slow, stepped back.

Drake thrust forward into his place, sped his own ball across the green apparently without even glancing at his target. There was a moment of silence, craning of necks, then a full-throated shout from the sailors of his *Revenge* and the people of Plymouth as Drake's bowl almost touched the jack.

Maurice, not particularly interested in Drake's triumphs, glanced away, his gaze traveling about the throng that edged the green. They made a motley colorful pattern, ragged seamen with scarlet kerchiefs about their heads, gold hoops in their ears, leathery bearded faces almost black from the sun; townsmen and women dressed soberly for the most part; a scattering of young gallants in blue and crimson and green and yellow satins and velvets, the richness of their dress set off by enormous lace-edged ruffs at their throats. The grass was gilded under the summer sun, and white clouds streamed across the intensely blue sky. The salty tang of the sea was in the air on his lips.

A pleasant scene, Maurice thought idly, which denied the hard fact of the Armada somewhere on the high seas between Portugal and Plymouth, and the fleet of England lying below in the Sound, bare poles swaying and ships rocking in the swells. Denied the need of Admiral Lord Howard's absorption in the discussion with his supply captain, his haste to revictual the ships and repair the damages sustained during the three-week cruise in the Channel when he had been out in hope to strike the Armada.

Maurice looked up as he saw Patrick moving through the crowd toward him. Patrick's sleeves were rolled up showing forearms black with gunpowder, and his white shirt torn along one shoulder was streaked with grime. He pushed the hair from his forehead with the back of his hand, said without preamble, "Did you notice that ship coming up the Sound, Master Quain?"

Maurice turned to glance toward the harbor. The ships swung in unison at their anchor cables as if guided by some unseen hand, facing into the wind which was blowing straight in from the sea. Small boats were rowing busily back and forth from quay to vessels, and sailors could be seen working along the yards and standing rigging. His eyes went beyond them to where a small pinnace was winding its way toward the anchorage, white sails contrasting with dark hull, a red and yellow pennon streaming from the top. Foam curled from her forefoot as she moved in and out among the ships.

As the anchor splashed into the sea, a small boat was put over the side. Its oars dipped in rapid stroke. Maurice stood up deliberately. His eyes went from Frobisher, who had stepped forward to take his turn again with indifferent luck, to Lord Howard, who had broken off his talk with the supply captain to turn his head sharply toward the harbor below. One of the men from the pinnace clambered out of the boat as it touched the shore, mounted a horse that was brought him. He crouched down awkwardly in the saddle. A trail of dust followed him, but the shouts of the spectators muffled the approaching hoofbeats until the rider had plunged into the fringes of the crowd.

They could hear his voice bellowing out, "Starboard! Hard astarboad, you brute! Easy now, easy! Heave to, you bastard! Hard over on your helm!"

The bewildered horse, mouth sore from the vicious jerking on the bridle, started to rear. A boy standing near jumped for the reins. The sailor slid from the saddle, gave the mare a malevolent look and turned to glance about for the Admiral. Howard moved forward easily, a tall fair man in crimson doublet and hose and high boots of tooled leather.

The seaman's voice carried clearly as the onlookers became silent one by one in a heightening expectancy. He clutched at his hair, feeling for his cap which had been lost in the first ten feet of his ride, saluted then instead. "My lord, Captain Weaver sends his respects and begs to inform you that we've sighted the Armada. The Spanish are off the Lizard!"

For one moment Maurice was aware of the rustling of the trees edging the green. Then the crowd surged forward in unbelief. The Armada off the Lizard? Impossible! Fear was stamped on every face. Each man turned seaward as though he half expected to sight the Invincible Armada driving across the tumbling water while the southwest wind bottled up the English fleet in Plymouth harbor. With the wind astern the Spanish could ride up the Channel, storm Plymouth or garrison themselves on the Isle of Wight. Then Parma could move his troop across the Channel from Flanders to England at his leisure.

A woman screamed. There was a quick growl from man to man, a touch of panic in the air that in a moment would sweep across the crowd like fire through a forest. The tension heightened dangerously as someone shouted, "Look! It's true news he brings!"

381

Far to the south on a hill overlooking the sea a spiral of smoke was rising against the blue sky, followed by a black smudge on a near by point, then another and another. The signal fires ringing England were carrying the word through the country that the Armada had arrived.

Drake's big figure suddenly moved from the center of the group around Lord Howard. Black hair ruffling in the wind, shoulders thrown back jauntily, he strode toward the grass. "Come, gentlemen, let's be on with the game!" His voice carried over the crowd. "We've plenty of time to even the score and beat the Spaniards too!"

As he spoke, he sent the ball hurtling across the green, striking the jack fairly. Men who had started to run wildly for the ships turned to stare. A quick wave of excitement passed through the crowd. Drake said arrogantly, "Match that delivery, Frobisher!"

Frobisher took the ball proffered by Drake. He judged his distance carefully, eye measuring the grassy space before he made his throw. Maurice noticed that even in their sport the two captains almost truculently made a point of their differences: Drake with his dash and daring, Frobisher with his wary preliminary weighing of the problem. Maurice was not sorry to see Frobisher's ball hit against Drake's, knocking the latter into the trench beyond while his own ball rolled to a stop within a foot of the jack.

Someone shouted hoarsely, "The wind, Sir Francis! We're holed in like rats, the whole fleet of England!"

Drake turned his head in the direction from which the voice had come. "One more strike, sir, and we'll show you what English seamen can do with an unfavorable wind!"

There was a laugh. The bravado was taken up, repeated and echoed back. The wild fire of panic had been quenched. Patrick looked at Maurice with a smile. "There's a man worth sailing under, Master Quain!"

Maurice glanced at Drake. "I'm afraid I don't share the enthusiasm of his admirers, though I am almost tempted to believe that he may manage the wind." He thought wryly that he was himself probably too much like Drake—arrogant, indifferent to others' opinions and feelings, but he had a cold deliberate courage where Drake's bravery was all heat and dash.

A young orderly came up. "My Lord Howard sends his compliments, Master Quain, and suggests that you repair on board at your earliest convenience as the *Ark* sails at once."

Maurice's brows lifted with mild interest. If Howard and Drake could sail English galleons down the Sound and into the teeth of the wind, he'd like to see it.

Patrick's muscles ached along his legs, up through his back, from finger tips to shoulders, as he pulled at one of the sculls in the longboat. He wondered if Maurice would be so interested in seeing the fleet sail down the Sound against the wind if he had to move the ships. The darkness was beginning to lighten, but the first rays of the sun would not be seen through the heavy mist. The shores falling away behind them were only a darker blue in the grayness, but just astern the *Ark,* which they were towing out to sea, loomed up, a huge towering hulk, its bare masts swaying gently.

About them through the haze could be seen other vessels in the fleet, some still under tow, looking like huge beetles dragged along by ants, others ahead of them breaking out sail as they swung around to follow the leading ships down the Sound.

The first few hours of pulling had been interspersed with acid comments by the sailors to the landsmen among them. "Ready to go back to the plow yet, lads?" . . . "Ye're at man's work now and want to call quits, I'll wager, before we're an hour out!"

Patrick had retorted. "Never knew a sailor yet who could pull an oar without wrapping himself around the shaft and breaking his neighbor's head into the bargain!"

But now every man was hauling with aching muscles and there was neither breath nor thought for gibes. As the swells increased, indicating they were reaching the sea, one and then another turned to search the horizon for sight of the Armada rising out of the fog, but only the English ships could be seen.

Patrick felt as though he were stuck forever to oar and rowing bench. He was wet with mist and perspiration that matted his shirt to his body, and every muscle cried out for release from the agony of exhaustion. But he was happy, happier than he had been since he'd seen Katherine in London and grasped finally how hopeless his suit had always been. No, he wouldn't think of that now. . . . Katherine . . . Edward Blount had still been in London when they'd left. He remembered Blount's face when the knight thought Katherine was carrying Maurice's child. He felt a momentary chill of dismay. But what could Blount do besides rage? Which, God knew, he certainly would, and to excess.

A whistle shrilled the recall for the longboat and the barges. The hawser was chopped, the boat was swung about and pulled alongside the *Ark*. The rowers shipped their oars, stood up stiffly from their cramped positions to clamber over the bulwarks and dropped to the deck to sprawl at full length.

"Stand by to make sail! I want her close-hauled on the starboard tack! Double the lookouts!" The crisp orders from the captain on the poop were repeated through the ship. Three long blasts sounded from the forecastle. Men tumbled up from below and scampered up the shrouds urged on by cursing quartermasters.

To the east there was a gradual brightening of the haze. The steady clanking of the capstan could be heard as it reeled in the towing cable. Overhead, sailors spread out on the yards removing gaskets, and then at a word from the deck the released canvas cascaded downward.

For a moment the *Ark* gathered sternway as the sails were caught aback, then it paid off before the wind, yards were braced around the sails sheeted home. The ship began to move forward, heeling gently to larboard. The thrashing of canvas and screaming blocks gave way to the rush of water under the transom. Patrick could feel the ship beneath him, a live thing moving gracefully over the gentle swells. The *Ark* was at sea under sail.

Maurice pulled himself carefully into the main fighting top and turned to look down at the deck far below him. His lofty perch gyrated in great arcs as Lord Howard's flagship swooped along over the broad Atlantic swells. Just beneath him the great bellying folds of the huge mainsail swelled out to starboard under pressure of the westerly wind, the top of the elongated golden lion of England visible occasionally as the sail swung with the wind and the motion of the ship. The long admiral's pennon fluttered above him.

Maurice had not particularly wanted to go aloft, but after the years of conjecture, rumor and counterrumor and his own firm belief that the Armada would never sail, he had felt a certain interest in getting a good view of the Spanish fleet to gain an overall impression of the impending action. So he had treated the somewhat amused ship's company to a picture of Her Majesty's envoy climbing up onto the bulwarks and ascending the main weather shrouds. On the deck below the gun crews, looking strangely small and squat, were hard at work removing tampions from the guns, checking priming and pyramiding shot. Ahead, the bluff bows of the *Ark* sent white foam cascading along her bulging sides as they plunged through the green seas.

Yesterday morning when the English fleet beat out of Plymouth Sound the Armada, evidently unaware of Howard's success in maneuvering his ships clear of the harbor, was far to windward. Apparently still unseen by the Spanish, Howard's ships had lain under bare poles during a midday rainstorm and then continued on a long reach toward the open sea as the wind freshened.

During the night they had come about and were driving in again toward the land, stretched out in single file. There were a few vessels ahead of the *Ark,* and astern Maurice could see them far out toward the horizon, white sails gleaming in the morning sun.

This line-ahead formation had been Drake's suggestion or rather demand, Maurice recalled. There had been some doubt at the council about the complete break from established naval warfare, but Drake had won Howard's assent, after alienating everyone else's

385

support by his dictatorial manner and overbearing confidence—usually justified but never palatable—in his own strategy.

He had said flatly that as the heavily gunned English ships were new fighting machines so far as naval tactics were concerned, a new and bold plan would be needed to use them efficiently. Maurice could imagine how the captains would be at Drake's throat like wolves if he were proved wrong—and if Spanish cutlasses hadn't slashed their own throats first.

Ahead and to starboard fanning out toward the distant coast, Maurice could see the Armada looking like a great half-moon. The yellow and blue of gold-embroidered sails and pennons made a moving tapestry against the deep green of the sea. His Most Catholic Majesty had sent to England an impressive proof of his naval might, Maurice thought, and if fighting capacity matched the size of the Armada the English fleet would need its Drakes and Howards and Hawkinses and Frobishers.

Maurice's eyes went over the Spanish ships shrewdly. Their formation as he studied them more closely seemed a double pyramid rather than a crescent. Ahead of the English line about a mile distant was a large compact squadron flanked by the dashing oars of two galleasses, while to starboard and almost abreast of them was a similar division. Between these two flotillas was a mass of smaller ships, including supply vessels and pinnaces, and beyond them, closer to shore, was the main battle fleet apparently consisting of most of the galleons. This must be the famous eagle formation that noted Italian admirals had developed for the galley warfare of the Mediterranean.

Maurice's observations were violently interrupted by the crash of the *Ark's* full broadside. It echoed across the waves, shaking the top and almost deafening him. A cloud of smoke rose to starboard and then dissipated as the shot fell harmlessly into the sea far short of the nearest Spanish ships. English galleons up and down the line following the flagship's example were firing now. Puffs of smoke from the starboard Spanish division indicated that they were replying although with no noticeable result.

Another broadside shook the mast. Maurice grimaced. He had no intention of spending the day in the top. It would undoubtedly be an easy target for Spanish snipers. He lowered himself onto the shrouds, refusing the assistance of the lookouts, and descended to the deck. The firing had broken off as Maurice reached the vantage point of the high poop, the *Ark* having moved completely out of range. The Admiral evidently was not wasting his time on the starboard and leeward division of the enemy but was bearing down directly on the Armada's rear guard and the weather-most flotilla.

Howard was standing at the weather rail. His controlled face was expressionless, but his eyes swept the horizon slowly from ship to ship. Breast and back plates and the steel gorget at his throat glinted in the light. He glanced up as Maurice moved over toward him.

"Today we have the weather gauge, Master Quain, and we'll direct our attack against the rear of the Duc of Medina-Sidonia's squadron. With his clumsy seamanship I hope the Duc will find it difficult to beat up to their relief with his main battle." He looked at Maurice sharply. "No armor, sir? As you are the Queen's envoy, I feel responsibile for your safety. I'd like you either to wear some protection or stay below while there's firing."

Maurice eyed the Admiral with amused surprise. "Don't trouble yourself, my lord. With the Armada between us and Parma, and the Prince not likely to smile at our suit anyway, I'm the one person in this fleet who should give you no concern. From aloft the Spaniards make an impressive picture, but as far as the size of vessels goes, to a landsman we look equal."

He gazed forward to where the mainsail was being clewed up to improve the maneuverability of the ship and to minimize its heel. Maximum gun elevation would be needed. Blocks screamed as slings were run up from below to deposit balls and powder on the deck. Gun crews, stripped to the waist, stood by their charges. Arms chests were broken out, cutlasses and boarding pikes distributed among the men. Sailors ran up the shrouds, while muskets and ammunition were hoisted into the tops.

The English ships moved on inexorably one ahead of the other toward the waiting Spaniards, white sails swaying against the blue sky. They were almost upon the first vessels of the Armada, their gun ports showing an ominous black against the red sides, their towering bow and sterncastles and decks lined with men. Burnished steel of helmets and breastplates glinted in the sun across the narrowing gap.

There was no sound save the rush of water under the stern, the muted creaking of the yards, an occasional shout from across the waves. An eternity passed, yet the fleet moved forward as if on parade, not showing the leashed power ready to be uncoiled against the greatest fleet ever launched for the conquering of England.

Howard said, "The Biscayan squadron, Master Quain. These are Recalde's ships, according to your friend Señor Huércal, who has incidentally proved useful."

As he spoke smoke whipped out from the leading English ship, the crash of the guns echoing back to them. The other ships ahead were firing now. Beneath them there was a splintering crash. The Spanish gunners had lost no time in finding the range.

The deck shook as the *Ark's* full broadside exploded in a torrent of smoke. At this range every weapon could be brought into play. Shattered gaps could be seen in the Spanish ship, smashed bulwarks, shredded canvas whipping wildly about yards and spars. Smoke sifted through the rigging up toward the clear blue of the sky.

A shot crashed through the rail and plowed along the poop deck throwing a shower of splinters. A small gray-haired officer coming up to speak to Lord Howard staggered, his eyes widening in a shock of horror as he clawed futilely at a jagged section of railing protruding like an arrow from his armpit. He collapsed, a dark pool of blood crawling stickily along the narrow scrubbed planks under him.

388

The English fleet was moving slowly now from ship to ship, guns pouring into Recalde's squadron the heaviest weight of metal, Howard said, that had ever been delivered in maritime history. The Spaniards, apparently unable to grapple and fling the crushing weight of their military might against the English crews, replied with vigor, but Maurice knew that most of their guns were of smaller caliber and he could tell that they were worked less efficiently.

Spanish soldiers, their armor and weapons flashing coldly sinister, stood ready to board, but Lord Howard kept the Spanish fleet just within range of his big guns in an attempt to pound the Armada to pieces before Medina-Sidonia could make his way toward Plymouth lying defenseless before him, ripe for plucking by the mailed hand of an invader.

Maurice noticed that the Spanish ship they had been firing against, visible now through a rift in the smoke, was suddenly smaller. Then he realized the vessel had turned and was making all possible speed to windward. Ship after ship in Recalde's squadron also swung about away from the withering fire of the English guns, and bore down in their flight on the Spanish vessels to leeward.

Ahead of them Maurice saw a great galleon turn slowly into the wind, white sails flapping. The scarlet and gold figure of the Madonna on the spread of canvas made a distorted pattern of color in the sunlight. Another galleon followed her, with dark wood glistening, the metal of the guns and the ready steel of its massed soldiery glittering as it swung about. But the rest of the flotilla fled down-wind leaving the two great ships alone facing the English.

Howard's voice rang out. "Up with your helm, Captain, and make for those ships! Signal the others to follow!" He turned to Maurice. "This is what we've been waiting for. The Spanish admiral in trying to rally his squadron has isolated himself. That's the *San Juan*, Recalde's flagship."

The *San Juan* resembled a floating fortress with bluff blows, high fore and sterncastles that rose in tiered decks high above the water. The decked balconies visible in the waist looked like the porches on a many-storied country house. Foresail lay aback against the mast, enveloping shrouds and halyards. Soldiers filled waist and foredeck.

"Fire at will, starboard battery!" Crews jumped to readiness and gun captains plunged slow match into the vents. The broadside crashed out, guns recoiling over the vibrating deck.

High on the poop Maurice watched the steady fire pouring into Recalde's helpless vessel and her consort while near by he could discern Drake's *Revenge* and Hawkins' *Victory* within pistol shot of the two Spanish ships, throwing a terrible concentrated fire. Gaping holes appeared in the *San Juan's* superstructure. The main yard cut loose from its slings crashed to the deck and trailed crazily over the side, shredded canvas flapped in the wind. But the *San Juan* was ringed with its own spouting smoke and the whine of balls through the *Ark's* rigging, and the occasional thud in the vessel beneath him showed that Recalde was fighting with every gun that could be made to bear.

Maurice felt a musket ball sing past his ear. He flung himself back instinctively, glanced with a faint smile at Howard, who had stepped to one side. "Half an inch of steel wouldn't have stopped that, my lord!"

"Armor is really of little use except in hand-to-hand fighting." Howard conceded. "May God and our captains preserve us from being grappled!" His eyes swept the horizon. Beyond the *San Juan* a group of Spanish galleons were beating up toward the melee from the distant shore. He eyed the ships, then the weather cloth to judge how long it would take the Spaniards to reach them.

Another broadside made even the planking under their feet shudder. Maurice gazed at the *San Juan*. If it came to the pass that she grappled with the *Ark*—— A sword in his hand again? No. And then, probably not. A musket ball ripped along the railing in front of him. He swung back abruptly, an ironic smile thinning his mouth. There was an easy end to too much self-questioning!

Patrick leaned against the bulwarks to look through

the gun port at the towering Spanish ship within range. His arms and shoulders ached from the unaccustomed labor of pulling at the oars and the constant heaving on the gun tackles.

He glanced at his fellow gunners, standing stripped to the waist like himself, bare feet spread wide on the smooth deck, teeth showing white in their powder-blackened faces. He grinned slightly. They looked like chimney sweeps. Slow match sputtered in a tub near by. Powder boys replenished their supply of ammunition, balls were pyramided neatly ready for reloading, while a few feet away sailors were mopping up the blood-smeared deck where sand had been strewed to prevent slipping.

Patrick was aware of the sun for the moment, hot against the cool breeze, searing his bare shoulders. The order was snapped out again, "Fire at will, starboard battery!"

The broadside roared out. The guns recoiled. The crew jumped to swab out barrels, ram home powder and wadding and ball. Then Patrick found himself tailing off on the tackle, with blistered hands throwing his weight against the line running the heavy gun into firing position. There was the rumbling recoil and he was back again with the swab, eyes smarting from the powder fumes.

A muffled scream sounded high above him. He turned to see a topman plummet to the deck with a sickening thud, then lie there broken in a pool of blood. Bits of line pelted about him and frayed ends of canvas drifted off in the smoke. He closed his lids tightly against the dry stinging sensation that seared his eyeballs, dropped involuntarily at a rending crash behind him where a ball had torn through the bulwark throwing splinters over the deck. His eyes flew wide. Beside him was the headless spouting body of a gunner. It swayed there for what seemed an eternity before it collapsed. Patrick thought mechanically that there was the weight of one less man now on the tackles.

Swab, load, heave, slacken off, stunning concussion followed one another until they became a rhythm with dark overtones of powder fumes, acrid smoke, thundering noise. He could see nothing but the gun before him, feel nothing but a grim urgency to keep it firing. It seemed impossible any ship could stand up under this pounding.

There was a sudden movement on deck. The chief gunner held up his hand as they slackened off on the tackles. They all turned to see a new flag fluttering on the signal halyard. Orders were shouted to the helmsmen and the *Ark* bore sharply closer to the wind. As the yards were braced around she began to haul away from the Spaniards, gun after gun falling silent as it ceased to bear.

Beating up from the north came the relieving squadron of Spanish galleons. It could be seen now that it was led by Medina-Sidonia in the *San Martin,* and it was nearing the belabored *San Juan.* The English fleet drew off to windward.

Someone called out, "We're east of the Eddystone, lads, and the Armada's past Prawle Point!"

Patrick flung himself down on the deck. The planks were hot under his shoulders and the sand grated into his flesh. "What does that mean?"

The chief gunner said patronizingly, "That means, my landlubber, that them Spanish bastards have been forced to leeward of Plymouth. So even if we haven't broke their formation or done any great damage, that's one port where they'll not land."

A ragged cheer went up, but there were few in the fleet who were not looking from the green hills of the English shore line to the squadrons of the invaders, ruffled for the time but still bearing on up the coast, past Plymouth toward the Isle of Wight.

Maurice looked around at the sound of rising voices. "An act of piracy, by God!" Frobisher growled at Drake. "A deliberate flouting of your duty, putting a prize ahead of the safety of the fleet."

Howard interrupted Drake's retort. "Gentlemen! Sir Francis was carrying out his duty as he saw it. But for a captain who is leading the whole fleet, Sir Francis, your tacking off after a disabled ship was perhaps too hasty. It disorganized us, left our vessels scattered for miles over the sea and might have led to disaster."

Maurice turned back to the weather rail in bored fashion, not listening to Drake's stormy rejoinder. They were only three days out of Plymouth, and he was already weary of Drake. He remembered that first night with the Armada sweeping on up the Channel pursued by the English fleet. The Spanish moved in ordered squadrons while Lord Howard's ships trailed the beacon of the *Revenge's* great stern lantern like a flock of cygnets swimming after a swan. Like the cygnets they were confused and disorganized when Drake at midnight suddenly doused his lantern and tacked off alone in pursuit of Don Pedro de Valdes' disabled flagship of the Andalusian squadron, leaving the fleet to guess at the whereabouts and activities of their leader.

Maurice wiped his face with his handkerchief. The sun beat down hotly. Not a breath of air stirred across the water. Masts and rigging shuddered as the *Ark* rocked helplessly in the swells.

Ahead of them just beyond range lay the Armada, formation unbroken and waiting only a wind to strike against Wight. The English ships were strung out along the western fringe of the Spanish rear guard rolling and pitching on the windless seas. It seemed like a picture on some vast canvas—invaders and defenders held immobile within sight of the stake for which they fought.

Howard's voice cut through the angry words of the two captains. "God's blood, gentlemen! We have no time to waste on past affairs. Let your quarrel wait. The Armada will not. I sent for you to outline my proposals for separating our fleet into squadrons—an arrangement we can well afford to copy from Medina-Sidonia so that we'll not repeat yesterday's fiasco. Because of our lack of proper co-ordination when we closed off Portland the Spanish came off with all the honors. By the grace of God the wind shifted or we'd still be trying to rally our fleet."

He grimly proceeded to call the roll of his ships, dividing the galleons, merchantmen and pinnaces into four squadrons. He assigned one to each of his chief officers, Hawkins, Frobisher and Drake, with the fourth under his own personal command. "And now, gentlemen, if we're to prevent a Spanish landing on

Wight, no time's to be lost." He eyed the becalmed Armada consideringly. "We must tow the fleet within gunshot of the Duc's rear guard."

Drake said, "Excellent, my lord! I'll give the word at once."

Frobisher nodded, made a parting thrust as he started toward the stairs. "We assume that the purpose of this move is the defeat of the Spanish, not scouring the ocean for the paymaster's ship."

Howard retorted, "Sirs, if you put your venom behind your cannon, the Armada will not drop anchor on the English coast."

A few minutes later the boatswain's whistle sounded through the *Ark*. Longboats and barges were lowered over the side and soon were tugging at the long cables to haul the flagship laboriously over the oily swells toward the Spanish galleons. A ball whined past the small boats, fell just short of the *Ark*. Two bow chasers fired in reply. A shot hit the barge, smashing thwarts and planking, killing two of the crew and dumping the others into the sea.

A whistle shrilled from the *Ark*, and the remaining boats eased off, then dragged the heavy cable to the port side of the ship to turn the big galleon. Maurice caught at the rail as the first broadside crashed out. Each time the guns barked the *Ark* twisted and shuddered, and the deck trembled beneath him. English and Spanish ships rolled helplessly in the swells. Smoke hung lifelessly in the air above the pounding gun, obscuring vision, irritating eyes and throat.

A breath of wind, damp and fragrant, stirred across the sea from the west, rippled along the glassy swells, dissipating the pall of smoke. Maurice looked around as Howard snapped out, "Make sail, Captain, with all possible speed, and continue to harass the enemy's rear!"

The great sails were unfurled and the *Ark* bore off to starboard. Howard said, "We'll have a gale before nightfall, Master Quain." His eyes searched the scene before him anxiously as the Spanish squadrons also made sail to maneuver into battle formation in response to the ensign flying from the *San Martin's* signal halvard.

The *Ark* swung past the rear guard pouring a withering fire into vessel after vessel. The Spanish guns roared out as they held their formation, but as the day wore on the Armada was pressed closer and closer upon the dangerous banks of the Owers.

Clouds piled high in the western sky obscuring the setting sun. A new signal flag was hoisted above the tattered remnants of the *San Martin's* mainsail. The great galleon came about on the starboard tack, breaking off the engagement. She plunged over the rising seas leading the well-ordered Spanish squadrons back into the Channel away from the treacherous lee shore, leaving the Isle of Wight hopelessly to windward.

Rain squalls blew out of the west. With the freshening wind the English ships shortened sail as they drove into the night after the Spaniards. Exhausted sailors made fast the guns, hastily replaced shredded canvas, rove new lines where enemy shot had sheared the running rigging. The rain pelted down about Maurice on the deck, wet through his doublet.

He turned to follow Lord Howard down the companionway to the quiet of the main cabin. He became aware of the steady clang of the chain pump against the deep hum of the rigging and the beating seas. Spanish guns had found their mark in the *Ark's* hull and she was taking water.

Howard, entering the dimly lighted cabin below, flung his cloak to the seaward, wiped the water from his tired face and dropped wearily into his chair. He motioned Maurice to do likewise. "Wight's to wind-Master Quain. The Spanish will not garrison that island. You'll soon be in a position to convey Her Majesty's compliments to Parma, unless of course some new difficulty arises."

Maurice took the glass of wine the steward brought up. He was amused at Howard's comment on Parma. "You do not like to sue the Prince for peace?"

Howard said, "We didn't arm the fleet of England, Master Quain, to convey Her Majesty's envoy across the Channel!"

"I suppose not. Where's the Armada heading?"

"I'd say without a doubt Medina-Sidonia plans to meet Parma's forces near Calais and the long threatened invasion is almost upon us. Seymour's and Wynter's squadrons have been blockading Dunkirk, but I'm ordering them to join us." Howard stirred in his chair, twirling his goblet thoughtfully in his fingers.

"Despite the pounding we've given it, Philip's Armada is still intact and in excellent formation, and they have twenty thousand soldiers aboard. With the short-sighted policy of the Court, we have again almost exhausted our ammunition. But perhaps more ships will come out with supplies——" He broke off as his tone grew bitter. For the High Admiral of the English Navy to be dependent on the dribblings of powder sent out from Whitehall and on the odds and ends of ammunition flung to him by citizens who were well meaning but had only limited supplies! Even the amiable Howard raged.

Maurice said unexpectedly, "Against a better prepared fleet, better armed and provisioned, you have something that I'd consider of far more value—a fighting idea. Even a landsman can see how effective at the crisis of battle is this line-ahead formation. One ship of yours after another hammers the Spanish, and you avoid all chances of being grappled into a land battle where your excellent seamanship would not count. A fighting idea. Imagination in war carries the seeds of victory." He added irrelevantly, "Just where are we in the Channel now, my lord?"

Howard glanced up in surprise. "About ten leagues off Selsey Bill. Why?"

"Nothing. I sailed this way once on my own ship on a voyage when we did not put in at a French port." It must have been near here, he thought, when he'd found out Katherine was aboard the *Falcon*, and he'd been fool enough to rage instead of thanking God for the gift. Katherine. He smiled, not sorry he was in the fleet guarding England from invasion that she might be safe.

21

The *Ark*, riding at anchor in the Calais roadstead, scarcely moved in the light swells from the southwest. Maurice shifted in his chair, aware again of the absence of the sounds of a ship at sea—creaking timbers, the wash of the waves, the feel of a moving deck underfoot.

Hawkins was completing a report Lord Howard had asked for, but Maurice could sense that the captains at the council in the main cabin were attending less to his words about the size of the fleets—the English with the arrival of the Channel squadrons now totaling over one hundred and thirty vessels while the Armada had been reduced to a score less—than on the difficulty of their position.

The Spanish ships were double-anchored and moored between themselves and Calais in a solid formation almost impossible to dislodge without an attack that would invite boarding. In every mind was the question—at any moment would the Duc de Guise wrest enough power from Henry of Valois to throw the weight of French men and ships into the struggle against them?

As Hawkins finished speaking, Lord Howard said absently, "Thank you, Captain—Sir John, rather." He glanced at Seymour and Wynter, the leaders of the Channel fleet which had until two days ago been blockading Parma at Dunkirk. "Captain Frobisher and Captain Hawkins distinguished themselves in our battles with the Armada and it was our pleasure to knight them after the engagement off the Isle of Wight. Now, Sir Francis, what have you to report on the Spanish position?"

Drake, who had been drumming with his blunt fingers on the highly polished table, brought his hand down sharply on the wood. "Report? Nothing except that the Spanish cannot be allowed to remain in the roadstead to form a junction with Parma." The sweat mark from his hand showed on the gleaming boards, dried in the moment of silence following his words.

Frobisher turned his head toward Drake. His hair stood out in tufts about his bearded face and his big shoulders in his worn leather jerkin were hunched forward. "You mean fire ships?"

"Aye, fire ships!" Drake's voice boomed out belligerently. Maurice's brows came together in a frown of annoyance. Drake always sounded as though he were carrying on an argument even when everyone was in complete agreement with his suggestions. "We used them at Cadiz and destroyed a quarter of their fleet, and I'll wager you the Spaniards have not forgotten the hell ships of Antwerp though there the Dutch gained less than nothing from their use."

Maurice said dryly, "Those ships were highly successful, Sir Francis. Victory was lost for lack of leadership and a certain—ah—dash and daring to pluck its fruits at the opportune moment. But of course we need fear no bungling here."

"Bungling? No, by God! But I thought you had some messenger work on the Continent for the Queen? Why not be about it?"

Lord Howard put in soothingly, "Fire ships would seem an excellent suggestion, Sir Francis. We will put the matter in your hands. As for the Queen's embassy—" he glanced from his captains to Maurice—"it would seem a pity to open negotiations with the Prince of Parma unnecessarily."

Maurice said, "I agree with you, my lord. For my part I'll be delighted if I never see Parma." He eyed Howard. Had the Admiral been in accord with Elizabeth's plans, he could easily have sent Maurice to Parma at Dunkirk in the pinnace that had been dispatched to Seymour and Wynter. He wondered how Howard would avoid the meeting now. He added, "Unfortunately I have Her Majesty's written instructions . . ." He let his voice trail off suggesting that if Howard could see a way out, he was willing to take it.

At his last words a long sigh went up from every man about the table. Wynter, gray-faced and slightly stooped, grimaced. "Her Majesty's instructions! We're to remain just off Dunkirk to blockade the city at all times! Any man who's been at sea ten minutes would know that at the first blow our fleet would be swept into the North Sea. One day we're to stay at our stations at all costs, the next join my Lord Admiral, then don't in any circumstances join my Lord Admiral!"

Hawkins ran both hands through his hair. "Commission the Navy! Decommission the Navy! Commission the Navy!"

"Master Quain," Seymour begged, "let's not discuss Her Majesty's instructions."

Howard grinned suddenly like a small boy. "It has just occurred to me, Master Quain, that really it would not be safe to set you ashore for several days. After that we can talk further."

Maurice smiled faintly. "I'm at your command, my lord."

Frobisher said, "Good! We'll deal with Parma in our own fashion. This is not the place for a woman's diplomacy."

Drake brushed the discussion aside impatiently. "We'll strike at once, gentlemen! The wind's favorable now and should hold. We can send the ships down the tide at midnight. I can provide five suitable vessels. Will you gentlemen let me know as soon as possible the number you can release? About eight should accomplish our purpose."

Lord Howard stood up to dismiss the council. "One thing more, gentlemen. If our stratagem works, we must attack the Spanish ships and destroy them before they can assume again that battle formation which we've been unable to break from the Lizard to Calais."

Drake said, "Aye, my lord. Now we'll need volunteers. I suggest that you pick your younger officers."

The ship stirred beneath them, and the sound of water gurgling past the sides indicated that the tide had turned and was running with the wind straight for the Spanish fleet. Patrick, knife in hand, stood in the small stern gallery of the *Margaret and John* where the heavy mooring cable passed aboard. He was waiting for the order that sounded now from the poop deck above. "Cut her!"

Watching his chance, Patrick hacked her loose as the cable slackened briefly at a wave passing under the ship. Then he ran through the main cabin, raced up the companionway to the half deck and mounted to the poop. The night was black, sky overcast, with one of the usual luminous sheen of the sea on a summer night. He could hardly make out the figure of Buckley, the young officer who had been assigned to guide the ship on her last fiery mission. Astern could be seen the twinkling lights of the English fleet, bobbing up and down as the vessels rolled in the short Channel chop. Below on the main deck men were tailing off on sheets and braces as the *Margaret and John* was brought squarely before the wind with topsails set.

"Crew away!" shouted Buckley. Topmen slid hastily to the deck and over the bulwarks to the waiting long-boat, only the helmsman and Patrick remaining with Buckley to work the ship. "North, now's the time for those fires!"

Patrick, battle lantern in hand, caught up the slow match from the waiting tub, went down the companionway to the main deck, swung over the main hatch combing and down the ladder into the hold. In a moment he had ignited the pitch-soaked waste in a dozen places. He waited briefly to see that the fire was catching before he went up to the forecastle. There he touched the slow match to the waiting powder trail. Sputtering flame raced along the powder.

The forward end of the *Margaret and John* erupted in a blazing volcano as Patrick joined Buckley on the poop. Flames licked up the pitch-covered foremast, edged along shrouds and stay. Tongues of fire fanned by the westerly wind stretched skyward from the hull throwing a billiant light over the tumbling black waves.

"Make sure the helm is secured and join me in the stern gallery!"

Patrick went into the forward section of the main cabin where the helmsman stood spread-legged, whip-staff firmly gripped. Lines were passed through ringbolts in the bulkhead and the whipstaff lashed.

The last bundle of faggots was ignited in the stern gallery before they swung down the long painter into the gig.

The first heady excitement had passed. Patrick was aware now that his arms had been burned, his hair singed, his shirt torn from him in his mad scramble through the *Margaret and John*. The acrid smell of powder, the pungent odor of flaming tar, still assailed his nostrils. Ahead they could see the fire ships plunging on into the Spanish anchorage like avenging horsemen, terrifying figures out of the Apocalypse. Guns exploded as the fire licked past them, adding another note to the crackling crescendo of the inferno. The yellow glare of the eight blazing ships spread out over the black waters.

Patrick could feel the cool spray against his back as they pulled steadily at the sweeps cutting through the crest of a sea, then sliding down the long slope of the swell. Aft the reflected light of the ships stretched out like ribbons of flame. The Spanish ships were shifting position, their lines lengthening out and their high sterncastles coming into view.

Patrick watched puzzled, then he realized that the Spanish must be cutting the cables in a panic-stricken effort to avoid the flaming hulks. With no time to make sail, the great galleons were running afoul of one another. The sound of the ships grinding together echoed across the water to give the last impact of horror to the flaming harbor. The whole Armada appeared a single heaving mass of entwined cordage and jumbled vessels slowly drifting up the Channel. The fire ships had unbelievably and beyond the wildest hopes dislodged the entire Spanish fleet.

"Hard up with your helm, Master Ashley! Our course will be east by south." The captain's order was followed by the shrill of the boatswain's whistle and the rapid-fire instructions of the chief officer as the *Ark* careened to port, pivoted suddenly on her course and headed shoreward the next morning. The great ship left a wide half circle of waters strangely calm in the midst of the tumbling waves as she slid to leeward with the momentum of her sudden turn.

Maurice caught at the taffrail to steady himself on the lurching deck, while he watched the English fleet sail up behind them out of the cold Channel dawn. Now that the *Ark* was doubling back toward the French shore, Drake's *Revenge* was in the lead, plunging ahead under full sail with a long line of the Queen's galleons stretching out astern. On Drake's port and some distance astern was Frobisher's great *Triumph,* and beyond him Hawkins' *Victory* led her own flotilla up the coast. Far to the westward and just clearing the anchorage could be seen Wynter's and Seymour's channel squadrons.

Maurice glanced at the flat coast stretching out northeastward toward Dunkirk where the Armada could be seen drifting in complete disorganization, scattered for miles along the banks. A league ahead of the *Revenge,* Medina-Sidonia's flagship and three other galleons had hauled their wind and were standing out into the Channel on a course designed to intercept the English squadrons and delay them long enough to permit the Armada to re-form. Whatever criticism the English admirals had for the Duc's sailing ability, no one could question his courage.

Maurice's eyes returned to the *Ark*. Just astern of her the *Golden Lion,* the second vessel in Lord Howard's flotilla, came sharply around and bore away on the same course as the flagship. One after another the ships in the Lord Admiral's squadron pivoted neatly to follow his lead back toward Calais. Maurice wondered what new consideration of naval strategy had prompted Lord Howard to draw his entire flotilla, almost a quarter of the English force, away from the battle line.

He crossed to the weather side of the poop where Howard was standing, his dark sea cloak whipping about him. "May I ask why the return to Calais, my lord? You haven't decided I should proceed with the Queen's suit to Parma?" He lifted his brows ironically.

Howard smiled. "Fortune, Master Quain, has delivered the *capitana* of the galleasses into our hands.

She lost her helm last night when the Spanish ships cut their cables and she's working back close in shore toward the protection of the fort there."

Maurice looked up the coast at the two fleets, the Spanish maneuvering desperately to achieve some semblance of order, the English pursuing them like hounds at a hunt. "What possible bearing can that have on the coming battle? With her helm gone the galleass is out of the fight anyway."

Howard said in surprise, "That *capitana*, Master Quain, is probably the grandest ship in the entire Armada—Spaniards claim she's the finest in the world. She carries Don Hugo de Monçada, lieutenant general of the galleys of Spain, and enormous treasure. What more fitting tribute could we present to Her Most Gracious Majesty than the greatest ship of Spain with her commander and her gold?"

Maurice stared at the Admiral. "Of course it was a week ago, my lord, but wasn't there some bitter comment when Drake left the fleet to pursue a prize?"

"Ah, but this is different." Howard spoke absently. "I am doing my duty as the first knight of England."

Maurice shrugged and turned to look toward Calais. Monçada, with the English gathering for the kill, was running his galleass aground directly under the guns of the fort before he turned to defend himself from the barges and launches Howard sent against him. Maurice could see how the boarders swarmed around the disabled leviathan pouring small-arm fire into her, then clambered up her towering superstructure to fight desperately in a hand-to-hand struggle with the Spanish soldiers.

Barges were riddled and sunk, boarding parties impaled on Spanish pikes and hurled into the sea. Time and again the English seamen appeared to gain the bloody top deck only to be driven back and slaughtered by the quick-firing artillery in bow and sterncastles.

A triumphant roar sounded across the water. The Hapsburg ensign was hauled down and chests of treasure were carried back to the waiting *Ark* which with the rest of the flotilla had been standing off and on in the roadstead. As the last man climbed aboard, Howard brought his ships before the wind and under full sail made for the Gravelines coast.

Maurice moved forward to the jutting prow of the *Ark* to watch the grim panorama of fighting ships stretching for a league along the coast. He could see English vessels operating in small squadrons wheel and tack about isolated Spanish galleons, guns blazing, sails wreathed in clouds of smoke. Further to the east Medina-Sidonia had gathered half a hundred of his ships into a loosely formed flotilla and seemed attempting to beat away from the French shore into deep water, but keeping to windward of Dunkirk in hope of making a junction with Parma.

English galleons hovering on the weather flank poured a vicious cross fire into the Armada and forced the nearest Spanish vessels to give away into the main body.

Howard drove his squadron straight toward four Spanish galleons that were to windward of the Armada and now less than a mile ahead. Above their smoke-shrouded sides could be seen the red and gold pennons and brightly blazoned topsails. Overhead soft white clouds scudded eastward across the brilliant blue of the summer sky. Sun glinted from polished ordnance, made whiter the flying sails, sparkled from the crest of an occasional sea as it broke into foam, and bathed in a golden glow the green hills beyond the low-lying shore.

Maurice felt a faint thrill of excitement as he worked his way back through the ship over a forecastle that bristled with small arms, past the waiting gunners in the waist and up the companionway to the half deck. The forward battery crashed out as he reached the poop, the thunder of the big guns shaking the deck. They were within musketshot now, the rattle of arms alow and aloft was added to the steady roar of the cannon. Smoke drifted upward, balls whined overhead, crashed into the hull beneath him, and the shrill whistle of bullets showed that the enemy gunners were shooting every piece that would bear.

The *Ark* drew clear of the drifting Spaniard. The second vessel in the Admiral's flotilla took its place.

Each succeeding ship poured its torrent of shot into the towering Spanish galleons. The helm was put over, the yards braced around, and the Ark tacked back so that its port broadside could be brought into action.

In the few minutes of unobscured vision before they plunged again into the pall of smoke, Maurice recognized the gilded sterncastle of the San Mateo and another vessel of the Portuguese squadron. The fluttering pennons on the other ships proclaimed one Castilian and one from the Levantine flotilla. The Armada must still be widely scattered when vessels from three different squadrons were fighting an isolated action together.

Again the guns roared out into the smoky haze. The smell of powder, the vibrating deck, the shattering shock of noise, the scream of shot and splintering crash of balls in bulwarks and hull stunned the senses. An officer beside Maurice stared stupidly at the bleeding remnant of his arm, then fell to the deck with a scream that was drowned in the thunder of the guns. The Ark left the cloud of smoke, and her cannon again fell silent. The San Mateo was in an unmanageable position, topmast shot away and hanging overside in a tangled maze of rigging. Fire blazed in the forecastle where men could be seen struggling to bring it under control, and gaping holes appeared in the topsides.

The Ark wheeled away, setting her course for the San Martín and the San Juan which had also been cut off a quarter of a mile to leeward of the San Mateo. Shot hoists rumbled on the deck, lines screaming through the blocks as fresh ammunition was brought up for the guns. Boys were strewing sand in the waist and additional men were going aloft to the fighting tops.

The San Martín looked tattered and disheveled as they bore up toward her, cut rigging dangling, shredded sails streaming in the wind, red topsides gray with powder smoke and torn and scraped from frequent collisions. The heavy oak sheathing that had ringed her huge girth hung in splintered sections. The capitana of the Spaniards rolled in the swells, but there was an indomitable air about her as she faced the English onslaught.

The two flagships were again face to face. Medina-Sidonia fired his bow battery into the approaching *Ark*. The Lord Admiral returned the salute with his bow chasers followed by a full broadside. The English ships sailed after Lord Howard past the *San Martín* raking her. Medina-Sidonia, who had hove into the wind to offer personal battle to the English Admiral, received instead the shattering fire of the entire flotilla. The *San Martín* trembled in the blast of lead, but she swung back on her course undaunted and defiant.

Sweeping up to and past the *San Juan,* the *Ark's* starboard batteries again went into action, and then they were bearing close-hauled upon the weather flank of the main battle of the Armada. The *Ark* hove to within a cable's length of the Spanish galleons to pour a tempest of shot into the enemy's ships.

The deck shook. Men lining the rails and the bulwarks with muskets and breech-loading pieces maintained a withering fire at the drifting Spaniards. Flying splinters, bits of shredded canvas, fluttering lines told of the heaviest weight of Spanish fire that the *Ark* had yet sustained. A body fell to the deck from the maintop. Men dropped here and there along the rail as the Spanish shot found its mark. A ball plowed across the half deck, hurling chunks of jagged planking in all directions, stopping with a thud against the mizzenmast birts.

Maurice watching the course of the shot in the murky pall shrouding the deck, moved mechanically to one side as a man raced up the companionway. It was not until the sailor in a familiar gesture pushed his hair out of his eyes with the back of his hand that Maurice realized the tattered and smoke-blackened figure was Patrick.

He gave Maurice a tired half-smile while he glanced about for Howard, caught sight of the Admiral and walked swiftly across the rolling deck to him. The message was evidently brief for after a moment's speech, Patrick started back toward the companionway, and the Admiral signaled to the captain and two of his staff officers to join him.

Another Spanish broadside crashed aboard. Maurice

406

swung aside involuntarily as shot whined overhead, spattered across the deck. He was vaguely aware of a thin tearing sound above, but it was almost lost in the roar of the guns and the scream of the wounded.

Patrick, one hand on the rail, turned, head tilted sharply back. His explosive yell of warning was indistinguishable as he leaped toward Howard before anyone could move. It seemed to Patrick that his feet were leaden as he ran and that Lord Howard's eyes, widening in amazement at the sight of a sailor charging at his Admiral, stared at him for an interminable time. Then his outflung arm, with the whole weight of his body behind the thrust, pushed Howard backward, sending him sprawling.

A tangle of rigging from aloft caught them both, bringing Patrick to his knees amid a rending crash that stunned him momentarily. He shook himself free from the folds of canvas and tangled lines. The great mizzen yard which had carried the lateen sail lay across the deck, protruding crazily through the shattered rail. Enemy shot had cut slings and halyards neatly, dropping the heavy yard onto the poop. As Patrick stood up unsteadily, he could see the crushed body of one of the junior officers beneath the wreckage where Howard had been standing a moment before, and the other lying motionless against the lee rail where he had been flung.

He turned quickly to Howard, but the Admiral was already on his feet. "I'm sorry, my lord! Are you injured?"

Howard, feeling his upper arm bruised from his fall, said wryly, "Not from the mizzen yard, young man!" He started to add a word of thanks but Patrick had already saluted and was gone.

The captain's voice rang out as he called men from the guns to clear the tangled rigging. Maurice glanced from the crew swinging axes against the wreckage to the smoke-sheathed muzzles of the vomiting Spanish cannon, then moved aft toward Howard. His words, chill and arrogant, were scarcely audible in the crescendo of sound. "Are you having difficulties, sir—

besides this obvious one of course? Perhaps I can be of service."

Howard looked at him in surprise. "The gun deck reports trouble, Master Quain. Your secretary—that gunner was your man, wasn't he?—told me the main starboard battery is apparently idle. You could go below and help serve on the tackles, but as a task for a royal envoy—I don't know."

Maurice smiled faintly. "As Her Majesty's mission seems to be of less than no moment, I have more time than employment."

Howard, adjusting the broken strap of his breastplate, said, "I didn't expect your secretary to have learned quite such prompt and vigorous action driving quills across paper. What is his name?"

"Patrick North."

"I won't forget he saved my life."

Maurice nodded absently, but he knew that in spite of the brevity of the words, Patrick had made a valuable friend today. He descended from the poop, walked across the length of the half deck, climbed by the thundering guns in the waist down the companionway and emerged gasping into the murky half-light of the main gun deck. One of the starboard culverins had exploded slaughtering its gun crew and filling the cavernous 'tween-decks with reeking powder fumes. He stumbled over a prostrate body, almost lost his balance on the slippery deck. There was stench of blood and sweat, and the fumes made his eyes smart.

Gun captains were urging their dazed crews back to the big culverins. Powder boys hurried through the haze with new charges. Near Maurice a half-naked sailor, blood streaming from his shoulder, plunged a water-soaked sponge into the sizzling muzzle of the gun, reached for the waiting powder charge, rammed it home, and the ball rolled down upon the charge. Under the desperate urging of the gun captain the remnant of the crew heaved their weight on the tackles, but the heavy gun moved slowly.

The forward cannon began to fire. The deafening concussion stunned Maurice. He reached automatically for a line that was undermanned, braced himself and pulled with all his strength against the weight of the big gun. A priming quill was thrust into the vent. The captain glanced quickly through the smoke-shrouded port, signaled with his hand to ease up on the tackles, plunged a lighted match into the quill, jumped clear as the gun recoiled to the limit of its breachings. Maurice staggered under the sound that he could feel rather than hear. Again the swab went into the muzzle. Someone yelled at him and he passed up the powder charge. The hot gun leaped in its carriage as the recoil flung it back.

Maurice felt the prickle of sweat on his brow, sweat streaming down into the ruff at his throat. He drew out his handkerchief, wiped fingers and face, then removed his doublet and jumped to the tackle again.

The battery was working rapidly. Guns rumbled steadily across the deck in their heavy carriages, grinding out pandemonium. He moved mechanically now, hardly aware of sore muscles, of the fierce burn on his arm where he had brushed against the hot muzzle, of his torn shirt. His nerves were dulled by the crushing weight of noise. They strained on the tackle running out the culverin, stood aside for the recoil and the concussion. Then the gun captain drew back. The entire battery fell silent. Through the gun port Maurice had a glimpse of green seas and sparkling sunshine that seemed another world.

The haze began to clear. The quartermaster came up with replacements, giving the gun that Maurice had been serving its full complement of men. He reached for his doublet, climbed back into the blinding light of the deck above, reeled as he filled his lungs with fresh salt air. His eyes ached from the bright sun. He winced as the sleeve of his doublet scraped his burned arm, and adjusted his torn ruff before going up to the half deck.

Howard stared at him a moment in rather amused surprise at his appearance, but he said only, in answer to Maurice's question, "The Armada's flank has been turned again, Master Quain. The galleons are giving way and running into the main body of the fleet forcing them to leeward. I'm sending flying squadrons against

409

the isolated vessels. We're running up to the *San Mateo* now before she can rejoin the main battle."

New halyards had been rove and the mizzen yard had been hauled aloft again.

As the *Ark* swung close, the *San Mateo* seemed a hopelessly shattered ship. Her rigging was shot down, her sails were riddled, long sections of bulwark were blown completely away and holes on the water line gaped like open wounds. Most of her guns must have been dismounted or put out of action. She replied with only small arms as the *Ark* sailed by discharging a fresh broadside, wheeled about to deliver its starboard batteries within point-blank range. The Spanish captain made heroic efforts to grapple, but as a fighting machine the *San Mateo* was a helpless wreck at the mercy of the English guns.

Lord Howard spoke for a moment to his captain. At a shouted command to the helmsman the *Ark* came up into the wind less than a cable's length from the Spanish ship. An officer was sent into the main shrouds above the level of the drifting smoke. His voice rang out across the narrow gap offering quarter to captain and command. There was complete silence from the *San Mateo*. He hailed the galleon again. "Soldiers so find should surrender to the Queen *á buena guerra!*"

This time in answer a musket cracked from the deck of the *San Mateo*. The officer's body splashed into the sea. Taunts rose from the Spanish crew.

Lord Howard turned to his captain. The *Ark's* broadsides thundered anew, riddling the hulk of the *San Mateo*. When the *Ark* finally bore away to avoid collision, Maurice had a fleeting glimpse through the ports of a tangled and bloody mass, of scuppers running red with the blood of men dying but refusing to be conquered.

An urgent hail sounded from the masthead. "Squall!" Every man's eyes turned to windward where a dark line of agitated water was racing toward them under lowering clouds.

"Bring her up to the wind! Shorten sail! Secure the guns!" Men were running up the shrouds, moving out on the yards and footropes before the boatswain's whistle shrilled through the ship. Crews jumped to secure their guns.

The wind struck, rolling the *Ark* onto her beamends and threatening to drive sails and spars out of the ship. Torrents of rain swept in with the wind, drenched everyone, sent blinding pellets of water into the faces of the men in the rigging as the ship lurched ahead over the foaming seas. Great sheets of spray hurled up from the bow dashed aft over the ship, leaving a salt taste in the mouth. Wind howled through the taut rigging with the high-pitched sound of a giant harp, plucking at the nerves of the sodden men, picking up the crests of breaking waves, sending foam and spray driving across the face of the sea, drawing a gray curtain about them until it seemed that the *Ark* was alone in the seething Channel.

The storm passed almost as quickly as it had come, but the wind in that quarter hour had veered to west-northwest. The Spanish fleet running before the blast had slipped out from between the English ships and the treacherous Zeeland banks.

Lord Howard was disgruntled. "We could have beaten the Armada to pieces and we had over a dozen galleons isolated as prizes. Well, we'll stay to windward through the night. If this wind holds, they're certain to be driven onto the shoals."

By dawn Maurice could see two of the big Spanish galleons aground, rapidly breaking up. The rest of the Armada continued up the coast drifting closer each hour to certain destruction under the eyes of the English. Drake's squadron led by the *Revenge* bore down on its weather flank. Medina-Sidonia again turned to draw the English fire.

"It's only a matter of hours now, Master Quain," Howard said. "Drake won't have to waste a shot. The sea will destroy the Armada for us."

Maurice watched the Spanish ships maneuvering desperately against the wind that would pile them up on the banks. Howard lifted his head sharply. "Jesus Christ! The wind's shifting again to the south!"

The Armada, almost on the coast, swung about to beat out into the North Sea. Maurice murmured sardonically, "The wind, Lord Howard, must have been taking lessons from Elizabeth Tudor."

Howard lifted his shoulders resignedly and signaled the captains to come aboard for another council while the fleet stood out after the Spanish ships. Launches brought the captains to the *Ark*. The report from every ship was the same. The ammunition was dangerously low, scarcely more than a round or two for the guns. Water was almost exhausted. The beer was sour. Even now, despite the hard battle the men had fought, rations had to be cut again.

Howard spoke to Wynter and Seymour. "You will return to your Channel stations." He went on above their protests. "We will continue northward. Medina-Sidonia may plan a landing in the Firth of Forth in hope of an alliance with the Scotch rebels."

The wind freshened every hour and the seas grew heavier. The *Ark* rolled constantly as she drove ahead. Off Newcastle Howard, deciding the Armada was too far north to go into Forth, gave signal for the English ships to run in to replenish supplies. Before they could change their course to Scotland, the wind swung to the northwest and drove down upon them in a full gale.

Lord Howard hoisted a new signal. The ships were to return home, making any port they could. The *Ark* flew southward under light canvas. The rising gale and tremendous seas scattered the fleet.

The battered flagship beat into Gravesend. Patrick and Maurice stood on the half deck watching the headlands sweep by. The ship was riding easier now with the wild seas of the Channel giving place to the short chop of the roadstead. Forward a party of men stood by the anchors and mooring cable.

Patrick fastened his doublet up to his chin. "There's one thing to be said for this wind, Master Quain. At least we won't have to row the damn ship back to England as well as away from it."

Maurice smiled faintly. "At any rate, Patrick, I hope that once we're in port, we can keep our feet on dry land for a long time to come."

412

The *Ark* was running through the anchorage. She came into shore, was brought sharply up to the wind. The anchor splashed into the sea. Sheets were let fly as the ship swung to her cable and topmast hands swarmed aloft to furl the sails.

"That anchor may mark the end of the Armada—we hope—but it brings with it all of our affairs at home which have been neglected for far too many months. The Eastern Company——" Maurice broke off. He wasn't thinking of his trade empire.

Patrick started to say, "And pleasanter——" He turned away. He couldn't speak of Katherine lightly—not yet. As though it were of significance he watched a pinnace with the royal ensign fluttering aloft come alongside the *Ark* and turn smartly into the wind. A young officer climbed aboard the flagship and disappeared into the cabin. Overhead, gulls swooped and wheeled about the tall spars. Wisps of gray cloud swept eastward before the gale.

"The Lord Admiral sends his compliments, Master Quain." A boy touched his forelock as he came up beside them a few minutes later. "He invites you to attend him in the main cabin at your convenience."

Maurice walked down the companionway and went through the cobridgehead. He hoped it was for the last time. He was weary to exhaustion and longed for a civilized dinner and a bed that did not sway with every sea.

Lord Howard looked gray and worn as he sat in his accustomed place at the gleaming mahogany table. "Dispatches from Her Majesty, Master Quain. I thought there might be something in them about your duties."

Maurice pulled up a chair as Howard broke the seal. "Elizabeth can't want anything of me at the moment, and has nothing she can possibly thank me for, my lord. To you and your captains she owes a debt of gratitude that from past experience I'd say she's not apt to repay." Not any sooner, he thought, than he'd get back again the thousand pounds he'd advanced.

Lord Howard read in silence for a few minutes, then looked up grimly. "Gratitude, did you say? There's another word for it here. Her Majesty is inquiring into a few matters of the Armada." He flung the rolled parchment to the table in exasperation. "Such as where are the Spanish prizes she was expecting, the treasures, the prisoners to ransom? Furthermore, I'm required to repair at once to Whitehall to give an accounting of the outrageous cost of the entire campaign."

Maurice made a gesture of sympathy, but it was denied by his quick smile. He also was bound for Whitehall—but not to see the Queen.

22

Mary Howard turned on Maurice like a fury. "It's time you came to ask about Kit, Master Quain. God-a-mercy!"

Maurice said coldly, "I'm sorry, madam, but I fear you have the advantage of me both in name and situation." They were in the hall outside the anteroom to the Queen's Chamber with pages and grooms going in and out past them, ladies hurrying by, courtiers, soldiers, sailors, in an endless stream to the Queen's presence. There were a rustle of silk against brocade, a clank of spurs on the carpeted floor, steel against steel; the gleam of satin, the dull shine of polished leather, the glitter of metal.

Mary Howard, small-boned and dainty, had to turn her head back to look up at Maurice towering over her, tall and impassive. She stamped her foot. "My name's Mary Howard, but what does that matter?" She looked like a kitten facing a greyhound. "As to the situation, you ask for Kit. The Queen knows and her Secretary, I suppose. God's wounds, where have you been all this time?"

Maurice smiled down at her involuntarily. "With Admiral Howard—a kinsman of yours. I'd think. Though he's of a gentler temper! But where is Katherine?"

She put her small hand on his dark sleeve. "I've been telling you, we don't know. She went out one morning, Master Quain, and did not return."

"When?"

"The day after you left London. And no word from her at all."

Maurice said mechanically, "That's impossible. What does the Queen say?"

"Nothing. That's what terrifies me. When I brought up Katherine's name, she just smiled and talked of other things—until one day she said she wanted to hear no more."

Maurice started to move past her. "I'll see Her Majesty."

Mary Howard looked at him mockingly. "You will? When? You won't see her this side of Michaelmas unless you're a foreign ambassador or the Lord Chancellor."

"Walsingham?"

She said grudgingly, "You might see him, Master Quain. I can get no word from him, but then he doesn't like the ladies of the bedchamber—he says they're forever interfering between the Queen and her ministers of state."

Maurice left her standing there looking after him with a small encouraging smile at the corners of her mouth.

Phillipps, Walsingham's most valued secretary for his ability to decode messages, looked up as Maurice entered the room. Maurice gave his name and demanded to see Sir Francis. Phillipps, lanky, sandy-haired and pock-marked, said arrogantly, "Sorry, Master Quain. Sir Francis is very busy. I'll send to you when he has more time."

Maurice eyed him contemptuously. This was the man who had been Walsingham's right hand in opening communication for Mary Stuart to the Continent so that she might be entangled in the last fatal conspiracy. "Tell Sir Francis I want to see him now." Phillipps started to shake his head. Maurice's mouth thinned. "Put it to him this way then. In my absence my agent lent him some money. Perhaps you were concerned in the business? Good! I didn't come here to discuss bad debts, Master Phillipps, but—— Thank you." The

415

secretary finally rose. "I'll appreciate your mentioning I wish to see him on a matter that will take little of his valuable time."

Maurice was shown into the dark paneled inner room almost at once. Walsingham drew a hand across his tired eyes, then nodded at Maurice. "A great victory that God has seen fit to give to his faithful servants, Master Quain. I'm so deep under reports I've really not come up yet to enjoy the free air that we may breathe after our defeat of the forces of Belial." His face looked thinner and darker than ever. His black beard was flecked with gray and his intense dark eyes were bloodshot from strain. "You wanted to see me?" He made a half gesture toward the piles of parchment, rolled documents and his own finely written reports that cluttered his desk.

Maurice's brows lifted at the apparent lack of neatness. "I'll take but one moment, Sir Francis. Where is Katherine Perrot?"

Walsingham's eyes opened slightly in surprise, but it was the only movement that betrayed him. "Lady Katherine?"

"She disappeared some time ago, immediately after I left London. I want to know where she is."

"Why, Master Quain?"

"I'm concerned, Sir Francis, as we're to be married."

"You—what?" Walsingham made no effort to hide his astonishment. He shook his head slowly. "I'm afraid that isn't a good enough story."

"I don't know what you're talking about, Sir Francis. But I don't like having my word doubted. What is all this mystery of Katherine?"

Walsingham leaned back in his chair. He looked over the tips of his fingers at Maurice. "I don't know why I should tell you, Master Quain. But you have done England such a good service that perhaps I can take you this far into my confidence. Katherine Perrot is under arrest for conspiring against the safety of the Queen's person."

Maurice said scornfully, "A child of two wouldn't believe a tale like that."

Walsingham's brows came together in a frown. "I regret to say it, but we have proof."

"You have?" Maurice's voice was cold.

Walsingham's brittle temper snapped. "We have, Master Quain. I have a statement written out and sworn to that Katherine Perrot is planning marriage—but not with a commoner. With the Earl of Leicester's stepson, the young Robert Devereaux, Earl of Essex."

Maurice said in a bored fashion, "I've never heard of him."

Walsingham retorted with a grim humor, "If you live long enough you will. He has been at Court a few times. The Queen is quite impressed with him. He has been made Master of the Horse, and the gossip is that he'll inherit the mantle of royal favor from his stepfather. But that's of no importance at the moment. The point is that he has some shadowy claim to the succession through his relationship with the Boleyns. Katherine Perrot also has a claim as far as blood goes, though not lawfully. As you know, Catherine Grey, a kinswoman of the Queen's, was put under custody for life because she married a man who might have hopes for the Crown. Katherine Perrot can expect nothing better. Those are risks of civil war that we cannot take, Master Quain.

Maurice said, "Did you go so far as to question this—what's his name, Robert Devereux?"

"He denies it of course. And we can't touch Leicester's stepson. But we can draw the fangs of the monster of rebellion by imprisoning Katherine Perrot."

Maurice could well imagine Elizabeth's anger if she thought anyone were planning to marry a young man she was beginning to favor. He said, "May I ask one question more? Who placed the charge?"

Walsingham picked up his quill to signify the interview was over. "I'm sorry, but that information we do not divulge. May I say only that it was lodged by a man who would be the last person on earth to make such an accusation if he were not assured of its truth? I was indeed amazed to have it come from him as I had done him the injustice of fearing his love for the lady would outweigh his duty to the State."

Maurice said, "Thank you!" bowed and walked out.

Patrick was waiting for him at the offices of the House of Bowyer in the Royal Exchange. Maurice went across the inner courtyard up the steps and directly into the office where Patrick and the elder Bowyer were going over his accounts. He said curtly, "Your pardon a moment, Master Bowyer. Patrick, I want you to find Edward Blount for me. I hope he's in London. I wish to see him today as soon as possible."

Patrick stood up, rolled down the sleeves of his doublet and fastened the clasps at the wrist. "Yes, sir!" He looked older these days and tired. He reached for his hat, smiled slightly then. "Though why you'd want to lift a finger to see Sir Edward, Master Quain, is beyond my understanding."

Maurice said, "To spur you on your way, Patrick, shall I mention that Katherine's safety depends on my seeing Blount?"

Patrick lifted his head sharply at that. "I'll find him."

Maurice watched him go, a considering look in his eyes. Then he turned to the elderly merchant. "I hope all my business is in good order, Master Bowyer. I may need rather a lot of money before morning."

Patrick returned to the Saracen's Head five hours later. "I finally discovered your man. He says he'll meet you in a private room at the Sign of Swan and Cygnet tonight just before curfew." He hesitated. "Master Quain, I know Katherine's troubles are not my affair, but could you tell me what that bastard has done now?"

Maurice told him of the charge against Katherine. Patrick said levelly, "I always knew that the time would come when I'd have to kill Edward Blount and take my chances on the consequences. I'll call him out today."

"No! Blount's death would be the worst luck we could have now. It's only if he's alive and will of his own volition retract the charge he's brought that we can hope to have Katherine released."

Maurice was picturing Katherine at the open door of

418

a manor house. He said abstractedly, "It's late. Send Tom to order dinner from the landlord." He looked at the garish room with disfavor. "We should really have had our own furniture sent here though it would be for only a brief time. To expect a man of taste to eat and sleep in these surroundings is to put too great a strain on his sensibilities."

Patrick, calling Tom from the inner room, turned to stare at Maurice. A man caviling about a room when his future bride was imprisoned and in imminent danger! Especially when that bride was Katherine. He wondered how long he could endure working for the man who was to be her husband. Not long by God! When Katherine and Maurice were married, he'd go away. He didn't know what he'd do but he couldn't stay near Katherine. He wouldn't trust himself so far. It should be enough for him to know she'd be happy. It was enough. No—but it helped somewhat because he couldn't endure it at all if he thought she wouldn't be happy. But this dull anguish——— Still, how could he say it was unbearable when he'd have to endure this ache in his heart forever?

Maurice said, "When we've dined, Patrick, we'll go to the Swan and Cygnet."

"How many attendants do you want, Master Quain?"

"Just you—if of course you have nothing more pressing to do." He eyed Patrick sardonically.

Edward Blount clicked the casement window to and turned as Maurice and Patrick came into the private room he had hired. Three armed attendants in his livery were in the hall just outside the door. He smiled charmingly, glanced from Maurice to his own companion standing at the head of the table that stretched down the center of the large square room. The visitors did not need Blount to bring the man to their attention. He seemed to fill the whole side of the chamber with his white turban and the immaculate robes over his huge body. Behind him stood the wizened little man who attended him when last Maurice had seen him in Paris.

Maurice murmured, "As always, Sir Edward, I find you in the best of company." He bowed. "Your servant, effendi."

Ali Bey gave the *témena,* knee, heart, lips and forehead. *"Hosgeldi!* Welcome!" He smiled.

Maurice said, "Close the door, Patrick." He seated himself at the side of the table.

Patrick swung the door to and came forward into the circle of light cast by the branched candelabra. He felt an icy chill down his spine and then a cold desperation. If it came to a fight—but Maurice of course would not fight. Ali Bey probably could not. It would be himself and Blount. What of Blount's attendants outside? He noticed Blount eying the sword he wore with a thin smile of contempt. He caught Blount's gaze. The knight's smile faded. Blount and himself. The blood surged betrayingly to Patrick's finger tips, but he felt steady and assured. He had waited a long time for this.

Maurice's voice cut across his thoughts. Maurice said arrogantly, "Don't you wish to be seated, Sir Edward, while we're reaching an agreement?"

Blount pulled forward a heavy high-backed chair. "What are we agreeing on, Maurice?" He twisted a ring on his index finger back and forth so that the diamond caught the light.

Maurice said bluntly, "Well, what is your price, Sir Edward?"

Blount lifted his eyes to Maurice. His smile deepened. "Do you know, Maurice, I always thought you'd have to come to me one day. My price——" He glanced at Ali Bey who had seated himself majestically at the head of the table, though still giving the impression of holding himself aloof from these Christian dogs.

Ali Bey said with prompt malice, "The establishment of Monsieur Chapé in the Street of the Three Angels in Paris."

Maurice said, "For just a woman?"

Ali Bey smiled, his eyes almost lost in rolls of fat. "After that, effendi, we can discuss the woman."

Maurice's brows rose. "Do you hold a lock to her prison?"

Ali Bey looked at Blount disdainfully before speaking to Maurice. "I could be said to hold practically all the locks."

Maurice smiled. His smile had a deadly quality that made Patrick shiver as Maurice looked at him. "Bear witness to that, Patrick." He turned back to the Turk. "Very well. The House of Chapé is yours."

Even Blount was surprised by so easy a surrender. By God, the man did want Katherine! His breath quickened, his face with its heavy jowls seemed to sharpen with avarice. Maurice at his mercy! He'd bleed him until—what was the limit Maurice would pay for Katherine's release? He thought savagely of her naked body when he'd forced his will upon her, the sense of power the act had given him, overlaying the terrible knowledge that he'd lost her to Maurice Quain. And then the brilliant plan, partly his, partly Ali Bey's, to have her imprisoned. The sweetness of his vengeance on Maurice and Katherine would have been almost enough payment without Ali Bey's soft insinuations that they had finally the key to Maurice's fortune.

Blount said, "That French house is not yours alone, Ali Bey. We were to share equally."

Ali Bey spoke scornfully. "Is the shop in Paris Effendi Quain's only possession?"

Maurice murmured. "Before we go farther, could we not sweeten this distasteful haggling with wine? Would you call the landlord, Patrick?"

There was silence while Patrick ordered a bottle of malmsey and the landlord, a portly genial man, came to serve it himself. Ali Bey refused a glass with a pious quotation from the Koran abhorring all alcoholic beverages. Blount drank the wine before him in one draught. The landlord refilled his goblet before leaving. The silence closed about them again, living and palpable and brutal.

The heady sweetness, of the wine crept through Bloun't veins. He said, "Constantinople. Now there——"

Ali Bey cut him short. "We'll come to his Turkish

421

commerce later, Sir Edward. Is there not a shop in Hamburg?"

Patrick pushed his wine to one side. "First, I'd like to know, gentlemen, just where Katherine is?"

Blount snarled, "What's it to you?" Then he thought better of it and added in a pleasanter tone, "At the Tower, my young cockerel—a trap not to be easily sprung."

Patrick sat back. "We are glad to hear she is not in your hands." He looked at both Blount and Ali Bey, reminding them there was still a score to settle for the way their hired assassins had mishandled Maurice. The score that would be settled tonight, however, would not be in Maurice's favor.

Ali Bey repeated, "Does not Effendi Quain have a place in Hamburg for you, Sir Edward?"

Maurice's hand was spread flat on the table. He stared at it unseeingly. Paris. Hamburg. He lifted his eyes to Blount. "Why not, Sir Edward? The house has never prospered quite as it should have anyway since it was moved out of Antwerp, but——" He stopped. He'd been about to say mechanically that Katherine's release was worth only so much to him. He added instead, "I can't feel that under this change the day of its glory will now descend upon the business. But that is no burden of mine."

Blount said, "How much is your place there worth, Maurice?"

Maurice looked bored. "Really, Sir Edward, I wouldn't care to hazard a guess. We will have to see Bowyer."

Blount finished off his wine, refilled his glass again. The sound of the malmsey pouring into the goblet seemed loud in the stillness. "Now about your Turkish house——"

Ali Bey's eyes half closed in annoyance at Blount's insistence, but he said dreamily, "Seventeen thousand pounds to be raised in twenty-four hours, a ruinous fine assessed against us in Paris for a shipload of silk that chanced to escape the eye of the customs officers—— You were not kind, Effendi Quain."

422

Maurice's brows lifted. "You must teach me, sir, the forgotten art of charity."

Ali Bey murmured, "Twenty thousand pounds of supplies lately from the Eastern Company, twenty-five hundred from your own house in Blyth shipped to Hamid in Constantinople. The value should be doubled in a good market. An agency at Aleppo, a shop opening in Smyrna—your name on a piece of paper, effendi, and perhaps we can forgive your barbarous demands in Paris."

"I fear I cannot sign the Eastern Company over to you. I only hold shares in the venture."

Ali Bey conceded graciously. "Since they are almost half the company's wealth, your shares will do well enough, effendi. But you need not sign them over. Your name on a confession that you crossed the will of Janfreda Kadein, and the holdings are mine."

"Ours," Blount corrected him. "Who, sir, discovered the deed, who made arrangements through the Chief of the Black Eunuchs to have the property confiscated? I!" His fist crashed on the table.

Maurice said, "If I should sign for you of course." He had thought they could not touch his Turkish property that went through Hamid's hands. They had shown more foresight than he had expected of them, at least of Blount.

Ali Bey's eyes disappeared again in wrinkles of fat. "You jest, effendi."

Katherine in a bare stone room, cold, possibly hungry, barred against sunlight and air, going mad, as other prisoners of Elizabeth had gone, with the creeping horror of imprisonment. Katherine my darling. "Sign? Why not? I can afford a high price for a favor." He turned to Patrick. "Write Webster to return to England at once. But now, gentlemen, I want your signatures on a sworn warrant that you have accused Katherine Perrot without proof and retract your charges, or make whatever other concession would satisfy Walsingham."

Blount twirled his glass. Gold! The feel of it in his hands. No more debts, no creditors hounding him, magnificent new suits to match his presence, a lavish gift to the Queen. Perhaps he could expect an earldom yet, prestige at Court, no doubt marriage to an heiress. What was Katherine compared with such riches? He might even—— He looked at Maurice. He'd had pleasure in Maurice's first wife. He smiled charmingly. "Why, I think that could be——"

Ali Bey's voice cut across Blount's like a scimitar through flesh. "Effendi Quain has branches in Rome and in Madrid."

Patrick felt a sickening at the pit of his stomach. They asked too much. Maurice would not face ruin. He could not believe indeed that Maurice had already paid so much for Katherine's release. He put his hand tentatively on the hilt of his sword. The laced metalwork of the guard felt reassuring under his fingers. Then he stopped. If he had Blount begging for mercy, he knew the knight would promise anything—until he faced Walsingham, and then he'd only buttress his charges with more manufactured proof. Maurice was right. Blount had to withdraw his accusations of his own will.

Maurice started to adjust the ruff at his wrist, stopped at the mannerism, then finished tightening the clasp with an odd half-smile. "Let's not haggle. The houses are yours."

Ali Bey said, "You grow generous, effendi."

"Thank you!"

The edge of the table cut into Patrick's ribs. He could see the end too clearly. Just how far would Maurice give before he'd say his final inflexible no?

Blount had his cue from Ali Bey pat to his tongue. "When I was in Blyth to see you, Maurice, I envied you your home. You showed excellent taste, if I may say so, in both architecture and furnishings. Your silver service alone—a lord's ransom if I recall it right."

"And Katherine's ransom now?" Maurice thought, No, not my house. The timber, plaster and lath exterior gracious toward shore and sea, the high, exquisitely furnished rooms, carpets from the East, tapestry from France, paintings and silver from Italy—and Katherine mistress there, her loveliness giving the last touch to make a home of what had been a shell of beauty. He shivered. The barricades of gold he'd built about himself were tumbling down. No wall so high it could not be leveled, no wall so strong it could not be breached. He lifted his head to look at Blount with a faint ironic wonder in his eyes. He did not need defenses. He needed nothing. And he knew that what he'd thought he must do would now be easy. "Why not? A lovely lady is worth a small sacrifice."

Blount wiped his mouth with the back of his hand. Himself master there? He could not quite believe his dazzling good fortune. How often had he envied Maurice's wealth and background, and now in one night's work they were his! He knew he'd never really believed his boasts that Maurice would one day pay his price. Yet here Maurice was being stripped as naked of wealth as he had stripped Katherine of her silken robes.

But always, always, when he had the upper hand, somehow Maurice took away the last taste of honeyed triumph. Maurice should be begging for mercy now, and instead he was handing out his fortune with little more concern than if he were giving away shillings.

He thought of Maurice Quain as a poor man. What could a destitute man nearing forty do to make a living? A beggarly clerkship perhaps?

Ali Bey put one fat hand over the other. His nails were long, cut to a sharp point. "I think then, Effendi Quain, there are left but your profits in the Turkey Company, the shares in the Muscovite Company, and a manor house in Sussex that Mendoza turned over to you in lieu of payment of a loan."

Maurice said politely. "Are you sure you have swept up all the leavings? I can oblige you in the matter of companies, but the manor house is no longer in my possession. There may be a few other odd riches lying about forgotten. I have for instance a government receipt for a thousand pounds of credit extended Admiral Howard for provisions. You are more than welcome to it. I wouldn't waste time, if I were you, quarreling over its possession. And now, gentlemen, shall we meet in the chambers of Sir Francis Walsingham tomorrow at nine?" He stood up.

425

Blount said. "Yes. But before you leave tonight, we want your signature to these promises you have made."

Maurice drew back his chair and sat down again. "No. You have my word, which is slightly better than your oath sworn on a Bible before a bishop. Tomorrow after we've seen Walsingham, after I'm assured of Katherine's freedom, we'll go to the House of Bowyer and I'll sign over to you the titles to my business houses and merchant shares. But I was perhaps over-hasty to think of leaving. If you have no great objection, I'd suggest we spend the night here together. Patrick, will you see if there are cards in the chest there in the corner? They might while away the time."

Patrick found a deck, brought it over. Blount said, "Good!" He felt Maurice had given up his fortune too easily and more than half suspected a trick to recoup his loses the moment he was out of sight. Ali Bey slumped down in the chair and went to sleep. His massive turbaned head dropped forward precariously for the safety of his neck.

Blount dealt. The parchment squares made a thin brittle sound on the table top. "We'll keep the stakes low, Maurice, within reach of your means. A shilling a game? Master North, will you send for more candles? We have a long night ahead of us." His day of triumph. The tip of his tongue ran about his lips.

The gray morning light crept through the windows. In the yard and belowstairs there was the sound of people moving about. Blount yawned, swept up the cards and tossed them aside. Maurice reached for them and stacked them neatly. "May I suggest, Sir Edward, we have breakfast and then send for a barber? Patrick, if you don't mind taking orders though you're no longer my secretary, would you go to the Saracen's Head? I'd like fresh linen and ruffs."

Patrick said automatically, "Yes sir!" He smiled. Today Katherine would be free. And Maurice, Maurice had unbelievably paid for this with his whole fortune. He could not quite imagine Maurice without half a dozen attendants, the aura that went with wealth. In Blyth—pity of God! there was nothing to return to in

426

Blyth. And Captain Fox and his *Falcon* would sail for other merchants. He glanced at Maurice. Maurice might be a poor man today, but his wide shoulders had the same arrogant set, his face the same impenetrable, slightly contemptuous expression as always. Of what was he thinking? Planning to recoup his losses? He'd started from nothing before, but he'd been younger then. Or were his thoughts on Katherine?

Maurice turned his head. He said coldly, "If you're going, Patrick——" Patrick grinned and left. He might have known Maurice's thoughts were on his own fastidious grooming.

Blount's eyes were bloodshot, his clothes awry, the flesh of his face was heavy with lack of sleep. He said, "You'll soon have to get used to meaner service and a less pampered sort of life, Maurice."

Maurice murmured, "Sufficient unto the day, Sir Edward—— What shall we order to break our fast?" He looked little the worse for the night behind him, perhaps harder, mouth thinner and more sardonic. It annoyed Blount. He'd always thought there was something inhuman about Maurice.

Phillipps looked up as Maurice and Blount, followed by Patrick, Ali Bey and his body servant, came into Walsingham's antechamber. Phillipps said sourly, "Really, Master Quain, Sir Francis does not have time to see you every day."

"Sir Edward and I have important information on a State concern," Maurice said curtly. "Be good enough to mention it to Sir Francis."

Walsingham evidently threw up his hands and said to send them in, for Phillipps was out almost immediately with permission to enter.

Maurice bowed. "Good morning, Sir Francis. Sir Edward here is the one who would speak to you."

Looking haggard but smugly satisfied, Blount swaggered across the floor, sat down in the great chair near the Queen's Secretary. "It appears, Sir Francis, that I was grossly misinformed in the accusations I placed against the unfortunate Lady Katherine Perrot. The

427 ·

paper was a forgery, as unhappily I have just discovered."

Walsingham looked shrewdly from Maurice to Blount. "And just how were you convinced it was a forgery?"

Blount's face lost its jaunty appearance. "But I say it is! I——"

Maurice put in smoothly, "Why Sir Edward would be duped so easily it is difficult for anyone but him to explain. If Ali Bey is the man behind the forgery, I believe the whole thing was a simple matter of revenge for some business affair. Since he could not move against me, evidently he decided to take vengeance on my intended bride. That is, if he's the man back of this. What say you, Sir Edward?"

Blount stared at Maurice at the unexpected twist against the Turk. But if Ali Bey were imprisoned—why, the whole fortune would come to him! . . . "Yes, Sir Francis, he is the instigator of this miscarriage of justice. I was duped, true, but my sins were on the side of too much zeal."

"Now, Sir Francis," Maurice put in shortly, "how soon can Katherine be released? Naturally I am anxious for her safety."

Walsingham said, "I will examine this Turk, Master Quain, and find out the truth of the charges he has placed against Lady Katherine. After that——"

Blount put in hastily, "Is it not cruel to hold an innocent lady one moment longer than necessary?" He'd not get a farthing from Maurice, he knew, until Katherine was freed.

Walsingham looked at the mountain of work before him and sighed.

Maurice said, "We expect of course that if you order her prison door unlocked, she will still be under surveillance. But in sheer justice——"

Blount looked up at that. Katherine released but under suspicion—why, he'd have her in his hand always! She knew how easily suspicion hardened into belief of guilt. He could hold that threat over her head so that she must do whatever he desired. As his wealth grew, his rising prestige at Court would make him a powerful enemy—or friend.

Maurice added, "Perhaps you'll be more willing to look kindly at our request when we can assure you Katherine Perrot will marry a commoner. Surely even you will admit her last shadowy claim will dissolve when she's united to one of no ranking."

"Yes, Master Quain, once she's married to almost anyone but the Earl of Essex, my last fear will be at rest. I'll order her release, but as you mentioned she'll be under surveillance until her marriage." He rang, looked up as his secretary entered. "Phillipps, call the guards. I want Ali Bey—is that his name?—held for questioning. And send orders to the Tower for Katherine Perrot to be released—under surveillance."

Maurice said cynically, "May I add one thing more, Sir Francis? Ali Bey has a considerable fortune at his disposal in spite of the fact that his Paris house has been ruined. If you should find him guilty of treason, the confiscation of his property would add to the Crown's revenues."

Blount snarled the moment they were outside, "You aren't turning over your possessions to a doomed man?"

Maurice smiled thinly. "I gave him my word, Sir Edward. As it's the only thing left me, I value it."

They crossed the room to Patrick and the unsuspecting Ali Bey. Maurice nodded to Patrick to accompany them. Blount said, "Sir Francis wishes to see you later, sir, on——" He stopped. What for indeed?"

Maurice put in helpfully, "Was it on some points that have arisen in the Turkish treaty?"

"Yes, yes, of course. If you'll wait here, I'll go with Master Quain to the Royal Exchange to witness the signing over of the deeds he promised."

Ali Bey looked at Blount impassively, then bowed his head. "But do not, effendi, attempt to get one ducat that's due to me." His voice sent a chill down the knight's spine.

Maurice said, "Sir, my promises as to the property will be carried out. Beyond that what fate brings you should match your deserts." He turned and walked out.

They were going down the great staircase before they heard a high-pitched unnatural scream that went on and on so that the air seemed torn apart. Blount's eyes darted about the courtiers, who held still with surprise, to the paneled wall, the painted ceiling. "If they should release him soon, Maurice——"

Maurice looked at Blount with scorn, then turned to Patrick. "Patrick, you go to the Tower and wait for Katherine. Sir Edward and I will go first to the Royal Exchange to see Bowyer on the assignments. Then we'll meet you at the Saracen's Head." He had no intention of letting Blount out of his sight until he was assured of Katherine's liberty.

Blount said, "Oh, no, Maurice! We'll meet at the Swan and Cygnet where my retainers will be."

"As you will."

Bowyer ran his hands through his white hair. "Master Quain, I can't do it. Sign over all your property to this—this gentleman? I can't. It's madness!"

Maurice said coldly, "I purchased a favor from Sir Edward and a friend of his. This was the price. If you don't care to have your clerks do the work, be good enough to call a notary."

Bowyer sighed. "I'm at your command, sir. But it will take days before I can complete a detailed record of all your houses."

Blount put in sharply, "Days? I was promised the titles at once." The lines on his face were etched deep with fatigue.

"Make out a paper for me to sign, Master Bowyer, covering the general picture. Sir Edward grows impatient." Maurice sat down, chin resting on his maimed left hand for a moment. But he was not tired. His body felt steel-hard, alive, poised for action. As he watched the pen scratch across the parchment, he thought carelessly that he could afford this. Stripped of all his wealth, he was at last a rich man. He had no need to shift with every wind, to be—as he had once said—only what it profited him to be. He could even afford to go to Mass again since he could now avow old beliefs, careless of whom he pleased or did not please, reckless of the credit and debit balances of his ledgers.

430

He could even afford—he lifted his head to look at Blount slumped on the bench against the wall—to be so imprudent as to have an enemy.

Bowyer said, "Here you are, Master Quain, Sir Edward. I don't like this. I don't like this at all." He shook his white head. "But I will have the reports copied as soon as possible and sent on to you."

Maurice signed paper after paper. "These are for Sir Edward; these to be held here for Ali Bey—or his heirs."

Blount scooped up the papers, read them through word by word. "In good order it seems, Maurice." He started to roll up the documents, stopped. "I think, Master Bowyer, I'd feel safer if you held these for me here and gave me only a receipt for them." He said smugly, "Is there anything I've forgotten, Maurice?"

"Nothing beyond your manners."

Blount laughed and reread the papers before handing them reluctantly to the clerk. "To think you worked all those years, Maurice, only to fill my coffers! Well, now to the Swan—and Katherine, we hope."

Katherine and Patrick were waiting in the same private room where the men had spent the night. Maurice stood in the doorway to look at her. His eyes smarted with sudden tears. She was pale, and the light in her eyes, the radiance that was all about her, could not hide how thin she'd grown in that short time, how tired she seemed, and how frail. But the beauty of her face and proudly poised head seemed accentuated rather than blurred by any hardships she'd undergone, and her slim body was alive and vibrant under her wine-red dress.

He was aware of neither Patrick nor Blount. He crossed to her, bent his head for one kiss on her sweetly soft mouth. She whispered, "Maurice! I knew when you returned you would help me."

He stepped back, loosened her hands that clung to him. "You and Patrick go now to the Saracen's Head. Wait me there."

Katherine said, "Not you? Oh, Maurice, can't you come now?" And then with the shadow of a smile because she'd said it often before, "You were very kind, Master Quain!"

Maurice caught his breath. He put out one hand toward her. If he could go with her now! Longing for her beat wildly through him, but he did not move except to turn his head toward Patrick. "Take Katherine with you to the inn. You'll know what to do now—and later." He had the sensation of everything moving too fast. There were too many things to do in the time given him. Katherine stood hesitatingly. Good God, would she never leave! He had wanted only to see her, and every moment she stayed made his decision more unendurable.

She looked at Maurice, her brows drawn together in a puzzled frown. These weeks of terror that had seemed like years—and here Maurice was more concerned with Blount than with her. And since she was the cause, there was something ominous in Maurice's request that she and Patrick leave. She looked at Blount, her eyes dark with pain. He was smiling at her, a considering half-smile on his lips. She groped involuntarily for Patrick's hand, a shiver of sheer panic going through her. His fingers closed around hers reassuringly.

Then Patrick dropped her hand, crossed the room to the knight. He said, "I was waiting for a better moment, Sir Edward, but it may not present itself. I would like to have you send your second to me—at your convenience. I will meet you any place, any time."

Blount yawned. "You don't want to die so young, Master North. I'm afraid I can't accommodate you. However, you'll be needing a new master and you should be useful to me. I'd like to meet you about that any place, any time." He smiled.

Patrick's expression did not change. He struck Blount across the face. Blount staggered at the force of the blow. He put one hand on his sword. "You young fool!" At the sound of Blount's voice, two of his attendants just outside the door came running in.

Maurice said coldly, "Save your quarrel for another time if you please. I have but one more thing to see

432

you about, Sir Edward." He glanced at his secretary. "I dislike violence, Patrick. Will you see Katherine to the apartment? And don't return." His eyes fell on Patrick's scabbard. "Just to be sure you don't court trouble on your way home, leave your sword here. Unless you're looking for a disturbance, you won't need a weapon in the London streets at midday." Patrick started to object. Maurice said, "Leave it here!"

Patrick shrugged. "Don't think, Master Quain, this will change my plans to meet Sir Edward." He unstrapped his sword belt, tossed it on the table. There was a steelike resolution under the pleasant voice.

Maurice smiled faintly. "As you put it, any time, any place, except here today." He looked beyond Patrick to Blount's attendants waiting for a command, then back at Patrick. Patrick became aware abruptly of their vulnerability. With the deeds signed and witnessed and with his retainers at his back Blount could make an unhappy situation if he chose. Patrick moved toward Katherine. She still hesitated, not wanting to leave without Maurice.

Maurice said, "God's wounds, go!"

Blount watched them leave. He was smiling. He could have Katherine when he wanted her. Katherine half-turned. She was framed in the doorway for a moment, black hair and wine-red dress and pale face poignantly beautiful. Maurice thought, This is right— Katherine in an open doorway. Only it was not greeting between them, but farewell. Katherine would be waiting at the manor house as he had dreamed . . . but it would not be for him.

All his life seemed to have come step by slow step to this. He had turned aside, held aloof, built up walls of defense about himself, but always he had been drawn back. "Greater love has no man that this, that he lay down his life for his friend." The remembered words gave warmth to his courage. Katherine's face blurred before his eyes so that he did not see the smile on her mouth, the way she held out her hand to him before she turned to leave. He sat down. He felt unbelievably tired now. If he could sleep for just five minutes! But that was a rather ridiculous wish in these circumstances.

Blount was still standing. "I hope, Maurice, your last piece of business will not take overlong. I must confess I'm weary. Am I right in thinking you intend to beg a position with me? I might consider that. Your knowledge of your own ventures would be valuable to one who is not a tradesman by nature—especially since your secretary is so bent on playing the fool. You and I are men who can take life as we find it." This he thought would be the dazzling crown to his achievement.

Maurice said, "I hadn't thought exactly of that, but . . ." He let his voice trail off. "Must we have those men of yours? I had hoped we could speak privately."

Blount murmured complacently, "Why not? I feel quite agreeable today." He waved to the attendants. "Wait outside!"

Maurice scraped back his chair, stood up to move toward the window as the door closed behind him. "One thing troubles me, Sir Edward. You are now a reasonably wealthy man, with every opportunity of becoming richer. You already have one foot in the Court. You should wield a fair degree of power." He moved as though aimlessly between Blount and the door.

"True, true, Maurice." God, Blount thought, but what wildest dream of his had ever matched this? "You want me to say a good word for you to Walsingham, perhaps Burghley, for some government position?"

Maurice's voice snapped out, "I am wondering how you will use your power? A poor man like me cannot always protect his wife."

Blount noted the words rather than the change in tone. "Don't fear, Maurice. I am fond of Katherine myself—as you know. A reasonable attitude on her part, on your part, and you will never need look farther than to me for a friend." He said sharply, "What are you doing?"

The bolt on the door clicked home in answer. Maurice walked deliberately to the table, took up Patrick's sword. "I dislike violence as I said, Sir Edward. But

434

sometimes it is a man's last and only choice." The blade flashed out of the scabbard, glittering and alive in his hands. He eyed the edge. "I used to have some small skill with a sword."

Blount stared at Maurice, his mouth agape, "You're mad, Maurice! What chance have you against a veteran swordsman like me? And if you should escape my weapon, my attendants are outside. You'll be hanged for this. Good God, man, be reasonable!"

Maurice flexed the blade in his hands. His wrist was stiffer than it used to be, but he was in better condition at the moment than Blount. He said arrogantly, "Draw if you'd defend yourself, Blount. Whatever happens to me, you will not leave this room alive." Blount's face was ashen. "And don't trouble to call out. Before your men can break in, it will be too late for you."

Blount ripped his sword out of the scabbard. "You overbearing fool! I gave you your chance. You, a ruined tradesman, against me? You should have let your secretary alone. I'd have been content to disarm him. But you—you're finished now, Maurice. And Katherine won't be marrying that commoner, will she? You'd have done better to stay away from her as once I warned you. Your fortune mine, your bride flexible to my will—you should have learned prudence after being ruined once."

Maurice's thoughts were racing. Webster and Patrick had enough experience to go into some trading venture together. They would do well. He might have made some arrangements for them through Bowyer, but Patrick did not need his help. Lord Howard, who did not forget easily, would stand his friend if necessary at Court. Katherine free of the Court and of Blount, free of the harder necessities of life! She'd marry Patrick, not at once probably, but soon. She was young. She'd love Patrick. She was half in love with him now, and his devotion would do the rest in time.

Maurice smiled, moved back away from table and chairs. He felt light, unweighted, alive under his fatigue to his finger tips.

Blount looked at his enemy patronizingly. He had

recovered all his bravado with the feel of the hilt in his hand. The gray sunlight through the window gleamed coldly on the steel. He drew his dagger, tossed his sword belt to one side.

Maurice also drew a dagger. He had not wielded one since he'd been in Constantinople. Without the index finger he hadn't the same strength in his grip, the same ability to guide the blade. Fortunate, wasn't it, that they'd started on his left hand? He needed his dagger only to parry.

He fell back on guard as Blount stepped forward. Blount moved with catlike quickness. His blade cut over Maurice's in a swift disengage. Maurice lifted his sword just in time. The point tore only the shoulder of his doublet. The sound of the rending cloth was loud in the room. Maurice counterdisengaged and lunged. Blount beat aside sword with dagger while his own blade dropped and flashed again. He overreached himself, was off balance a moment. Maurice held the point, slid his sword down the length of Blount's almost to the hilt. It made a shrill scraping sound. Then he disengaged and straightened out his arm. Blount made a half step back and saved himself. Maurice's blade cut only across his upper arm, drawing the first blood.

They moved in again, more warily, circled in the small space between table and window and door. There was only the noise of their soft leather shoes, then heavy breathing, the ring of steel. Outside was a louder noise, a hammering at the door, voices crying their names, but neither was aware of the clamor. Their eyes were on the deadly lengths of steel, twisting snakelike about each other. Trained hand and wrist responded to the engage, the thrust, the parry, the riposte, before the eye could follow the flicker of steel.

Blount stepped back. A chair crashed over. He moved forward swiftly. His blade held Maurice's in quarte, disengaged to tierce, lifted. Then as he straightened his arm in the lunge, he dropped the point and thrust. Maurice's parry swung down a hairbreadth too late. He felt a stinging pain in his loins, but as though it were another's pain. He felt warm sticky

436

blood mat cloth to flesh, but as though someone else told him of it and he responded, Yes, I know. He must move carefully. He had not much time.

His sword made a circle of light about Blount's, beat it aside to aim for the heart. The point ripped a button from the doublet, but Blount was not touched. Blount's sword followed Maurice's, held it to one side, snapped back to strike sharply at the dagger. With only Maurice's maimed grip against the strength of that blow, the weapon went clattering to the floor. Blount smiled, but sprang to one side as Maurice's sword came ripping back. He parried.

And then the person outside Maurice said, You're losing blood, you grow slower, and Blount has two blades against your sword. Swiftness won't help you. Only one thing will do it—a slow deadly approach that will not waver no matter what hurt you take, an attack that aims for his life at any cost. He is still trying to save himself.

While Maurice was listening to that voice, his sword was a tongue of flame. He parried, stayed for an instant with his leg against the table edge just beyond Blount's reach. Then he lunged in so that their blades crossed almost at the hilt. And after that he did not retreat again.

Blount leaped back, struck aside Maurice's weapon with his dagger, came in with his sword. Maurice's blade swept down in a half circle, parrying the blow. Blount's dagger followed as swiftly, stabbing his right arm. Maurice went down on one knee under the assault, swayed there precariously. The point of Blount's sword was aimed at his defenseless throat.

Maurice half sobbed in the anguish of getting his breath. He gathered his failing strength of sinew and spirit with arrogant and indomitable pride. He stood up with his sword rigid in his hand. He thrust. He sensed the point cutting deeply into flesh. He saw a widening stain of blood on a pale-blue doublet. He heard the thin scream of agony of the man above him mortally hurt, and then the crash as Blount fell.

Maurice could feel himself plunging forward into

437

blackness. May God be kind to Katherine! A splintering of wood, men's voices came to him, but from far away. The dark was lightening before his eyes to a dazzling whiteness. This was the end, he knew. And he was content.

THE END

Another tumultuous romantic novel
by Patricia Matthews,
author of the multi-million
copy national bestseller,
LOVE'S AVENGING HEART

Love's
Wildest
Promise

P40-047 $1.95

Sarah Moody was a lady's maid in a wealthy London home. But suddenly her quiet sheltered world
was turned upside down when she was abducted
and smuggled aboard a ship bound for the colonies. Its cargo—whores to satisfy the appetites
of King George's soldiers in New York. Was Sarah
destined to become one of these women? Or
would she find the man she was searching for,
the man who would help her to fulfill Love's Wildest Promise.

If you can't find this book at your local bookstore,
simply send the cover price, plus 25¢ for postage
and handling to:

 Pinnacle Books
275 Madison Avenue, New York, New York 10016

The epic novel of the Old South,
ablaze with the unbridled passions
of men and women seeking
new heights for their love

Windhaven Plantation

Marie de Jourlet

P40-022 $1.95

Here is the proud and passionate story of one man—
Lucien Bouchard. The second son of a French nobleman,
a man of vision and of courage, Lucien dares to seek a new
way of life in the New World that suits his own high
ideals. Yet his true romantic nature is at war with his
lusty, carnal desires. The four women in his life reflect
this raging conflict: Edmée, the high-born, amoral
French sophisticate who scorns his love, choosing his
elder brother, heir to the family title; Dimarte, the in-
genuous, earthy, and sensual Indian princess; Amelia,
the fiery free-spoken beauty who is trapped in a life of
servitude for crimes she didn't commit; and Priscilla,
whose proper manner hid the unbridled passion of her
true desires.

"... will satisfy avid fans of the plantation genre."
—*Bestsellers* magazine

If you can't find this book at your local bookstore, simply
send the cover price plus 25¢ for postage and handling to:

Pinnacle Books
275 Madison Avenue, New York, New York 10016

PN-15